RED LINE

Blake Rudman

A HellBound Books Publishing LLC Book
Houston

Dedicated to my beautiful daughter, Selah, as this book was written during COVID-19 when you were a magical hopeful thought soon to be a reality. You're a supreme blessing, and the world is your oyster.
Love, Dad

RED LINE

Prologue

She never felt more alive than when she was bathed in sweat.

The sour stench of booze, thumping pulse from the club's speakers, and pheromones exuding from the other dancers all played their part, but her body's response to heat set Yasaman free. Red-faced and shiny with perspiration, she felt like Venus born from the sea-foam. Arms swaying, hips gyrating, Yasaman tossed her long brunette locks and whooped at the ceiling, which was barely visible through the dense, acrid fog of cigarette smoke.

Wearing a short, metallic-silver club dress, which scooped immodestly low at the front and clung to her sweat-dampened curves like a second skin, Yasaman felt so wickedly decadent and *alive*. In her culture, for any woman, let alone one of her standing, to wear such revealing clothing was incredibly taboo. She was by no means the most scantily dressed there, however. Her fellow hedonists wore barely-there dresses, skimpy catsuits, bikini tops, and micro miniskirts that showed off far more skin than they hid, while many of the young men chose to dance shirtless, their toned, glistening bodies further adding to the debauchery.

The man she danced with was the tall, muscular, swarthy type she rarely went for, but something about the depth of his darkly brown eyes had drawn her in that night. He leaned forward to whisper something into her ear, his breath warm against her skin. Yasaman couldn't quite make out what he was offering—drink or sex or adoration—but the details didn't matter. She accepted his worship by pressing her hands to the back of his silk shirt to pull him close and kiss him in full view of the other revelers in the room; that they watched her wanton display added to its excitement.

A beauty such as Yasaman Karami could easily have chosen any man in the room, but she'd chosen him. She sensed weakening as she focused directly on him with her wide, brown eyes and couldn't help but feel exultant at the power her taut, curvaceous body held over men.

Cheers erupted from a dozen throats. The dancers were vibrant, liberated! Yasaman didn't care that half were students at the Tehran University where she was *Dr.* Karami—the tenured professor of linguistic anthropology. The unspoken rule was for no one to speak of what went on inside the four walls of the private home that accommodated the roving nightclub that night.

Clasping her handsome admirer by the hand, she pushed through the crowd and exchanged casual caresses with the fevered bodies she brushed by along the way. The hallway she came out onto was brightly lit. As she turned to her paramour, Yasaman realized she knew him. His name was Davoud. Or was it Sadegh? No, *definitely* Davoud. Not that the man's name mattered to her; she never allowed familiarity to detract from her pleasure.

When Davoud's mouth opened, she was sure he was about to call her "Dr. Karami." She reached up and gently bit his lip. Looking into his eyes, she tugged at his belt buckle to express an interest no man could mistake for academic. With her head half turned over her shoulder, Yasaman led her prize up a staircase and down a hall.

The first door she tried was locked. Moans of sensual delight came from within, which was impressive, given the volume of the club music. Yasaman knocked at a second door and got no answer. The knob turned freely. She pushed the door open to reveal a small office. Turning to

Davoud, she invited him in with pure lust flaring in her eyes.

Yasaman didn't know the homeowner who played host to the club, but she admired his confidence. Books sat on shelves fixed to the wall on her right. On the opposite wall was an elaborate hanging, the calligraphic words of a prayer done in metalwork. It loomed over a wooden desk with an ornate Tiffany lamp. If she or Davoud—or any one of the revelers, for that matter—had cared to, they could have so easily strolled from the office and out of the house with arms full of priceless treasures. The dancers would do little more than watch them go. But, of course, she and Davoud harbored other ideas.

She waved his hand away from the light switch. The only illumination they needed was the moonlight streaking in through narrow windows above the desk. Yasaman danced into a moonbeam, swaying as she tugged down the zip at the front of her dress. Davoud kissed her neck, her breasts. His hands caressed the muscles of her arms and back. She responded by tearing open his shirt, springing buttons in all directions. Davoud gasped, then grinned, eager to play along. Lifting Yasaman out of her high heels, he helped her lock her long, bare legs around his waist, and carried her over to the antique mahogany desk.

With the light behind his head, Yasaman saw little of Davoud but his shadowy shape, and that suited her just fine. She'd imagine him as any man she chose—young or old, fierce or yielding, a perfect stranger or a familiar face. If she wanted, she could picture the hand sliding up her thigh as the hand of the only man she'd ever loved. She didn't want that, as it happened; when that man appeared in Yasaman's mind's eye, she banished his image at once.

As Davoud planted Yasaman firmly upon the desk, the spaghetti strap of her tiny purse slipped from her shoulder. As she shifted position to offer his eager fingers the opportunity to explore within the tight confines of her white thong, Yasaman's near-naked butt rolled on the purse. Feeling the firm rectangle of her cell phone pressed against her buttock, she gently shoved Davoud away.

"Wait," she said, fearing a collision between her cell and apartment key within the confines of the purse would leave her with a cracked screen. After a grunt, Davoud gave her breathing room. She took out the phone.

"You're joking," Davoud groaned. "Who can you possibly want more than me?" He spoke Persian like the son of an Azeri banker, balancing each consonant on the tip of his tongue before spilling it out; his arrogance was far from attractive.

"No one, my soul." To tease, Yasaman awoke the phone. All she wanted was to see Davoud's astounded expression in the liquid crystal glow, but the name of her last missed caller jolted her like a splash of cold water.

Davoud reached for the phone.

Yasaman fended him off with ease. He was half drunk, and she'd never felt so sober. The name—M Farbod Namdar—burned on the phone's display. Without looking at Davoud, Yasaman said, "I'm sorry. I need to leave. I must return a call."

"You're not serious." Davoud's tone held more than a hint of menace.

How could she have been so damn foolish as to shut herself away with a man she knew only by sight? His broad shoulders held a considerable capacity for violence. She recalled seeing him ground an opponent during a game of lacrosse. Frowning, Yasaman tilted the phone to see his eyes.

"I am serious, Davoud. Stand aside, please. Let me out."

Davoud's lower lip stuck out in a pout. He stiffened his stance. Yasaman almost *heard* the aggressive impulses crackling in the man's brain.

Reaching down, Davoud unzipped his pants. "You can't turn a man on and off, like a machine."

"Can I not?"

"Not this man," Davoud growled as he pulled out his dick with trembling hands and took a step forward.

There was no denying it, the guy was certainly impressive; seeing Davoud's long, engorged member pointing accusingly at her as he advanced almost had Yasaman reconsidering her phone call.

"Don't be a prick tease, Dr. Karami," Davoud leered as he aimed himself between her legs.

It took only a heartbeat or two for Yasaman's judo training to kick in. Before Davoud could even react, Yasaman grasped the hand holding his dick and twisted herself around. Davoud yelped as Yasaman bobbed down and hurled him with expert ease over her shoulder, her full breasts swinging free from her dress.

Davoud crashed onto the desk where, mere moments ago, he'd discovered just how ready the professor was for him. He let out a winded grunt; the desk's contents fell alongside him as he tumbled headfirst onto the polished wood floor.

Stepping back into her shoes and zipping up her dress, Yasaman walked around the desk and stood over Davoud. She'd been taught to always ensure an opponent was no longer a threat before walking away; poor Davoud was no such thing—he looked so dejected lying there with pain etched upon his rugged face and his wilting member jutting from his pants, she actually felt sorry for him.

Yasaman bent over and touched her palm to Davoud's bare chest. He tried to reach for her, but instead of leaning in, she raked her fingernails diagonally down his chest to raise red welts on his skin. Davoud flinched and gasped, pressing a hand to his wounds.

"You can tell them I was a lioness," she said and walked out.

1—The Living Man

The opulent white stone home hosting the club was barely able to muffle the thunder of the party inside. The stink of cigarette smoke and sweat clung to her body like some unearthly smog, yet Yasaman already missed being inside, surrounded by all those lithe, dancing, jostling bodies.

Despite the fact the weather bureau had predicted a smattering of snow, the air was uncharacteristically warm for a February night in Tehran. Yasaman found the knee-length jacket she'd fetched from the house's sitting room to be handy only for modesty's sake—after all, she was barely dressed, which she knew very well was most inappropriate for a woman outside. Yasaman did, however, wish she'd worn a thicker headscarf; seeing a dead man's name on her phone had cooled her blood, a chill she felt mostly in her cheeks.

"Forgive me," said the voice on her voice mail. It was, unmistakably, the voice of Mohammad Farbod Namdar, though he sounded far more serious than she'd ever heard him before. "I know your fun lasts until the dog's horn. Alas, my business could not wait."

Yasaman shook her head at Farbod's half-hearted attempt at humor. She had known the man for twelve years, first as her professor, then as a colleague. She should have cheered any indication his personality remained intact. But she couldn't help remembering the morning six months ago when Fatemeh Namdar—called Fatemeh the Patient by those who knew her husband—appeared in the common room of the faculty of letters and humanities, Tehran University, with a tale of Farbod's kidnapping by armored car.

They had planned to meet for breakfast, Fatemeh explained, at the Chez-Vous Café. Farbod had been crossing Darakeh Street when a blocky black van swerved in his direction. Fatemeh thought she was witnessing the start of her widowhood, but the brakes screeched as the van lurched to a halt. As Farbod dropped his cane and clutched his chest, men in cloth hoods leapt from the vehicle and lifted him by the elbows through its back doors. The driver started off while one of the men was still standing on the bumper.

Mentally, Yasaman reviewed all the fates she'd imagined for Farbod. Most of her nightmares ended with him shot in the head. Her recent past had been dominated by fretting over his disappearance, hassling NAJA—the uniformed police force in Iran—for news, and offering what comfort she could to the mourning Fatemeh. She began to feel closer to Farbod in his absence than in his presence. Listening to him after all that time was like hearing footfall in a tomb.

"I need you, Yasaman joon," said the voice mail. "Please call as soon as you can."

Was it a trick? Could someone have spliced together clips of Farbod speaking to fool her into taking some action? She tapped through a series of informational menus to verify the call was from Farbod's personal phone, the one he'd been carrying when he was captured. It had. But that was impossible. Farbod was dead. No scenario she could ever envision allowed for his continued existence. The phone, the police had informed her, would have been destroyed by the kidnappers.

And yet, it had just called.

With an effort, Yasaman stopped questioning what she knew to be true. Skepticism was a comfortable old blanket, but tenting in it got her no closer to the truth. Steeling her nerves, she called back.

The phone rang once, twice, three times. Yasaman considered hanging up.

"*Salām*, Yasaman."

She swallowed. "*Halu*, Farbod."

"Thank God you have kept this number. I need you to come to me. Tonight."

"Where are you, Farbod? Where have you been?"

He sighed. "There are things I can only say in person, *joonam*. You will meet me, please, on Pol-e Tabi'at?"

He'd rehearsed the speech, she was sure. What was more, he was delivering it with deliberate flatness. Even the term of endearment, joonam, addressing her as a dear one, rang hollow.

Before she could insist on knowing what was wrong, he said, "Come alone. No police. Tell no one. Do you understand?"

Hesitating, she weighed the unknown danger he'd asked her to walk into against the consequences for him if she refused. Could she face Fatemeh if anything she did or refused to do slammed the lid on Farbod's coffin?

She could not.

"Fine. I will do as you say. Pol-e Tabi'at? I'll come."

"Thank you. God support you." Farbod coughed. The next words he spoke warmly, sounding more like himself. "Will you be coming from Elahiyeh or the pharmacy?"

Had anyone been watching Yasaman's face, they would have seen her forehead crease in thought. She rarely got the chance to party in the wealthy Elahiyeh district, but Farbod was correct in thinking she wouldn't have spurned an invitation. He was also right in the fact that the wild parties she frequented were often fronted by shops, whenever a private home was unavailable. His mention of a pharmacy was nothing to do with that, however. The reference was obscure; few in her circle would have caught it at all.

Professor Farbod Namdar esteemed Attar of Nishapur above all great poets. He made a habit of speaking about Attar's works at length. Since *attar* meant pharmacist, the members of the Tehran U's Linguistics Department had adopted "the pharmacy" as code for procrastination. When two researchers chatted pleasantly instead of starting work, they were said to be "going to the pharmacy." When a lecturer lingered over her notes for minutes before starting class, she was said to be "coming from the pharmacy." Farbod was giving Yasaman a chance to play for time.

As casually as seemed appropriate, she said, "The pharmacy. Why?"

Farbod hummed in contemplation. "Oh, a matter of the distance. You can arrive in, say, forty minutes if you come as you are?"

"Of course," she said. In fact she could be on either side of the bridge in fifteen minutes, smack in the middle in under twenty-five. Farbod was inviting her to take her time, to prepare ahead for whatever was about to happen. She knew exactly how she would prepare.

"*Sepas*," he said. "I will be on the first lookout from the Ab-o-Atash entrance in guise as a blind man. Find me, Yasaman. Come as quickly as you can."

A beep told her he'd hung up.

Yasaman frowned at her phone before dialing the taxi service. When a car approached the curb a few minutes later, she gave the driver her home address. She didn't tell him to hurry. It would take only a minute to fetch what she needed.

***

The illuminated, gleaming metal of the Pol-e Tabi'at was a futurist's dream; lit up in glowing blues and whites, the crisscrossed struts resembled some kind of surreal honeycomb. The bridge itself, the largest pedestrian walkway in the city, meandered gently between Taleghani and Abo-Atash parks like a gently snaking river. As a glittering background to the spectacular bridge, the bright, sparkling lights of Tehran's cityscape lit up the night sky; on such a clear night, Yasaman could make out the unmistakable outline of the spectacular Azadi Tower, along with that of the Milad Tower—the city's tallest—where she had enjoyed many fine dinners in its revolving restaurant. And, as a backdrop to that, the dark, brooding shape of the white-capped Alborz mountains cast a malevolent silhouette against the velvet of the night's sky.

The Nature Bridge, as its name translated, was popular among the common people too. From her position fifty meters from where the walkway through Ab-o-Atash Park gave way to the bridge, Yasaman saw couples walking together and small groups milling under the artificial lights, despite the lateness of the hour. The presence of the crowd should have calmed her, but having lived through three major protests and the police crackdowns that followed, large groups of people made her anxious instead. Farbod's manner and the message hidden in his words convinced Yasaman he was being pressured to draw her out. His captors intended to add her to their collection of academics, or kill her for reasons unknown. The fact they meant to carry out their plan in view of bystanders did not fill her with confidence.

As she walked out onto the bridge, pleased she had changed into much more appropriate footwear for the occasion, questions flooded Yasaman's mind—the most salient being, *"Why me?"*

Who was she to attract the attention of fortune hunters, radicals, government agents, or whoever else might have orchestrated the plot? The only answer that made sense was she was a linguist with qualifications like Farbod's. She assumed something in the professor's personal life had set him in the crosshairs, but if his captors were interested in her as well, it could only be because of something in their shared work.

But what?

All she ever did, professionally speaking, was feed the curiosity of fellow academics. She was an antiquarian, not an activist. She worshiped at the temple of words, offering prayers to the grammar gods. Nothing in her work was a threat to the people in power—it was neither political nor religious, similar to her.

A speech she often gave to undergraduates when they asked her to defend a linguistics major came back to her. "Words are the world," she would say. "They mold how we think of people, places, things. Why is a person your friend and not your lover? You love your friends, do you not? Yet the distinction remains sharp. Words define our boundaries. They can tear down our walls. We can do nothing, which cannot be expressed in words. Words are the world. Without words, there is no meaning."

She believed the mantra to her core. Some of her recent discoveries bore it out in a manner she hoped never to express in concrete reality. Perhaps, in those discoveries . . .

As she reached the steps leading up to the first lookout, the view derailed her train of thought. The glow of her city was so bright, it illuminated the Alborz mountains. Every home Yasaman had ever known inhabited the sweep of metropolitan excess that was visible from where she stood. She climbed three steps and saw Tehran unroll like a carpet at her feet, climbed three more, and realized from where she stood, she was able to survey nine-tenths of her personal life map. Breathless as if she were cresting Everest, she finished her climb and stood still, afraid that if she blinked, the city and all it meant to her would vanish.

A faint drumming to her left alerted her. A man was standing at the railing, striking it rhythmically with a folding cane. Yasaman recognized the meter of Attar's poem, "Speech of the Birds." Suppressing the urge to call Farbod's name, she turned to look. At the same time, she reached into her jacket pocket, seeking the textured handle of the revolver she had discreetly brought along. Her fingers gripped the handle while her thumb worked the safety.

Farbod was leaner than she remembered. His skin was more wrinkled but still retained its typically healthy glow. The silver hair, once neat and trim, draped Farbod's shoulders like a woolen veil. Before the kidnapping, her former professor had worn a beard; this *new* version of Farbod was clean-shaven. What all these changes added up to, Yasaman didn't know, but at least they showed he was allowed to care for himself. The pea coat he wore was of a good cut. It hugged his shoulders without appearing to restrict his movement. A pair of dark glasses combined with the cane suggested blindness, though if anyone had been looking at him when Yasaman appeared, they'd have seen a stiffening of limbs and a tremble in the chin before he looked away. Doing her best to seem casual, Yasaman moved to the railing a meter to Farbod's right. If any of the twenty or so night owls ringing the lookout took notice of her nerves, they didn't let it show.

As Yasaman assumed her position, the friend she thought was long dead dipped his head, jolting his dark glasses to the bridge of his nose. It was a familiar affectation, one he repeated often in the lectures Yasaman had attended as an undergrad. The glasses had been different back then, but the meaning they conveyed was the same: "This is where we are," they announced. "What are you prepared to do?"

By way of an answer, Yasaman glanced at the pocket in which she was gripping her revolver. At her apartment, she'd changed into jeans and a moto jacket, complementing the outfit with a warm blue hijab and a pair of new Nikes. After indicating the gun, she glanced at the sneakers. I can fight and I can run, was the message her eye movements conveyed.

Farbod returned his glasses to their place. Whispering, he said, "Forgive me, Yasaman joon." Aside from the term of endearment, he spoke in French, a language known by many, but not all, of their countrymen.

"Dear one, what have you done?"

Farbod slowly pivoted. The other visitors ringing the lookout were grouped in six to eight parties, depending on how one counted the stragglers. The dark panes masking Farbod's sightedness settled briefly on two men. One, a tall man with a mustache, stood on his own. The other, shorter and bearded, stood close enough to a group of merrymakers that Yasaman would have thought him one of their number, if not for his grave expression.

Returning his attention to Yasaman, Farbod said, "On the phone, I told you I needed help. It was a lie. I have drawn you here, my dear, as a spider draws a fly. Until a moment ago, I thought it was what I wanted. But the moment I saw you—ah! Forgive me, Yasaman joon." His lower lip quivered. Turning his face to the city, he lifted his glasses and wiped away a tear. "I have placed you in danger, little flower. By my own weakness, I have placed you in danger."

"How can you say such a thing, baba jaan?" said Yasaman. By calling him "dear uncle," she hoped to remind him of their closeness and his old confidence. "You were kidnapped, dear. Whatever you did, it was against your will."

Farbod gave a wry smile. "Our ancient debate. You remember? If the mind is of the brain and the brain of the body, the will is but an illusion to excuse the body's urges."

"*That* was never my opinion."

"Ah, no. As I recall, you opposed the notion vigorously, even when the fight was two to one against."

For the second time that night, Yasaman was forced to remember a man she'd striven so hard to forget—Farbod's ally in their debate over free will, and their mutual colleague, Bizhan Al-Kabir. It was more than a year ago when her young, wonderfully eager, and energetic lover had stood in their bedroom doorway, enshrouded in dense mist from the shower, and ranted about how his academic growth was stunted by the shadow cast by her career.

"Of course you cannot see it," he'd said in answer to her protests. "Even now, you look away, as always."

She'd looked back at him, then, sitting cross-legged on the bed as he told her he had taken up a position at a university he refused to name because he didn't want to be followed. When Bizhan finished his speech, she'd asked him why he was so determined not to tell her the truth; not one single word he had spoken was accurate. Their careers had grown together and could grow still; she loved him and wanted what was best for him. If another woman was in the picture, Yasaman was prepared to give him time; if he had wild oats to sow, she was sure they could work something out.

She'd spoken in a tone that stopped short of pleading, but nothing in her words or the gestures of her unashamedly naked body had been able to change Bizhan's mind. She remembered with bitterness how he'd dressed in the shirt and trousers she'd stacked neatly for him on a chair and stormed out of her life. After he was gone, Yasaman scalded her flesh in the heat of the shower, preferring to burn than to live another minute with his scent on her skin.

Aside from a few involving her mother, the memory of parting with Bizhan was Yasaman's least favorite. She clamped her eyes shut to dismiss it. When she opened them again, Farbod had removed his glasses and was looking at her tenderly. His moist eyes were shockingly bloodshot.

She said, "Whatever you've done, I forgive you. Come away with me now. You look strong. I'm sure we can lose your minders in the park."

As she started away from the railing, Farbod replaced his glasses and glanced once more at the men Yasaman had referred to as his *minders*.

"I am lost," said Farbod, "but you must go. The men who took me will hunt you. You have a car? Leave the city. Flee wires and Wi-Fi. Destroy your phone. Find a cave to hide in. You won't be alone for long. There are days coming . . . but if I say more, you will hate me. Go now. Save yourself, Yasaman. Save yourself!"

With a powerful shove, he propelled Yasaman in the direction of the stairs. One of the minders, the man making a poor attempt to blend with the crowd, took notice of the sudden burst of action and began advancing on Yasaman and Farbod. Yasaman, reeling from Farbod's unexpected roughness, spun on her heel to take hold of her old friend's wrist.

"Come with me." There was desperate urgency in her voice; she knew in her heart that to leave him now would be to lose him again—and forever.

Farbod snapped back at her. "No!" He broke away and turned to face down the pursuer. As he did so, Farbod slipped a hand into his pea coat, as if making ready to draw a gun. Acting on instinct, the man watching the pair ducked to one side and mirrored the gesture.

"Idiot!" his partner said in plain English. "He's unarmed." The partner had been standing to Yasaman's right, and the suddenness of his harsh, baritone voice startled her. As Yasaman looked on him in horror and bystanders on the bridge turned around to see who was shouting, the man took a few rapid steps at Yasaman, closing the gap between them.

The urge to run flashed through Yasaman's mind as she stared Farbod's minder straight in his eyes; she wondered if he could see the fear in hers. Fearful for her life or not, Yasaman couldn't find it within herself to leave Farbod to the mercy of the thugs who clearly meant to do him harm.

She drew her revolver.

The man stopped dead in his tracks, his eyes wide open and staring at her gun as if it were something entirely alien to him; Yasaman had no doubt the last thing he'd expected was for her to be armed.

Around them, sightseers scattered, scurrying away from the crazy lady with the gun and the two burly, black-clad men who confronted her. For all they knew, Yasaman was the dangerous one and the men law enforcement.

The man closest to Yasaman took a tentative step toward her with a conciliatory smile playing upon his thin lips. He spread his hands out in front of him, palms upward, reminding Yasaman of a cheesy street magician she'd seen as a small child.

Pushing aside the fond memory, Yasaman pointed the gun directly at the guy's face; let the bastard look into the lethal darkness of its barrel while he contemplated his next move.

Another step.

As if seeking support, he cast a quick glance at his comrade, who stood several strides away. But that guy remained still, his hand hovering over the gap in his opened jacket.

The man took another step toward Yasaman—only a few steps more and the muzzle of her gun would be making a red indent on his forehead. He kept his eyes fixed firmly on Yasaman's, as if *daring* her to pull the trigger, as if he knew full well she had no more desire to carry out her unspoken threat than he had to allow her and Farbod to escape Pol-e Tabi'at.

Suddenly, the first minder produced a pistol. Yasaman saw the flash of metal in her peripheral vision and, acting purely by reflex, she turned and pulled her trigger. The sharp *crack* of the revolver's retort split the cool air and elicited squeals of panic from the fleeing tourists as the gun bucked in Yasaman's hand. She heard a low, guttural grunt from her target and, as she looked on in abject horror, a dark fountain of blood spurted from his chest.

As he fell, the man clutched at the rapidly spreading patch of wet soaking through his jacket, which appeared almost black in the bridge's lights; he coughed up a thick, scarlet spray that misted about his head like some ghoulish halo. The dull, metallic clank of his pistol on the planks was swallowed up by a loud roar in Yasaman's ears.

Through the cacophony and ringing inside her head, Yasaman heard a woman behind her scream. Someone else shouted, "Was that a shot?" from somewhere below.

Then, Farbod was squeezing her shoulder. "Go quickly. Take the ramp."

The fallen man's pistol was in Farbod's hand, though Yasaman had not registered seeing him grab it. His facade of being blind now broken, Farbod kept the weapon trained on the remaining minder, who stood where Yasaman had stopped him in his tracks; the minder's attention was still on her and Farbod—he appeared to have little concern for his fallen colleague, who lay quite still in a spreading pool of his own blood.

Yasaman said, "I can't—you—please, Farbod, think of Fatemeh."

"May she never think of me," she *thought* Farbod said; the roaring had gotten so loud, she couldn't be sure.

Giving Yasaman a final shove in the direction of a ramp, Farbod aimed the pistol high at a distant stand of trees and fired. The minder surged forward a half meter before Farbod stopped him with the gun pointed directly at his forehead. The bystanders in the fleeing crowd ducked and covered their heads. Impelled as much by fear as the momentum Farbod conveyed, Yasaman glanced once at the dark puddle forming under the fallen man before breaking into a sprint.

The ramp Farbod indicated was mostly empty, so Yasaman was able to make it to the bottom while the bystanders on the lookout huddled in terror. The bridge below was crowded; about fifty night visitors occupied the same amount of space that held twenty-five above. The confusion was also greater, as no one seemed to know where the shots had originated, only that they *were* being fired. With her revolver back in her pocket and hijab adjusted to hide her face, Yasaman was able to blend in quickly and easily with the general stampede headed to Ab-o-Atash Park.

When she nearly reached the exit, it occurred to her she was putting the fleeing innocents in danger. She didn't know the minder's disposition or his orders. If he overpowered Farbod, would he shoot at her from the lookout or allow her to get away? She had no idea, so she ran on, doing her best to open a space between herself and the rest of the panicked mob. One man's blood on her hands was enough. If anyone else was shot because of her, she wouldn't be able to live with herself.

With adrenaline driving her body, Yasaman wasn't sure it was safe to stop running, so she glanced backward over her shoulder instead. The crowd had scattered, so she could clearly spot the minder, who wasn't aiming a weapon at her as she'd feared. He was standing at the top of the ramp, searching the crowd as he talked into a phone. Farbod and the pistol were nowhere to be seen. Yasaman shuddered at the thought of what had happened to the professor, and shuddered again when she tried to imagine what would happen to him next. Would they kill him or merely subject him to torture? Compassion cut through her fear. This was Farbod! Her colleague, her mentor, and husband to the finest woman she knew. She couldn't leave him behind. As the crowd swarmed onto the walkways of Ab-o-Atash, Yasaman wheeled around. Her foot slipped and she rolled on the ground over her shoulder, barely managing to save herself from a cracked collarbone.

When she rose, a man was watching her from his position beside a sign. He lowered his phone and stared at her for a moment. An insincere smile spread across his lips as he stepped forward. "Don't try to run," he said. "There's nowhere to go."

"So I'm told."

As the kidnapper reached for her, Yasaman's decade of self-defense training kicked in. Catching his arm, she turned and flipped him over her back. He cried out as he landed on the pavement. Even as Yasaman backed away, she saw another man charging up the path ahead of her. He, too, was holding a phone. She had time to draw her revolver, but even as she felt for the handle in her pocket, an image of spurting blood, vivid against the night sky, flashed before her eyes. She had shot one man too many already. Her capacity for violence was spent. With numb fingers, she gripped the gun to keep it from bouncing as she turned to run back to the bridge.

Security agents had begun arriving on the scene in a golf cart with flashing lights. It pulled up as close to the bridge's entrance as possible, given the fleeing crowd. Fewer people were running now than before—many had already fled while those remaining stopped to ask what the panic was about. A man was fetching a medical bag from the back of the cart. Jogging up to him, Yasaman's adrenaline had abandoned her, leaving her breathless. "A man fell," she said between gasps and pointed at the way she'd come. "There. Right there."

The medic jogged off in the direction she had indicated. Yasaman pretended to watch for a fraction of a second as a pair of girls, younger than she was but similarly dressed, caught up to where she was standing. Her heart was aching as she fell in beside them, and not only from exertion. In a tremulous voice, she asked the girls if they had seen the trouble. The roar in her ears obscured the answer. Together, the trio climbed a hill. Yasaman was tempted to stop and look back. She clearly couldn't save Farbod, but she wanted to check on him. Was he still on the lookout? The distance was probably too far for her to tell, and the man from the path was likely close behind. Yasaman decided not to break stride.

At the first branching path, she left the girls, darting into the trees to hide among bare trunks and evergreens. Seconds into her sojourn, she heard a man only a short distance away swearing in Arabic. A minute later, someone came stomping through the pine needles. Yasaman crouched behind a tree. Her pursuer paused. Peering around the tree that was her shelter, Yasaman saw she was facing the man's back. Silently, keeping low, she padded away on tiptoe.

Winter wrapped her like a wet blanket, turning beads of sweat into creeping glaciers. She reached a more open area on the edge of the woods, found a sheltered wall with clear vision in several directions, and shivered with her back against the wall for what felt like an hour, watching for signs of pursuit. None came. Tears did, though she fought them. It was too cold to cry, and she needed clear sight. When she was sure she could wait no longer, she shook out her cold muscles and made a mad dash to the parking lot, where she'd left her car.

Surely they'd be watching it?

The realization hit Yasaman like a hard slap in the face.

Yes, if Farbod had been coerced into luring her into a trap, then every angle would have been covered; it was an easy assumption that they'd stake out her car.

Yasaman switched course without breaking her stride toward another car park nearby but far enough away from where her car awaited her—so tantalizingly close.

Her senses keen, on high alert, Yasaman walked slowly into the car park; it was dimly illuminated, as all but three of the tall street lamps around its periphery were dead. On any other occasion, she would have thought twice about venturing into such a poorly lit place, but now its darkness gave her a sense of security. She saw no one loitering around the desolate square of cracked tarmac, and no signs of life from any of the dozen or so cars clumped together between two of the functioning lights.

Yasaman picked out an old Peugeot, which had definitely seen better years; it was battered and rusting, at least one of its tires worn down to the wire, and as far as she could tell beneath the sodium orange glow of the street lamps, the vehicle was a dark, shitty brown color. Perfect.

As one of countless other nondescript cars that were so common on Tehran's roads, she'd blend in nicely.

As Yasaman administered a quick heel kick to shatter the left-hand rear window, she muttered a silent prayer of thanks to Bizhan. He'd gotten a kick out of teaching his older, more sophisticated lover how to steal cars; it was a skill he'd picked up as a reckless youth who'd fallen in with the wrong crowd, and one he told Yasaman she may need one day, when dark times came and the infidels came to take their country.

At the time, it had been a thrill that had led to the some of the most electric sex between them in the back seat of Bizhan's car—she'd never agree to *actually* steal a car, so they'd used his for practice. Yasaman would never have believed back then that the skill would one day save her life. She popped the rear door and slipped in.

Using her phone for light, Yasaman crawled between the front seats and reached beneath the steering column. There, she located the bunch of wires that led to the engine; wrenching hard, she yanked them out of place and tried her damndest to remember which one to touch to which to fire the ignition.

After three tries, Yasaman's heart was sinking fast. Her luck had held thus far, but sooner or later, somebody would come to the car park, maybe even the owner of the shitty brown Peugeot.

"Please," Yasaman hissed through her teeth as she touched two red wires together.

The old car coughed to life like a phlegmy old man. Its entire chassis shuddered and creaked, but the ignition held and the engine rattled and churned beneath the rusted hood. With a sigh of relief, Yasaman twisted the wires together and squirmed her way into the driver's seat, allowing herself a brief moment to slump against the steering wheel. Pounding the wheel with the heel of her hand, she eased her foot onto the gas and drove out of the car park at a sensible pace; any kind of speed would have drawn attention.

For forty minutes, she kept the speedometer low purely by force of will. By the time she reached a filling station in Garmdareh, she was exhausted. Fueling the car strained her nerves, as every splash of neon in her field of view made her remember the blood she had pumped from the minder's chest.

Before Yasaman drove into the night, she took a moment to replay everything Farbod Namdar—the man dead, then alive, now current status unknown—had said. Remembering his prompting, she wedged her phone under the right front tire of the car. She rolled down the window and heard the crack and snap as it was crushed into the concrete. A sad, flat pile of scrap was all she left behind.

2—Red Line Day

Eight-and-a-half time zones away, a young boy sat fidgeting in the back seat of his father's car.

"Do you like this movie, Daddy?"

Out of habit, Detective Mitch Wilson of the Baltimore Police Department checked that the cars darting in front of him through the intersection still had the green before he glanced behind.

"I don't know, bud. Haven't seen it yet." Mitch rubbed at the roughness on his chiseled chin; although it was only midafternoon, he was already sporting the beginnings of a five-o'clock shadow that mirrored his short, dark hair with a few gray streaks. He didn't bother to color either—Jessica thought they made him look mature and dignified.

"Spex likes it."

Mitch shot a look at Jessica, his wife of eight years. She sat quietly in the passenger seat and tipped him a wink. He thought she looked so beautiful, even more with her flaxen locks cascading into waves a little past her shoulders instead of tied back into the blonde ponytail she normally wore to accommodate her daily workout. Jessica's bright blue eyes sparkled with the excitement of their family outing.

"We downloaded the app at lunch," Jessica told him. "It's *really* cool. Right, Ethan?"

"Very cool," said Ethan.

As Mitch smiled in the rearview, the faint lines around his brown eyes crinkled. He knew nothing about the app, but he did know the kid was crazy about the movie it advertised. The Hollywood hype machine had done a thorough job. *Spex: Your Electric Friend* was in its first weekend of release and already breaking box office records. Mitch couldn't remember the last time a kids' movie had been so successful. *Toy Story 2*, maybe? He was too young to have been around for *E.T.* but had heard about the buzz. The buzz around *Spex* was close.

Ethan held up his tablet. It was a 7.9" Stadion J-Tab with custom decals of dinosaurs, giant beetles, and cartoon flames shooting out of a golden crown. Grandma had given it as a gift at Christmas, having ignored protests from Grandpa, who'd favored a carpentry kit.

"See?" Ethan turned the screen to the mirror.

All Mitch managed to make out were shapes and colors. Nonetheless, he said, "Great, bud," before returning his attention to the stoplight ahead. The green flashed and he drove across the intersection onto a stretch of road lined with scraggly trees. It had been a warm first week for February in Baltimore, and some of the trees had sprouted delicate sprigs of green that were doomed to die in the next frost. Dumb trees should have known better. There were still patches of snow on the ground; spring would be a long time coming.

After ten minutes of slow driving, Mitch turned his gray Nissan Rogue onto Rosebank Avenue, the one-way street beside the Senator Theatre. All the parking spots on Rosebank were taken, which was a phenomenon he'd never seen before. Driving to the corner of Rosebank and York Road, he looked York up and down, only to discover its spaces, too, were at capacity.

A line of moviegoers had formed in front of the Senator Theatre, beneath the retro-style half-circle marquee jutting out over the sidewalk. Above the marquee, the building's second story alternated between large vertical rectangular panels of limestone and translucent glass, with four regal stone pillars encasing the circular architecture. The line of moviegoers snaked around the corner, running a good thirty feet up Rosebank.

Ethan spoke up, "Dad! Can we go see Spider-Man after the movie?" Across York was a comic book shop, where a life-sized statue of the superhero made like it was about to spray webbing at the inside of the window.

"We'll see, bud," Mitch told him.

Ethan sighed. "That means no."

"It means *we'll see*, bud. Somebody stayed up too late on his tablet last night. He might need a nap after *Spex*." Mitch turned his attention to Jessica. "Babe, it looks like I'll have to park at Belvedere. Wanna get out here?"

"Thanks," she said. "We do." She patted her hair down in preparation to cover it with a wool cap.

"You won't need that," said Mitch.

"Oh, yes I will. Ethan, put your hat on."

Mitch grunted, but when Jessica offered him a kiss, he leaned in. There was no traffic behind the Rogue, so he lingered, his lips barely touching his wife's so as not to smear her lipstick.

"Oh, brother," groaned Ethan.

Mitch reached back to pinch his son's leg. "You just wait, little man. One day, you'll be happy to take time for kisses too." He gestured toward the line of people stomping their boots on the sidewalk. "Take care of Mommy, okay? It looks like you'll have to wait awhile to buy tickets."

"You're confused," said Jessica playfully. "Daddies wait in line to buy the tickets. Spoiled mommies and kiddies wait inside to hit the concession stand."

"Can I get jujus?" Ethan asked.

"We'll see." Jessica smiled.

After Mitch watched them climb down from the SUV and step up on the sidewalk, he rolled down his window to say, "You sure you want to go, Ethan, not stick with your old man?" He made it sound like a tease. The truth was more complicated. The only thing he hated more than leaving Jessica or Ethan on their own individually was leaving them both on their own together.

Gripping Ethan's hand, Jessica tightened her jaw. "Not across York. It's too busy."

"For this big guy?"

"I'll hold Daddy's hand," said Ethan.

Of course, Jessica was right about the traffic. Mitch said, "Hey, don't worry about it. I forgot Mommy needs her burly protector." It was a family joke, a routine Mitch and Jessica worked out to keep Ethan at her side.

Ethan took his cue. "I'm not burly."

"Yeah?" Mitch reached out of the window and gave Ethan's ribs a squeeze. At the first slight touch, the boy broke into giggles. "You feel pretty burly to me."

"Enough, you two," said Jessica. "Come on, Ethan. Babe? Love ya. Don't be long."

"See you in a sec," said Mitch. He would have added, "Love ya too," but a car approached him from behind. Another driver wanted the curb. No biggie. Jessica knew how he felt. He could say it anytime. After a quick check of traffic, he pulled onto York, turned left, and swung right into the parking lot of Belvedere Square Market, a small, charming mall with unique shops and eating places snuggled under a green metal roof. Since the market boasted over four hundred free parking spots, Mitch figured at least one of them would have his name on it.

The unroofed portion of the lot was small, and it was packed. Mitch quelled a sliver of panic; he had to get back to his wife and kid.

His fear was not an entirely irrational one. As a young child, he'd looked up to his dad like he was a superhero. Mitch loved the hugs and attention Dad always paid him. His dad always enjoyed looking over Mitch's schoolwork, driving him to soccer practice, or roughhousing with him on the living room floor. But Dad also traveled a lot for work. Mitch always hated when his dad left for a trip. Six years old was the age where his dad was everything, and more than simply disliking the fact he would leave, it terrified Mitch. What if Dad never came back?

Then one day, he woke up to find his mom in his bedroom with tears streaking down her face. As Mitch rubbed his eyes and tried to comprehend what she was telling him, she explained how Dad had suffered a heart attack and would never be coming home, but he would always love him. Having his worst fears realized affected Mitch in such a way that he'd never completely healed. From that point on, he'd felt vulnerable loving anyone. As a grown-up, he had two such someones in his life; Mitch preferred to keep them close, to let them out of his sight as little as possible.

It still amazed Mitch he'd ever even given his heart over to Jessica. After losing his father, he hadn't opened up to anyone in years. But Jessica, the younger sister of one of Mitch's college buddies, had refused to let him go. They dated for two years before the vulnerability of being in a serious relationship got too much for Mitch.

"I have to let you go, Jessica," he'd quietly informed her one warm summer evening as they walked a trail near the Patapsco River at Middle Branch Park in Baltimore.

Faraway traffic sounds from the Hanover Street Bridge joined with those of the crickets. Lightning bugs flitted in looping patterns on either side of the path.

She had stopped, looked him in the eye, and instead of making a big scene, had asked only one question. "Why?"

The simple question took him aback, and he'd stumbled over his words. "B—because I'll be starting my job as a cop, and I—I'll be working a lot and . . ." He'd stopped there, afraid and unsure of what was in his own heart.

"Those don't sound like very good reasons, Mitch," Jessica had responded, the softness of her voice matching his. "I love you. You know that, right?"

Mitch had nodded imperceptibly.

"Mitch?" She'd looked him directly in the eye, taking his hand in hers. "I think something else is going on here."

When his eyes met her loving but confused gaze, he'd reacted with an unexpected torrent of tears. Somehow the emotions triggered tears he had never cried when he'd lost his father. He and Jessica sat down together on a large rock away from the path, and he had poured out his heart to her—about his vulnerability in loving someone, his fears for the future, and his belief he could never be a good lifelong companion. She had listened to everything he had to say, the tears streaming down her cheeks as well, while he dug patterns in the sand with the toes and heels of his shoe.

"Mitch, I hear what you're saying, but I think we're good for each other. I'm not perfect either, and I need you as much as I think you need me. Let's do the difficult thing and keep going forward in this relationship." She refused to let go of his hand.

Six months later, they were married.

Mitch shook off the memory and drove as fast as he dared to the larger, sheltered lot in back of the Belvedere

Square Market. He found no empty spaces there either. He rolled his eyes; if even half the cars in the lot belonged to theatre patrons, all four auditoriums showing *Spex* were going to be packed. Would the Belvedere folks even put up with moviegoers using their lot? Thanks to the badge in his glove box, Mitch didn't mind risking parking the car in the Belvedere lot, but the desperation of the other drivers to see the film on opening weekend spoke volumes about its destined success. He regretted not buying the tickets ahead of time online; it might just have been one of those times it was worth paying the five-dollar service charge to guarantee seats.

In his peripheral vision, Mitch noticed a pedestrian making his way up the stairs from a lower level. The guy seemed distracted and wore an ankle-length coat that appeared too bulky, despite its threadbare material. Unseasonably warm though it was, the coat was too thin for any February in Baltimore since the beginning of time. The man's sneakers were wrong too. Melting snow had made them soggy, which surely made his feet uncomfortably cold. He wore no hat, only a scarf scrunched up around his ears. In one ungloved hand, the man held a phone up in front of his face. The other hand he'd shoved, Napoleon-style, inside his coat.

Mitch's cop radar pinged. Back when he'd worked a beat, Mitch had developed a keen eye for drunks and dope heads. The guy in the coat didn't quite fit the profile, on account of his steady tread, but he had the fidgets and dazed look suggesting his brain had been altered by *something*. Gaze fixed on the phone, he bobbed his head in time with the dancing lights glowing so bright from its screen that Mitch saw them from several feet away.

Intrigued, Mitch feathered the SUV's brakes. The Rogue was a hybrid, so by switching off the heat and crawling along, he was able to still the gas engine. Cracking the passenger window, Mitch crept up on the walker, thanks to the almost inaudible electric engine. He heard a pounding rhythm coming from the man's phone—blasting bass and rattling snares interspersed with bursts of gunfire. On the vocal track, a man's voice alternated between trilling and rapping in a language Mitch couldn't have named for a million dollars.

After a moment, Mitch braked the Rogue and let it roll back slowly to give the man some distance. What he'd heard was troubling, but what worried the cop most was the man hadn't glanced from his screen when Mitch's car pulled alongside. The level of concentration from the guy suggested a dangerous fixation. If Mitch let the guy leave the parking lot, he might wander into traffic, if he did nothing worse. The last thing Mitch wanted on his Saturday off was to tangle with a mental case. Still, he felt he had to do something. He reached for his phone, which was clamped to a bracket on the Rogue's windshield; he'd put in a call to dispatch before he confronted the screen junkie.

As he tugged the phone loose, Mitch felt a jolt, a crunch, and the furious honk of a horn. Slamming on the brakes, Mitch realized too late he'd still been rolling backward while some other driver had tried to back out. The phone flew from his fingers, bounced off the passenger seat, and slipped between it and the center console. Ignoring his loss for the moment, Mitch glanced in his side mirror and saw a dust-brown Buick pressed up against the Rogue's bumper. A door opened, slammed, and a moment later the Buick's driver appeared, thumping a fist on the SUV's rear panel.

The driver, who looked to be little more than a kid, was built short and sturdy, like a mini-fridge on legs. From the way he swore, he clearly thought he was all grown up, though Mitch estimated he was too fresh-faced to be much more than a year out of high school. He wasn't a dropout, or at least didn't dress like one. His chinos fit, his flannel jacket looked sharp, and his black Timberland dress boots had a shine so bright, they glowed.

Ten feet ahead, the man in the coat had left the sheltered lot. He stood in place, looking around as though giving his eyes a moment to adjust; Mitch saw they were wide, bloodshot, and cushioned by sallow, puffy skin. They made him think of Alex in *A Clockwork Orange* when they held his eyes open with metal clamps. After a shake of the head, the guy's unblinking eyes returned to the phone's screen and he resumed his walk.

Frowning, Mitch grabbed his badge from the glove box and flung open his door, considering the best way to get rid of the hothead driver, who was stomping around and thumping his fist on the Rogue's hood.

"Hey yo, what's up, man? You backed into me. You stupid or something?" the young guy shouted.

Mitch showed the badge.

"A cop? That don't scare me." The guy's fresh face soured into a sneer.

At the word "cop," the man in the coat paused. Mitch took a half step to the angry guy's right just in time to see the guy mesmerized by his phone breaking into a jog, then a sprint. As the guy ran, he let the hand with the phone swing free, while the other stayed where it was inside the coat—unnaturally so.

In a flash of insight Mitch prayed was wrong, he tallied up the bulk of the coat, the rage rock filtering out of the phone, that hidden hand, and the man's troubling, fidgety intensity. The nightmare scenario awoke Mitch's basic instincts. Ignoring the Buick's angry driver, he made to run after the man.

The young guy caught Mitch's sleeve and wrenched him around. "Hey, yo, I'm—"

Mitch slammed him hard against the side of the SUV. At six feet tall and 190 pounds of mostly muscle, he was capable of putting out some power. The young man was stunned but didn't lose his hold. "Let go," Mitch growled. The guy let go.

Mitch ran. Between his lean body and long legs, he could blow most of the cops he ran with off the track. The man in the long coat had a good lead, but by the time he reached York Street, Mitch was only an arm's length away. He made a grab for the shabby coat but missed. Without an instant's hesitation, the man charged between two parked cars and into the street . . . right into the path of a blue sedan.

The driver blew his horn and slammed on his brakes, but there was no time to stop. He swerved right, almost sideswiping the parked vehicles and sending Mitch backpedaling out of harm's way. Mitch looked up, seeking his suspect, and his breath caught in his throat. The guy had nearly been run down by another car coming at him from the opposite direction. If Mitch's insight was right—the man was likely hiding a suicide vest under his coat—being hit by a car might either simply kill him or transform him into a fireball.

A symphony of horns blared as the man pounded across York to disappear among the line of dumbfounded moviegoers. Mitch vaulted the trunk of the blue sedan, his mouth open to shout at somebody to stop the man. He swallowed the words. The bomber's Napoleon pose suggested he was holding a dead man's switch. If he let go, either voluntarily or because somebody jostled his elbow, the vest would explode, killing the people in line, in the cars nearby, and likely those in the lobby. If Jessica and Ethan had gotten no farther than the concession stand, they would surely be caught in the blast.

Mitch couldn't ask anyone else to stop the bomber. His specialized training had prepared him for such a moment.

His only hope was to reach the guy and stop him from releasing the trigger. It would mean clamping the bomber's hand through the fabric of the coat while he cut the blood to his brain with a chokehold. It was an illegal move, but, given the circumstances, that was the least of Mitch's worries. It could work . . . but only if Mitch got to him in time.

Ignoring horns from ahead and swearing from behind, Mitch darted in front of a stopped car and zigzagged past one that was still moving. From the middle of the street, he saw through the glass front of the theatre into the vestibule. The bomber, standing in the center of the circular lobby, looked strangely alone under the domed ceiling, notwithstanding the line of theatregoers snaking around him.

Sweeping his gaze to the right, Mitch saw Jessica. She was in the middle of a line leading to the concession stand. He couldn't see the stand from his position, but over the roofs of the cars parked in front of the theatre, he saw Ethan's hand holding on to Jessica's.

Mitch launched himself forward, barely avoiding being run down by a panel truck. He'd just reached the row of parked cars when the bomber dropped his phone, his mouth open, shouting something Mitch couldn't hear.

Time stood still.

As Mitch watched, the bomber's phone tumbled toward the floor of the theatre's vestibule. Time oozed forward and, as Mitch braced to scream Jessica or Ethan's name—afterward, he'd be unable to remember which one—he saw the room filled with people vanish in a blinding pulse of white light.

Mitch's racing brain told him it was a fireball; not that it mattered. What did matter was one moment there was a lobby packed with people, and the next, there was no lobby and no people—only that terrible brightness.

Everything Mitch loved—his entire life—was gone so fast it hardly registered. The detachment of watching everything in slow motion detached him from the cataclysm; an SUV in front of him flew up toward him as he flew backward, and every nerve in his body lit up with searing pain.

Then the pain was gone, along with sight, and sound, and motion. The world turned gray, the air filled with a wash of white noise, and he was utterly still, body and soul.

Was he dead, or was he in Death's lobby? Perhaps all he needed to do was wait. There was nothing else he could do. Mitch thanked God for that much. Death would reunite him with Jessica and Ethan. He would see Mama again and get to introduce her to the grandson she'd never known. She had been a pillar of the Grace United Methodist Church and had taught Mitch what it meant to be human. She'd also taught him songs that had never left him, even years after he had joined Jessica as a lapsed Wesleyan; "Nearer My God to Thee" played through his mind as the Senator Theatre burned and people screamed.

3—A Quiet Morning

Darren McGann watched with curiosity as the idiot cop who had stopped his SUV in front of Darren's gold Buick LaCrosse raced across the parking lot and over to the theatre. He seemed to be chasing an odd-looking guy who was in love with his phone. The cop skimmed the roof of a car across the street, only to be sent head over heels seconds later by a monstrous explosion. The blast lifted Darren's high-shine Timberland dress boots off the asphalt and tossed their owner to the ground. Twenty-five years old, yet appearing much younger, Darren brushed himself off and checked his short, dark blond hair for debris. Anyone who had not spent his entire high school career as an all-state wrestler would have broken a bone. Not Darren. He landed on a forearm, a hand, and the toe of a boot. Changing his vertical direction with a kick, he was back on his feet in time to see the same cop literally fly across the roof of the car he'd leapt only moments before, skim the back window, and tumble across the sidewalk to strike the wall of the building opposite. A second afterward, an SUV parked in front of the theatre echoed the move, smashing the roof of the car and rolling up against the same building, no doubt crushing the cop beneath it. A second blast wave followed, accompanied by bellows of smoke so thick, it might as well have been a concrete wall.

"D!" shouted Darren's wife, Vanessa. A stately, brunette Amazon compared to his stumpy self, Ness was tall enough to meet his eyes with her baby blues over the Buick's top while she was still half in the passenger seat. How he'd ever managed to catch such an awesome woman, he wasn't sure. But he had hastened to put a ring on her finger, and soon after, they were blessed with a son. Their four-year-old, Jeremy, was crying in his car seat behind the driver side.

Darren waved for Ness to sit down. "Stay with Jer. Wait for me. I need to help."

What he could do was beyond him, but Darren had watched too many cartoons growing up to retreat from a disaster. Lately, he had been compiling a playlist of old shows to show Jer. They had already explored *SpongeBob* and *Rugrats.* How would they ever move on to hero shows like *Dragon Ball* and *TMNT* if Darren was a coward in real life? Besides, it's what his dad would have done. Yep, Colonel McGann would have jumped in without any thought to his personal safety to help rescue the injured and wounded. He would never expect his small, cowardly son to do the same. Darren could almost hear his father's voice in his head. "I'll take care of this mess. You go play . . . like you always do. Where exactly I got a son who's afraid of his own shadow, I'll never know. Someday maybe you'll grow up to be a man."

He puffed out his chest and ignored Ness, whose cries of "What?" and "Don't go!" trailed after him all the way to the wall of smoke. As he passed into darkness, another wall hit him—one of heat. It sucked away his breath and beaded his skin with sweat. He dropped to his knees, hardly able to move.

Dust and smoke had swallowed the world. Even the cars inches away were barely visible, as was the hand he held to his face. The only visible light came in orange pulses from several directions at once and in lurid, neon sparks from somewhere ahead. Horns and screaming came from all around. As the sparks were the only things holding their place, Darren faced them as he rose. He felt his way forward, hunching low and taking shallow breaths.

It wasn't long before he slipped in a patch of something wet. His boot kicked flesh, and he found himself looking down at a body. The darkness was so complete he had nearly stepped over the woman, but he knew she was there and was able to make her out. She was lying with her face to the sky. At first, Darren thought her head had sunk partway into the pavement. On second look, he saw the back of her head had been smashed flat. Blood oozed from her brain to form the gooey crimson puddle in which he'd slipped. One of the dead woman's eyes dangled from its socket on a bloodied cord of gristle. Moved by a sudden humanitarian impulse, Darren lifted the eyeball and set it on top of where it belonged. His stomach was too queasy to shove it all the way in. A flash of the memory of his ten-year-old friend Trevor lying bleeding on the floor blazed through his brain. He shook it away.

Everywhere Darren looked, bodies littered the street. He danced over so many, they stopped being people and began to blend in with the rubble. Whenever he found someone who seemed mostly intact, he would stop to grasp a hand or shake a shoulder, but he never got a response, only sightless stares. Nearly every piece of glass in every car had been shattered by the blast that had come, he came to realize, from the theatre's lobby. Everywhere he walked, pebbled safety glass crunched underfoot.

Once, when he had drawn close to the source of the sparks he had followed, entering a region of cleaner air and unbearable heat, a gust of wind blew a hole in the smoke. Off to his right, Darren saw the burned wreck of a body jammed through what remained of a driver's window. The body was too small to belong to an adult. Its head had smashed into the head of the driver. Heat had welded their faces together with a seam of melted flesh. As Darren recoiled, a sound like a groan issued from the demolished driver. It seemed impossible he could be alive. Before Darren was able to check, the wind shifted, shrouding the scene again.

The whole setting was too much for Darren. Why had he ever thought he could help anyone in such a hellish scenario? No, no, the blood and guts, the feeling of utter helplessness. He recoiled back to his childhood. Sounds of cruel laughter from other kids, adults, everyone. He was always the smallest. The shortest end of the stick. The one chosen to do what no one else in the group wanted to do. The one who was always too small to defend himself.

A memory assaulted him—the one he tried to avoid thinking of. Somehow amid all the smoke and carnage, the other brush with death in Darren's life came rushing back . . . a group of boys alone in the basement of a farmhouse one afternoon after school.

"I bet you wouldn't even have the guts to try." Austin was the kid with the confidence to be leader of the pack of fifth-grade boys. All the others laughed; no one was brave enough to stand up to him.

"I know where my dad keeps his guns. And I know where the key is too." To prove his claim, Austin led the group up to the office where his dad worked on his books in the evenings and weekends. There, a large mahogany desk was covered with papers, pens, and a closed laptop, and a pair of bookshelves were crammed with oversized, important-looking leather books—except for one reserved for trophies and a major league baseball displayed on an aluminum stand. A gilt-framed painting of a hunter taking aim at a sky full of geese adorned the opposite wall. In the back corner of the office sat the gun case. Sunlight streamed through the slats of the thick wooden blinds, its brightness the antithesis of what was to transpire in mere moments.

Austin stood on the desk's matching chair to locate the key on top of the gun cabinet. Then, hopping down, he unlocked the cabinet and removed his father's revolver—the one he'd been instructed countless times never to touch. Like a pro, Austin clicked open the empty chamber and popped in a single bullet from a box stored in the cabinet. Holding the loaded gun out to show it off to his friends, he declared, "See? One bullet. Let's go back downstairs."

The boys trooped back down the stairs; those doing the talking did so in voices quicker and high pitched with excitement.

"Yeah, I saw this on a movie once."

"I think my older brother tried it with his friends."

A couple of the boys fell silent.

"So, this is how it works." Austin boldly looked each boy straight in the eye. "We'll choose one of us to point the gun at Trevor."

"Hey, why me?" Trevor protested.

"What? You scared? It's just one bullet." Austin chastised. "You have *five* chances nothing will happen—and only one chance something will."

Trevor's face turned deathly white.

"Okay, now we'll vote for who's going to be the shooter." Austin picked a small Mead notebook from his schoolbag and tore out a strip of paper for each boy. As Austin handed out the paper and a pen to each boy, Darren saw him whisper something to three of them. When Darren got his, Austin whispered nothing to him. Each boy wrote down a name, and Austin collected the papers in a baseball cap.

With dramatic flair, Austin made a game of opening each slip of paper. "First slip. One vote for Darren." He removed another and unfolded it with a flourish. "One vote for Matt. Next. Another for Darren." He glanced at Darren with a wicked smirk on his face. "One vote for me. And . . . the last slip? Looks like you're the winner, Darren." Austin laughed, but the other boys held their silence.

Oblivious to the unease in the room, Austin carried on as lighthearted as if he were merely calling names for a game of pickup softball. "Trevor, you go over there by the wall. Darren, here, you take the gun. Now, you're gonna go over by the other wall and point it at Trevor. On the count of three, you'll shoot once."

Trevor's face appeared as ashen as the dirty, half-melted snow outside the window. Darren's short legs quivered, but he didn't dare stand up to Austin; last year, he hadn't even been in the running to be part of the popular group of boys—he was just grateful to be a part of the gang. Darren took the gun in both trembling hands, walked to where Austin had directed, and raised it in Trevor's direction. Trevor stared blankly at him from the other side of the room, and Darren was pretty damn sure the dark spot on the front of the kid's jeans hadn't been there before.

"On the count of three," Austin announced, and had the rest count down with him. "One . . . two . . . *three*!"

Running on automatic, Darren squeezed the trigger.

Trevor's shriek matched the thundering boom of the bullet's release. Darren tumbling over backward with the recoil, and every single boy screamed out at once.

"He's hit!"

"Darren shot him!"

"Call an ambulance!"

"I'm getting out of here!"

One of the boys rushed over to check on Trevor. The others, minus Austin, shot up the stairs in a thunder of footfalls like demons escaping from the flames of hell itself.

Austin stood staring silently into nothing. Darren lay on the floor and covered his face, too terrified to look.

For his part, Trevor continued to emit ear-piercing screeches as blood gushed from the wound Darren had given him; his T-shirt was soaked with a bright red stain. "I'm dying! I'm *dying*," he gasped before finally passing out on the cold cement floor.

That sudden silence hit Darren harder than Trevor's blood-curdling frenzy of noise. He sat up but lacked the strength to stand. He crawled across the basement, past the shocked, still-staring Austin, to the boy who sobbed next to Trevor.

"He's d-d-dead," the kid said.

As deep shock set in, Darren was suddenly overcome with a detachment way beyond his years. Feeling he had to be the one to take charge of the situation, he examined the source of all the blood: Trevor's shirt was torn atop his shoulder, where the bullet had grazed him. Darren noticed the boy was breathing—at least he wasn't dead. Forcing himself to examine the wound, Darren discovered the bullet had barely nicked Trevor's shoulder, despite the pool of blood beneath him. "He's fine. He'll be fine," he declared.

"What?" The sobbing boy quit crying enough to weigh up Darren's pronouncement.

"The bullet barely touched him."

As Darren shook Trevor gently until he came to, the full realization of what he'd done just to remain in good standing with the popular boys hit Darren head-on. He crumpled into the fetal position and sobbed, not caring anymore what the other guys would think of him; he'd not cried that hard since the day his dog died.

Time stood still as Darren's tears flooded his face to soak through the front of his shirt. Vaguely, he became aware of Trevor and the other boy sobbing alongside him. Austin slipped quietly from the room.

Somehow Darren made it back to his home in base housing that day. Telling his mom he didn't feel good, he went straight to bed. Dad was deployed again and would never have to know how close he'd come to having a murderer for a son.

Darren never spoke to any of the boys in the group ever again. When they went out for football, basketball, and baseball, Darren took up wrestling. He worked out with intensity to build muscles to make up for his small stature and to compensate for some hole of shame inside him he would never be able to fill. When he'd see Trevor in the hallway at school, he'd avert his eyes. The mere sight of Austin made Darren seethe with out-of-control anger, even years later. He vowed to never again let anyone control him, and his appetite for violence died.

The rumor around school was Trevor had climbed a shelving unit in his basement and knocked a set of tools from the top shelf. Something had scored his shoulder and knocked him to the floor. Other than receiving a stern talking-to about doing something so lame-brained, Trevor had emerged unscathed. As far as Darren knew, none of the boys' parents ever learned the truth about what had happened that day. Their shame was buried deep in their souls, and the fraternity of fifth-grade boys kept their secret into adulthood.

Back in the present, feeling shaken, sick, and on the verge of fainting from heat, Darren turned back. His dash into hell had accomplished nothing. He was no hero and should never have pretended to be one. His job was protecting his family. What had he been thinking, leaving Ness and Jer?

Then the obvious truth hit Darren like an internal shock wave.

Stupid! Of course! Why didn't I see it?

The whole scheme, the crazy cop, the bombing—it had been meant for him! He'd known for years people were after him. Ever since the day he'd almost shot Trevor, Darren had realized people were following him, wanting to point the finger of guilt at him. They'd upped their game—big time. He checked to the left and right to see if someone was eyeing him but couldn't see through the smoke.

He was struck with the sudden terror he wouldn't be able to find Ness and Jeremy through the smokescreen. What if they had wanted him to leave his family alone so they could kidnap his wife and son while he was gone? He started back in the direction he'd come. He wandered until he fell, adding his groan to the screams, the horns, and the crackle of the burning theatre. The building itself was shrieking as wood warped and portions of brick work gnashed together like teeth. Any second now, the flaming ruin would crash down on Darren's head.

In a blind panic, he ran from the sparking lights, inhaling painful gulps of superheated air. He collided with someone lurching the other way in the dark; his exceptional balance was unable to save him. He crashed onto gravel that had once been sidewalk. As he scrambled to his feet, he heard a wheezing gasp coming from underneath a twisted metal doorframe. A hand reached out, touching his arm. An innocent person caught unaware in the plot to snatch Darren. Maybe he could help before returning to his family?

"Hold on," said Darren. "I've got you."

He put his shoulder to the edge of the frame and managed to heave it an inch. When he took hold of the hand to drag out its owner, the skin and muscle sloughed away, like smoked meat off a rib. Darren panicked and tried to say he was sorry, but all that came out was a gagging cough. Trevor's face and bleeding wound flashed again in his memory.

Overhead, the shrieking of the wood and brick changed its pitch. Letting the limp hand fall, Darren fled, stomping on corpses and shouldering the injured out of his way. He broke free of the smoke and saw the parking garage, just as the arched upper story of the Senator Theatre collapsed behind him. The thunderous roar of twisted metal, wood, and dust dispersing suddenly in all directions spilled him onto his side, but he didn't lie still. Scrambling to his feet, he glimpsed Ness running toward him from across the parking garage.

"Go back," he cried. In his head, his voice was a roar; it came out as a hoarse whisper. His lungs were scorched. He was bruised all over. Still he rose, croaking when he would have shouted: "Drive. Go home. We have to go home."

4—City to City

Yasaman woke to shouts and laughter. She checked the backlit clock, saw it was three in the morning, and decided to go for her gun. She had reloaded the double-action revolver in the car, though it had seemed at the time like she was courting bad luck. When would she need to shoot six bullets in one go? Straining to hear any sound from inside her hotel room, she knelt on the bed. The grainy bed sheets felt itchy around her knees. As a fugitive, Yasaman knew sleeping nude was a habit she'd have to give up, but it was the first night and, although her panic bag contained two tight-bound wads of US dollars, it didn't have nightclothes. It was short on many things, though it contained extra underthings, stockings, and a toothbrush. She'd used the most important item it had contained to shoot a man.

Never in her bitterest dreams had Yasaman imagined she would take a life. Perhaps she still hadn't. The man on the bridge might have been wounded, not killed. He could be sleeping, now, beneath warm covers, while she shivered in the dark, her skin prickling thanks to the cold night air.

She made out the shape of her panic bag in the dark. She crawled to where it lay, retrieved the revolver, and squatted with a shoulder against the wall, facing the door. Would the first man through be distracted by her nakedness? If he looked fast and didn't blink, he might be able to catch an eyeful before she added his death to her list of sins. Merely warning him off wouldn't do. Yasaman loved life too much to risk it on a thug's discretion, however traumatic destroying him might prove to be. She waited with a steady gun barrel and deadly intent.

No one came through the door. After Yasaman gave herself time to listen, she discerned the noises that had woken her were coming from outside the hotel window. The frenzied assassins she'd imagined to be the source were in fact a crowd of five or six young men. They were chanting, swearing, and screaming jokes. Something had excited them past the point of vulgarity. As she peeked out of her curtained window, the guys started singing. The song's beat was familiar to Yasaman, though the lyrics were not.

If someone had asked for her opinion on the original, Yasaman would have been hard pressed not to roll her eyes. In original form, the song was a saccharine ballad urging all discontented youth to hoist the flag of Iran. The extremist pastiche being sung by the men outside was far worse. It blended calls to jihad with misogynist murder porn. America was named a nest of devils, and the rape of its women was prescribed as a response.

Yasaman still gripped the revolver. After a few seconds watching the men through a crack in the curtain, she set the safety and let the gun hang at her side. As disgusting as she found their sentiments, the men gave no hint they were agents of the group that had tried to have her kidnapped. So long as she was inside and they were out, there was no reason to worry about them.

Then she heard another voice. Looking to the right, Yasaman recognized the night manager. He was standing a dozen meters from the men, shaking an angry fist. "Shut up!" he said. "There are decent people sleeping here. Do you know the time?"

The singers laughed. One said, "Do you know the time, old man? It is time for revolution."

"Go home," said the manager. "Leave my property. Don't trouble my guests."

"Your guests must wake up," said his opponent. "The Great Satan staggers. It has suffered a killing stroke."

Yasaman cringed, away from the window. The speaker's tone and his phrasing reminded her of Father. For the seven years he had lived with her and Mother, he had talked glowingly about his years as a basiji. To hear the brute tell it, he had personally been responsible for the overthrow of the Shah and the commencement of the Cultural Revolution that had followed. Certainly, he had broken the heads of liberal demonstrators; she definitely believed his bragging about that. Once, he had caught young Yasaman mouthing the words of some Western pop song she had heard in the schoolyard. He'd pressed her little body against the wall, mashed her windpipe with his forearm, and dared her to utter such deviltry in his home again.

A woman's voice brought Yasaman back to the present. "Shame!" shouted the woman, who was peeking around a door at the group of men. "You are celebrating the work of those madmen? Go away. Be donkeys in your own homes."

The singers mocked the woman and the manager for several minutes before the shouts of other guests moved them on. Yasaman didn't know what to make of what she'd heard. She set the revolver on the bedside table and stood chafing her gooseflesh. What could have happened to drive the hatemongers into the streets? She switched on the TV, tossed back the quilt, and sat cross-legged on the top sheet, flipping through channels. Fire, smoke, and sirens were on every one. At first, Yasaman thought she was looking at stock footage, historical archives of history's disasters. The building she saw burning—was that One World Trade? The people fleeing the subway—were they in London or Tokyo?

The truth dawned gradually. It was no historical footage. The word "Live" appeared in the corner of several newsfeeds. There the camera panned over a scene at a baseball stadium, where police in riot gear were barking at a crowd of people who ran with arms above their heads in a scattered line across the playing field, hastily exiting through a hole that appeared to have been knocked in the fence by a nearby fire truck. The on-scene camera operator pivoted to show stadium seats, where starburst muzzle flashes from at least two assault rifles were keeping a half dozen paramilitary officers pinned down. Bodies draped the bleachers. Yasaman could have traced the gunmen's position by the distribution of corpses, if the crackle of their weapons hadn't made it obvious.

She flipped the channel and a new scene of horror appeared. It, too, was "Live," according to the thick red banner underscoring the action. Two men in plain clothes were carrying a woman along a sidewalk. Each man held an elbow of the woman, who was twitching spasmodically. Her face appeared frozen, but her head jerked side to side and her arms and legs shook so badly, the men had to shift their positions every few steps. They practically wrestled her past the camera, which was evidently someone's phone, as it promptly flopped into landscape orientation to show rescue workers in gas masks dragging people from a narrow doorway. The first two evacuated were twitching like the woman. The next was a child, a little gold-skinned girl with hanging braids, who lay in her rescuer's arms as still as stone.

Yasaman took a respite then, setting aside the remote control and holding a hand in front of her eyes. For the first time in a decade, a rote prayer sprang unbidden to mind. She dismissed it, selecting instead a Vedic mantra to hum under her breath until her heart settled down. When she no longer heard her thoughts, Yasaman returned to switching channels. At last, she found BBC Persian. The story explaining the "Death to America" zealots was reported as a series of bombings, shootings, and gas attacks in "city after city, town after town." Nearly all the cities and towns seemed to be in the United States, though there were rumors of similar incidents in London, Paris, and Brussels.

At the bottom of the screen, names of cities and brief summaries of what had happened in them went scrolling by. Yasaman knew a few city names. New York, Miami, and San Francisco had all been targeted. Kansas City, Baltimore, and San Antonio—all of which sounded familiar, though Yasaman couldn't have placed them on a map—were on a list of sites with the highest potential body count. All the reports were preliminary but astounding. Yasaman had to remind herself the events were taking place thousands of kilometers away. She was safe, comparatively speaking. Her numbness was a natural response to cold. Her vertigo was an illusion. Trembling, she pulled the quilt around her shoulders.

"What we will now show is footage provided to the BBC by an affiliate of the American Cable News Network. A warning to sensitive viewers: the scenes are upsetting. We will wait a moment for children to leave the room."

Yasaman switched off the TV. The world had gone mad—madder—overnight. Who knew how people on the street, not to mention the zealots and extremists and political leaders, would respond? Her encounter with

Farbod's kidnappers had made her think like a hunted animal, and she scented wolves on the wind. She would have to flee, but where? What was happening in the United States was clearly a transformative event, as surely as 9/11 had been. Security everywhere would tighten, as it always did after outbreaks of mass terror. It might just be to her benefit, if the people who had taken Farbod and whom she believed would continue to try to take her were criminals or foreign agents, as she suspected, but it would also make her own movement around the country more difficult.

She also considered the possibility her enemy was the Ministry of Intelligence or some other Iranian state agency. They might pounce on her the first time she showed her ID. She had told the night manager it was forgotten at home, weeping a little to imply she was fleeing an abusive husband. He had proven to be softhearted, but she could not count on tender treatment from every official in her path. If she marched into Tehran International Airport without her passport, she would be marched right out, probably under guard. And even if the national government wasn't out to get her, the Tehran police might well be. Witnesses had seen her shoot the man in the public park, witnesses who might not know she had been acting in self-defense, or might not care.

For an hour or more, Yasaman sat silently in the bed, playing out scenarios in her head in hopes of settling on her best course of action. In the end, she decided to remain where she was for a few days, to see what new shape the events in America gave her situation. In the morning, she would pay the hotel manager in advance for her stay. If he claimed there were no vacancies, she would offer to let him visit her in the night. Her panic bag was strong on cash. Tomorrow she would search out the black market, buy a new phone, and maybe have a fake passport made. If her name did not show up on a wanted list by Wednesday, she would drive back to Tehran, park in an out-of-the-way place, and hire a taxi to the airport. If her name did show up, she would make plans to emigrate by land instead.

She dared not wait too long. All the countries she'd ever pictured herself settling in—ancient lands she would be happy to explore for the rest of her life—might be declared enemies of Iran before the week was out. Only by moving swiftly could she be sure of escaping to their shelter. She would wait and watch a few days, then sprint as fast as possible for the border.

She rose at dawn and was in the hotel office minutes later. Despite her promptness, she found herself standing at the back of a queue. Had her fellow guests assembled to complain, perhaps refusing payment for the interrupted night's sleep? No. They were mostly men in business suits. Their neat hair and restrained nervous energy precluded incivility.

"Pardon me," she said to a fat, baby-faced specimen near the back.

"Hello, good morning," said the businessman. "You are stranded, mademoiselle, as we are?"

"Hello. I am sorry. Why do you say you are stranded?"

"Ah. You have not heard. The world changes so quickly. You know of the attacks in America, yes?"

Another man invoked Allah's protection. Yasaman said, "I do."

"Good. You are not far behind the times. Their president, the strutting peacock, insists the leaders of all nations should swing wide their doors. He withholds aid, threatens sanctions against any country that does not welcome the diplomats with open arms. This is funny, yes? Very droll to our countrymen."

Yasaman felt a chill. "What does the Supreme Leader say?"

"What else? There will be no welcome, no so-called diplomats. From this day, we reject American blood money. Our borders are closed to any country that cannot control its criminal element. For now, it means *all* countries."

"They have closed the borders?"

"Firmly. International travel is to be by special permit only."

"How does someone get a permit?"

"Who knows? If I did, mademoiselle, I would be on my way to the airport, bound for the ten o'clock to Riyadh. Ha! Emirate Air isn't even allowed in our airspace. Ah, what can we do? Only wait another day. Perhaps the peacock will apologize, yes? The world turns on such chances. For now, I can only beg the hotel to let me keep my room. You will do the same, mademoiselle?"

Yasaman gave no answer. The thought of closed borders had made Iran seem to shrink to the size of a birdcage. She was the bird, and the whooshing she heard was the claws of a cat swatting at her through the bars.

"Mademoiselle? I have made you upset. Forgive me."

She touched her hand to her heart. "What? Oh, there is no need. I am grateful, sir. Thank you for sharing this news."

The businessman bent his neck slightly and touched his right eye with four fingers, to indicate his sincerity. Yasaman nodded to acknowledge the antique gesture before backing away and jogging all the way to her room. She couldn't stay, now. With air travel impossible, she would have to spend every minute seeking a way out.

She left money on the nightstand to cover her bill and swung her bag onto her shoulder, keenly aware of the weight of the revolver inside. Would extra police forces be assigned to the roads? She would have to avoid checkpoints. Leaving her key card in the door slot, she fled along a hallway and down a flight of stairs, humming her mantra the whole way.

5—Against Medical Advice

"Sir?" said a voice Mitch didn't recognize. "Detective Wilson?"

He moved forward in time, an experience indistinguishable from sinking in the ocean.

"Mitch?" said a different stranger.

"How are you, Detective?"

"Mitch?"

"Detective Wilson?"

"Mitchell? Can you hear me?"

He knew the last voice at once. There had only been one woman in the world who called him *Mitchell*. How Mama could have gotten to Baltimore from heaven, he didn't know.

"Can you hear me, baby boy?"

Of course he could. Even his deaf aunt Karen would have heard Mama speaking so loud and so close. It sounded like her voice came from the middle of his head.

"Time to get up, Mitchell."

I'm tired, Mama. Let me rest. A building blew up. I flew through the air. A car landed on me, I think.

Through billows of glittering sea-foam, Mitch Wilson swam back to life. His vision was a narrow tunnel showing a mostly flat world, but he saw enough to know he was in a hospital bed. His mother, the venerable Elizabeth Cullen, née Pontefract, ex-Wilson, was a backlit cumulus levitating off to his right. Mitch tried to greet her and realized his jaw was splinted. The rest of his body was similarly restrained. Not even his arms and legs were free of wrappings; he was bound in more bandages than Boris Karloff, the mummy who came back to life in the old film.

The cloud that was Mama began to drift away. Mitch opened his mouth wide enough to whisper, "Mama. Help me, Mama." He was tugged into darkness before she could respond and rode for a while on a silent tide.

When he opened his eyes again, the world had broadened and taken on depth. He was able to move almost freely but was in too much pain to want to. He recognized he was in a hospital room, albeit an empty one. Mama was long gone. He was no longer wrapped in bandages but had some kind of goo covering the exposed skin of his arms and legs. Something else was gone too, but Mitch couldn't remember what. His memories were splashes of yellow paint on a white wall, which he could barely make out. Images of a brown Buick, a coated stranger, a brilliant white flare, and a levitating SUV appeared in his mind, but he couldn't make them fit together.

Flying. He'd flown. Or had been hurled through the air like a human fastball.

A TV hung on the wall. Spotting the remote lying on the bed, he picked it up and switched the TV on, groaning at the realization that even that simple movement made his tight, burned skin ache. Keeping his arms as still as possible, he cast about for news channels, hoping the information would help jog his memory.

He flipped past a dozen old movies and half as many again morning talk shows before he found CNN. Jim Acosta was adding his two cents to a review of the president's speech. He agreed with the panel that it had shown great leadership. Mitch waited for Jim to add a caveat, but he didn't. The panelists all nodded their heads, and then fell strangely silent, clearly uncomfortable. Mitch didn't know the panelists and didn't much care what the president had said, nor that his critics were tongue-tied. He was about to try Fox when a woman whose looks split the difference between stunning and relatable announced the next segment would feature images some viewers would find disturbing.

The aftermath of a series of disasters played out on the screen. Buildings burned. Shattered bodies of adults and children were wrestled from rubble by first responders and civilians alike. Whole families fled a stadium with their arms above their heads. A police chief broke down sobbing in a professionally filmed news segment. Smoke clouds hovered above neighborhoods in a dozen cities, said a reporter. SWAT teams roamed the streets of a dozen more. The US Attorney General announced at a press conference there *was* a pattern to the attacks. Most had been carried out at movie theaters, although sports arenas, bowling alleys, and concert venues had also been targeted. A symphony hall in Indiana had been the site of a mass shooting with deaths in the double digits. A famous ballet dancer was among the victims of a Houston apartment fire assumed to be started by an arsonist.

Mitch tried to sit up when images of the Senator Theatre appeared on screen. Pain decked him and memories came flooding back in graphic detail. He remembered pulling up to the curb on Rosebank Avenue. Ethan had been excited about a movie. Jessica had taken their son to wait where it was warm while Mitch found a parking spot. She had said, "Love ya," and Mitch hadn't said it back.

He clamped his eyes shut, not wanting to see more, but the memories played out against the curtain of his eyelids. He opened his eyes and searched the railing of his bed for a call button. Fail.

His first shout was weak, but with practice he made it louder. "Nurse. Nurse. *Hey! Nurse!*"

He found the button and thumbed it. On screen, the woman who had introduced the news clips explained the targeted theaters had all been showing *Spex: Your Electric Friend*. The stadiums and other targeted locations all had advertising for the highly anticipated children's film. Billboards showed baseball mascots playing catch with Spex, some kind of cartoon owl. Promotional videos showed trailers on concert screens. Even the ballerina's torched apartment complex had gotten in on the act, accepting money from studio marketers to display a huge *Spex* banner.

Some of the attacks had nothing to do with the film, but most experts believed these were distractions—deliberate attempts to obscure the pattern. Newscasters gave the same explanation for the few attacks outside the US. On the day after the attacks, a member of the Senate Judicial Committee had given an interview that gave the mass terror event its name.

"The tragedies we all witnessed have inscribed a bright red line between the world we used to have and the world we have now. The peace and security we fought for after 9-11 is gone. The War on Terror is over. We lost. There's no getting back to the other side of the line we've crossed. We can only move forward. God help us all."

A middle-aged black woman in nursing scrubs appeared in Mitch's doorway. "Detective Wilson? You shouldn't be—"

"Where's my wife?" said Mitch. "Where's Jessica? Where's Ethan?"

The nurse swept in, motioning for him to calm down. As soon as she was in reach, he grabbed her and pulled— the adrenaline rush enabling him to ignore the pain signals shooting to his brain—dragging her to him with shaking limbs.

"*Where are they?*" he demanded.

His throat was finally clear, his arms strong despite the trembling, but he only managed the one outburst before releasing the woman and flopping back against the bed. Mashing an eye with the heel of one hand, he lifted the TV remote with the other and smashed it against his forehead. On the third smash, the plastic shattered. Mitch firmed his grip on the broken remnant, preparing to grind the jagged edge into his flesh.

The nurse lunged across his bed to grapple his wrist and hold his hand down with the full weight of her body.

"Stop that, Detective. *Stop*! Mr. Wilson, listen to me. We're short-handed today. I can't call anyone to help. Are you going to make me hurt myself to get you to act right? I raised two boys; I'm that stubborn. Don't try me; I won't give up."

Her motherhood reached him. The nurse was somewhere between Jessica's age and the age Mama had been when she died. He saw the resemblance in her determination. Easing the pressure he had been exerting, he let go of the broken remote. She swept the bits into her hand.

"How long have I been out?" asked Mitch.

"Nine days on and off. Nine days and some hours. I was here when you arrived with most of your clothes burned off and covered in and ash; the paramedics told me they pulled you out from under a car—you're lucky you weren't crushed or burned to a damn crisp, Detective; it looks like the Volvo saved your hide." A pained, wistful expression crossed her handsome face. "Compared with a lot of the others, you've gotten off lightly with a few second-degree burns." It was obvious to Mitch the nurse stopped herself short of telling him he was one of the lucky ones.

"Were there . . . other survivors? From the theatre, I mean."

"Your partner came by, Mitch. I'm sorry. Your wife and son didn't make it out."

Mitch swallowed, clenched his fists, and closed his eyes. He shut out the world as best he could, willing it to go away.

When he had been silent for several seconds, the nurse said, "I have to leave you in a moment, Mitch. We're short-handed, like I said. Can I trust you not to hurt yourself, or do I need to strap you down?"

He said, "Why did I live? I wanted to die. Why didn't I?"

"I need you to stop that talk, Detective. We can't afford such thinking on this side of the bright line."

Looking at her, Mitch felt his neck hairs rise. He couldn't accept the full weight of his losses yet. He needed proof. But then the rational side of his brain kicked in. He would never get to bury the bodies of his wife and son. They had been incinerated. Knowing they'd been at the epicenter of the bomb was all the proof he'd ever get. Denial would get him nowhere. He moved quickly to the next stage of grief, anger. Thoughts of how horrific the ending had come for his wife and son crept in, like a tiger ready to pounce. They hovered directly behind a heavy curtain he was unwilling to open, yet snatches of despair threatened to creep beneath and between the panels of the drape. He held the anguish at bay as two competing instincts awoke in his brain. He wanted to either fight the tiger or run from it, but he didn't know how.

Eyes blurring, he glanced away from the nurse, at the TV, where the CNN analysts were commenting on the terror investigation, which was already in its second week. Local law enforcement in the victim cities were scooping up suspects, inciting concerns over civil liberties. The FBI had been silent, so far. The only statements they had issued were that they were on the case and were marshaling their resources. Suddenly, with a surge of energy, Mitch's decision seemed plain.

"You're right," he told the nurse. "Talk won't help." He lifted his arm, indicating the IV tube in his arm. "Can you get this out?"

"I can talk to your doctor about having it removed."

"You take it out. Or I will."

"No. I'll talk to Dr. Gammage. It's her call."

"Take it out, and get me my clothes, my badge, and my cell phone."

The nurse placed a hand on her hip. "You came to us just about naked, Mr. Wilson. You don't have a cell phone or a badge. How's your hearing?"

"Huh? I hear fine."

"That's a miracle. Try to listen: You were covered in so much blood, we were sure your eardrums had burst. You sustained second-degree burns and you're still at risk of infection—which is part of the reason there's an IV."

"Thanks for that," said Mitch. Bracing himself, he tugged at the IV.

The nurse swore and grabbed his hand with just enough force to send pain shooting up Mitch's arm like an electrical charge.

He snarled. "I need you to call my partner. Tell him to get here quick and bring me some clothes. If the doc wants to talk, she can walk me to the door."

"You're not going anywhere, Detective. Look, I get it," she said when he opened his mouth to roar at her. "I understand you want to *do* something—anything—not just lie there and get right. But if you hope to do anything for anybody *ever* again, you will lie there until your doctor says your IV can come out."

"I don't need—"

"Where'd you get your medical degree, Detective? This is *my* bailiwick, not yours. I will tell you what you need. Is that clear?"

Mitch swallowed the litany of things he wanted to snarl and lay back against the raised head of the bed, glaring at his tormentor.

"Good. The first thing you *need* to understand is the IV is what's making it possible for your skin to heal and fight off infection. That and the gallon or so of Silvadene you're wearing. I should also mention your left knee is wrapped like a burrito, and the shushing sound you hear is the ice therapy machine working on your right hip, which—by the way—was seriously mashed by the Volvo that saved your life. Now, you will lie there while I call your partner and page your doctor, or I will restrain you. Is that *also* very clear?"

Suddenly exhausted, Mitch closed his eyes. "Painfully."

He expected the woman to return to the nurses' station to make her calls, but she clearly didn't trust him. Instead, she called Ben and paged Dr. Gammage from the phone in Mitch's room.

6—Exit Strategy

Compared to navigating the labyrinth of Tehran's Grand Bazaar, Yasaman found making her way around Tabriz Bazaar a joy. She enjoyed the sunbeams streaming through the open skylights of the arched, vaulted red brick ceilings, which joined with the wonderfully ornamental wall lamps to provide ample lighting, and was pleased to nod at fellow shoppers and share pleasantries with the vendors and excitable hawkers. The rustic stone paths led her from one storefront to the next, where each shopkeeper's wares—everything from wool to rugs to blankets to produce and exotic spices that filled the air with such heady scents—tumbled outward from each shop into the path, considerably narrowing the area available for walking. No one got so caught up in the hustle and bustle of commerce to brush her off when she asked for directions. She didn't want to make a spectacle of herself, but she did need help. She was happy so many gave it willingly.

She was, however, aware that she might stand out as a woman alone. She was used to the more relaxed, cosmopolitan atmosphere of the capitol, in which unaccompanied women were accepted and not always assumed to be of dubious moral standing. But this was away from Tehran, where the majority believed that a woman must always have a *mahram*—typically a male relative—by her side.

And the very last thing she needed was to draw attention to herself, especially since the anonymity of the crowd helped quell her paranoia that any one of the men in the bazaar could be someone out looking for her.

Turning a corner she'd been told would lead to the bazaar's pottery section, Yasaman was confronted by a pair of armed soldiers. The insignia on their headbands identified them as basiji—militiamen—like her father had been. Yasaman had noted an increase in their population since the American "Red Line" attacks. Before, there were too many. Now, they were common as stray dogs. Keeping her head down, she shuffled past. One basiji looked her over, visually probing her outfit for any feature he might expose as immodest; she could see from his demeanor he was displeased she was unaccompanied. The chador she had on left him disappointed; the pure white garment covered her from crown to ankle.

Yasaman busied herself at the closest lace seller's stall until she was sure the soldiers had walked on. The stall's owner, a wizened old woman with a leathery face etched deep with lines, grinned at her with the few teeth she had remaining.

"Pretty lace for a beautiful lady?" she said. "Perhaps a handmade tablecloth for your husband's dinner table?" She made a big show of peering around the bazaar for Yasaman's nonexistent husband.

Yasaman shook her head. "Perhaps something smaller," she said.

"I have tea napkins." The old woman rummaged through her hodgepodge of seemingly random merchandise and plucked out a handful of delicate lace napkins. "I made them all myself."

"They are wonderful." Yasaman took the offered napkins and turned them over in her hands with great care. They were, indeed, quite beautiful, but she'd seen many others like them on other stalls around the bazaar. Either the old woman was impossibly prolific at napkin making, or she sourced her goods from the same wholesalers as everybody else. "How much?"

"I have a special price just for you—one hundred and twenty thousand rial."

"I was thinking fifty," Yasaman replied, amused that the woman was still working in the old currency. While the old woman's offer put the napkins around three US dollars, she was playing for time; the basiji were still within sight.

"The lowest I can go is eighty," the old woman said with a theatrical sigh. "But only for you."

Yasaman produced a bunch of notes and pressed them into the woman's hand. "Thank you," she said with a genuine smile. A quick glance around told her the basiji had moved on, swallowed by the bustling crowds. It was time for her to go.

Not that Yasaman particularly wanted the napkins, but she figured nothing would be more likely to stick in a shopkeeper's memory than a woman who feigned interest when the authorities were nearby only to lose it the moment they were out of sight. The last thing Yasaman wanted to be was memorable. She'd stopped in Tabriz on a journey she hoped would take her out of Iran, and there was just one man in all of the market she wished to meet. To everyone else, she intended to be invisible.

Yasaman's journey simply to arrive at the bazaar had been remarkable. Retrieving an old memory from her earlier life, she'd acted on her hunch. It had then taken four hours on a hotel phone to contact a great aunt who knew

Mother's rabbi. Yasaman hadn't seen her elderly relative in an age, and had been surprised, in fact, to learn her great aunt was alive. They had spoken briefly, using formal, overly polite language designed to preserve their detachment from each other's lives. Finally, Auntie had given Yasaman what she wanted: the rabbi's phone number.

A day had then passed before the rabbi's granddaughter returned Yasaman's call. The rabbi had been able to put her in touch with a friend of his, a man Yasaman could vaguely remember speaking at their *kenesa*, or Persian synagogue, in those long-ago days when she had been too young to refuse to go.

In his sermon, the rabbi's friend had told how he had fled Iran as a boy. It had been somewhat after the Revolution, at a time when the status of Jews in the new Republic was unclear. He had settled in Israel with his family and, as a young man, had then returned to Iran, the home of his youth, which was a nominally more tolerant place than many had feared.

The rabbi's friend, a plump, gray-faced man somewhere in his middle age, had the knowledge Yasaman needed, and she'd offered to pay him to help her escape from Iran. Being much in need of money, he agreed to help her, and the two had set off together from Tehran in his car, heading toward the northern border of Iran.

After three hours on the road sharing small talk and trivial facts about their respective lives, Yasaman had felt safe enough to try to glean some information from the rabbi's friend. "You have relatives in the Israeli homeland?"

"Of course."

"You must know many interesting people there," she'd fished. "A man of your means must know Mossad?"

The man had bristled at hearing the name of the Israeli secret service. "Maybe I do. Maybe I don't." Clearly, he was not to be drawn on the subject.

"Forgive me," Yasaman replied. "I did not mean to pry."

Ignoring her apology, the man said, "I am driving you to a place where you can speak to my rescuer—the man who helped me flee the country. He is retired now, I think. Makes his living as a ceramics seller in Tabriz. He would like to meet you. The company of a woman who knows she is beautiful is always a delight to him. He will know to expect you."

"Are there such women?" Yasaman had maintained a casual air. Inside, her heart had leapt. Was she really on the verge of finding a man who could get her out of the country after a week of abject failure?

The two drove the rugged Iranian roads by night to avoid daytime crowds and questions. He'd then dropped her off at a hotel within walking distance of the Tabriz Bazaar and instructed her how to reach the rescuer.

Yasaman felt refreshed after several hours of sleep, a shower, and a cup of hot Persian tea with her lunch. By late afternoon, she was ready to enter the bazaar and begin the search for the man who would hopefully transport her across the border.

Which was how she'd found herself standing amid a jostling crowd with lace napkins in her hand, scouring the bazaar nervously in case the basiji returned.

"Excuse me," she said to a woman selling dishware at the stall adjacent to the lace seller, "do you know the ceramics seller Bilel Sarraf Nezhad?"

"He has the best plates in the bazaar," the woman said with a smile. "Even better than mine." She tipped her head toward her own wares as if they were terribly subpar. "But his prices . . ."

Yasaman smiled back. "I will be sure to come back to you if Bilel doesn't have what I'm looking for."

"But what if I have sold out?"

Having no time or patience to stand and argue, Yasaman plucked a plate with a rich, Persian blue pattern from the woman's stall and had her wrap it up in brown paper.

"The man you are looking for is over there," the woman pointed across the bazaar as she carefully slipped the plate into a plain brown paper bag. "Tell him Frida says hello."

Bilel was tall and stout, with a shiny bald head. When Yasaman spoke his name, he turned to face her and flashed a smile she was sure he'd practiced in the mirror. With smoky eyebrows and an orange beard, the guy's face made Yasaman think of a campfire. His uneven teeth were the dull yellow of parchment paper, his eyes dark and somewhat clouded, though they peered at her with crystal clarity.

"How can I help you, little flower?"

The allusion to her name startled Yasaman. She wondered if he'd said it as a test. The man who'd set her on Bilel's trail had said she would be known. Shrouded in her chador, Yasaman didn't see how.

She glanced around for eavesdroppers. There were none, so she said, "I have come a long way to seek a man of your ability."

"I am humbled," said Bilel. He bowed and swept a hand at the multitude of teapots, cups, and saucers set out on chest-high shelves. Each set was painted with a different geometric design, every one intricate and precise. "You will examine, please. Make me an offer."

She was glad to get down to business. Nodding, she lifted a dainty cup by the handle, setting it down. "I don't have much time."

"You will need little, madame."

"Madame?"

"Forgive me, mademoiselle. Perhaps you will tell me how much you wish to spend. I can then explain what that amount will purchase."

Yasaman lowered her voice. "Are you always so mercenary, monsieur?"

"I live to serve, mademoiselle." Bilel patted his paunch and added with a laugh, "But I must eat, eh?"

"I can pay you in dollars," Yasaman offered.

"American?"

"Of course."

"Then I believe I have just the perfect merchandise for your exquisite tastes." Bilel gave Yasaman a crooked smile as he mopped the top of his head with a filthy old rag.

"That is my understanding," Yasaman was growing weary of the ridiculous double-speak; she was in the Tabriz Bazaar, not some James Bond movie. Even so, she understood perfectly the necessity to be guarded—in Iran, there were inquisitive ears everywhere. "I am sure I have more than enough money to afford anything you have on offer—even your most exclusive items."

Bilel's smile evaporated. "You understand such items come with great responsibility and risk?"

"For which you will be more than adequately compensated, Mr. Nezhad."

Bilel's eyes narrowed. He fished around in his pocket and pulled out a slip of paper, which he slipped into Yasaman's hand. "Be here tonight, no later than ten," he said with a quick glance around the bazaar.

Yasaman purchased the dainty cup and its accompanying saucer, which she secreted in her bag alongside the blue plate. Then, with the negotiations swiftly concluded, she stepped back into the crowd.

That night, under cover of darkness, Yasaman entered Bilel's home. She carried the bag containing everything she had run away with, along with the few clothes she had purchased since. A small, round table stood in the middle of Bilel's tiny kitchen. He rapped a knuckle on the rough wood. Yasaman set down the bag where he had indicated. With a sigh, she opened the bag and handed over an envelope containing the remainder of the currency she had managed to hide away over the course of the past eight years. Bilel accepted it without comment, then motioned Yasaman into a chair. He laid out tea before retreating to another room, taking the envelope with him.

The tea was strong and bitter. It tasted of haste and desperation, as if Bilel had shaken out the tin, pounding the sides to free the last clinging tea leaves. Yasaman helped herself to sugar. She preferred all things in balance, if not a little sweet.

"Is it enough?" she called to Bilel when she could bear waiting for his verdict no longer.

"Of course," said Bilel. "More than enough, little flower." He didn't offer one single toman back.

Yasaman sipped her tea until dawn. The sun found her and her new companion rumbling southeastward out of Tabriz in a Jeep Yahoo that was her senior by decades. The outskirts of the city of Tabriz provided something to look at, at least; the picturesque views along the Quru River valley offered a wealth of verdant green, and Yasaman had always taken great delight in the stunning views across the majestic volcanic plugs of the Sahand and Eynali mountains. The city itself was a sprawling mix of modern towers and quaint, traditional housing, interspersed with straight, tree-lined roads. Yasaman had always considered Tabriz to be a city best appreciated from afar, for one to truly take in its beauty.

When they got farther out, the landscape was desolate, with barely a tree to see anywhere on the horizon. When Yasaman asked where they were going, Bilel winked and retrieved a cigar box from under his seat. She opened the box in her lap to find the other item she had purchased, aside from Bilel's service as a smuggler. It was a cell phone, sitting naked on a bed of white paper.

"Encrypted," said Bilel. "Untraceable as any of one of those things can be. Don't call anyone. When we are farther from the city, I will mount the satellite receiver." He pointed to the Jeep's ceiling. "You can get caught up on YouTube, eh?"

"Thank you," said Yasaman. In spite of the protective shell around the phone, the screen had cracked. When she powered it on, images flickered on either side of a jagged seam. With nothing to watch, she tucked the phone away and tilted her seat as the Jeep slurped up pavement and the morning sun painted the desert pink.

7—Last Known Address

Nothing remained of the Senator Theatre. At least, nothing to indicate that only a little over three weeks ago, it had been a place people wanted to visit, a happy place they *loved* to go. The upper story of limestone and glass was gone, replaced by open sky. Where the box office and sidewalk had been were domes of rubble covered by construction tarps. A backhoe had done some digging before being abandoned. Police tape fenced off half the block, stretching from the corner of the building next door to the far side of Rosebank Avenue, then cutting in front of the house behind the theatre before making a return to York.

Cleanup had been focused on Rosebank. Mitch had asked storeowners across the street if they knew when the tape would come down, but nobody had any idea. He had a keen desire to park on the corner and shout, "Love ya!" out the window, as he should have done on the fateful day. They would have been decent last words, an acceptable thing to say before he blew his brains out.

No. None of that thinking. He wasn't going to run away. He was going to fight. To emphasize the point, he ground the end of his metal single-point walking cane into the pavement of Belvedere Market Square parking lot.

"Mitch!" said a voice from his right. Detective Ben Martinez strode into view. Based on the volume he had used, Mitch guessed he had missed the first couple times Ben had called his name.

"What?" said Mitch, turning.

"It's freezing out here. Let's get in from the cold." Ben was a little guy, a whole head shorter than Mitch, with a pudgy face and large, deep-set eyes, which he scrunched up, as though in concentration. He was trying, Mitch realized, not to dart a look across the street.

"What's wrong?" said Mitch. "Think it'll hurt to look?"

Ben mumbled something Mitch didn't catch.

"Speak up, Benny Boy. You scared of a few bricks, some busted concrete?"

"Don't— Let's go in, Mitch. Please."

"What did you say just now?"

"Huh?"

"You mumbled something a second ago. What'd you say?"

"It was nothing. Come on. Let's go."

"What, you keeping secrets from your partner now?" Supporting his weight on his good left leg and grimacing with each new movement, Mitch pointed his cane at Ben. "Speak up. Tell me what you said."

Ben let out a breath as thick as the frozen mud around the bombsite. "I said, *Maria mater gratiae*. Mary, mother of grace. Now come on. It's too cold. Let's get some coffee."

They drove up York to a Panera and sat warming their hands for a full minute before Mitch said, "You got what I asked?"

Ben drew a thumb drive from his jacket, but when Mitch reached for it, he pulled it back. "Tell me your plan, first."

Mitch suppressed the impulse to lunge across the table and grab the damn thing. "Who says I've got a plan?"

Ben balanced the drive on his palm. "Looks light, huh? Heavy inside. The Feds made us turn over the hard copies and erase everything digital. The information in here, you can't get anywhere else. If you had stayed cooped up in the hospital one more day, you wouldn't have been able to get it at all."

He'd already been in the damned hospital two weeks longer than he'd wanted, with Nurse Indomitable or one of her minions watching over him like wicked, cherubic hawks. He'd decided the woman must have been a sadistic dominatrix in her spare time. "What do you want from me—money?"

Ben laughed. "If I wanted money, I'd charge you rent. I want to know your state of mind. If I give you this information, what will you do?"

"I told you, I'll take a look, get to know the case."

"Then what?"

"Then nothing. Nothing I can do. You don't think you'd get like this if you lost—" He broke off, not wanting to mention Ben's family, even as a hypothetical. Maybe he was just superstitious, but realistically, he still couldn't let the thoughts of his own lost family seep in. In fact, even the shadow of their memory created in him the strong urge for some whiskey. Panera's hazelnut coffee, though good, lacked the numbing effect he currently needed.

"If you were me," he told Ben, "you'd want to know everything. I guarantee it. And I'd get you everything I could."

Ben sat back, flicking his eyes from Mitch to the thumb drive still balanced on his palm. "We had some close calls, partner. Those days back at GT. I got you out just in time."

He was referring to the Baltimore Police Department's Gun Trace Task Force, on which they had served together for three months, ten months prior to eight of its officers being busted for corruption.

"Way I remember it, I got *you* out, Benny Boy. Checking traffic cams for stolen cars was more your speed."

"Exactly my point. I'm the brains of this operation. You're the muscle; it's the way we've always worked it. And that's why I need to know your plan, bud."

Mitch flinched, his forehead creasing. He unconsciously clenched his fists.

"Whoa, what's wrong, bud?"

"Don't call me that," said Mitch.

"Don't call you—oh." They had been friends for a long time. Ben had heard Mitch call Ethan his "bud" a thousand times. He said, "Sorry. Won't happen again. Listen, uh, Mitch. You know I ain't above a little street justice, but you can't go all Death Wish on a federal investigation, if that's your plan. You can't curb stomp Al Qaeda, or whoever did Red Line. I know what you're going through. I mean, I don't understand, but I get it. If it had been Liza or the girls, I couldn't have left the hospital. I get you, man. I do. If you want to spend the rest of your life going through case files in my basement, I'll bring you snacks on a TV tray. What I won't do is help you get locked up, or killed, or—"

"Don't worry," said Mitch. "You won't." It was the fastest he had ever told a lie, and he pulled it off with a straight face. He extended a hand.

"You promise you're not going to do something crazy?"

"You're the brains, right? You tell me."

Ben mumbled another prayer to Mary and passed Mitch the drive.

"This is everything?" said Mitch.

"Crime scene photos, notes, witness testimony. Our friend in Homeland was generous."

The Homeland Security Investigative Taskforce was a sister division to their own Regional Auto Theft Taskforce. Both men had contacts in HSIT, mostly acquaintances, but also a guy from Mitch's old precinct and a woman whose name they never spoke out loud once Ben was a married man. Mitch didn't ask which friend had provided the thumb drive. If he was caught with it later, he couldn't give up a name he didn't know.

Mitch removed his laptop from the courier bag he'd brought with him. Liza had fetched it from his place in Towson on the first night he'd crashed in the Martinez guest room. She had also brought him the clothes on his back and the spare credit cards he had yet to use, since Ben and Liza had been feeding him the past week. Benny had retrieved the Rogue from impound and topped off the gas. Remembering his friend's generosity, Mitch gave him a smile over the laptop lid before he plugged in the thumb drive.

Their friend had indeed been generous. It would take hours to go through the documents, to say nothing of the video evidence and interviews. Ben coughed to grab Mitch's attention.

"I have to get to work. You know I don't want to hassle you, but the brass would like to know when you'll be coming in for mandatory counseling. There's a report they need to file to figure out your compassionate leave."

Mitch mentally bookmarked the passage he was reading. "Say I'll be in tomorrow."

"Will you?"

"Sure."

Ben looked unconvinced, but he said, "Good. That's good news. How 'bout tonight? Will you be home for supper?"

"Sure," said Mitch. "Liza's doing those pork chops with the mushrooms—"

"And the cheesy rice. What do you call it?"

"Risotto. How could I miss risotto?"

Ben rose, leaving his half-full cup of coffee on the table. "Great. I'll see ya then, bu—uh, man."

Mitch showed him another smile. That was four smiles total he'd dispensed since he'd woken up. He'd given one to Liza, one to the older Martinez girl, Cella, and those two to Ben. He wondered how many more he'd have to put on before he got his hands around the throat of somebody—anybody—responsible for taking his family. He'd be able to smile without faking, then.

Ben waved from the door. Mitch waved back. As soon as his partner was gone, he got back to reading. He found what he was looking for sooner than he had expected. As he was typing the address into his phone, it occurred to him, if he hurried, he really might be able to finish his work in time for supper, as he had told Ben. That would be nice. Everything he had eaten since the coma had tasted like chalk. Liza had assured him her pork chops were the cure for whatever ailed him. He had smiled at her and lied in agreement. Unfortunately, whiskey and revenge were the only true cures for him at this juncture. He thought about praying—something that came so naturally to Ben and had once come naturally to him—but he wasn't sure he should be talking to God right now.

It had taken mere hours for HSIT to identify the man Mitch had failed to stop from destroying the Senator Theatre. CitiWatch, the guardians of Baltimore's CCTV, had captured his face from multiple angles. The bomber, Akhtab Mattoo, had been born on September 8, 1994, at

Jersey City Medical Center, where he'd been a guest at the Neonatal Intensive Care Unit for a month. Finding out Mattoo had been born in the States was a slap to the face. Learning that doctors had fought for the man's sick, twisted life turned Mitch's stomach.

Mattoo had grown up in and around New Jersey, the son of Pakistani immigrants. Exactly what had brought him to Baltimore, HSIT's report didn't say, but they had been meticulous in laying out his travel history and known associations. He had made two trips to the country of his parents' birth, spaced eight years apart. The most recent had been in 2012. That proved nothing; the domestic contacts Mattoo had made were more interesting.

A man by the name of Mohammad Ali Khan, who was brother to Mattoo's wife Hanifa, had been on the national No Fly List for seven months in 2005 and again from April 2010 to June 2013. Khan was in FBI custody. Mrs. Mattoo had been questioned by a team of Baltimore PD and FBI agents. Finding she had no insight to offer as to how her husband had been radicalized, the joint task force had released her, then been disbanded prior to BPD handing the investigation to the Feds.

It was ten before noon when Mitch cruised by the Mattoos' last known address. The squat row house had a padlock on the front door and boards over every window. Mitch parked down the street and hiked up the sidewalk. The going was slow. His right hip ached and he wasn't used to walking with the cane. He kept losing his rhythm, slapping the cane down when he meant to plant it and pull. His new, pink skin was still healing and delicate to the touch. Every time he moved, the new-grown flesh on his arms and legs reminded him of that hellish night.

One particular patch of skin on his arm had started emitting a foul odor and oozing a thick, yellowish liquid. He suspected it was because he'd been lax about the course of Bacitracin and Silvadene he was supposed to be using. He promised Dr. Gammage he was keeping an eye on it, mostly by using whiskey to forget. In the back of Mitch's mind, the words of the overbearing nurse reminded him he was no good to anyone if he wasn't good to himself. She'd gotten her way and managed to keep him in the hospital for an additional two weeks; he figured she was probably still gloating.

A kid's sled had been abandoned in the front yard of a house Mitch passed. Spotting it, he jolted to a halt. For an instant, he was sure the boot prints connecting the sled to the home's front porch belonged to Ethan. It took the rest of his walk to put the notion out of his mind.

Nobody came in answer to his knock at the Mattoos' front door, so Mitch circled around. The side windows were boarded and too high to access if they hadn't been. Bracing himself on the handrail, Mitch climbed the steep back steps, relying on leg muscles he formerly kept strong via regular trips to the gym. The back door wasn't padlocked. When Mitch tried the door handle, it twisted in his hand. A deadbolt had been deemed sufficient to keep the riffraff out. Like the windows, the glass panels in the door's upper half had been boarded over. Mitch tried to pry the edge of the plywood with his fingers but couldn't. Whoever had nailed the board knew how to swing a hammer.

He saw no faces in any adjoining windows, and nothing was moving outside, not even a cat. Mitch heard the usual tumult of city life—distant music, braying horns, rumbling engines—but no voices, nothing to suggest anyone was close by. He lifted the back of his jacket. The .38 was in a holster at his waist. He drew it carefully and backed down a step, listening carefully for any break in the silence.

"Stand clear of the door," he said. "This is your last chance. Stand clear."

Covering his face with his sleeve, he fired. Pausing to correct the aim of each shot, he blasted the top-right corner of the sturdy board. With four ear-aching cracks, the bullets opened a hole the size of a bread plate. Mitch bashed splinters out of the hole with the gun barrel. Quickly as he could without gashing the tender skin on his arm, he reached inside and felt around, praying the deadbolt was a single cylinder and operable by hand. If it was a double cylinder, requiring a key to open, he'd risked a criminal charge for zero gain.

His fingers found the deadbolt's rosary. He twisted the rosary and worked the doorknob. A shove of the shoulder later, he was inside the house. Before moving on, Mitch took a moment to relock the door. If anybody was going to come after him, he wanted to hear their fumbling. Holding his weapon in front of his body, he searched the two-bedroom home. It was empty, completely abandoned. A bed frame had been left in one room. In another he found a mattress. A dresser was in the mattress room, and a love seat had been shoved against the front door. The major appliances were gone, and the place had been professionally cleaned. The only dust was sawdust from the door and particles of drywall from holes the bullets had punched. He saw nothing else of interest in the house.

Mitch was putting the SUV in drive when a squad car drove by, running its lights but not bothering with sirens in a neighborhood where the patrolmen knew most folks by name. When the car had passed, Mitch pulled away from the curb, glad his "Plan A" hadn't ended with him in handcuffs, even if it had failed to put him in touch with the woman who had known Akhtab Mattoo best.

"Plan B" was nearly a complete success. At one fifteen p.m., Mitch pulled into a parking spot on Wright Avenue, opposite the driveway to Armistead Gardens Elementary School. He'd already synced his new phone—purchased at the Apple Store minutes north of Panera—to his streaming dash cam. Rather than wait until somebody noticed he was spying on kids, he locked the Rogue and took a stroll down Wright. He killed thirty minutes wandering aimlessly, practicing with the cane and making frequent stops to rest his hip and stinging skin. The temperature had turned frigid, but he was grateful for it. He took a couple swigs from the flask he kept in his upper pocket but stopped at two so he'd stay alert. Shivering gave him something to focus on.

If Ben had called to ask what he was doing, Mitch would have said he was following doctor's orders—walking, moving. It was better than sitting at home, brooding. All true, so far as it went. Of course, by home, he would have meant the Martinez place. The modest three-bedroom house in Towson, Maryland, he'd shared with Jessica and Ethan was strictly off limits. Every time he imagined going back, pictures from his dead life hijacked his thoughts. Memories of the good times would frequently fill his brain. Even as he planted the end of the cane on the sidewalk, scenes of making love on the sofa came back to him. He saw himself spilling wine on the tablecloth when Jessica made a joke, and Ethan squinting up at him with his gnomish newborn face as he settled into his crib for the first time.

What a gift Ethan had been. All those long months of trying to get pregnant slowly merged into years. Jessica took her temperature daily upon waking, timed their lovemaking, and used fertility drugs in a process emotionally draining for them both. Remembering the two miscarriages, Mitch had barely let himself look forward to his son's birth. After the long wait and many disappointments, he was afraid he'd have trouble bonding with the baby when it finally came. But one look at the helpless, screaming infant, and Mitch was a goner. He would have killed anyone who even hinted at harming his son.

Following Ethan's birth, Mitch and Jessica decided that, after all the emotional ups and downs, any future pregnancies would happen organically—or not at all. Thus, Ethan was their one and only. He completed the picture and made their family whole.

As Mitch pushed the memory away, he felt a light tug on his coattail. He turned, expecting a three-year-old Ethan with a welt on his check where he'd run into a potted plant. Nobody was there.

Parents started forming a pick-up line around one forty-five. Mitch didn't rush back to the Rogue. He sauntered like a man without a care, keeping an eye on his phone at all times. Occasionally, when he felt someone watching, he pretended to swipe, as though scrolling through a feed or a dating app. His finger never quite touched the screen. He had panned the dash cam feed to exactly the angle he wanted, zooming just enough so he was able to make out the colors and shapes of the vehicles as they entered the school's driveway. License plates entered and exited the frame as he watched. He'd memorized the tag number of Mrs. Mattoo's Chrysler. When she showed up to retrieve her fourth-grade boy, Mitch would be ready to follow.

He climbed into the Rogue, marveling there was heat to be had so long after leaving it parked. He cranked the engine, turning to scan the next few license plates in person. A squad car was parked behind him, on the other side of the street. Two of its wheels were on the sidewalk. The bored officer inside lifted a hand to return somebody's wave. Mitch wondered if he'd come back to the SUV too soon. Would the officer notice him, question him, insist he move along? He considered flipping his turn signal. All the other drivers were making a right turn into the drive, pulling around, and exiting to the right. If he made like he wanted to turn in left, would they interrupt the flow or make him wait forever? He didn't want to turn. His plan depended on staying put, but it could all go south if the officer got suspicious.

Suddenly, the Chrysler was there. Mrs. Mattoo had waited in line and was turning in. Mitch felt a surge of relief, the first since waking up. His lips curled into his fifth smile of the day. The woman at the wheel of the Chrysler wouldn't see him any better than he could see her through the windshields of their respective cars. They were just suggestions of people, their facial features and expressions distorted and blurred by the curving glass. Mitch glanced away anyway.

After she made the turn onto school property, Mitch opened his glove box. He transferred a ski mask he had bought at a Walgreens near the Apple Store into a pocket. If all kept going as well as it had, he would have need of it soon.

Running errands took nearly two hours. Mrs. Mattoo went to McDonald's, then CVS. She used the drive-thru at both places. Shopping at the halal market on 33rd consumed the biggest chunk of time. Mitch monitored his gas closely, opting to shiver rather than run the heat while he waited. He'd been on plenty of stakeouts in his life, but always with a partner. Waiting on his own took a different brand of patience, especially since he couldn't trust his own thoughts. His mind kept returning to the heaps of rubble that had been the Senator. Had Jessica known what was happening at the end? Would the coroner call him in soon to hand him a box of bone fragments to bury? He was beginning to crave another drink but again resisted to keep his head clear.

Mrs. Mattoo exited the market at 4:26 p.m. The drive to Eldersburg took another forty minutes. The whole of the trip, Mitch wished he had backup. It was tricky staying far enough back to avoid notice yet close enough to spot all the turns. If Ben had been pacing him in a separate car, they could have kept Mrs. Mattoo's vehicle between them, swapping positions at intervals. The rhythm of a good tail was impossible as a solo act. Mitch got away with it only because Mrs. Mattoo was distracted, either by her thoughts or her son.

The sun was sweeping the horizon when she turned onto Piney Ridge Drive. There was no need for Mitch to follow right away. He knew where she was going. The map on his dash showed an alternate route to her brother's house. He made two lefts following its directions, passing a school where Mrs. Mattoo was no doubt looking to get her son transferred. Two lefts later, he parked in a cul-de-sac. A service road led behind the houses. According to the map on the SUV's display, the road accessed a utility building of some kind close to the Khan residence. Mitch couldn't believe his luck.

He exited the Rogue. If Mrs. Mattoo had lingered twenty minutes more at the market, he would have hiked up the service road in darkness. On the cusp of twilight, the best he could do was keep his face down and do his best to stay out of sight.

He left his cane in the SUV. He couldn't afford to look weak in front of the woman he planned to intimidate. His height would help, as well as the bulky jacket, which made his shoulders look even broader than they were. He slipped his .38-caliber pistol into the jacket pocket. Remembering his struggle with the plywood over the Mattoos' back door, he got a small crowbar out of the Rogue's cargo hatch. The Lord only knew when it would come in handy. The crowbar didn't fit in a pocket, so he slid it up his sleeve, buttoning the cuff to keep the flattened, fourteen inches of forged steel secure.

Shuffling through the snow beside the service road took longer than Mitch would have liked, but his luck held. As he peeked around the corner of the privacy fence running around the Khans' side lawn, he saw Mrs. Mattoo exit her house's front door. The trunk of her Chrysler was open. Mitch had watched her stow the groceries at the store; thankfully, she had taken her kid inside before returning for the bags. He wasn't sure what he would have done if the child were still with her. There was no telling how many trips she had already made. If he wanted to confront her without adding another count of breaking and entering to his crimes, it looked like it could be his last chance.

He waited until Mrs. Mattoo was hidden by the trunk lid, then he slipped on the ski mask and attempted a sprint from the corner of the fence to the driveway. It turned out to be the most painful, least elegant run of his life. A spike of hot metal stabbed his hip with every long stride, his healing skin stung, and the area of his arm he figured was likely getting infected ached. The pain nearly forced out a scream, but Mitch pushed through. Glimpses of his shadow stretching out on the snowy lawn made him think of the Senator as it had been, moments before the collapse. Swirls of snow reminded him of smoke. The *shush* of his boots sounded like the murmur of the crowd.

Mrs. Mattoo slammed the trunk, saw Mitch, and dropped the bag she was holding. She took a tiny step back and covered her mouth. That piece of luck shook Mitch from his stupor; he had meant to cover her mouth himself. As she pulled her hand away, no doubt to scream, Mitch swung his arm up; his mind was once more fully focused on his plan.

He'd stop her cry for help, give her a good shake, and demand she tell him what she had kept from the investigators. How had her husband fallen in with the terrorists? He had to have had a communication channel.

How else would he have coordinated the bombing with the other attacks that day?

In his haste to ask questions, Mitch forgot the crowbar in his sleeve. He was gripping the gun in his right hand, so it was natural to swing up the left, but the extra weight of the bar made him misjudge his force. Instead of cupping Mrs. Mattoo's mouth, he struck her across the face hard enough to feel the shape of her cheekbone. She dropped to the concrete, saved herself within an inch of cracking her forehead, and stared at Mitch, a dazed look of terror in her eyes.

Mitch considered running for the trees. He hadn't meant to hurt Mrs. Mattoo, only to scare her, and only as much as it took. He would have run if not for his hip and aching skin, which were in agony, as well as his desperate need to know what she could tell him. Seizing her by the arm, he prepared to set her on her feet, then thought better of it. She was scared now. That much of the plan had worked. Why shouldn't he press his advantage? Instead of lifting her, he hunched over her, showing his teeth through the mouth hole of the ski mask.

"Don't scream," he hissed. "Stay down. I've got a—"

He didn't get a chance to say "gun" because a black sedan screeched to a skidding halt at the end of the driveway. A squat, dark-skinned woman whose large breasts strained against the front of her dark-blue jacket jumped out, shouting, "Freeze! Don't move!" She had a semiautomatic aimed at Mitch's head.

Over the roof of the sedan, a man's head and shoulders appeared. He didn't shout as the woman had done, but said firmly, "Stay where you are. FBI."

"I surrender," said Mitch, raising his hands. "I'm surrendering."

"Get back. Get away from her," said the woman, not waiting for him to obey before she advanced.

Mitch did what he was told. The woman's partner, a blond, baby-faced guy with the bulk and build of an NFL fullback, came around the car with a gun in hand to cover Mitch, while the woman took a knee beside Mrs. Mattoo.

The woman swore and glared at Mitch like she would have liked to blow a hole through his middle before telling her partner, "She needs an ambulance."

"No," said Mrs. Mattoo. "I won't go."

The woman protested. "Hanifa, you—"

"No."

The bull moose spoke calmly, never taking his eyes off Mitch. "You don't have to go anywhere, Hanifa. We'll get a doctor to look you over here."

Again, Mrs. Mattoo said, "No." She pushed herself to a sitting position, rejected the hand the female FBI agent offered in favor of the car's bumper, and pulled herself up. Mitch could only watch as Mrs. Mattoo stumbled up the driveway and climbed the steps to the front door, which had been opened by a woman in a peacock sari, who reached out to draw Mrs. Mattoo inside. The door closed, and Mitch heard the click of locks.

"Give me an excuse," said the female agent. She had rounded on Mitch and was aiming dead at his heart.

"Leave it, Wells," said her partner.

Snarling, the woman the agent had called Wells kicked a clump of slush from the edge of the driveway in Mitch's direction, her narrowed, intensely brown eyes staring him down. She thrust her gun an inch or two closer to Mitch, her slender finger poised over its trigger. "Try something. Come on!"

"Wells. Stand down."

After a final grimace Mitch barely detected in the light of the setting sun, she lowered her weapon. "Get him out of my sight," she said before turning away.

"Deal," said the soft-spoken giant who had talked her down. He motioned to Mitch. "Let me see your back. Hands where I can see 'em."

Mitch pivoted as he'd been told, though his foolish run at Mrs. Mattoo had strained his hip to the point he could barely stand. When his back was to the agent, the man approached. He patted Mitch down and took his gun. He clicked his tongue when he found the crowbar.

"It's not what it looks like," said Mitch.

"Hope not," said the agent. He pulled off Mitch's ski mask. After he had locked his prisoner in handcuffs, he added, "I'm Neil Parker, FBI. Are you going to give me trouble, Detective?"

"You know who I am?"

"We had you on satellite. Would have scooped you up earlier, only we thought you'd given up when you took your little detour."

"Sure," said Mitch. "And no. I'm not gonna give you trouble, Agent Parker."

Meanwhile, Agent Wells had gone up to the house to knock on Mrs. Mattoo's door. "Hanifa? Please let me in." A moment later she entered the house.

"It's Neil," said Neil. He turned Mitch gently and braced his elbow all the way to the sedan's back seat. The "door open" bell dinged as Neil climbed behind the wheel. "Slide to where I can see you, please."

The hip combined with the handcuffs clamping down on his sore skin made the move trickier than it sounded, but Mitch chose not to complain. He lurched to the middle seat and kept his head low as Neil executed a three-point turn.

"Neil, if you're turning me over, can we do it out here? Eldersburg, I mean. Give me to the county PD."

"I'm not turning you over," said Neil. He drove down a block and parked on the cul-de-sac where Mitch had left the Rogue. "Before we do anything, I want a word, Detective."

"Mitch."

"Okay. Mitch, how about you tell me what you're doing out here?"

For as long as he dared, Mitch kept quiet, staring at his knees. The absence of leads in task force files proved somebody needed to lean on Mrs. Mattoo until she gave up her husband's contacts, but he couldn't say as much to Neil. It sounded too much like an excuse to hit a woman. Which it wasn't—seeing Mrs. Mattoo fall had shaken Mitch, though not half so badly as knowing how terribly he had failed on the day of the attack. He had meant to scare Mrs. Mattoo, that was all. He hadn't meant to hit her, and if the FBI agents hadn't shown up, he would have tried very hard not to hit her again.

"I'm looking for answers," said Mitch.

Neil said, "Aren't we all?"

"You know I was there, right? At the bombing. Senator Theatre."

"I know. I'm sorry for your loss."

"Did you know I saw the perp? He walked right by me in the lot across the street. He was looking at his phone. This video. Some kind of chanting, a rock beat, gunfire. I figured he was pumping himself up for something, so I followed, but I was too late. Too slow. I couldn't do anything. I got within feet. Did you know that? Before he dashed into the street. If I'd have rushed him, dropped him like—"

Softly but certainly, Neil broke in to say, "You did what you could."

"I failed," said Mitch. "I didn't stop him. Everybody, all those people. It's all on me."

Neil was silent. If he had argued with Mitch, tried to console him or said anything else, Mitch would have shouted him down, insisting on taking the blame. The agent's stillness and his calm stare in the rearview mirror made Mitch pause. He studied the other man. The smooth skin and quiet eyes clashed with Neil's size, but they suited his demeanor. When Mitch started talking again, it was in a lower tone and a slower pace. He didn't rush to make excuses but spoke carefully, wanting to get his theory out.

"After what happened, I saw the profiles of the attackers on the news. Everybody who's been identified— Samowitz in Houston, Elmore in Denver, now Mattoo— Americans, mostly, the rest here legally. Clean, barely a parking ticket on record. Nothing in common, no connections, and nobody with any idea how they got radicalized. The internet's the obvious answer, but which part? Nothing on the dark net or they never would have found it in the first place. I started to wonder; maybe the video Mattoo was watching wasn't just a mood booster. Maybe it was a message, telling him what to do."

Neil was quiet for a moment, then said, "Some kind of code, you mean?"

"No. Not quite. Mattoo's eyes were buggy, bloodshot. He looked like he was on something. But like I said, clean record. No drug use in his history. He didn't smoke or drink. Everybody who knew him said he was a man of faith, straight as an arrow, up to the day he destroyed a building full of innocent people."

Another pause, then Neil asked, "You heard all this on the news?"

"I heard it. That's what's important." Mitch hesitated, unsure how much he should say. Neil was a good audience, and maybe, just maybe, in a position to help. Mitch said, "I think there was something about the video Mattoo was watching before he got to the theater. Not just a beat. Some kind of brainwashing. It hooked Mattoo like a drug. I think it told him—told all the Red Line attackers—what to do, and when. I thought if Mrs. Mattoo told me the websites her husband was into, his YouTube channels, whatever, I could figure it out. His internet history is only so helpful. He's been using a VPN."

Neil's calm facade flickered. He turned his head to look at Mitch eye to eye. "No news channels told you that."

Mitch gave a shrug to acknowledge the agent's guess. Sure, he had sources. What cop didn't?

Neil seemed to accept the shrug. "You say this video hooked Mattoo somehow, and it told him what to do. How's that supposed to work?"

"I don't know. My hunch is, some kind of posthypnotic suggestion." Mitch waited for Neil to laugh, but no laugh came. "Whatever was on his phone, it was life and death to Mattoo. If we could find it, we'd find out a lot."

A crease appeared in Neil's brow, giving him the look of a grade-school kid trying to puzzle out algebra. "We? Listen, what happened back there, with Hanifa. Nothing like that can happen again. You understand? I sympathize with what you've gone through, Mitch, but there's no 'we.' You're not FBI. According to your files, you're not even active BPD. You're on leave, and that's exactly where you need to be. Don't take this the wrong way, but if I were you, I'd be with family now, or friends. Anyone you've got."

Mitch answered on impulse. "Would you?" He stared at Neil until the agent looked away.

After an uncomfortable silence, Neil swallowed and said, "Since you're a survivor, we were going to ask you to come by the office." He produced a card from the car's ashtray. Mitch couldn't take it, as he was still handcuffed. Apologizing, Neil got out of the car and set Mitch free.

The card read:

U. S. DEPARTMENT OF JUSTICE
FEDERAL BUREAU OF INVESTIGATION
Special Agent Neil Shaun Parker

Printed at the bottom was the field office address on Lord Baltimore Drive, along with Neil's phone number and email.

"Call me tomorrow," said Neil. "Or drop by. It's my boss I want you to talk to, Special Agent in Charge Trent Falwell. He's spent the last three weeks sleeping on a cot in his office, so anytime is fine. Though, we should maybe give Wells a night to cool off. She only let us go because she thinks I'm cracking your head up against a tree."

"Is that the sort of thing you do often?"

"Hardly at all."

"Likewise."

"Good to hear. You won't go near Mrs. Mattoo again?"

"Nowhere close—trust me."

Neil considered for a second. "I didn't tell you this, but the thing with her husband came out of left field. A nice, quiet guy, like you said. The Mattoos and Khans—their world is in pieces now. Hanifa can't tell you what you want to know."

"I won't ask."

Neil looked troubled, as though unsure he actually believed what he was hearing. Mitch pinched the card between his fingers. It was a lifeline he hadn't expected to be tossed, and he didn't know what to do next if Neil took it away. If he could get to Neil's boss, make him listen to what Mitch had to say, Mrs. Mattoo would remain safe; there'd be no need to go back on his promise.

"Let's get one thing straight," said Neil. "You're coming in for an interview, that's it. I'm telling you now. Don't try to stick your nose in FBI business."

Mitch gave him smile number six since the coma. "Hey, I wouldn't dream of it."

The puzzled grade-school Neil came back, but before he could rescind Mitch's invitation, an ambulance sped past the cul-de-sac, pulsing its siren.

"Whoa," said Neil. "You better go. Keep your lights off until you're around the corner. It'll be better if Wells doesn't see you go."

"I'll do that," said Mitch. "Thanks."

Neil went to the car and returned with Mitch's gun. "I'll keep the crowbar, if it's all the same to you."

"Sure. Don't need it."

When Mitch's hand was on the Rogue's door handle, Neil called his name. Mitch turned in time to catch his ski mask. After tossing it inside the SUV, he gave Neil a nod. Fumbling for his keys, his eyes fell on the camera affixed to the dashboard and an idea popped into his head: he would show Neil's boss the footage it had recorded in the Belvedere parking lot. The special agent in charge wouldn't have to take his word about Mattoo's strange behavior— he'd see that for himself.

Mitch frowned. If the cam had been at a different angle, it may have captured the video playing Mattoo's screen. What a shame to have missed such a crucial clue by a few degrees. There was CCTV on the thumb drive, but none of it had caught a clear image of the phone screen either. If only other dash cams had caught the footage. But, of course, there were, he realized. Mitch had license plate numbers for dozens of cars that had been in the lot or driving along York Road. There was a chance, just a chance, someone had caught precisely the right angle . . .

He slammed the Rogue into gear and zoomed out of the cul-de-sac with newfound energy, spotting Neil's taillights as he turned. In his head, he was already sifting through the names of BPD contacts who could help him link license plates to cars and cars to drivers. It was going to be a long night. He hoped Liza didn't mind him wrapping his pork chops to go. He had phone calls to make and people to visit. If he was lucky, he'd be able to sit down for breakfast. Maybe he'd even postpone that drink for another day.

8—Special Delivery

A pair of headlights flashed from the end of Darren McGann's street. He went to the window and watched the lights come closer. The yellow glow of the street lamps revealed, instead of the delivery truck he'd hoped to see, an SUV slowly rolling up the street. It was coated in thick dust, even the windshield, where the wipers had cleared a pair of eyebrow-shaped trenches for the driver to see out. As impatient as he was to call his brother, Rod, and ask when the truck would arrive, Darren leaned against the window, watching the SUV go by. The left rear quarter panel was dented.

Darren straightened, glancing at the driver. A streetlight gave him a glimpse of the guy's face. He jumped, feeling his heart flip.

It couldn't be the cop from the terrorist attack, the one who'd bumped Darren's car in the parking garage. Red one he'd seen thrown clear across a four-lane street and buried under an airborne SUV. There was no way the guy wasn't dead. Everyone who'd gone under the dust was deceased—all except Darren. The mainstream media said there were survivors, but Darren knew better. All the independent reporters he followed online agreed. No one had come out alive from any of the Red Line attacks. Those who gave interviews on fake news were all crisis actors. Besides, if there had been anyone alive under the dust when Darren ran in, he wouldn't have run out and driven off but would have stayed to help with the rescue. He would have made his dad proud. Which he hadn't. Case closed.

The SUV moved away, and Darren stood back from the window. "Nice try," he said under his breath. Those Deep State strategists were thorough, he had to give them that. To think they'd sent a make-and-model duplicate SUV down his street with a crunched fender and a lookalike driver behind the wheel, only to make him doubt himself! The effort they put in was crazy, but Darren wasn't about to fall for their tricks.

His distrust of people had started long ago—first and foremost with his dad. A memory from when he was a kid flashed through his mind, to a time when he couldn't wait for his dad to get home. His mom said his dad had been gone for nine months fighting for freedom in some faraway country. Freedom—some elusive concept, which made him mighty proud of his dad. Nine months seemed like forever—almost since his last birthday when he was only seven. He'd turned eight and, though barely taller than last year, was old enough to know how things worked. His busy dad had never spent much time with him before he was deployed. The couple times they'd played catch with the baseball before his dad lost patience and left to go spend time with his friends at the bar—those times meant the world to Darren. He was so much older now and had been working hard on being able to catch a baseball. His dad would be proud of him—and he'd grown, at least a little.

He ran to the window every five minutes to be the first one to see Dad pulling up in the driveway. He'd been working for days on a special gift for his dad, something he would for sure like. He'd be so proud of Darren. The eight-year-old had been dreaming of the moment for weeks. His dad would scoop him up, a big smile on his face. He'd love Darren's gift and want to go in the backyard right away to see how well his son caught the ball now. Then, they'd laugh together like only a father and son could do.

Then Darren caught a glimpse of the black Ford truck coming down the road. "It's him! It's him, Mom!" He ran outside but then realized he'd forgotten the gift and scrambled back inside to retrieve it from the kitchen table. By the time Darren got back outside again, Dad had pulled into the driveway. Darren couldn't help but jump up and down as he ran to the driver's door. "Dad! Dad!"

Dad opened the truck's door, climbed out, and lifted up Darren to give him a big hug. In his excitement, Darren dropped his gift for Dad on the ground. Dad's booming voice was such a welcome sound. "How's my big boy? You've gotten almost too big for me to pick up."

Little Darren beamed and gave his dad a kiss on the cheek.

"Okay, okay, let's not get crazy now. No kissing between men. And another thing, don't be skipping. I'm glad to see you, but you won't see me skipping, right?"

"Right, Dad." Darren looked down at his feet as his dad set him back down on the ground. He hadn't even remembered skipping.

"All right, then. Give me a second to get my gear. But first I need to say hello to this fine-looking lady here. What a sight for sore eyes."

Darren was proud of the tall, broad-shouldered man in the military uniform as he hugged and kissed Darren's mom, who had been right on Darren's heels in rushing out to the front driveway. Darren stayed close by as his father gathered some belongings out of the back seat.

Then he remembered his gift. Young Darren scampered after the paper that had blown a few feet away.

He stepped up and proudly handed Dad his masterpiece. "Dad, look. I painted you a picture. It's a picture of a bird I saw outside."

"What's this? A painting? Hmm, nice." Then he turned to his wife. "Sharice, we've got to get this kid enrolled in a football program. Teach him some more manly pursuits."

Darren's face reddened. But with the boldness of an eight-year-old, he knew he would find some way to make Dad proud. "Dad, do you want to go play catch?"

Dad laughed. "Well, son, maybe later. I remember what it's like to play catch with you. Later I might feel a little more up to running all over the yard to retrieve baseballs. Right now I gotta get me some grub, and then your mom and me have an appointment down at the bar. Gotta check in with some of my buddies."

Darren couldn't remember if he ever did get to play catch with his dad on that visit home; the remaining emotional memory was the rejection.

Darren's eyes twitched at the thought. After the incident with Austin, Trevor, and the other boys, and no adult to help him process the emotions, Darren got in the habit of always watching his own back. Someday, someone was bound to knock on his door to accuse him of nearly killing his friend.

Throughout high school, Darren poured his excess emotional energy into working out. As a short guy, his muscles responded pretty well to the intense workouts and bulked up. In avoiding the other boys from the fifth-grade posse, he discovered wrestling, a sport that suited his frame well. He became remarkably good at it. And, although Darren's dad barely noticed, some of the girls did. Vanessa seemed to appreciate his fit, bulky appearance and didn't mind she was taller than him. She and Jeremy were the only two people he loved in the whole world. Sure, he had some affection for his mom and his brother, Rod, but not quite what you'd call love.

Again remembering the mysterious SUV, he checked the window to see if it would pass by his house again. Nothing was out there now, but he made a mental note to keep an eye out for it to return. He remembered well the times he was aware people were watching his movements. One time when he was out on a date with Vanessa, while they were still in high school, a car had tailed them for miles down the freeway. Darren had exited and pulled into a gas station, and the other car followed right behind. Trying to hide the stalker from Vanessa was difficult. He couldn't exactly go beat up the guy in front of her. He had quickly gotten five dollars of gas and then rushed out of there. The driver of the other car was caught by surprise at how quickly Darren left and never caught up with them again. Darren had a good internal laugh over being so much smarter than the other guy.

Other times, he was sure certain teachers were on to him—sometimes they would look at him for no reason at all. He was always able to tell what they were thinking. *You're guilty, Darren.* And the one time Trevor had made direct eye contact and half smiled at him in the school hallway, Darren had nearly taken off running. He shut the blinds when he got home, and secretly unplugged the phone for the next three days. His mom never knew.

Vanessa had been such a godsend. He was different when he was around her, a better man. And Jeremy—all Darren wanted to do was protect his son from harm.

He drew the curtain, shutting out the street where the fake dead cop had been, and reached for his phone, which was resting on the windowsill. A comparison of portable water filters played on the phone. Darren wanted only the best for his family. He was thinking that when the phone slipped from the sill to land with a thud on the wood floor.

Ness called in from the kitchen. "Who's at the door, D?"

"Huh?" said Darren. "Nobody."

"I heard a knock."

"There wasn't a knock."

"You sure?"

Darren grunted. He picked up the phone. The screen wasn't cracked, but there was a split in the casing. As Darren turned the phone over, the back fell off and made a clatter.

Ness said, "Seriously, what was that?"

Carrying the busted phone, Darren loped across the hallway and into the kitchen. "It was nothing, babe. Don't worry. I dropped my phone is all."

She was sitting on a bar stool, hunched over her own phone. Even with the bad posture, Ness's tight jeans and crop top did a great job showing off her coke-bottle body; it was a body she loved to show off, much to the chagrin of the dried-up old frumps in the neighborhood. Darren didn't mind so much—let them all look at whatever skin she chose to show off; she was his wife and he knew damn well he'd done well to grab himself such a looker.

Vanessa straightened herself up, spun to face Darren, and leaned back against the granite countertop of the kitchen island. "That ain't like you, babe. You're usually so careful with your toys."

Darren knew what her off-kilter smile meant. She was ready to be complimented, ready for him to turn a compliment nasty, and ready to let him chase her into the bedroom, where they'd have some fun together. Jer was awake, somewhere in the house, so they'd have to be quiet and quick, but Ness prided herself on being able to get a job done right under any circumstances.

"Yeah," said Darren. "Sorry, baby. Wish I had time to play."

"Sorry?" said Ness. "That's all I can get from you lately."

"I'm stressed, okay? There's a lot going on."

"Like what?"

Darren's mouth hung open. He shut it with a grimace. His wife's ability to bury her head in the sand was enough to make his own head spin.

He said, "Don't worry, Ness. I got you. Mind if I borrow your phone?"

"Wow, you dropped yours good," she said, noticing the pieces for the first time.

"Yep. Should have had the stupid case on it." Darren set the scattered phone bits on the counter. "I can fix it; I just need to make a call."

"I'll dial. Who?"

"Uh, Rod."

"Rod? You know I can't stand the man. I don't care if he is your half brother. What do you want to call that fool for?"

Darren hadn't told her about the delivery, of course. He didn't want to spoil the surprise. "Something good's coming, babe. Trust me. You'll love it."

She squinted at him, then handed over the phone. "God, D. We've got to get out of this house."

"You know we can't, babe. Just wait. I've got it covered."

On his way back to the living room, the front doorknob rattled. Darren hung up and pocketed the phone before retracting the deadbolt. The porch light shone off Rod's bald head.

"Yo, it took you long enough," said Darren.

"Don't be like that, bro," said Rod. "You haven't seen the stuff yet."

The two men didn't look alike. They both took after their moms, instead of their shared dad. Darren was short and compact, Rod tall and broad shouldered. He was built almost as big as the ghost cop Darren had seen driving by. When Rod turned sideways, Darren saw that the delivery truck was idling in the street. The truck had been hidden by Rod's bulk. Rod was gesturing wildly like an inflatable waving-arm man outside a cheap car dealership.

Darren was eager. "All right. I'll help you unload."

"No need, bro. I've got my boys on it. Yo, how's the nephew?"

"Jer's fine. I think he's watching TV."

Jerking a thumb at the shadowy figures unloading the truck, Rod said, "This stuff is gonna blow his mind."

The truck Rod had borrowed—or boosted, whatever—was twice the size it needed to be for its cargo. The McGann brothers watched as Rod's boys lugged box after box up the steps to the row house and through the front door, then around the corner and down to the finished basement. It had been a concrete block when Darren, Ness, and Jer had moved in. The Sheetrock had thankfully been up before the world went crazy. In the past week, several friends of Rod had wired electrical outlets and plumbed the three-quarters bathroom. Darren had paid them with cash under the table, the last cash he expected to see. Over the weekend, he had personally bricked up the hopper windows, closing the only source of outside light.

Darren opened the first box. "Ah, sweet!" He waved Jer to his side. The boy had been too excited to stay out of the basement, despite Ness's feelings about Uncle Rod. "Hold this, little man," said Rod, handing Jer an extendable tripod. There were four tripods, total, in the box. Over the next several minutes, father and son arranged them in a square with eleven feet to a side.

"Is that a new computer?" asked Jer as Darren unpacked a box he had cut with his pocketknife. The plastic tower inside was, indeed, the brains of the new setup.

"How much did all this cost?" asked Ness. She hadn't been helping unpack, only glaring as the men carried in packages.

Rod said, "What's a few Benjamins between brothers, sis?"

"You loaned him the money?"

"A buck or two. Don't worry. Your man's good for it."

"How much, Rod? Don't lie to me. How much?"

"Twenty-three hundred. About that."

Ness rounded on Darren. "Are you kidding me, babe? That's more than we have in the bank. More than we've *ever* had."

"Credit, sis." By that, Rod meant he was happy to bankroll his brother, so long as Darren understood the strings attached.

Swearing softly so Jer wouldn't hear, Ness stomped upstairs. Darren went after her but couldn't get her to talk. Half an hour later he sent Jer up in his place. He came downstairs leading a steaming mad Ness by the hand.

Everything was ready—the VR headset, the motion controllers, the sensors mounted on the tripods defining the play space, and the PC that would run the whole rig with no more sound than a soft whisper. The crown jewel of the collection rested on a stand in front of a wall opposite the stairs. It had personally been smuggled by Rod out of a Best Buy loading dock. As Ness looked on with folded arms and shaking head, Rod left Darren's side to hand her the remote control.

"Go ahead, Jer," said Darren. "Show Mom what we've got."

"You'll love this, Mommy. For real."

Jer ran to the center of the tripod square. After a wink at his mother, he waited while Darren fitted him with the bulky headset. With the space age hunk of plastic strapped to his face, he looked less like a boy than an oversized action figure, some Chinese knockoff of a background character from Star Wars. Darren attached a motion controller to Jer's hand.

"My game's on pause," said Jer. His ears were blocked by headphones, so the words came out as a shout. "Watch, Mommy!" He held up the controller so the adults could see him press a button.

Darren stepped away in time to avoid Jer's jab at an invisible prompt. He watched as his son's body language changed, switching from nervous anticipation to frenzied excitement. Jer ran a few steps, stopped, and reversed course. He swung the controller like a sword, laughing at the defeat of an invisible foe.

"C'mon, Spex!" said Jer. "Let's get the key!"

Rod said from the sidelines, "You get it, little man."

Ness hadn't moved from her place in front of the stairs. She looked amused at Jer's antics, but when Darren came over, she said, "We can't afford this, babe. You been out of the warehouse three days. Do you even have a job?"

"Chill, babe," said Darren. He pulled himself up to full height. With his forehead level with his wife's nose, he recited the lie he had prepared. "I didn't tell you before, because I wanted to do this right. I got me a new job, doing scheduling for the fork trucks. It's all online. I'll be working from home. The company's hooking me up with a laptop. Soon as it gets here, I'll start on the training. First paycheck is in two weeks. There's a one-grand bonus and two fifty more a week. We'll get all this paid for, then we're on easy street. Don't worry about money, baby. We've got it good from now on."

Ness screwed up her face. She wanted to believe in their luck, but could she, after all the craziness last month? "You for real, babe?"

"'Course I'm for real. Look at Jeremy. This is the start of the good times."

In the days they had spent sheltering in the house, Jer had broken a lamp, two dresser drawers, and a glass soap dispenser. His energy was finally being focused in a safe direction. He laughed and loped around the sensor square, cutting at imaginary enemies and ordering Spex around.

Darren saw Ness was ready for his killer argument. Gently, he lifted her hand, the one holding the remote, and showed her the button to push. He had cleaned out their savings to make the first payment to Rod. On the same day, his boss had called to fire him from the warehouse job. None of that mattered if his family was safe. Ness just couldn't see it yet. Keeping her calm required lies. Darren had learned, mostly from Rod, lies went over better when they came tied up in a bow. And she had no idea about the danger they were all in—because of him. All the news reports were about the bombings. Bombings even in many different locations in the nation to distract from the true goal: Darren. If anyone knew where he was hiding out, they'd all be in trouble. He had always been careful—even at his jobs—to never give his address. Only a PO box. He had to stay vigilant. Everything he'd been watchful for and dreading for years came down to this moment in time.

"This is awesome, Mom," said Jeremy. "Are you watching?"

"Push the button, babe," said Darren.

Ness did. A rollable TV screen began to unfurl from its case on the stand on the other side of the virtual reality play square. Even as the flexible material stretched itself, Darren saw vibrant images and heard Jer's VR game soundtrack pump from the speakers. Ness gasped as a virtual version of Jer came into view. He was standing in a fantasy forest, dueling goblins with a wooden sword. The armor he wore came equipped with a visor covering the same part of his face hidden by the headset in real life. But, the mouth and jaws were unmistakably Jer's. The digital double dashed and slashed, copying Jer's movements—though with some exaggeration—and a stutter step behind.

A creature resembling an owl swooped over virtual Jer's shoulder. Ness jumped, as if she expected the thing to fly off the screen and orbit the basement. Darren nodded at Rod, who gave him a wink. The setup was perfect. It was all he had asked from Rod, and more. No longer would Jer give Dad a hard time about missing his school friends. He would be too busy making new friends online. In between his VR sessions, Ness could use the basement as a workout space, complete with exercise videos, cutting her need to go to the gym. Darren and Ness would have virtual dates to replace their neglected nights out. By the time Darren enacted the next part of his plan, the family would be used to a life lived indoors, where the bombers and gunmen and cops from the Deep State couldn't get at them.

He motioned to Rod. They went upstairs, leaving Ness and Jer, neither of whom seemed to notice. Outside, Darren fist-bumped Rod.

"Good job, big brother. Did you, uh, bring the other thing I asked for?"

"D, how many times I have to come through before you know I got you?"

He opened his coat and showed a pocket secured to the inner lining. A moment later, Rod was handing over a Glock .44, fully loaded, and an extra magazine of ammo.

"Careful, yo. You remember how to shoot?"

"'Course I do." Rod, of course, didn't know about the shooting he'd done earlier in his life. Nearly killing his friend. Or maybe he did? Darren had vowed to never talk about it, though, so unless Rod brought it up, they'd never have a conversation about it.

"Right. I forgot you're the stone killer in the family. Maybe you ought to take some time this week, go out to the 'burbs, practice popping cans. Don't take too long, of course. You want to be here when that laptop arrives. Got to get a hustle on the new job." It was plain from his tone Rod didn't believe in any such thing. And no wonder. The lie had been crafted to sooth a sweet, loving wife, not a hard-nosed, lying thug like Rod who happened to have been around to change Darren's diapers. "About my money, though. You know you don't have to pay. You can work it off."

"No need," said Darren. "You'll get your money." He belted the gun behind his back and tucked the magazine into a pocket.

"For real, though," said Rod. "The offer's open. See Donk down there?"

It took a moment for Darren to make out which of his boys Rod was indicating. It was a tall dude with tattooed cheekbones leaning against the back of the truck with a cigarette in not-so-steady hands.

"I found the crackhead on the street. Picked him up, paid off his dealer, took him to my man Doc Jeff for a one-day cure. For saving his life and whatnot, I figure he owes me four months of light work, then he's free to go. I take care of my boys, little bro. Wine, women, all that. I teach skills they need to know. I even cut them in on the take for our last jobs together so they've got something to build on. Some of the boys don't leave, you know? It's a nice life."

Darren's jaw tensed. He felt exposed in the open. He wanted to get back inside with Ness and Jer. There would be no money for Rod when the second payment came due at the end of the week, but as nervous as Darren felt, he doubted if anybody not boarded in their basement would be alive to care. "Yeah, yeah. I told you before, it's not my life."

"No?" said Rod. He stepped close, looming over Darren. Deftly, without a look, he thumped the magazine in

Darren's pocket. "Seems to me it's real close to how you're living."

Darren backed away, eyes lowered, being careful not to form his hands into fists. "I just want to be left alone."

Rod took a pause before answering. "Yo, that's fine, bro. Not a problem. You get the money together. See you get my money by Friday and it still won't be."

"I will," said Darren. "Friday." He turned to leave.

Rod said, "Hey, I'll drop by tomorrow with a spare headset for your rig. No charge, okay? A gift for the family. And then I'll give you time. Time to think. All the time you need. Until Friday."

"Cool." Darren left Rod standing with the boys looking on and bolted the door behind him. What would he do if the worst didn't happen by week's end? He had only instinct to say it would, a sort of slow panic that had stayed with him since the theatre bombing; it rose and fell depending on what news feeds he looked at. Darren wished he had his phone to check on the news. Remembering he still had his wife's, he fished that out.

Searching for a video from his favorite real news outlet took only a moment. As soon as the video started, he felt better about his purchases and his future plan of action. He was doing what he needed to keep his family safe. Rod's nonsense didn't matter. Darren would find some way to deal with the money problem if the crazy, out-of-control world didn't deal with it for him. Still watching the phone, he went to his bedroom to hide the gun before returning to the people he loved downstairs.

9—The Assassins

There was no end of comings and goings in the nameless smuggler village. Yasaman said as much to Bilel as they hiked along an elevated trail a kilometer above, watching people rove the streets like ants. Bilel gave a shrug but said nothing. Yasaman pulled a blanket tighter around her, struggling to keep warm on the mountain. She was a woman more accustomed to the much, much warmer temperatures in Tehran.

They were making their way back following a somewhat subdued meeting with Hashem Mehrad, who was supposed to be guiding them across the border. Hashem, an old, decrepit individual with white, thinning hair and a lined face, had seemed less than pleased to see Yasaman, despite the promise of a fat payday that came with her.

"I must beg your pardon," Hashem had relented upon seeing Yasaman's poorly hidden disdain toward him. "I have been waiting all day for some cargo I'd agreed to transport for my nephew."

"I am sorry if we are inconveniencing you too much, Hashem," Bilel had chastised the old man. "I am sure we can always find another—"

"No, no." Hashem waved away Bilel's apology with the flap of his hand and offered his guests fresh-brewed tea. "But if my nephew is late, it may be better that we put off our journey to another day."

At that, Yasaman and Bilel had declined the offer of tea and made their way from Hashem's house.

"When your nephew arrives, let us know when we can make our way to the border with you," Bilel had said.

Looking down on the village with time to reflect, Yasaman asked Bilel, "Is it safe for us to wait? Would it not be better for us to go alone?"

"It would not," Bilel said. "You don't know the way, and I am not going, remember?"

"So you keep saying." Yasaman kicked a stone with the toe of her boot and watched it skip down the snowy path. "You won't tell me what is keeping you here, however."

Bilel put on an affronted tone. "I am a businessman. There are people, grandmothers mostly, who depend on me to supply their tea sets."

"There are grandmothers everywhere, Bilel. Israel, for example."

"Keep your voice down. You know what else is everywhere? Anti-Semites."

Yasaman made a show of glancing around. There was nothing to see but shrubs and trees. She wouldn't have been able to discern the trail if her host at the hostel hadn't pointed it out.

"You're paranoid," said Yasaman.

"Am I? Good! I'll live longer. You know, little flower, that I have been here before. The people, the ones you see coming and going, are farmers and shepherds and tradesmen. Simple folk, but they know the value of money. It is mostly petrol they take over the mountain. The work is profitable. If it were easy, more would make it their business. You must be patient. Our time will come."

As they hiked, Yasaman gripped the straps of her knapsack through the mittens she had purchased earlier that morning. A biting wind blew down from the mountain. Traveling up and over was going to be chilly.

When they reached the women's hostel, Yasaman said adieu to Bilel, ate a late lunch shortly after Asr—the wailing call to afternoon prayer—and tried to forget her frustration by getting up to date on the global security crisis. There was no cell reception so far from civilization, but the clear weather allowed Bilel's satellite transceiver to get a decent signal.

Her news feed was crowded with commentaries on the injustice of America's response to Red Line. In addition to insisting they cooperate with the US investigation, the president had curtailed foreign aid and was threatening sanctions against Muslim-majority countries. It was old news to Yasaman. She dismissed the commentaries and scrolled through what was left. A video less than an hour old stood out. It was entitled "Billionaire to blame for Red Line??" In a bed across from Yasaman's own, an old woman was snoring peacefully. Not wanting to be rude, Yasaman put in her earbuds and, with the outside noises muffled, tapped the video link.

A young woman in a dingy gray hoodie appeared. In American-accented English, she explained the footage she was about to show had been broadcast the day before on a US news program. "Y'all know I'm no hater, but this dude? No spoilers, but this is like, 'Oh my God, is he serious?' I don't know what to say, y'all. I really don't."

The woman disappeared, replaced by a scene from an interview set. The program's hosts, an attractive man in a crisp suit and shiny tie and an equally attractive young woman in a short skirt and tight-fitting blouse, sat next to each other on one end of a semicircular couch.

The woman welcomed the viewers back, her expression most grave. "Last month's mega-terror event left a thousand questions in its wake. Among the most urgent is, 'What motivated eighty-one individuals, most of them American citizens, to commit such heinous acts?'"

The camera switched to a close-up of her co-host's face. He added, "Nearly all the perpetrators have been identified. While all are believed to have been practicing Muslims, no solid links have been established to known terror networks. Officials don't know how they communicated or what their motives may have been."

The camera zoomed out so viewers could admire her perfect, bare knees. "The children's movie *Spex: Your Electric Friend* was the top draw at sixty-three of the sixty-four movie theaters where attacks occurred. Nine of the non-theatre targets were in some way involved in promoting the movie. Ever since these facts became known, experts and civilian investigators have been struggling to explain the connection."

The camera zoomed farther out to show both hosts. A man had magically appeared, and he sat patiently at the far end of the couch.

The woman introduced the next segment and the man on the couch with the air of a teenager about to blow the best-loved member of her favorite boy band. "Lars Aaugstad is chief creative officer of Stadion Technologies International."

It took but a moment for Yasaman to recognize Aaugstad. The outspoken inventor had been a household name before the Red Line attacks. Days after a bomb blast carved out a chunk of the Chicago Board of Trade Building while "The Nordic Steve Jobs" was visiting the fourteenth floor, a sea of cameras had captured him rising from a hospital wheelchair. Square jawed and dauntless, he had slotted into the role of unofficial spokesman for the fractured American dream, despite his Scandinavian origin, which was easy for Yasaman to discern from the way he spoke.

The tailored suit Aaugstad had on made him look healthy and slim, while his open collar lent an air of casual authority. He sat with crossed legs, smiling with visible teeth from behind a trim and tidy beard. No saint of the church had ever been less worried about accounting his sins than Lars Aaugstad—that much was clear.

"Good morning, Helen, Brent," said Aaugstad.

After the hosts thanked him for coming by, Helen said, "Lars, you haven't been shy about advocating for the aggressive pursuit of truth. How do you respond to *The Daily Beast*'s allegation of the Red Line terror acts being sparked by a scene in *Spex: Your Electric Friend*? Your company, Stadion, provided financial backing for the film. It also pioneered several of the revolutionary animation techniques."

Based on the living legend's head bob alone, accompanied by blue eyes sparkling like sunlight on the ocean, millions of admirers earth-wide would have immediately dismissed all charges. Aaugstad was a decade older than Yasaman and not her type. Still, she found herself sympathizing with him, as she would have a lover. She reminded herself not to judge the technocrat until she had listened to his response.

Aaugstad said, "There's nothing to respond to, Helen. People grasp at straws when there is nothing else to grasp. That's all that is happening here."

Brent said, "Isn't it true there's a scene depicting the Prophet Muhammad in the film? Such depictions are a strong taboo in fundamentalist Islam. After the *Charlie*

Hebdo incident in 2015, surely putting something like that in theaters is just asking for trouble."

"You know, it's funny," said Aaugstad. "Politically speaking, I couldn't be more different from the victims of *Charlie Hebdo* unless I was a terrorist myself. Which is naturally ridiculous. Still, I am deeply sympathetic. They have license as artists, yes? So do my animators. Though, of course, the current accusation is unfounded. There is no religious depiction in *Spex* or in any other work Stadion has supported that is in any way controversial. We are not simply a technology company. We are a family company. We make technology for the family. That is why we financed *Spex*. It is a family film. Uplifting, safe, fun . . . wonderful is the word I'd use. *Spex* is full of wonder for all the family. Everyone who sees it falls in love. You will see. When we get it back in theaters, you will see."

Brent said, "As I understand it, there's a class action going on, which may prevent it from happening."

"Frivolous," said Aaugstad. "It's sad what lawyers can talk people into. Sad. Look, the scene you're referencing, Brent. You have the clip. Show it. Go on! Show it, and everybody can make up their own minds. You have the clip, Brent. Let us see for ourselves. Let us all see."

Brent looked reluctant, as did Helen. Yasaman understood their trepidation. At last, Helen held a whispered conversation with Brent. Afterward, she said, "We do have a clip. Before we show it, we want to assure viewers we have obscured the controversial image—the representation of what some have said is the prophet Muhammad. This isn't a political statement on our part. It's in our charter to avoid giving offense. We will show enough so you can see what we're talking about, no more. Jerry, can we roll the clip?"

The faces of Helen, Brent, and Aaugstad faded, replaced by the image of a pre-teenage boy standing in a room filled wall-to-wall with shattered bookshelves. Books were strewn everywhere, both loosely on the floor and piled in heaps. Some had their covers splayed like birds in flight.

"We've muted the audio," Helen said in voice-over. "What you're seeing is the main character—"

"Saul," said Aaugstad, "played by Tim Nadir. Amazing kid. Bright future as an actor."

Helen said, "You see actor Tim Nadir as Saul. He's walking through a library in—sorry, where is this?"

"Detroit. Not the real city, but a place much like it. Times are tough, you know, but there is so much potential."

Saul had taken several steps as they'd been talking. He stopped and looked expectantly at a floating, semi-transparent shape. It looked roughly like an owl with a bulbous body and thin legs. They were not bird's legs, but a child's depiction of dangling human legs with a cartoon boot on each foot. The face was not that of a bird, either. It carried a whole hodgepodge of influences: a snout, teeth, and ears that split the difference between dog and cat. The mouth was pensive, the eyes distant.

"That's Spex, correct?" said Helen.

"Yes." Yasaman heard Aaugstad's pride. "His main avatar. This next bit is—"

"Sorry," said Brent. "We came in a bit early. For the sake of time, Jerry, can we fast-forward?"

Yasaman heard a snort of annoyance, presumably from Aaugstad. In a rapid jumble, she saw Spex draw attention to a cloud of shimmering, multicolored flames dancing upon the shelves of the decrepit library. Saul showed fear, then interest as one aquamarine flame lifted above the rest, zipped over, and transformed into a sturdy woman wearing an antique gown. She spoke to Saul as they shook hands.

Brent said, "That's it, Jerry. Right there."

The playback resumed its normal speed, and there was sound.

". . . to meet the rest?" said the creature identified as Spex in a reedy, childish voice.

"Will they be nice," said Saul, "like her?"

"Ain't he sweet," said the woman. Her accent was American. Midwestern, Yasaman thought.

"They'll be nice to you, Saul," said Spex. It flicked a feathered wing. The flames swelled. So did the musical score. Figures in a variety of historic costumes began to shape themselves out of the flames. Before they could quite solidify, Brent said, "Whoa, pause. Toward the back . . . There. Jerry, zoom in."

Jerry zoomed in. A yellow circle appeared in the cloud of ghostly figures, highlighting an area where shape and color were obscured by blocky squares.

"You can see where we've covered the original image," said Brent. "Lars, in the original film, there's a figure standing there. He wears a beard, a blue robe, and a white turban. Are you telling our viewers, on the record, that is *not* a depiction of the prophet Muhammad?"

"Your *viewers*?" said Aaugstad. The director and the camera operator must have been mesmerized by his smirk. Otherwise, they would have recognized the plastic tube he proceeded to pull out of his suit jacket. With a swift motion of the fingers, Aaugstad unfurled a flexible electronic display. "They can tell me."

The display flicked on. Across its surface burned an unedited version of the image Brent had described— bearded man, blue robe, white turban. The producers of the *Charlie Hebdo* cartoons had been murdered for less clear, though more crass, depictions of Islam's founding figure.

For a second more, the cameras kept rolling. Muhammad was displayed just long enough to capture a gasp from Helen, then the picture on Yasaman's phone went black. The woman in the hoodie, the one who had posted the TV clip, reappeared.

"Like I said, y'all. Oh. My. God. Seriously, what was that dumb motherfu—"

Yasaman plucked out her earbuds. She had heard enough and seen far too much. It made her sick to her stomach to think she'd felt sympathy for Aaugstad when his smug expression first appeared on screen. Personally, she didn't care if his movie depicted Muhammad or not. What disgusted her was Aaugstad's willingness to risk lives for—what, exactly? What had he hoped to accomplish by repeating the sin that might or might not have inspired extremists to carry out the Red Line attacks? The celebrity he had gained from becoming the most famous survivor had clearly fed his ego. The only motive Yasaman imagined for him to pull the stunt he had on the day-old clip was to stoke it to greater heights.

She needed to clear her head, so she strolled into the hostel's common area. Sunset was approaching, so the sky outside offered waning light. Bilel had urged her to sleep, holding out hope the smuggler's missing nephew would appear in time. But it was no good; Yasaman couldn't force herself to relax. After fetching her knapsack, she hurried out the front door, intending to seek out the trail to the old smuggler's hut and convince him to leave without the nephew's cargo. Whatever it took, she was going to cross into Iraq tonight.

Trees grew thick around the base of the mountain. It was several minutes before Yasaman caught her first glimpse of the village below. The setting sun was bleeding pink and she had no trouble spotting the line of canvas-covered trucks entering the village via the main road. The lead truck turned aside, blocking the entrance to a warehouse housing several shops, including the one at which Yasaman had bought her mittens. Another truck continued on in the direction of the mud-roofed huts in which lived most of the villagers. Yasaman watched a third truck peel off, heading at speed for the men's hostel, where she imagined Bilel pounding the table as he jovially demanded his tea.

They were border patrol trucks. Bilel had warned her what to look for and showed her images on her phone. Yasaman studied her feet, unsure what she should do. She was sure the old smuggler, Hashem, would flee over the mountain. She could go ask to go with him. If she didn't, if she went back for Bilel, what good would she be able to do?

She didn't take long to decide. On her gallop down the mountain, she pulled out her phone but found there was no service. She replaced the phone and fished her gun from the knapsack. Even as she checked the magazine, she heard the first shots. The distance made them sound like pebbles rattling a tin roof. Dozens or hundreds came in rapid-fire spurts punctuated occasionally by screams. Yasaman held the knapsack to her chest as she ran, though she knew it would be no protection against machine gun bullets.

Bilel had parked the Jeep by the women's hostel so Yasaman could use the transceiver. As she fished in the knapsack again for her keys, the woman who had been snoring on the other side of the sleeping room emerged from the hostel's front door.

"What is it?" the woman said in a country accent so heavy, she might as well have been speaking a nomad patois.

"A raid," was all Yasaman thought of to say. "Come. I'll get you out."

The woman clutched the tail of her headscarf, reminding Yasaman of Lars Aaugstad's words about grasping at straws.

"Come," repeated Yasaman. She fitted the key in the Jeep's lock. Mutely, the woman returned to the hostel, apparently preferring to take her chances. Yasaman had no time to try and convince her otherwise. She had to adjust the seat before she was close enough to work the clutch, cursing Bilel's big belly as the tide of gunfire turned her way.

When she got the Jeep turned around, she floored the pedal. A border guard, armed with a rifle, stepped into the street. He stood directly in Yasaman's path. She couldn't stop, so she tried to swerve. The barrel of the rifle got caught between the driver's mirror and the triangular side window, carrying the guard a few meters before he let go. Yasaman heard a man's shout a moment before the wheels bumped over something that might have been legs, or a back, or merely a hump in the road, and it sickened her that she felt little remorse.

The killing was getting easier . . .

Instantly, Yasaman was back on Tabi'at bridge, looking over the gun at her armed attacker. The air was clean and cool with a scent of cypress. She squeezed the trigger, the gun jumped, and the attacker fell in a spray of blood so abundant her brain rebelled against its vividness. The memory of the sickly sheen of the scarlet fountain thrust Yasaman out of the memory and back into reality, where she immediately slammed on the Jeep's brakes. The vehicle skidded sideways, gouging the dirt road until it came to a halt.

Heart racing, Yasaman eased open the Jeep's door to see what she'd driven over. Three sharp cracks from an automatic weapon swapped the window glass for spider webs, then empty air. Whatever she'd run over ceased to matter. Yasaman slammed the door and jammed the gas pedal. The Jeep's wheels spun for a moment before they caught. The side mirror was shattered, so Yasaman never got to see if the man she had likely run over was the same man who'd fired at her. It seemed an absurd thing to hope, but hope she did as she sped through the village.

Twice she had to detour to avoid gunfire. Once, her headlights picked out a cluster of low shapes in the road ahead. She had the choice of backing up or rolling over. She told herself they were only sandbags meant to impede traffic, but she backed up anyway and found another way around. At last, she reached the men's hostel.

It was ablaze. Fire roared from every window as bits of roof crackled and fell in. Timbers jutted out at odd angles, forming a burning pincushion, and a pillar of gray ash spiraled up to the heavens. Yasaman leapt from the Jeep without a second thought and screamed for Bilel. It seemed unthinkable he'd still be alive, but more unthinkable to leave him. She was far from sure she'd make it out of the village alone.

On their way in, Bilel had showed her an alternate escape route. In spring or summer, he had said, it was entirely hidden under a canopy of leaves. Even now, covered only by snowy branches, the road was easy to miss. The border patrol might not know about it or might not care. It was the village they wanted to destroy. What did it matter if a few souls escaped? A distant drumbeat brought Yasaman back to reality. The assassins who ran her country had sent an elimination squad.

The smoke from the hostel was overwhelming. She paused to swath her mouth in her headscarf and lurched forward, shouting for Bilel once more. After a few steps, she had to lurch back when the front wall of the hostel collapsed. Yasaman danced away from the tumult, covering her ears and screaming into the scarf.

"What are you doing?" said a strained and rasping voice. A soot-blackened hand caught her and spun her. She swung a fist. Bilel took the punch on the chin. His lower lip twitched. Otherwise, he was unmoved.

"It is good to see you embrace violence," said Bilel. "You will live a long life."

He was covered boot to brainpan in ash. His nose had been smashed flat, and his right eye was a blue-black knot. He was bleeding from a ragged gash connecting the crown of his bald head to the puffy tissue around the eye.

Yasaman flattened a hand against his cheek. "Oh, no! Forgive me, baba."

Bilel scoffed and trudged to the passenger door of the Jeep. Yasaman popped the old-fashioned lock from inside. Only when Bilel was firmly seated did he allow himself to slump forward, smearing the dash with blood and ash.

Shifting into reverse, Yasaman said, "Someday you will tell me how you survived."

Bilel said, "I'm not sure I did."

They drove through streets clogged with smoke and lit by fire. When the last distant screams dipped below the volume of wind rushing past the absent window, Yasaman stopped briefly to sob out her grief and stress by the side of the road.

10—Point of View

Special Agent In Charge Trent Falwell greeted Mitch at the door and personally conducted him through security. He was slim, shorter than Mitch by inches, and had thinning salt-and-pepper hair. He wore circular John Lennon–style glasses that tended to make him look like a professor. Mitch was still keeping a close eye on the patch of his arm that he was pretty sure was getting infected. In addition, he was feeling a little warmer than normal.

He said, "Thanks for coming, Detective," as Mitch was placing his keys in a bowl for the X-ray machine. "Can I call you Mitch? Call me Trent. Don't stand on ceremony."

"Uh, sure," said Mitch. "Good to meet you, Trent."

"Likewise. Do you know what you are to me, Mitch? You're why I do this job. My reason for getting up in the morning and staying late at night. I'm a lone wolf, Mitch. The type of loss you've undergone is unimaginable to a man like me. I won't pretend I understand. I'm sorry for your loss, for America's losses. If there's anything I can do for you, I'll do it. You know Young Parker over there?"

Neil stood sentry on the other side of the metal detector. He waved as Trent pointed. Mitch was about to say, "Yes, and thanks," but Trent didn't give him the chance.

"I call him 'Young Parker' because I knew his father and it helps me remember who the hell I'm dealing with. You can keep on calling him Neil, if you like."

"Young Parker" made a wry face, but at what part of Trent Falwell's explanation Mitch couldn't tell. Aside from a bit of snow at the temples, Trent didn't look old enough to be calling anyone "young" anything. Mitch didn't argue. The dizzying welcome was a relief. He had been worried Neil would be the only FBI agent who regarded him with sympathy. If the rest responded as Wells had done, it was likely they'd show him the door, if not a jail cell.

What he had told Neil about Mrs. Mattoo was true. He hadn't meant to hurt her. When the opportunity presented itself, however, he hadn't hesitated. He had been lucky the woman hadn't cracked her skull. Had it been her confession he was after when he swung at her, or his revenge? He couldn't be sure. He hoped Trent wouldn't ask. If he could only keep his head in the game, the interview might put him a step closer to justice for Jessica and Ethan. If not, the alternative was back in his glove box with a bullet already in the chamber.

He followed Trent and Neil up a flight of stairs and along a hallway. Trent talked the whole time. "Summer is usually the busy season. Heat breeds discontent. The world's first mega-terror event, and it happens in February? I'll have to add a chapter to my memoirs about adapting to change. Maybe you can help me figure out the ending, Mitch." He opened a glass door, held it for Mitch and Neil, then stepped through. "My office is on the far side. Get it, Mitch? You've been around. *The Far Side*—like the comic. Gary Larson?"

Mitch faked a chuckle and wiped his sweating brow. He had seen reprints. "Sure. Good title for the memoir, if you can get the rights."

"I should be so lucky," said Trent.

They had entered a room striated with long tables. Monitors and phones divided individual workstations where men and women in outfits ranging from slacks and tees to business formal attire glared at their keyboards. Maybe two-thirds of the workstations were occupied. Dark blue jackets hung on the back of several chairs.

Trent slowed his pace, cocking his head at Mitch. "If you see someone you know, keep walking." A dozen workstations away, Agent Wells stood talking to a colleague. One hand was on her hip, her fingers touching the grip of her weapon. She watched Mitch from behind a cascade of tightly woven braids she'd tied back the night before; set loose, they were as thick as a beaded curtain and were highlighted by barely perceptible blonde streaks. Trent put a hand on Mitch's shoulder to steer him away from the woman and into his office. Neil closed the door.

"Have a seat," said Trent. "I'll stand."

Chairs were arranged in a circle around the small room. A desk had been pushed into the corner, its purpose apparently to give Trent somewhere to stack papers. He picked up a folder, opened it, and handed Mitch a printed photo.

Mitch sat and was able to concentrate on what he was hearing only because the task was his lifeline. Nothing else in his life mattered except getting justice for Jessica and Ethan. The picture was a still of Akhtab Mattoo crossing the Belvedere parking lot. The original CCTV footage was on Mitch's thumb drive, though of course he didn't say so. Clips like it had been shown on the news.

"That's your vehicle, right?" said Trent. He tapped the image of the Rogue's side panel. Mitch nodded. "You were the first guy I wanted to see after this landed in our laps. 'Who's the stalker?' I said. 'He knows something.' You can't tell from the still, but you're a second away from doing that roll-up, roll-back thing. I liked that. I checked the make and model on your SUV. Did you know Porsche invented the hybrid? The Agency has been modifying gas-guzzlers since the 1980s, fitting them with electric motors for long-distance pursuit. They used to fake the engine noise. You believe that?"

"Sure. I'll believe whatever you tell me. I hope you'll return the favor." Mitch wasn't as confident as he tried to sound. The sparkle in Trent's eye made it easy to pretend.

"I want to believe," said Trent. "I wanted this meeting. Seeing as you're here, I guess you wanted it too. What can we do for each other, Detective Wilson?" He tucked his hands in his pockets and leaned back against the window frame.

Mitch had rehearsed his answer. He unlocked his phone and held it out to Trent. Trent flicked a finger at Neil, who carried the phone to his boss. Together, they watched the video Mitch had cued for play. Neil returned the phone.

"Not the first dash cam evidence I've seen for this case," said Trent, "but new to me. Came off *your* dash, I take it?"

"That's right."

"What did you want me to see?"

Mitch looked at Neil. "You explained my theory? It's not what you can see, Trent, but what you can't." He cued another video. Trent and Neil came to him. "You have this one already. I know because the guy I got it off said so. I'm showing it for context."

He played the video. Like Trent's screen grab, it showed Mattoo walking across the lot from a different angle.

"Did you catch it?" he said after running the clip a second time. "It's the same shot, different point of view. Here's a close-up." He exited the video player and brought up his picture gallery to show a still of his own. The dash cam's resolution was HD, so even close up, the image on Mattoo's screen was reasonably clear. Glare dimmed it partially, but the colors and shapes were enough to suggest a crowd of men in bandannas, each holding an assault rifle over his head.

Trent gave a tight-lipped smile. "As it happens, I asked cyber to find the video the still is from. They cranked the footage through a supercomputer or two, got something like 350,000 partial matches. I understand the list's been whittled down by half. You said it was for context. I take it you have more?"

"I do," said Mitch.

"Great. See, Young Parker? I told you the detective wouldn't waste our time."

"BPD did a round-up of dash cam evidence," said Mitch. "But only from living owners. Probate takes time, and there were plenty of vehicles in the parking lot or passing by whose drivers didn't make it out. I'm guessing you've got people on that." Mitch wiped his brow.

Trent hunched his shoulders, confirming nothing. Mitch leaned back in his seat.

"Something wrong?" said Trent.

None of the versions of the interview Mitch had imagined had been quite as friendly, so he had to chew his lip for a second before working up the nerve to say, "I'm waiting to hear your offer."

"What's that?" said Neil.

Ignoring him, Mitch said to Trent, "I've got something you want. What's it worth to you?"

Neil said, "Anything you have, you need to hand over. Otherwise, it's obstruction of justice."

"All right, Young Parker," said Trent. "Mitch, in simpler times, I was a profiler. There's nothing I've read before and nothing I'm reading off you now to suggest a mercenary streak. What are you after?"

"I think you can guess."

Trent took a step back, searching his face. "You want in on the investigation."

Mitch didn't deny and didn't elaborate.

Neil said, "Whatever ace you think you're holding, you know we'll find it eventually."

"No," said Mitch, "you won't. Image matching is above my pay grade, but is it fair to say the more images you have, the easier it'll be to find that video?"

"It's fair," said Trent. He squinted his eyes and looked more closely at Mitch. "Mitch, on another note, are you feeling okay? Your face is awfully red. You look almost feverish."

"Yeah, I mean, not really. My arm is . . . I kinda left the hospital about a week earlier than they wanted. Didn't take care of my burns the way I should have."

Trent glanced down at Mitch's arm and stepped back, taking in the deep redness of his wrist below the sleeve of his jacket. Mitch quickly turned his body so the older man couldn't easily examine his arm's condition.

"That's messed up," said Trent. "When we're done here, you gotta get it checked out."

"Yeah, I will."

"I mean it, Mitch," said Trent. "You put yourself back in the ICU, you're no good to yourself or anyone else."

"So I've been told. Regarding the investigation, then, you'll want the password to my encrypted hard drive. It's the only place those images now exist."

Trent gave Mitch a sad smile. "You bought the dash cams."

"I got 'em."

Neil looked incredulous. "You preyed on people's grief—"

"No," said Mitch. "I used mine. Do you know how many kids died at the Senator? How many grandparents? I do, Neil. I've got names and faces in my head. There was this one family, the Kurtzes. Oma and Opa took the two girls to see *Spex*. They were standing maybe ten feet from my family when Mattoo blew up. The girls' dad is Joe Kurtz. He showed me pictures when I picked up Opa's dash cam. He showed me a note from his wife, too. She left it before she shut herself in a car in the garage and left the engine running. Joe found her body—only two days after losing his kids. You can imagine the agony this guy was in. Joe and I talked for an hour. I didn't have an hour to spare, but I didn't want to read about another Kurtz in the obituaries, you know? We hung until Joe was good. If that's preying on grief, I guess you've got me. I'd call it something else."

Trent found a spot of ceiling to stare at. "You're willing to risk your career on an obstruction charge? Interesting. I'm not biting yet, Mitch, but I'll nibble. You want in. How do you imagine we'll work it?"

"Like professionals. You hire me as a consultant. Then everything I have, it's yours. I don't care what you pay me. A dollar a day, if you want. All I ask is you keep me in the game. When your people find Mattoo's video, I'm there. When you trace it to his bosses, I get names and faces. When you're ready to move in, I'm there at the arrest."

Neil was frowning. "That—there's no way. Sorry, boss. I shouldn't have brought him in."

Trent held up a hand. "Is that all you want, Mitch?"

"Yeah. I'm not asking for special treatment here, just to be part of the team. Give me orders, Trent. Put me to work. You've seen my record. RATT's busted four major carjack rings since I made detective. I'm not saying it was all me, but ask anybody who was there, they'll say I did my part. And since I feel the need to give you a bit of a resume here, my partner and I served on Baltimore's Gun Trace Task Force—"

"Ah, man, I thought you were trying to help yourself out here."

"Wait, hear me out. Eight out of ten of the guys got busted on corruption. The two who didn't? My partner Benny and me. Put me to the test. You won't regret it. Not once you see what I can do."

"If Wells was here," said Trent, "what do you think she would say?"

Mitch felt a cold stab of regret. He wondered if the former profiler was reading his feelings. "I'm sorry. I've never—you gotta know, I never hit a woman before. Not on the job. Not in my personal life. I didn't mean to hit Mrs. Mattoo. I was amped up. That doesn't justify what I did, so I won't give excuses, only a promise I already gave. It won't happen again. Put a stack of Bibles in front of me, I'll swear on every one."

"You go to church much?" said Trent.

"Not as much as my mom. More than my wife."

The men passed a few seconds in silence. Speaking to Neil, Trent said, "It's not a democracy, but I'll hear what you think."

Glancing between Mitch and Trent, Neil said, "I think if my opinion mattered, we'd be talking in private. On the other hand . . . I told Detective Wilson yesterday I get where he's coming from. I guess I still do."

"Faint praise. Mitch, I'll level with you. At the moment I can't show my face outside this building. The press and the victim support groups are tough enough to deal with, but it's my boss, Deputy Director Solomon, I'm most worried about. He paid a personal visit, said in no uncertain terms what would happen if I fail to establish Akhtab

Mattoo's ties to a known terror network. I've never gone in for hemorrhoid surgery, but after hearing his predictions for my career path, I know what it feels like. If I put you on the team, will you do everything in your power to get justice for your family?"

The surprise Mitch felt was reflected on Neil's face. Neil said, "Sir?" as Mitch got abruptly to his feet.

"You notice I said justice, not revenge? I need to make sure you know the difference."

"I want justice," said Mitch. "Justice is all I want."

"Lucky you. I want justice and peace and my boss off my back. Fine. We can do business. A dollar a day is an insult. Let's make it thirty-five hundred for the month. Still insulting, but you make rent. I'll get somebody from HR to write up a contract. You sign, I sign, then you give me the password. No holding back once the ink is dry. Deal?"

"Deal."

They shook hands. "Now go get your arm checked out, Mitch."

"Yep. And I'll pick up some celebratory whiskey on the way."

11—Run or Hide

Bilel dozed in the Jeep, but never for more than a few minutes at a time. The road—if it could be called a road—was rocky and winding and pitted with holes. Yasaman steered them through switchbacks and down steep gullies. Whenever she was sure they would not make it out, Bilel roused himself to say, "She's fine. She'll make it. Go on." Yasaman didn't know if he was talking about the Jeep or herself, but either way, he was right. They arrived at the place he directed her to in mumbles in time to watch dawn break over the mountains.

The place had no name, so far as she could ascertain. It was on the Iranian side of the border, but so remote, so primitive, it might well have been from another century. It was not truly a village—just three stone huts within bow shot of one another. Yasaman was fairly certain the inhabitants were a single family. The woman who greeted Yasaman and Bilel might have been forty or seventy. It was impossible to tell. Her cheeks were like creased linen; the braid hanging down her back was black as jet. When she took Yasaman's hand, her grip was firm. Yasaman thought if she ever had to get old, that was the sort of old she wanted to be.

The woman, whose name was Medya, didn't speak any language Yasaman had ever heard before, though she picked out Qashqai influences. Medya obviously knew Bilel well. She whispered in his ear as she half carried him from the doorstep to the hut's only bed. Yasaman took the open door as an invitation and fell promptly to sleep on Medya's couch.

Hours later, Yasaman awoke to the sizzle of sausages in a hot pan. The heady, pungent mix of turmeric, cumin, and paprika, which vied with the unmistakable tang of garlic spices, wafted her into the kitchen. There, Medya was busy preparing *Sosis Bandari*—otherwise known as Persian sausage and potato skillet; it was Yasaman's favorite comfort food from way back in her childhood, although there was no possible way the old woman could have known that.

After she had eaten more than her fill, Yasaman fetched a teapot from the Jeep. Medya sat knitting while Yasaman carried a tray to Bilel.

The teapot she had chosen was a custom creation, elaborately painted to show devils cavorting in a fiery hell. "You didn't make this pot for one of your grannies," she said to Bilel as she poured the clear, amber-colored, steaming brew into two cups.

"No," he said. "This one, I made for an Artesh general. We had a dispute over payment, so I strangled him." He flexed a hand so thick it was easy to imagine it killing a man unarmed. The expression on Bilel's face was too flippant to take the boast seriously, however.

"You're lying," said Yasaman.

"Never."

"You're a spy. Spies always lie."

"You're confused. I'll instruct you. There's no such thing as a spy. There are patriots. In the homeland, there are saviors. Do you know how many families I've rescued from oppressive regimes?"

"How many?"

"I would like to tell you, but it's classified. Besides, 'it is God who guards the city.' The rescuing is his work. I merely do his will."

"You believe in God?"

"Of course. I'd be wrong to strangle generals if I didn't think they'd get a fair shake in the afterlife."

"When do you think we'll be able to leave here?" Yasaman switched the subject; if Bilel was teasing her, she didn't want to encourage him or seem gullible, and if he was not, she had little desire to become entrenched in a theological debate with the man.

Bilel shrugged. "The old woman is insisting I stay until this has healed." He tapped at the thick poultice Medya had wrapped around his injured head. "To hear her talk, it could be weeks."

"That's just not practical at all," Yasaman protested and immediately realized how desperate she sounded.

"You are right," Bilel replied with a sage nod. "The way she feeds me, I'll die of a heart attack long before that. What of you, little flower? If you'll take my advice, you'll stay. This place is not exciting like the city, but it's safe. You can hide with me; give the world time to settle down. Later, we'll go somewhere else. Gather your strength, Yasaman. Then make a life for yourself."

She was tempted. Running for her life held no savor. Since pulling the trigger on the bridge, she'd felt only disquiet.

"You invite me to stay," she said. "Does that mean this place is yours?"

Bilel folded his hands. "No place is mine, *joon delam*. I belong everywhere."

"I don't." Yasaman unlocked her phone. She showed Bilel the screen. He gestured for his reading glasses, which she retrieved from the bedside table.

It wasn't the best picture she'd ever had taken, but her face had a symmetry that photographed well. The accompanying article from the Islamic Republic News Agency was not as flattering. Dated less than a week after Red Line, it described her as a terror suspect. She had opened fire on official security agents, it said, while in the presence of women and children. Yasaman didn't remember seeing any children on Pol-e Tabi'at that night, but the article quoted eyewitnesses who said they were there.

Bilel looked up to show he was done reading. "You knew something like this would be said. All the more reason to hide away."

Yasaman scrolled to the line she wanted and zoomed in. "Read it out loud."

"'The victim, Bizhan Al-Kabir, died in hospital.' I'm sorry, little flower. Many men die."

"You don't understand. The man I shot was not Bizhan Al-Kabir. I know because Bizhan Al-Kabir is the man I was going to marry last year."

"Oh?" said Bilel. His expression made Yasaman think of a farmer she had seen on a documentary, explaining why he never gave names to the beasts he meant to slaughter. "You think he is the only one of this name?"

"It is too great a coincidence. Bizhan disappeared eight months ago. First Mordad." Yasaman used the Solar Hijiri name for a day in late July. "I thought he had abandoned me. Now I know he was taken, like Farbod. When he disappeared—my God! I have never felt such rage. If he had appeared before me, I would have strangled him, like your general. I felt like a cigarette, smoked and stubbed out. It made me so angry, I didn't think. When Farbod was taken, I didn't question. Why would I? Why would I think it strange a man who loved me body and soul would think twice about leaving me behind? It was stupid. Stupid!"

She scrubbed her eyes with the backs of her hands, forced herself to sit down, and wrapped her fingers around a teacup.

"They are hunting me, Bilel. They took Bizhan and they took Farbod. Who knows what they have done? Who knows what they can do? They tracked us to the village."

"No. What happened at the village was not your fault. Smugglers and Kurds breaking the border at a time like this? It is plenty to draw the assassins' wrath."

"Assassins? That is what I call them too. The military, the government. Who put them in charge? Not God, eh?"

"Not *my* God."

Yasaman set down the cup, tired of feeding off its heat. "I can't stay. Not here. Not anywhere in Iran."

"You're convinced the assassins are hunting you?"

"Who else?"

Bilel had no alternative theories. "You are as far from them here as you would be anywhere. Israel, America, even Australia."

"There is one difference. In Australia I would be alone."

Bilel laughed so loudly, Medya looked in to make him shush. When she was gone, Bilel said, "A woman like you? You'll never be alone for long. If you're worrying about me, don't. I'm a soldier. A killer."

Yasaman looked at the pink flesh that replaced the brown of his skin and found nothing more to say. After sipping his tea in silence for some time, Bilel promised to make arrangements to send her away.

Four hours later, she was standing before a mirror laughing as Medya held up a dress that was floor length to the smaller woman but would have struck Yasaman at the knee. Bilel called to Medya. She looked in at his doorway, grumbled assent to a request for more tea, and motioned Yasaman to sit by the bed. As Medya busied herself with boiling water, Yasaman sat patiently while Bilel brought up a message hidden in the source code of a defunct website on his phone.

The message looked like nothing but a string of numbers to her, but Bilel showed her a page from a handwritten codebook he'd conjured from somewhere, which allowed him to translate the content. On a separate page was a jumble of scrawled notes he instructed Medya to burn when she brought in the tea.

"You'll need a car," Bilel told Yasaman. "Medya's nephew will sell you his Renault for a fair price. Will you miss me when you are gone?"

"As flowers miss springtime," Yasaman said as she hugged him.

12—Symbols

The creak of a door woke Mitch from the sleep of pure exhaustion. On top of everything that had transpired, from losing his family, to attacking Mrs. Mattoo, to being involved in the bombing investigation, he'd gone to an urgent care clinic and been diagnosed with an infection of his healing arm. He'd left with antibiotics, more ointment for his arm, and a promise he didn't intend to keep about taking it easy. A few swigs of whiskey had guaranteed sleep.

Pawing at the air in response to a vanishing dream, he nearly fell out of his chair when Wells shoved his boots off the desk. "Ow." He looked at Wells from the level of her knees, bracing to absorb whatever abuse she intended to pile on. Whether she attacked him verbally or physically, he knew he deserved what was coming.

"Get up," Wells said. "We've got something."

"What's that?"

"Get up and come on."

Now fully awake, Mitch decided he'd prefer not to take a kneecap to the eye. He rose, protecting his face with his hands. Wells glared, but he was used to the way she looked at him now. He had spent most of the past several days watching the best FBI analysts in Baltimore pore over candidate stills from image-matching software. Whenever the analysts thought they'd found a hit, they sent the video to Trent's office for the special agent in charge's personal team to take a look. Mitch got an invitation to each private showing.

Naturally, so did Trent's best and most accomplished analyst, Agent Wells; Mitch actually found some kind comfort in the ironic synchronicity of the agent who hated him the most being the most indispensable member of the team—it told him the world post-Senator was still a bitch. Rumor had it there wasn't a system Agent Wells couldn't get into, not a password or firewall she couldn't hack her way through, not a level of encryption she couldn't render invisible. For as much as the woman hated Mitch for being a woman-beater, he was pleased to have her working alongside him.

Not that the one-sided animosity dissipated any; between his hip and her energy, Wells would beat Mitch through the door to any gathering, then would stand fuming and muttering beneath her breath at his lack of speed.

The intensity of her dislike was a stress on the team dynamic, but the insights she brought to their discussions were invaluable. Her knowledge of foreign and domestic terrorism was encyclopedic. She was conversant in Arabic and knew Middle Eastern culture like the back of her hand. The most useful tool she brought to the table was a confidence in her own intellect, which was untainted by arrogance or false modesty. For every "I think" anyone else offered, Wells had a simple yes or no. She never hesitated to express her opinion, and Mitch had yet to see her judgment on which video deserved another look proved wrong.

"Falwell said to wake you," she said. "You're awake." And turning her back, she left Mitch to hunt for his cane.

There was a buzz in the air when Mitch entered Trent's office. Also, there were at least double the number of bodies it could comfortably fit. Mitch recognized analysts he thought had gone home for the night. He wasn't sure if it meant he'd slept longer than he'd thought or they, like him, had been camping out.

"This is big," Trent said. "Maybe bigger than we thought."

Mitch looked at the wall, where a forty-inch TV had been hung. He had watched a dozen disappointments play out on that screen. It showed a freeze-frame practically identical to the one he'd used to sell his services the day before. Neil stood motionlessly beside the TV, looking breathless with anticipation.

A chill touched Mitch's spine. "Let me see."

"You heard the man," said Trent. Somebody must have pressed a key, because the mass of robed and turbaned men on the screen started chanting, *"Allah'u'akbar! Allah'u'akbar!"* and shaking what Mitch saw clearly were AK-47s above their heads. There was a filmic quality to the video that hadn't been apparent on the dash cam recordings.

"This looks professional. Like news footage."

"That's because it is," said Wells. She had moved to stand beside Trent. "Pause, please. The clip is from a 2002 documentary on the Taliban done by the BBC. Let's keep watching."

The chanting resumed but was cut off abruptly by a scene change. A hard rock soundtrack played over the scene. A young man dressed in full combat gear with black hair and dark, bushy eyebrows above intense deep brown eyes read a printed statement to the camera. When he was done, he shifted the rifle slung across his shoulders before stepping aside to reveal a man dressed in an orange jumpsuit tied to a chair behind him. The man's head was covered by a black hood, and his hands were tied behind his back.

"Uhhh," groaned someone behind Mitch, speaking what all those watching together in the office felt.

Then, in the video, a third man holding a huge two-handed sword stepped up behind the seated man. He looked directly into the camera, expressionless, and recited something he had memorized, presumably a prayer to Allah. While the other man stood looking on, the one who'd said the prayer lifted the enormous sword above his head, then with a loud cry brought it down, severing the seated man's neck in one blow.

"Oh God," said Mitch, reacting more than he intended to in the present company. Blood squirted in every direction, covering the two men in red droplets. The severed head rolled off camera. Then both men, not pausing to even wipe a drop of blood from their skin, each looked at the camera, their cold and lifeless eyes a picture into their dead souls, while their lips moved in unison for another ten seconds. The hard rock soundtrack continued playing. The tape ended with the two killers still staring into the camera. By the time the victim's head had dropped out of the frame, Mitch was nodding.

"I recognize the music. Mattoo was listening to this."

Trent said, "The software flagged a couple of stills as a ninety-eight-point-nine percent match to some composites Wells put together. Eckerson, over there, and DeLuca flagged the winner." He gestured at a pair of agents standing together. "Let's have a round for teamwork, people."

The agents in the room applauded. Once he understood what they were doing, Mitch joined in.

When several seconds had gone by, Trent said, "OK, quiet down. It's been a long road and we're not home yet.

Eckerson, dim the lights. Mitch, are you ready for the interesting part?"

Squinting at his ally through the sudden darkness, Mitch pointed at the screen. "More interesting than this?"

"You'll want to keep a firm grip on that cane," said Trent. To the unseen video operator, he added, "Go."

The image on the monitor showed the same rifle-shaking militants, their movements slowed to a fraction of normal speed. With exacting slowness their jaws stretched and their elbows bent. It took a full ten seconds before anything out of the ordinary happened. When it did, Mitch spotted it immediately.

"Whoa, what's that?" A curving shape had appeared in the middle of the screen. It looked something like a sickle, or a snake making a U-turn. The symbol faded in and faded out. "How long in real time?"

"Milliseconds," said Wells.

A second symbol appeared on screen: a stick like a shepherd's crook, straight on the vertical and slightly hooked up top. It didn't occupy the middle but faded in near the screen's left bezel. In a few slow-motion seconds, it faded out. Mitch held his breath as a third symbol appeared, then faded. Then a fourth and a fifth. Each filled its own section of real estate, all clustered around where the first, the sickle, had appeared.

Mitch took a breath after the eighth symbol vanished, but the show wasn't over. After an interval, the sickle appeared again in the center of the screen. It burned a little brighter than before and remained a little longer. Before it faded, the crooked stick appeared to its left. The stick was still visible when the third symbol appeared. While it faded, the fourth appeared. The pattern was then repeated through all eight symbols. A second run-through made it clear that, together, the symbols formed a complex shape of loops and hooks and lines that would connect if they all appeared together.

There was a considerable pause after the second run. When the sickle appeared again, it flared at the center of the screen for less than a second of snail-pace footage before its partner symbols blazed in sequence. They flashed faster, appearing and fading multiple times in a short span. After fading for a brief interval, they cycled once in reverse order before blazing all together, a burning nest of asymmetric scratches.

How long the woven symbol pulsed against his retina, Mitch didn't know. When Trent said, "Enough," Mitch was startled. He shifted his weight and hefted his cane, feeling the warm rush of blood to his cheeks. All of a sudden, he was on York Road, being battered on all sides by traffic, seconds away from losing his wife and kid. He was ready to fight, for their lives and his. The panic that had moved him to attack Hanifa Mattoo was nothing compared to his surging rage. He looked for a head to swing the cane at, feeling spoiled to have so many choices.

A strong hand seized the cane as an arm enfolded Mitch's middle. A moment later, the light snapped on. Mitch knew where he was and how he had gotten there. He had no clue how a nest of meaningless symbols had sent him into a fight-or-flight response.

"It's okay, Mitch. You're safe. You want me to let you go?" This came from Neil. It was his long arm cinching Mitch in a half bear hug. At Mitch's request, he returned the cane.

"Steady," said Trent. "Don't worry. Bunch of us had a reaction." He helped Mitch to a chair, winking at the analyst who got out to make room. "We don't know why, but everyone who watched felt some kind of effect."

"The symbols," said Mitch. "If you hadn't slowed the playback, would we have known they were there?"

"Not visibly. They're gone too fast."

"Like . . . what do you call 'em? Subliminal messages."

Trent smiled broadly. Mitch envied his good cheer.

"I've had a breeze through the literature," said Trent. "Those aren't supposed to work."

"Says who?"

With a last shrug at Mitch, Trent turned to address the room. "Folks, a month ago the FBI was tasked with finding a link between the deadliest terror attacks in America since 9-11 and some known entity, some state or terror network we can bring to justice. We hit nothing but dead-ends until our friend from the Baltimore PD pointed us in the right direction. We've got a break now. There's something about these symbols, something about them popping up in the videos our subject was watching on Red Line Day, that's going to lead us to the answers we need. I feel it in my old and dusty bones. You feel it, Wells? How 'bout you, Eckerson? We all feel it. The pieces are in front of us; we just have to make the connection."

After a rummage in a desk drawer, Trent held up a bottle of honey-gold liquor.

"I have questions, people. What are the symbols? Where did they come from? What do they do? How do they do it? Is their placement on the screen important—is it part of the message? If you put 'em all together, do they make something? The first person with answers to those questions walks away with this thirty-year-old Glenlivet, or the cash equivalent for you teetotalers. I know you're tired. Those of you who need to sleep, get some sleep. The rest of you know what to do."

There was subdued cheering, followed by a general exodus. Watching the faces of the departing agents, Mitch doubted any were on their way to a bed. They were hunters, energized by the prospect of taking their shot. In seconds, most had filed out, leaving only Trent and Neil with Mitch in the office. Agent Wells was the last to go. Pausing at the door, she glared at Mitch, then at Trent.

Trent said, "Something on your mind, Noreen?"

It was the first time Mitch had heard the star agent's first name. Considering her feelings toward him, he made a mental note to keep calling her Wells.

"We're off the record here," said Trent. "You can speak out."

"I'm not sure I can," said Wells. "I'm not sure you're open to the idea 'our friend' should be arrested for battery instead of given credit for the job we did."

"I'm open to all ideas, Noreen. I don't see the utility of that one. We'll shelve it for now. Anything else?"

Wells worked her jaw. At last she said, "No, sir."

"Keep up the good work then."

The dark eyes of Noreen Wells attempted to burn Mitch where he stood before she left.

Neil said, "I'm sorry about that."

"Wells can say what she likes. Tell me what I can do to help."

Trent looked thoughtful. "You had a strong reaction, Mitch. Maybe if you watched the video again—"

"Sure," said Mitch. There was nothing he wanted less than to be thrust back into the memory the symbols had evoked. But what he wanted didn't matter. "You can count on me."

"You wouldn't be here if I didn't think I could," said Trent. He cued the footage for another run.

13—A Man in Textiles

Yasaman passed back through Tabriz on the way to the city Bilel had directed her to. Again, most of the landscape was desolate save for an area that piqued Yasaman's interest because it was clearly a dry lake bed with sand so white, the reflection hurt her eyes. Then she was driving on a bridge directly over the largest lake in Iran, a salt lake they called Lake Urmia. She recalled taking a vacation here with her family when she was young. She had floated so easily in the magical waters. The still lake appeared reddish in areas due to deposits of the microscopic organisms that accumulated as the lake's water evaporated and became thick with salt.

Urmia, the city Yasaman had driven seven hours to shelter in, would have made a disappointing vacation spot, though perhaps it was more attractive in spring. There were shops, some parks, even a university, but no nightlife to speak of. Yasaman was frustrated she couldn't distract herself by swirling a room full of multicolored lamps into her personal kaleidoscope. Still, with modesty a ready excuse to veil her face, at least she didn't feel the need to hide out in her hotel.

So, on a gray, snowy day, not long after the city paused for sunrise prayers, she sat in the café Bilel had told her to visit twice a day and wait for one of his "saviors" to make contact. He hadn't told her what to look for, only where to be and when, and how to verify the identity of her contact. Looking out the window at the dismal Urmia weather, peering hopefully at a break in the clouds, she wondered if she'd been a fool not to accept the offer to stay longer at his backcountry home. But if anything happened to him because of her proximity, she wouldn't be able to live with herself. She had enough trouble putting the strangers she had hurt (or killed) from her mind. To put someone she cared about in danger was unthinkable.

In simpler times, she had developed a love of drawing. It had been weeks since she had last picked up a pencil. She did so now, to kill time. With a blank page in front of her, she could forget the dread of being a hunted animal. When Bizhan had been in her life, they had worked together on a revolutionary theory concerning the origin of languages. It had stayed in the back of her mind ever since he disappeared. As she bent over her notebook, she tried to remember where they'd left off. The protolinguistic characters central to their hypothesis sprang readily to mind. She sketched them eagerly for several minutes.

She quickly became engrossed, so much so she didn't notice the man standing at her shoulder until he said, "Pardon, madame. It is rude of me to eavesdrop, but what you are writing there . . . it is a sort of code, yes?"

He was tall and not unattractive, despite some weight around the middle. She raised an eyebrow and he backed away, parting his lips to say farewell. Aware he might be the reason she had been coming here twice a day for the better part of a week, she said quickly, "Did you mean to say madame? Not mademoiselle? Never mind. I do pardon you, monsieur. And yes. What I am writing is a sort of code. At least, I believe it to be so."

"How mysterious." The stranger spoke Persian with an accent she thought at first was French and then decided was Belgian. "I thought you were recording intimate thoughts for a lover, but if the alphabet is uncertain, how can he read what you write?"

Yasaman laughed. She liked confident men, even confident men who ate too much cake. But her laughter was undergirded with wariness. How did a complete stranger find it acceptable to approach a lone woman—a veiled woman—so boldly, hinting about lovers? In normal life, she would relish such a meeting, but there was nothing normal about life now.

"I can't read it, myself," she told him, pointedly adjusting her hijab. "It is not a language of words."

The man looked intrigued. "There are other languages. The mouth is not the only organ of communication."

She raised her brows anew but said nothing—which somehow prompted him to sit, uninvited, at her table. Her heart rate picked up. Perhaps her wait was over.

His name, her new acquaintance explained, was Michel Dubois. A wool merchant by trade, he had come to Iran on business and been stranded when the borders closed. She gave her name as Munireh Firoozi, and said she was a student of language and folklore, also stranded by closed borders.

He gave her a sly glance. "It is an inconvenience, but an inconvenience that has allowed us to meet."

Yasaman swirled her coffee and fixed Michel with a look he was sure to find rich with meaning. What meaning depended on whether he was the man she was waiting to meet or merely a slightly foppish admirer . . . or something else again, entirely.

"I wonder if you know my uncle," she recited. This code phrase, given to her by Bilel, would be answered in a certain way by her contact.

Michel said, "I'm sorry. Perhaps my ear for your tongue is not so good as I supposed. Your uncle? What is your uncle's name?"

Yasaman was torn between a sigh and a shiver. Would-be hookup or . . . ? Either way, she needed to be rid of him—quickly, before her window of opportunity closed. "Never mind. I had a notion you might be someone he spoke about. You would know if that were the case."

"Your pardon. I don't see how. We are both far from home."

"Forget I asked." Yasaman picked up her pencil and turned pointedly back to her notebook.

Michel Dubois declined to take the hint. "Well, as I do not know your uncle, does it perhaps clear the way for us to do as we like? I find you intriguing, Mademoiselle Firoozi," he said, "and I should like to further our acquaintance, perhaps find out more about your lovers' language."

"I am not sure that is wise, monsieur."

"Why ever not? Do you have family in town who would miss you, should you fail to return at a certain hour?"

The question fanned Yasaman's shiver and sent it into her bones. She was about to agree she had such family, when Dubois spoke again.

"Of course you don't. You have already told me that you, like me, are stranded here. Alone."

Yasaman checked her watch. The fifteen-minute window she was to allow for her contact had ended. Was he still here, waiting for the pushy stranger to leave? She gave the room another swift scan, but none of the several other customers seemed to be at all aware of them.

"You have an appointment to keep?" asked Dubois.

"No, but I think I should go." She closed her notebook, dropped it into her bag, and stood.

The disappointment on the man's face was almost comical—or it would have been if she had not also read a flash of anger in his eyes.

"Won't you at least allow me the opportunity to talk you out of leaving?" he asked.

She opened her mouth to say no, then hesitated. There was risk in using the word with men who felt they had earned something by having deigned to flatter you with their attention. Instead, she said, "Very well, monsieur, but first I must use the lavatory. It will give you time to prepare your case."

Shouldering her purse, she made her way to the short hallway at the back of the café and the entrance to the women's restroom. The men's facility shared a hallway with the kitchen entrance on the opposite side of the coffee bar. She knew Michel (if it was even his real name) could not observe the rear of the hallway from the table and so he would not see her walk past the door to the women's lavatory to slip out through the rear exit at the end of the hall. She opened and closed the door carefully, then padded down a short flight of steps into the alley, where she broke into a run, heading for a north-to-south cross street.

She slowed to a walk at the end of the alley, then stepped out onto the street and headed north. She would walk up several blocks, she thought, then turn onto the major thoroughfare running past her hotel. She might have hailed a cab, but the setting sun was peeking at the city through the clouds on the horizon, and shadows grew long between the buildings, making Yasaman in her dark colors all but invisible. In her anonymous garments, she was just one more woman in a hijab. She pulled her head covering closer around her face and walked briskly as if she had somewhere important to be.

She had just turned onto the boulevard leading to her hotel when she felt the prickling sensation of being observed. Without altering her gait, she dug into her purse for her phone. She activated the camera, set it to selfie mode, and held it as discreetly as possible to allow her a view of the sidewalk behind her. At first, she saw nothing alarming. There were people on the street, of course—men and women alike. A few of the women were unveiled. She was on the verge of chiding herself for being more paranoid than was warranted, when she saw Dubois; he was on the other side of the intersection she had just negotiated.

Yasaman's heart rate spiked, but she clamped down hard on the urge to panic. He might not have seen her but simply given up waiting. He hadn't told her what hotel he was at; perhaps it was along her route. How ironic if they were at the same hotel. If that were the case, Yasaman told herself, she would simply slip in by a side entrance and wait for a chance to return to her room.

She figured her wisest move would be to step into one of the storefronts and wait until Dubois had gone past. She looked ahead for a likely candidate—a clothier, perhaps, or a hair salon. She saw a confectioner's shop a mere three storefronts up.

Perfect.

She glanced again at her phone. Her plan collapsed around her. He was closer, walking swiftly, his eyes sweeping from side to side like a pair of radar antennae. The expression on his handsome face made her breath catch in her throat; it was grim and his cheeks red . . . with embarrassment or something else?

Heart hammering in her chest, Yasaman lengthened her stride. Sailing past the confectioner's, she looked up the block toward the hotel. To the near side of it was a broad access to the parking garage. Her thoughts fragmented, running down a branching set of options: the Renault was in the garage; perhaps she should simply get in and drive. But no, she still needed to make her contact, and the satchel containing her few belongings was in the hotel room. She could simply stride into the hotel and go to her room—what might her stalker do in such a public place?

Make a scene, that's what he could do. Call attention to her. Make people look at her. Or perhaps worse, if he was not what he had purported to be.

Bilel had given her a new perspective. Despite his assurances, she couldn't believe the raid on the village had been carried out for reasons having nothing to do with her. If her enemies had tracked her there, they could track her here. How many villagers had died, screaming, because of her? It made her want to scream, herself.

As she drew level with the garage access, instinct took over. She dodged into the alley and ran, thankful she was not wearing heels. She thought she heard a shout behind her but didn't slow or turn to look. Roughly ten yards down the alley, she slipped in through a pedestrian access to the car park and made a beeline for the nearest hotel entrance. It offered her three choices: elevator, stairs, or a glass door to the ground floor of the hotel.

Choice, she realized, was not always a good thing. The stairwell would make her too vulnerable. The elevator might force her to wait. And both required she use her key card. The door, then; it opened into the rear of the lobby, but she might be able to make an interior elevator before her pursuer caught up with her.

She had nearly reached her goal when someone said, "Wait."

The voice was gruff. Annoyed. It sounded nothing like Michel Dubois. Looking back over her shoulder, she saw a man in a gray fur cap and an overcoat as black as the new moon step out from behind a panel van. Though he was less than five meters away, she had heard no sign of his approach.

She said, "Who are you?" and hugged her purse to her chest, feeling the pistol, hard and heavy, within it. It was useless to her.

"A friend," he said. "Your uncle taught me."

It bothered her she couldn't place his accent.

"A friend," he said again, even more annoyed than before. "Your uncle taught me."

The venue, combined with the man's sudden appearance, had confused Yasaman. The import of his words were slow to reach her, but she grasped their meaning at last. Haltingly, she spoke the lines Bilel had taught her: "My uncle is a private man. He—I'm afraid he didn't speak of you."

"I'm sure he did. I was a difficult student. No doubt he sought to spare my feelings by changing the details. Reverse the description of his most wayward pupil. You will see it is me."

She looked him up and down, as she had rehearsed. "I do see, now."

With a bounce on the heels and a bob of the head, the contact she had awaited brought the recital to a finish.

"Why are you *here*?" said Yasaman. She knew she sounded breathless, rattled. "You were supposed to be at the café."

"I *was* at the café. *You* were talking to a tourist. Or was he your boyfriend?"

She shook her head. "He was a chance meeting. I found it difficult to extract myself." She flicked a glance toward the garage entrance.

"You should have tried harder. He followed you."

"Yes. Which is why we should go."

"No."

"Why not?"

He lifted an eyebrow. His look chilled her. "I want to meet your new friend. I'd like to know what he does for work."

Her rescuer's eyes were small and widely spaced. The pale blue irises were never still. The whole time Yasaman looked into them, they refused to focus straight ahead but kept twitching to the right. She focused on the bridge of his nose to keep from getting distracted.

"He's in textiles," she said.

The man gave a laugh that held equal parts amusement and scorn. "Really? So am I." He held up his sleeve, pinching the heavy fabric. "See? Textiles. You've never heard that line, clearly. An old trick to get around intuitive women—the ones who can easily spot a lie."

"I don't know he was lying, nor do you. Anyway, it doesn't matter. You can take me away and we won't have to worry about Monsieur Dubois again."

"No, no. I will make sure." He followed her glance toward the garage's pedestrian entry, then took a step back toward the van. "Go to your room. Get your things. I promise he won't see me."

The implication of his last statement wasn't lost on Yasaman. The contact man intended an ambush. He was asking her to leave him alone with Dubois.

"You would shoot him like a wild dog?"

"Go get your things," he repeated, then tilted his head, looking past her. "Ah. Too late."

Yasaman spun back toward the hotel to see Michel Dubois standing on the other side of the glass door. Before she could react, he opened the door to beckon her in.

"You are a difficult woman to know," he said.

"She is also a dangerous woman to know," said her would-be savior. Feigning indifference, he stood with his hands jammed deep into the pockets of his black coat.

Yasaman did not doubt there was a gun in one of those pockets.

Dubois started, looking from the stranger to Yasaman. "Who is this?"

"That," said her contact, "is also dangerous knowledge. Ms. Firoozi, step aside so your friend can come out where I can meet him properly."

"No." She shook her head. "I won't let you—"

"What is he?" Dubois demanded. "An overprotective brother? A jealous husband?"

"No," said Yasaman.

"Yes," said the man in the black coat, and added, "Go get your things." He took a long step forward and pulled a semiautomatic pistol from his pocket.

The hotel door swung shut as Yasaman's aspiring lover let go and stepped back into the lobby. The fear on his face was dreadful. She had only seen its like on the faces of terrified children. She found herself doubting he was anything more than an overconfident and aggressive man whose ego had been rudely deflated. He proved her intuition when he turned and ran back into the safety of the hotel.

Yasaman sagged against the door, weak with relief.

"Stupid," her contact said. "He might be able to identify you."

A flash of anger leapt from Yasaman's mind to her tongue. "Oh, yes. This is the woman who spurned me and left me sitting in a café alone—the woman who literally ran away from me."

He returned his gun to his pocket. "Do you want my help?"

"I do."

"Then you must trust me."

"I don't know who you are. You are nothing like the man who set up our meeting."

"No. I'm Max. If a name is not enough for you to trust me, at least don't insult me again."

"How did I insult you?"

Max moved closer. "I'm charged with keeping you safe at the risk of my own life. When you put yourself at risk, you threaten your safety and mine. That is an insult to me. Now, will you go collect your things?" He tilted his head toward the lobby. "Take the closest elevator."

Swallowing her sarcasm and her relief, Yasaman did as he instructed.

14—Repeat Viewing

Like a sailor watching the tide, Mitch waited for new videos to roll in. Whenever one of the analysts approved a video flagged up by the pattern-matching software, it appeared on Mitch's screen. He played it at full speed or various degrees of slow motion. His job—his role on the team—was that of a screener. He watched videos and then gave detailed reports on any effects he felt. Early on, these were the briefest swings of emotion, but the more videos Mitch watched, the more he got the impression he was being influenced to take specific actions. The pressure was subtle, more like the tug of a creek than the rush of a river, but it persisted between videos, gradually strengthening the more he watched.

"It's mostly like it wants me to keep watching, to look at other stuff. It kind of makes me feel like it was what I wanted anyway, like there's a sort of hole in my mind I want to fill. I'm being pushed to find shapes—uh, *videos*—that are the right fit."

Trent hummed to himself before he said, "Are they all like that?"

Mitch said, "No. The Mattoo Clip"—the moniker they'd given the video Akhtab Mattoo had been watching on the dash cam footage—"makes me angry. A little scared. It's complicated."

Neil was the third participant in the review of Mitch's findings taking place in Trent's office. He said, "Maybe the others are a hold signal. Like when you're on the phone. 'Your call is important to us. Please stay on the line.'"

"Well reasoned, Young Parker," said Trent.

"Maybe," said Mitch. "In that case, is the Mattoo Clip the operator? These other videos are to let the attackers know instructions are coming, then Mattoo hits, and bam! They go blow up something?"

"I think there's more to it," said Trent. "It's not just a code. Inserting frames in a video is hardly sophisticated. Producing a visceral reaction with invisible squiggles is something else. The academic consensus on subliminal messaging is it's not worth the effort. Hiding a message doesn't make it more persuasive. It makes it less. Even running repeats won't work. The brain senses it's being signaled, but it doesn't care. There's no threat, no offer of reward. The brain ignores useless information all the time. That's how it interprets subliminal messages. They're worthless, not worthy of attention. You can't be influenced by something you don't really watch."

"But these are influencing me," said Mitch.

"That's right. There's a clear emotional response. I wish we knew how it was being triggered."

A young analyst poked her head in the office. "Sir? Wells wants to see you."

"Just me, Olivia?"

"*Everybody*, sir."

Trent strode out into the main workspace, rubbing his hands together. "You're about to see a show, Mitch. Wells is the best I've ever known."

The woman who most wanted Mitch arrested was leaning against the corner of one of the long tables. Her hands were in her pockets and her nose was in the air. A number of colleagues were standing nearby. The first thing Wells did after Mitch staked out a space between onlookers was point her chin at him and say, "We don't need any consulting on this one."

Trent answered before Mitch replied. "If it concerns our mysterious symbols, we do. Detective Wilson has been binge-watching the candidate clips for hours. He's the closest thing we have to an expert on their effects. Tell us what you found, Noreen. We'll figure out together what it means."

Wells scowled but left off staring holes in Mitch. Seating herself at a workspace, she brought up a document on the monitor, then wheeled her chair to one side so the gathered agents could see. It was some kind of technical paper. At the top left was a caption, FIG 1.4. Below it, arranged in rows and columns, were a collection of lines, dots, crooks, knots, and pinwheels. Mitch recognized all of the symbols he had seen in video clips, alongside a dozen others. Viewing the symbols in that way had no discernible effect on his emotions, aside from stirring his curiosity.

Trent started a slow clap. "Where did you find this, Noreen?"

"The Library of Congress Web Archive. There are references on the net, but every copy, in every language, has been taken down."

Neil said, "And what is it?"

"A proposal," said Wells. "A funding request."

Trent said, "Why not? They took Capone down for tax evasion. Don't leave us hanging, Noreen. Who's the author?"

Wells tabbed to another screen, bringing up the headshot of a woman in her midthirties or remarkably youthful forties. Even Mitch, whose knuckles ached to choke the life from anybody who had played the slightest part in the bombing, blew out breath at the sight of her sculpted features, luminous eyes, and dark hair.

Trent tipped his round glasses for a better view. "Wow. Not how I picture a terrorist mastermind. What would you say, Young Parker, more of a Rossetti or a Gauguin?"

"Too skinny for a Gauguin," said Neil.

Wells minimized the headshot and brought up a listing for the University of Tehran's faculty of letters and humanities. She highlighted a name. "This is her. Karami, Yasaman. Professor of linguistic anthropology, Tehran University."

"Tehran," said Trent. "There goes our luck."

In spite of Mitch's presence, Wells allowed herself a smile. "Don't be so sure. I passed the name around ICON, got a hit back from K-Group. Seems the Iranians have a warrant out. Karami has a Jewish mother, so she put in a request for asylum in the homeland. An Israeli agent caught up with her something like thirty hours ago."

"Where is she now?" asked Neil.

"Our attaché is working on finding out."

Trent set a hand on her shoulder. "Amazing work, Noreen. People, we're taking our show on the road. Young Parker, Noreen, my office. Mitch, head on home, pack a bag, get some sleep. I'll call when it's time for wheels up."

Wells pulled away from Trent. "Sir, you're not serious—"

"My office, Noreen. We'll talk."

Glaring at Mitch so hard he was afraid his head would explode, Wells stomped in the direction of the office, followed by Neil.

Before Trent took off, he said to the room, "Good work tonight, folks. I'm going to be all your Secret Santas next Christmas. For now, overtimers clear the floor. The rest of you, get everything we know about Noreen's professor, conditions on the ground in Iran, and the disposition of our friends in Mossad. The field team will need twice the usual support, as I'll be leading it. Now, before we break, give yourselves a round of applause."

Retreating from the hoots and hollers Trent had solicited, Mitch snagged his coat and left the workroom.

***

He got back to Ben's so late, it was early. After retrieving the spare key hidden in a crack between two bricks, Mitch let himself inside. Twenty minutes later, he stood in front of the bed that had been his for the past weeks, wrapped in a towel and dripping from the shower. A gym bag lay open on the bed sheets. He was thinking how to fill it when his phone rang. It was Trent.

"Sorry, Mitch. Looks like you'll have to sleep on the plane. Our man in Tel Aviv came through. We're meeting Karami at the US consulate in Milan."

"Milan? As in Italy?"

"That's the one. Pack a tie. I'm sending Neil to pick you up."

"No need. I can meet you at the airport."

"Yeah? Fine. I'll tack on long-term parking to your already exorbitant fee. The flight out is at five fifteen. Grab breakfast on the way."

"I'm fine with airplane food."

"Mitch, you know you don't really work for me. I can't give you a promotion, no matter how much you suck up."

Mitch smiled. "I'll meet you at security in twenty minutes."

"God! This guy. Make it thirty, okay? No speeding."

Mitch hung up. In record time, he was wearing his nicest suit. In the gym bag, he packed a pair of jeans, a denim jacket, a shirt, toothpaste, toothbrush, comb, and the electric razor he used on trips. And, of course, the salve he was expected to dutifully apply to his healing burns. As he shut the door to the guest room, he saw the flickering light of a TV down the hall. A mild thrill went through him at the thought of telling Ben the good news, but it wasn't Ben who sat watching cartoons in the darkness before dawn. Therese, a big-eyed, brown-haired girl of seven, spun to face him over the arm of the couch.

"Are you leaving, Uncle Mitch?"

Mitch froze. The sight of the slim silhouette against the flickering widescreen threatened to drag him into the past, when he and Ethan had acted out a dozen similar scenes. He concentrated on Therese's nightshirt: the frilly collar and cuffs made it like nothing Ethan had ever worn.

"What are you doing up, sweetie?"

"My show's on." Therese indicated the TV, where an episode of a pony-centric cartoon Mitch was sure she could watch anytime was playing.

"Gotcha. Yeah. I'm taking a trip. I won't be gone long." The look of distress she gave him was so intense, he was worried she would run after him if he left it there, so he added, "You'll barely have time to miss me."

She said, "I miss you now. Stay with me, Uncle Mitch. There's bad people outside."

"I know. I know there are, sweetie. That's why I have to go, to stop the bad people."

"But you're hurt." With a delicate finger, Therese tapped her chest. "Inside. You need time off."

"I'll take some. I promise. Look, can you do something for me?"

Therese tilted her head, intrigued but wary. "What?"

"When you see your dad at breakfast, tell him I'll give him a call."

"Oh. That's easy. I will."

"Thank you, sweetie. Enjoy your show."

"I always do," said the child, sounding wiser and more world-weary than her years. "Be careful, wherever you're going."

"I will."

When Mitch reached airport security, he found Neil propping his back against a wall. Neil had his phone out, but he wasn't tapping buttons, only looking at the screen.

"What've you got there?"

Neil's head rolled on its corded neck. After blinking the Morse code for "I haven't slept in days," he showed Mitch a picture of a smiling boy holding a fishing rod and a trout as long as his arm. There was no question of paternity. He could have been Neil in miniature, only with messier hair.

"That's my little man, Justin," said Neil.

"He looks like you."

"Possibly why my ex bailed on both of us."

"Ouch. Sorry."

Neil shrugged. "She had . . . issues. Not wanting to be a mom was only one of them."

They waited to see if the rest of the party would appear. It occurred to Mitch his coat might be too warm for the grilling under hot light Wells was likely to put him through. Once they were in the air, she would have a captive audience.

"Hey, when you met at HQ, did Wells say anything about me coming on this trip?"

"Sure she did. She's not happy, but it won't stop her from doing her job. Wells is the best, remember. She doesn't let feelings get in the way."

"She's right about me, though. I crossed the line with Mrs. Mattoo. That stomping she wanted you to give me was one I had coming."

"You were out of line. Okay. It's in the past. Don't worry about Wells. Trent believes in you. That's what counts."

"You two are pretty close, huh?"

"I was holding Dad's right hand when he died. Trent was holding his left. He sort of picked up the mantle, I guess you'd say."

They waited in silence for a time. Finally, Mitch said, "You want some breakfast?"

"Yeah. No caffeine, though. Trent said to sleep on the plane."

"He said the same to me. How long do you think it'd take for a moose like you to sleep off a stack of pancakes?"

"I don't know. I owe it to the country to find out."

Mitch gestured down the concourse with his cane.

15—Digging In

The knocking was the worst. Darren was able to drown out the shouting with his earbuds, but not even Drake had enough bass in his throat to cover the sound Ness made pounding on the basement door. After he'd gotten weird looks and a complaint from a neighbor, he'd resorted to running a satellite rock 'n' roll station through the stereo, knowing the neighbors wouldn't be able to distinguish Ness's pounding from the drums. He wished she would understand how it was all for her own good. He loved her and Jer, which is why he needed to protect them.

Back in high school, when he'd first become aware of people watching him, he'd learned to get real good at avoiding detection. He avoided meeting new people, sticking to going to class, wrestling practice, and spending time with Vanessa. He'd known Ness for years and knew she was okay.

When at home, he'd usually hole up in his room to avoid questions from his parents. He never wanted to give too much information about his life even to them. They could too easily pass it along to people at work or to friends, and anything his dad knew about him might become common knowledge to everyone in the whole military.

He remembered the time Dad had come to one of his wrestling matches, when he'd brought along his buddy—some highly decorated guy from the military. He was so nervous his dad had shown up, and had worked harder than ever to quickly pin his first opponent. He'd gone on to pin the next guy too and won the third match on points. Afterward, his dad had commented he'd done pretty well for a small guy—about the most of a compliment his dad ever gave. But afterward, Darren's dad had introduced him to his military friend. "Darren, I want you to meet Colonel Rogers. He wanted to come see what my son was all about."

"Good job, son," Colonel Rogers said with a smile and a wink.

And that's when he knew the military was gathering data on him. He could tell by the look in Colonel Rogers's eye.

Shaking off the memory and frowning at the ceaseless rhythm he was already sick of, he turned down the music, picked up the brown bag he had been packing in the kitchen, and carried it down the hall to the basement stairs.

Ness must have heard him coming, because she stopped pounding for a moment to shout, "D? Let me outta here!" before taking up pounding again.

"Chill with that," said Darren. He dug in a pocket for the key to the padlock. "Chill, Ness. I'm not playing with you."

"Open up, D. I'm not playing with you, either."

He was going to open up, but not because she insisted, and not to let her and Jer out. It was sad Ness couldn't see the reality of what their life had become. She had been with him almost two months ago when the world had gone crazy. Why couldn't she understand the need to dig in?

He let the door reverberate between thumps of her fist. When she took a brief pause, he said, "Yo, you hungry?"

A thoughtful silence followed. Ness hadn't eaten since breakfast the day before. The soup he had brought her for yesterday's lunch had been slammed to the floor, so he had let her skip a couple meals. At least Jeremy knew better than to waste food. He had been burning calories swinging his virtual sword and whatnot in games. If Ness could learn to appreciate the provisions Darren gave them the way Jer did, they would be able to eat together again. Food, shelter, and family togetherness. Wasn't that what every mother wanted?

"Stand back from the door and I'll pass in a bag. There's subs for you and Jer, some baby Snickers. Cold like you like. Stand back, okay? Don't try anything. Maybe after you eat, we can talk. I miss you, baby."

He pictured her standing on the other side of the door, processing, probably pursing her lips in that cute way she did when she was thinking. Finally, he heard a creak on the stair as she descended.

"Good girl. Go on down bottom. I'll wait."

"One sec."

From the sound of her voice he gauged she'd reached the bottom of the stairs. Why did she want him to wait? The arrangement they had come to was simple. He would crack the door, set the bag on the stairs, then tell her when he was ready for her to come get it. It was a shame he had to be so cautious. He would have preferred to give her the run of the house, but couldn't until she grasped the importance of staying indoors. Lying on the floor to his right was a set of metal brackets and a bar he intended to fit to the inside of the basement door. He had already installed a similar setup on the row house's front and back doors. Once Ness picked up her food, he would get back to boarding up the windows.

"What's the holdup?" asked Darren. Without waiting for an answer, he popped the padlock and opened the door. If he had respected Ness more as an all-around athlete, he might have guessed her plan. She hadn't spent her whole high school career as a wrestlerette; she had medals in the closet she had earned at track and field. In high school, she had the upper body strength to throw the shot put—a talent she'd transferred to the javelin during her stint at community college. Darren regretted he'd ever praised her for her accomplishments in the event. As the pole she hurled javelin-style struck Darren's cheek, there was a brief moment he felt he deserved the pain, if for no other reason than he'd been slow to dodge.

The middle of the pole bounced against the half-open door, causing the pole to pivot. The end jabbed Darren in the eye. He swore, sure Ness had struck him blind. When he heard her feet on the stairs, he reached out, dropping the food bag.

He didn't mean to shove his wife. She hadn't actually tried to blind him. A split second before his palm smacked against her chest, he heard the concern in her voice when she cried, "D!" But by then it was too late.

She was a strong woman. The first time they had held hands had been after a challenge to arm-wrestle. He had almost let her beat him then, and every time after. As she sped away from him, her palms slapped the unpainted drywall and, for an instant, the force she exerted was enough to hold her upright. Then she fell, tumbling head over heels so, by the time she landed, it was impossible to tell if she'd fallen on her back or her neck. She crashed and lay motionless at the bottom of the stairs.

"Mama?" Jeremy cried out. Darren heard a clunk as the VR helmet hit the floor. Then Jer shouted, "Mama!" and stooped over her. He glanced up the stairs at Darren, wide eyed.

Darren said, "Don't touch her." It was the first thing that sprang to his mind. "Stay there, Jer. Mama's okay."

Blinking, Darren descended the stairs. He could see perfectly well, aside from a few tears. The pole had stunned him without doing much damage. He stood bent over the silent Ness, guts in a quiver, sure he had murdered the woman he loved.

"Ness, I'm sorry. I didn't mean—"

Darren, overcome with emotion and uncertainty, missed Ness's windup but felt the full force of the sharp crack of pain as Ness's foot landed square on his shin. He jumped back. "Ow!"

"You tried to kill me," she said between breaths, rolling away from him.

"I'm sorry, baby. It was an accident. You hit my eye." Darren bent down and rubbed his sore shin, not moving closer to Ness but keeping his body strategically between her and the stairs. He had never intended to hurt his wife and truly didn't want her to feel threatened.

"Jeremy, get Mama's phone."

Jeremy looked from Mama to Dad and back again, tears running down his cheeks.

Darren said, "Go back to your game, Jer."

"I can't," said Jer, rubbing his puffy eyes.

"Go."

Sniffing, Jer slouched away. Ness tried to sit up. The arm she used to brace herself collapsed.

"Ah! It hurts, D. My right arm. I think it's broken. I need a doctor, D. You have to take me to the hospital."

The idea of visiting a place with so many people, all strangers who could be bombers or shooters or any other kind of nut made Darren's skin itch like he'd just crawled through poison ivy. He shook his head vigorously, limping away from Ness.

"You don't. You're fine. Remember when I cracked my elbow? I've got the sling upstairs. I'll bring you the sling and some aspirin. You'll be okay, babe. Just lie there. I'm sorry I pushed you. Don't worry about the eye. Just lie there, okay?"

She glared at him. Her eyes were bloodshot. He would bring her a sleeping pill in addition to the aspirin.

"You can't go out, Ness. Ain't you seen the news? It can happen anywhere, babe."

"What can happen, D? Are you high or something? I need a doctor."

How could she not understand the danger they were in? He was the protector of those weaker than him. He lurched away as she lunged at him. She screamed in pain as she landed on the bad arm. In a hurry to get away, he put a foot on the stair. Then he noticed Jeremy standing in place, watching him.

"Jer, what are you doing? I told you to play your game."

The boy stood unmoving in the middle of the VR play space, helmet on and controller in hand. The foldout TV showed the word "PAUSE" in wavy text on a frozen screen.

"I can't," said Jer, his voice cracking. "The pole—"

Darren clenched his jaw to keep himself from screaming at Jer. He had been so proud of how his son was adjusting to life indoors, but it seemed like Ness had erased his progress with one senseless act of rebellion.

Wait . . . *senseless*?

Then he understood. The pole Ness had hurled at him was one of the four sensor poles defining the play area. With one of the four gone, poor Jer was stuck in a directionless game, drifting around until Darren could put things right.

Darren took a deep breath. "It's okay, little man. I'll help, just as soon as I can. Watch *SpongeBob* or something while I help Mama."

"D!" said Ness. She managed to stand, though she cradled her arm and swayed, clearly in pain.

"You wait," said Darren. "I'll make everything okay, I swear." He hustled upstairs before Ness made more trouble. The moment he clicked the padlock, the walls seemed to wobble, as though they might collapse in on him at any moment. He told himself it was his blurry vision. His lungs didn't believe what he said. He gulped air like a fish breathing water. His heart sped up to keep pace with his swimming thoughts.

The aspirin was in the medicine cabinet. He had the bottle in hand when a text came in from Rod. It was one character long, the simplest possible message: $

Darren almost dropped the phone. He still had no money to give his brother. He had maxed out the last of his credit cards buying boards for the windows. Anxiety flooded over him, so he pulled out Ness's phone, watching the first video recommended on YouTube. It happened to be a recorded session of some shooter game he didn't play anymore but had thought about getting back once Ness cooled off enough for him to share the VR system.

When a commercial interrupted the video, Darren hit pause. He went to the bedroom and brought out an old Amazon box from under the bed. The gun Rod had sold him was there. Darren lifted it, testing the weight on his palm. Holding the gun brought back memories of the incident so long ago with the boys from school. The revolver seemed much lighter, but then again he'd been a ten-year-old the last time he shot a gun.

Rod wouldn't give him a hard time about payment. They were brothers. And if he did, maybe it wouldn't be so terrible to work with Rod for a short time. He hated the thought of leaving the house, but one or two stick-up jobs wouldn't take long. He would get Rod off his back, give Ness a few days to calm down, and then shut himself in with Jer and Ness to ride out to the end his instinct told him was coming.

He slid the gun away and went back to searching for the sling. Very soon, Ness, or maybe Jer, would start knocking on the basement door again. Anticipating the racket, Darren turned up the stereo, from which Tina Turner demanded to know, "What's Love Got to Do With It?"

16—Common Interest

The taxicab pulled up to the curb across the street from the Enoteca Ombre Rosse wine bar on Via Plinio, which was virtually identical to any one of the myriad other fashionable drinking establishments in Milan.

The bar was cozy, modern, chic. Its outer deck was covered by a faded blue awning, though nobody in their right mind would have sat outside on such a cold day. The awning was attached to an L-shaped building, the base of which was six stories tall, the leg closer to twelve. Yasaman couldn't see the top of the leg due to sleet and rain and the frost partially obscuring her window. Turning away from the outdoors, she watched Max run a credit card through the slot on the back of the driver's seat.

Were spies actually *supposed* to use credit cards?

Yasaman suspected "Max" wasn't her companion's real name. She also figured his buzz-cut hair was dyed to conceal its true color—unless the guy was prematurely graying and vain, of course. And there was something about how his face fell into a permanent scowl that had Yasaman thinking he'd had work done there too.

Max's lack of concern over having his movements tracked seemed to confirm her suspicions as fact. So-called Max refused his receipt, retrieved a suitcase from the trunk, and came around to open her door. Though he took care to unfurl a black umbrella, offering shelter from the storm, Yasaman didn't exit at once but sat watching his pupils flick back and forth, back and forth.

"What are you waiting for?" he said. They had both been practicing their English since landing at the airport. Yasaman thought it most strange, but Max insisted it was practical.

"I'm sorry," she said. "Is there something you want? How would I know? You haven't told me why we're here."

"I did tell you. We're here to do a friend a favor. That's not enough? I've been good to you. I bought you those clothes, let you clean up at the hotel. Now, you be good to me. We're late."

"Late for what?"

Max grinned but didn't say.

The cabbie wasn't in a rush. He seemed to enjoy leering at Yasaman in the rearview. If she'd shouted, "Drive!" she was sure he would have taken her anywhere in Milan. So, why didn't she shout? She'd been debating doing something of the kind from the moment Max had told her they wouldn't be flying to Israel, which came after taking her across the border into Turkey and passing through checkpoints with what he called his "magic pass." All he had to do was flash the paper and, abracadabra, their car was waved through.

Yasaman had been impressed by how easily Max had managed to get her out of her country. If she'd thought M. Dubois was confident, Max made the guy look like a monkish mouse. His aggressive, rough manner might have intrigued her if she had not witnessed him threaten to kill an innocent stranger. She had no doubt he would have carried out the threat, too.

After Max made her shiver outside in the car for twenty minutes while he made a call via a Turkish cell phone tower, all of her remaining lukewarm feelings toward the spy had evaporated.

"I won't be taking you to Israel," Max had grunted upon returning to the car.

Yasaman had been taken aback; just who the hell had he been talking to on the phone that had elicited this sudden sea change in plans? "That's not what you are being paid for," she said.

"I am being paid to get you out of Iran." The flat bluntness in Max's tone didn't court any argument from her. "And that's what I'm doing."

"So, where are you taking me?"

"That has not been determined yet." Max closed her down. "We are to wait at the next town until I receive further orders." He gunned the car's engine and, mercifully, the heater kicked straight in.

Yasaman opened her mouth to speak as Max pulled the car back onto the road, but thought better of it. Whatever was happening, she sensed it was to be the end of her association with the dour man, and she decided at that moment she would ditch him the first chance she got; she'd strike out on her own in the country that was, after all, stranger to him than to her.

Scarcely an hour after Yasaman made her decision, they'd stopped for gas at a station-cum-bus stop. Yasaman saw her chance, but so did Max. He turned and fixed her with his most penetrating gaze yet and said, "You're plotting. Why? Maybe you don't like or trust the new plan." He offered a wan smile in an attempt to reassure her. "Look, it's fine. We're doing a favor for a friend. My superiors— this is *their* idea. You should talk to them; they'll be happy to explain. There's Wi-Fi in the gas station. Take my phone. I'll show you how to start a teleconference. Go on, it's fine. I should check in anyway. They're like *bubbes*, always waiting for a call. Take the phone. You'll see."

It was the longest speech Yasaman had heard the man string together, although by the end of it, his eyes were shifting again. It was also the first time she'd heard him use Yiddish. Yasaman's own grandmother, known only from postcards and as a voice over the phone, had wished to be called "Bubbe" by her grandchildren. Yasaman had never granted the wish; perhaps guilt over the ancient sin made her do as Max instructed at the gas station.

Yasaman keyed the combination of letters and numbers Max dictated to her into his phone.

Nothing.

There was a gap—a blank page in her memory from after she keyed the last digit to when the teleconference was over. She didn't remember anything of what Max's superiors looked like or what they'd said. She recalled none of their assurances, only that she no longer felt compelled to translate her umbrage at being carted around a succession of countries into action.

Instead, Yasaman questioned Max's plans but failed to actively oppose him. When opportunities arose to flee, she simply allowed them to slip by, though not without some internal debate. Ultimately, the winning voice informed her she had to trust Max; she had no *choice* but to trust him. As he'd told her in Urmia, he was putting himself in danger to escort her to safety. Why would she want to do something stupid?

As she sat in the cab outside the fancy wine bar, utterly perplexed she'd come so far with a man she hated, Yasaman couldn't bring herself not to do his will. For every destination she thought about calling out to the cabbie, her heart gave an irregular beat. By the time she leaned forward to tell the cabbie *ciao*, she felt physically sick. Not daring to look at Max for fear she'd either spit in his face or kiss him, she stepped from the cab to the sidewalk. Beads of ice tap-danced down her back as she was shunted to the fringe of the umbrella's protection so Max could slam the cab's door.

Crunching slush underfoot, Max loped away. Yasaman was obliged to jog at his side to keep from being soaked.

They stopped under the bar's awning. Yasaman said, "Won't you tell me what to expect? A lady likes to know the proper demeanor to put on."

"Look," Max said, gesturing.

Past the drinking establishment and a span of exposed sidewalk stood a pair of guards in uniform. A shelter a good deal sturdier than the one they were under cast a shadow over a side entrance to the L-shaped building. Yasaman judged it must be an important place to warrant protection by soldiers with automatic rifles. Max pointed at the circular emblem on the wall beside the guards. It depicted an eagle with a shield protecting its breast. Over the eagle's head was a cloud of stars.

"American," she said.

"US Consulate," said Max. He led the way across the exposed span, closing the umbrella the moment he was no longer in danger of getting wet. Nodding to one of the guards, he said, "Mr. Barroso and guest. We're expected."

One of the guards, a woman, relayed the information over walkie-talkie. A minute later, a buzzer sounded. Both guards stood at attention as a man in a less weather-appropriate version of the same uniform opened the door. He twirled his hand like a fisherman drawing in line. Then he said, "Barroso and guest, this way, please."

They bypassed a security counter as their escort signaled for the guard manning it to stand down and crossed a marble floor to where a tall man in an expensive suit stood conversing with a shorter man in a dark suit and round-rimmed spectacles. Behind and a little to the left was a woman who had taken great pains to constrain her tightly braided hair in a thick ponytail. She wore a dark pants suit, which was tailored tightly enough to taper from thigh to ankle instead of falling straight down like a shapeless curtain. Unlike the chatting men, the woman stared silently at Yasaman and Max as they approached. She first probed one, then the other, as though looking for weaknesses. If Yasaman had been carrying a weapon, she was sure the woman would have read the fact on her face or in her gait.

Both men looked up as Max and Yasaman halted. The tall man's smile was not exactly fake, but certainly calculated. He nodded to the military escort, who bowed and left.

The short man said, "Salām, Dr. Karami." He produced a badge from inside his suit and held it out for her to see. "Special Agent Trent Falwell. With me is Special Agent Noreen Wells. On behalf of the FBI, thank you in advance for your cooperation."

Yasaman craned her neck to read the badge. She felt more confused about what was going on than ever, and half expected Agent Falwell was pulling her leg. The expression on the face of Agent Wells told her it was entirely impossible.

"I'm sorry," Yasaman said. "I wasn't expecting this. I don't know what you want. If we have some common interest, this is the first I have heard it suggested."

The tall man's smile brightened. "Don't apologize. You're not at fault." He looked disapprovingly at Max. Extending a hand to Yasaman, he said, "My name is Vincent Joval. I am the consul general, mademoiselle. I am your host. Max was supposed to prepare you for this meeting. It is not often he falls down on the job."

The familiarity implied by his choice of words struck Yasaman as mysterious. She had been trying to reason out why she'd been brought to such a place. The difficult history between the US and Iran brought to mind a number of possibilities, but a personal connection between Max and a senior diplomat wasn't one of them. From the ages of eighteen to twenty-nine, she had seen a vast array of cousins and friends married off. At every wedding, there had been at least one moment when she had turned a corner to find herself alone with an eligible bachelor of about the same age. By the third or fourth encounter, she had learned to distrust coincidence.

"How interesting it is that you know each other," she said.

Agent Wells shot the consul a sidelong glance. Her face was unreadable, but her eyes said she found the coincidence curious as well.

"We've worked together a few times," said Joval. "You'll find I make fast friends, Professor."

"I'm sure. Please, call me Yasaman."

"You see? We're friends already. Call me Vince."

"Thank you, Vince. I will."

Falwell clapped Vince on the back, drawing everyone's attention. "All right, the ice is broken. Yasaman, here's the situation. You and the United States do have a common interest. If you're willing to come with me and Agent Wells, there are questions we'd like to ask in private."

"Privacy is relative, of course," said Vince. "Yasaman, my background is as a human rights attorney. If you don't mind, I'd like to be present at your questioning. Nothing against the FBI, you understand. I feel responsible for the comfort of my guests."

Falwell's glasses slid a half-inch down his nose, but he didn't voice an objection. Yasaman considered refusing the interview, but she doubted it would be allowed. She was broke and far from home. Max was looming at the edge of her vision. If the United States was the friend who had asked him to do a favor, Yasaman was sure he'd see to it she complied.

"Thank you, Vince. That's a generous offer. I would be pleased to have your input."

Max surprised everyone but Vince by saying, "Me too."

"Forgive me," said Vince. "I should have mentioned. The . . . *arrangement* . . . that brought Yasaman to us was made with Max's people. It requires his presence in the room."

Falwell cleared his throat. "I see what you mean by relative privacy. Do you mind a few extra ears, Yasaman?"

Yasaman got the distinct impression he *wanted* her to mind. What he would have done if she did was an interesting question. For her part, she would have been happy to see the back of Max's trench coat. But that wasn't to be. A pang of nausea compelled her to say, "I've nothing to hide."

"Fine," said Falwell. "Fine."

Vince rubbed his hands together. "It's settled, then. A room has been prepared, as my good friend Agent Falwell instructed. There is coffee, Yasaman. Say the word if you hunger for something substantial."

"Coffee is perfect."

Offering his arm, which she accepted, Vince agreed. "It can be, my dear." With a spring in his step, he conducted the party to a bank of elevators.

17—Yesterday's Future

The long, narrow meeting room on the third floor of the Palazzo Montecatini where Mitch and Neil sat waiting for the others gave Mitch the creeps. Before Trent took off with Wells to fetch the guest of honor, he had guessed the furnishings in the room, and throughout the consulate building, to be retro-futurist. The sleek lines of the metal chairs and the Bakelite coffee table reminded Mitch of Spaceship Earth, which he'd last seen on Ethan's first—only—visit to Disney World and Epcot. The designs conjured visions of an atomic tomorrow, as seen through the lens of an extinct past. It was amazing, really, how hopeful the older generation had been. They had come through war and influenza only to look back and say, "The best is yet to come." Every hygienic surface in the room proclaimed the same message.

Mitch's hip was still bothering him—it probably would for quite a while—but at least his burned skin was healing nicely, and the arm infection had been arrested with the help of the antibiotics. He felt more energetic today and realized how truly run down he'd been while dealing with the infected arm.

In such a setting, Mitch couldn't help but feel like a tourist. Or worse, a trespasser. He didn't belong in a place built on hope—no matter how naïve that hope turned out to be. The question running through his head was, "What would Jessica think of this place?"

He knew how she would have felt about the company he was keeping. Jessica had never been totally comfortable around his cop buddies, aside from Ben. There were things cops could only say to each other, so there was a point in every get-together when Jessica would walk into a room and conversation would cease. "Guess you had to be there," someone would say, and the talk would start down a new path. During his time with the Gun Trace Task Force, Mitch had often taken it upon himself to change topics. He didn't want Jessica to know how close cops often came to sounding like criminals.

Jessica would have liked Neil on a personal level, Mitch was sure. She would also have liked Trent Falwell, who was the kind of man who didn't forget how funny he looked naked the moment he put on pants. There was a good chance Jessica would have liked and respected Wells. But she wouldn't have been pleased about Mitch riding shotgun with the FBI. It would have been another part of his life he couldn't share openly, another source of secrets he felt obliged to keep. Given the sort of people Trent's team was trying to track down, it was also another way Mitch could get killed. Though death seemed to come from all angles these days.

Neil was sitting at the other end of the faux-leather couch. They had cracked a few jokes after the others had gone, speculating if they knocked the dirt off their shoes, Rosie the Robot would roll in with a dustpan. After awhile, Neil had poured himself a cup of coffee from the ornate, stainless steel urn in the middle of the table. Ever since, he had been fidgeting with the cup, not drinking but blowing across the top, rotating the blue-and-white china in his big hands. Mitch got tired of his fidgeting.

"What's with you?" he said.

"Huh?" said Neil.

"Keep feeling up that cup and I'll have to ask if it wants to press charges."

Neil chuckled. "Sorry. I miss my gun."

"Seriously?"

Neil gestured at the high ceiling with its strips of concealed lighting, then down at the pale, almost featureless floor made of a material neither man could name. "It's this place. I keep thinking Darth Vader is going to walk in."

"Well, if he did, and you shot him, he'd catch the bullets anyway."

"Yeah. But I'd *make* him do it."

The agents had surrendered their weapons to the marine security guards on entering the consulate. Mitch had flown unarmed. Before Neil said something, it had seemed natural to leave their defense to the rifle-toting marines. But there weren't any marines in the hyperclean room, or anywhere nearby, so far as Mitch had seen. He began to feel nervous and tried to combat the effect by downing his own cup of coffee. It made him jittery.

He was popping his knuckles to work off spare energy when the automatic door hissed open. Instead of the fictional dark lord, General Consul Vince Joval stepped inside. Earlier, the consul had introduced himself, passing out limp handshakes and failing to meet eyes. Instead, he acknowledged Mitch and Neil with a tilt of the head before stepping aside to let Trent into the room.

"Neil," said Trent. "We'll be a little crowded. Do you mind waiting in the hall?"

"No problem," said Neil, who was, after all, wide enough to fill two seats. On his way out, he gave Joval a subtle once-over. A quick backward glance made sure Mitch got the message. With a silent understanding, Mitch agreed to keep an eye on the slender diplomat in his three-piece suit.

When Neil was gone, Trent said, "Mitch, I told Dr. Karami to give us a moment. Are you ready to meet her?"

"Did she give you trouble?"

"Not a bit. She's been perfectly helpful."

Joval said, "If your man has a problem with the professor, Agent Falwell, I don't see why he needs to be here."

"Oh, I do," said Trent. "I mean it, Mitch. If you need a moment—"

"I'm good," said Mitch. "Happy she wants to play ball."

Trent walked to the door. "Noreen? Bring her in, please."

For several seconds, the sound of footfalls was the only noise those in the room heard. Wells evidently retreated a short distance before returning, accompanied by the steady tap of boot heels.

The instant Dr. Yasaman Karami appeared, Mitch knew he'd lied to Trent. The thirteen hours, more or less, since he had first heard her name hadn't been time enough to get his mind straight. No sooner did the lights fall on the delicate contours of her neck than he wanted to close his hands around it and demand she spill all she knew about the symbols on the Mattoo Clip. He didn't know if she had personally done anything to inspire Red Line. He didn't care. She had knowledge that would get him a step closer to what he had told Trent was justice, no matter how much it smelled like revenge.

And yet, there was something about the woman's flawless, honeyed skin, classically beautiful face, and stunningly proportioned figure that stirred feelings up inside of him that he'd not felt since . . .

Jessica.

Suppressing the sickening wave of guilt that swept through him, Mitch pressed the tip of his cane into the floor and got to his feet to acknowledge the newcomer. Squeezing the cane's handle was no substitute for wringing the truth out of an enemy, but it helped him keep hold of himself. He knew he wouldn't be able to look at the professor long without making plain how he felt, so he lowered his eyes to the coffee urn.

"Yasaman," said Trent, "this is Detective Mitch Wilson of the Baltimore Maryland Police Department. Mitch is working for the FBI in a consulting capacity."

Mitch waved a hand. It was all he could trust himself to do.

"It is . . . nice to meet you, Detective," said Yasaman. She had a smooth, confident voice and was not above weighing her words. When Mitch didn't respond, she took a deliberate pause before adding, "We are both a long way from home."

The comment was so shrewd, Mitch almost laughed in the woman's face. "Yeah," he said, "we sure are." A fleeting glance into Yasaman's eyes and Mitch felt himself sinking deep into their dark, exquisite beauty.

In response to Trent's invitation to sit, Yasaman chose a chair across the coffee table and slightly to the left of Mitch. Joval took a chair on Mitch's right. Trent occupied Neil's place on the couch, waving Wells to a chair across from Joval.

"I'll stand," said Wells.

Joval raised an eyebrow, but Trent shrugged as if to say, "You try." Producing a key card from his pocket, Joval said, "Max, didn't your mother teach you not to lurk in doorways?"

There was, as Joval had indicated, someone standing partially in shadow on the other side of the doorframe. Mitch hadn't noticed him, and until he stepped inside, had never seen anyone like him in person before. With his slim build, black trench coat, and slicked-back hair, he looked like he should have either been curating a Goth museum or sucking the blood out of its visitors. His eyes met Mitch's for an instant before darting away. It took Mitch a few repetitions to realize the man wasn't prompting him to glance sideways. He had a tick of some kind, which made his eyes bounce. Back in junior high, Mitch had known a kid with the exact same condition; teachers were constantly telling him not to look at the other kids' work.

"Come in, Max," said Joval.

The stranger slouched inside. Ignoring the empty chairs Wells had scorned, he stalked to the room's single window, some yards behind the consul's chair. The consul wasn't in it, as he had gone to the door.

"It looks like we have room after all," said Trent. "Mind if I pull my man in?"

Acting like he hadn't heard, Joval passed the key card in front of a sensor. Following a whir of motors, the door hissed shut, and with a clunk, locked.

Trent chuckled, though not convincingly, as Joval returned to his seat. "Well, never mind. How 'bout that coffee, Professor?"

She accepted with grace. While Trent poured, Mitch scanned the crown molding, trying to rein in his thoughts. Wells, he noticed, kept her eyes on the new guy, Max, who appeared to be fascinated by the view from the window.

The professor took a sip of her coffee. "Wonderful. That was all I lacked in life. You said you had questions, Trent. Perhaps if you like my answers, you'll pay me back by answering some of mine."

"I'll try," said Trent. He picked up his tablet, a Stadion S-Tab Pro, from where he'd left it on the table. "A little background, first. Yasaman is your given name, Karami your paternal. Correct?"

"Yes."

"Do you have a middle name?"

"They are not common in my country."

He quizzed her about contact with terrorist organizations. To her knowledge, she'd never had any. After listing the usual suspects—HAMAS, Hezbollah, Al Qaeda—plus several Mitch had never heard of, Trent said, "You're sure you've never communicated with any member of these organizations?"

"I'm sure I have not knowingly. Certainly not by choice."

"Thank you. And thanks for hanging in there. Next I have some questions about your family."

Joval lifted a finger. "Excuse me, Trent. I know you have your procedures, but I have an appointment within the hour. For the sake of time, could we skip to what you're here after?"

"Fine," said Trent, only mildly annoyed. He tapped at his screen. When he had found what he was looking for, he rotated the tablet to show the image of a sinuous line curling upward from a flat base. Mitch recognized the symbol from the Mattoo Clip and Yasaman's grant proposal. Trent said, "Are you familiar with this?"

The placid look the professor had worn evaporated. It was replaced by confusion. She leaned in for a closer look, sat back, and hugged herself. "I am. Before I say more, do you have other examples to show?"

Trent swiped to the next page and handed the tablet over.

Mitch knew exactly what was on the page. While airborne, Trent had asked him to edit FIG 1.4. Working from memory and clips saved on his phone, he had circled all the symbols found by the team.

"I know what these are," said the doctor.

Joval held out his hand. "May I see?"

Mutely, she passed him the tablet.

Trent said, "Care to enlighten us, Professor?"

"How familiar are you with my work?"

"We've only seen the one paper. Translation was in the works when we got on a plane. No one here has had time to read the fully translated text."

"The details are mainly technical. Language is my life. Tracing its origins is my life's work. I have made an intensive study of protolanguages. Are you familiar with the term?"

"I'm here to learn."

"Very well. There is a debate among experts in my field about how much of human history has been lost because we no longer think as our ancestors did. I believe the answer is: 'A great deal.' Words, as I'm sure you're aware from interviewing witnesses to a crime, are a poor substitute for meaning. A protolanguage is a set of sounds that had meaning once, which have since passed their qualities down the line to modern languages. Note I say, 'qualities.' Usually, it is not meaning that is remembered, but sounds, word order, plus some niceties of grammar and tense. All such elements change over time, but *meaning* is the most subject to change. I tell my students the history of language is a chain with rusted links. There are many breaks, but they are rarely complete. It is possible, in most cases, to see the shape of the chain, how the links fit together. Each link, in a way, is a protolanguage."

Trent reached to get his S-Tab Pro back from Joval, but the consul swiped, pretending not to see Trent's hand. Trent said, "So, the symbols. They're some kind of alphabet for one of these protolanguages?"

Yasaman shook her head. "In a sense, they are the opposite. Alphabets, generally speaking, are meant to encode speech. These symbols, I believe, are always silent and are used to encode meaning directly."

"You mean like *kanji*?" asked Wells. "I know kanji characters aren't letters or even words per se, but they stand for objects directly."

"That is a similar situation, and it's why Japanese fiction is so difficult to translate; there is no word-for-word correspondence. But this goes deeper. Some years ago I asked a colleague of mine to run several computer analyses on a collection of grave markings. My theory was these markings, found carved into stone at archaeological sites around the world, predate the very concept of written words. This idea is not new; many in the field have proposed theories to similar effect. What I brought to the exploration was breadth of scope. Or rather, my colleague, a man by the name of Bizhan Al-Kabir, brought that depth."

It was at this seemingly random point in the interview the pale, window-obsessed Max turned his back on the city. He leaned against the windowsill, watching Yasaman intently. Out of habit, Mitch had been checking on him periodically and happened to catch the movement.

Yasaman went on. "It was Bizhan who parsed out portions of the symbols algorithmically. He cut them, you see, as one might cut letters drawn on paper. Using angles and width of line, we delineated the portions into isolated shapes. Bizhan's program compared those shapes with cuts from known alphabets and ideograms."

Mitch had stopped feeling the need to hold his tongue. The woman was being helpful, after all. There would be no need to choke the truth out of her. He was able to speak without fear of shouting.

"Hold on," he said. "What's an ideogram?"

"A written word that resembles its meaning, like the kanji characters Detective Wells mentioned or the figure *shān* in Mandarin Chinese. It looks like, and means, a mountain."

"I'll take your word on that. So, you say you cut these symbols from something bigger, then compared them to letters. That right?"

"Bizhan cut the symbols from grave markings. There are standard tables of common written-language shapes we used for comparison. When I asked Bizhan to make the program, I didn't know if we would find similarities. I only suspected, and I was right. Bizhan found more than I was looking for. As Trent suggested, I had thought the cuts might form a sort of alphabet. Phonetic, most likely, a means of preserving sounds over time. They might have been ideographic, suggesting likenesses strange to us because of the disconnect between present and past. But these symbols, the ones in the paper Bizhan and I authored, do not preserve sounds or a semblance of meaning. They preserve meaning itself. They seem strange because it is not a meaning expressed in words."

"You're losing me," said Trent.

"Yes. Because words fail. Let me try an illustration. Please, imagine you are a member of an ancient tribe. Your great chief has died in battle. You are marching in his funeral procession. This man was a leader, a warrior, a literal father to half your tribe. Skilled workmen have carved a resting place for him in stone. Your priests have scribed symbols on a marker. As you descend into the dark valley that is to harbor your chief's soul, the torchbearers lift up their torches. What you see written stirs something inside. The symbols make you weep. Then your grief becomes pride. You remember all the chief did for the tribe. You feel love and courage. You are ready to defend the tribe, as the chief would have defended it in your place.

These emotions well up from inside, but they are not summoned by your will. The symbols draw them up like a bucket drawing water from a well."

Wells glanced away from the stone-faced Max. "It sounds like mind control."

"Not control," said Yasaman, "and not of the mind. It took some time for Bizhan and I to understand the symbols, but long before then, we gave them a name. *Al-zban ghraza.*" She spoke the term with a heavy Persian accent, which was difficult for Mitch to repeat in his mind. "The language of instinct. It does not implant ideas. It awakens feelings, isolates impulses, and amplifies them. They are your impulses, your feelings. Sometimes, they are a part of your personality you have worked to suppress. But they are a part of you. Al-zban ghraza does not control. It makes you true to yourself, though not always in a way you would consciously will."

"So, some people are more apt to respond to the symbols than others?" asked Mitch.

"At one level, yes. Some people would be more suggestible after viewing the symbols for only a short time. Since anger is such a powerful underlying emotion, the symbols might work to stir up those who have anger just beneath the surface. Someone who tends to be naturally patient or mild-mannered might only find symbols invoking anger mildly unnerving or annoying."

"They sure affected me—I've been awfully angry lately," Mitch mumbled.

Trent leaned forward, elbows on knees. "We all have some anger in us, Doctor. If people were to be exposed for hours to anger ideograms, what would be the effect? Could they, in a way, hypnotize people to act on their suppressed anger? To commit acts they might not normally contemplate?"

"I suppose it *might* be possible."

Mitch thought there was something in the doctor's tone to suggest she was holding back. Whether it was an avoidance of too much technical speak that would confound the uninitiated in the room, or an unwillingness to share something she saw in the symbols, he couldn't ascertain. Nonetheless, he decided to err on the side of caution and run with his instinct to not trust her, no matter how attractive and open she appeared to be.

"Could it work the opposite way? Could people be soothed, even convinced to have peace on earth and good will toward men?"

"Yes. Love and hate are both intense, deeply felt emotions. A tweak in the symbols you use or in the way you use them might stir a person or groups of people into a humanitarian response."

Mitch said, "When you were researching this alzaban thing—"

"Al-zban ghraza—yes."

"Were you trying to come up with something like that? Something to control people's emotions?" Mitch appreciated how open the doctor was in sharing the information but still did not yet feel anything like trust.

Her dark gaze was wary. "Our interest was academic. We wished to piece together a part of the language chain. The link we found was older, more primal than we expected."

"But you realized your research could be used for something nefarious, like what did happen?" Mitch couldn't help but pin the blame on the woman who sat so close to him he could quite easily reach over and strangle the life out of her and her pointless research.

The linguist looked Mitch directly in the eye. "I never—*never*—imagined any of my research would have been used in this horrific way . . . to do such evil."

"Okay, let's talk about what we might deal with in the future." Trent cut into the tense conversation. "It seems highly unlikely scores of people across the globe could be convinced to expose themselves to enough of these videos to get them to act on their anger impulses. How much viewing would be needed to provoke a mass response?"

Yasaman shook her head. "We never tested the symbols in such a way. I'd be conjecturing."

"Please, conjecture away," Trent said.

"I think it would require many hours of viewing within a short span of time. Emotions are powerful, but people tend to be drawn toward what makes them feel good. Consider how masses of people of all ages watch their TV screens, their mobile devices, or play games online, neglecting other activities, simply because it feels good to do so."

"Addiction," said Wells.

"In a word," the doctor agreed. "Or a form of hypnosis."

"So, an evil mastermind," said Trent, "could conceivably mask what is essentially hypnotism of his audience behind seemingly harmless content."

Yasaman stared at him for a brief moment, her lips parted as if to respond. She glanced at Max, her brow furrowed, then turned her attention back to Trent. "An evil mastermind? That sounds so far-fetched . . ."

Trent shrugged. "Someone with *ill intent*, then."

"That . . . that might be possible."

"Let's assume it's possible. How would it work?"

She considered the notion for a moment, then said, "The hypnotizer would seek to gain rapport with a broad audience by finding common ground, common interests, or a common set of images that are pleasing in some way. Those images—used with symbols evoking a sense of belonging—would incline viewers to feel included, special.

Your 'mastermind' would set up what we call anchors. Think of a song that takes you back to a special moment at your high school prom, or the smell of baking bread reminding you of your grandmother's kitchen."

"And it would work the same way with negative emotions, right?" Trent proposed.

"Yes. That's essentially how PTSD works. For example, the sound of a door slamming or fireworks forces you to recall being in combat, or the sight of a playground swing set takes you back to a time a group of school kids bullied you."

She glanced again at Max, paused, as if temporarily losing her thought, cleared her throat, and then continued. "The next step would be to attach those anchors spatially. By that I mean, in effect, the hypnotizer trains the audience to react when they're in a particular place, or they see particular objects or people, or have specific interactions. So, to go back to our schoolyard, seeing a swing set might fill you with the strong urge to run. Or hearing a particular word your tormentors used to taunt you might compel you to fight."

Wells looked as if she'd just had an epiphany. "That's . . . a sort of call and response."

"Yes," said Yasaman. "Because the anchor produces an emotional reaction in the audience."

Mitch felt in his gut he *needed* to understand the mechanism, even if he couldn't quite pronounce the term correctly. "Okay," he said, "so it's all about hypnotism. But how about the symbols? The alzerban graze?"

"Al-zban ghraza." Yasaman smiled.

"I'll get it eventually. I'm not great with foreign terms—*obviously*," stated Mitch.

"The al-zban ghraza would take a normal hypnotism experience and expand its emotional effect exponentially. In conjunction with a—a mastermind producing video content using hypnotic suggestion to manipulate an audience, the symbols have the potential to captivate that audience, to keep them spellbound . . ." She hesitated.

"Then make them do bad things?" asked Trent. "It sounds to me like you're suggesting the symbols drive deep emotional responses, which, combined with hypnotic suggestions, could . . . *recommend* a particular behavior to susceptible members of the audience."

She fixed him with her "look" again—the one saying she wished he'd not brought her to that point. She nodded. Once.

"And," Trent went on, "once the audience's emotions are engaged and directed, the mastermind could use the symbols to create anchors to serve his purpose—whatever that might be."

Yasaman Karami took a deep breath and looked down at her hands, which were knotted in her lap. "If the ultimate goal of this person or persons is violence, the symbols could help create an anchor suggesting the victims channel their intense, buried anger into action. Possibly, it could suggest a target or targets."

"And methods? Bombing, shooting, fighting, whatever?"

Wells was shaking her head. "I studied psychology as part of my field training. One thing I learned was, even under hypnosis, people won't do things that are harmful to them. It isn't like making some poor joker cluck like a chicken whenever he hears the word 'popcorn.' What hypnotically implanted suggestion would be strong enough to make anyone hate so hard they'd blow away innocent people?"

"I can think of one," Yasaman said quietly. "Betrayal."

"So," said Trent into the following silence, "let's propose that, after hours of watching videos, unaware that these ancient symbols are being programmed into their consciousness, our audience could theoretically behave like an army if the mastermind wants it. Could he do that? With some combination of emotions, anchors, and perhaps even the suggestion that they've been betrayed in some way?"

"Theoretically," said Yasaman. "But it would require a broad array of anchors. Not everyone shares common experiences. And it would require a sequence of them, built up over time. It would require an unprecedented control of media or at least access to it."

"But theoretically—"

"Theoretically, yes: If those elements were combined by someone with ill intent."

Trent finished the thought. "Masses of people could be driven to erupt in a frenzy of violence? People who would never normally be violent?"

The doctor looked as if she'd been gut punched. "Yes."

Wells's eyes narrowed. Trent shook his head and blew out air. The only person who seemed to have no reaction at all was Max.

"Fascinating," said Joval. He had been swiping through pages on Trent's tablet with such contentment, Mitch had forgotten he was there. "I think we've heard enough, Professor."

Trent's annoyance at the interruption was obvious. He turned to the consul and said, "Vince, that's not your call."

"I merely meant you should give her a break, Trent. You've had your quid. How about some pro quo?"

"I don't mind going on," Yasaman told them.

"A minute, my dear," said Joval. His tone was friendly, but Mitch saw the professor found it patronizing. "When we talked before, Trent, you said the FBI found evidence of these symbols subliminally inserted into online videos."

"Is this true?" Yasaman was shocked out of glaring at Joval.

"I wasn't going to bring it up," said Trent. "But yes. We think your—please say the name once again."

"Al-zban ghraza."

"We think it may have played a role in radicalizing some of the suspects implicated in the recent mega-terror event."

"You mean Red Line."

"Yes."

Mitch felt a surge of panic. He thought about going to the window. The scowl of the man already there changed his mind.

"My God," Yasaman murmured. "Bizhan . . . About a month before he disappeared, Bizhan theorized perhaps our research would yield a more potent form of the indoctrination cultists or terrorists go through. When I asked what he meant, he said he thought it might prove useful in psychotherapy—deprogramming."

Trent sat up. "He disappeared? Tell me."

A blush had risen in Yasaman's cheeks. "I thought he had left for personal reasons. Then another of my colleagues, Farbod Namdar, also disappeared. We—"

"Sorry to interrupt," said Joval. "Before we move on, Trent, I'm trying to understand these annotations your people have marked beside the circles, here." He indicated Mitch's work on the figure page.

Hurrying to get back to Yasaman, Trent said, "The letters code the source video. The numbers are time stamps for where symbols can be found."

Mitch saw Wells shift her weight from one foot to the other. The wallflower, Max, had decided to join the party. He strode over to stand behind Vince's chair, leaning over its back to peer over Joval's shoulder. The consul did nothing to dissuade him.

"The letters run A through J, inclusive," said Trent. "We eliminated a couple of candidates, so it picks up with M through R."

Joval asked, "Is there a key?"

"Last page of the document."

The consul tapped, swiped, tapped. "Excellent. That's very efficient. You have this backed up on the cloud, I guess. Is it only the three you brought along who have knowledge of the material?"

"No. My whole team."

"Ah. What about Washington? Have you phoned the commander in chief?"

Trent shook his head. "We wanted to know what we had." Leaning forward, he scrutinized the consul. "Vince? How 'bout you tell your buddy to step back. It's got to be uncomfortable, him breathing down your neck like that."

"I want his opinion, first," said Joval. He lifted the tablet a fraction of an inch. "You see what we have here, Max?"

"Yeah," said Max.

"Anything more you'd like to learn?"

"Nope."

Before the word was out of Max's mouth, a gun was in his hand. Mitch heard a pop—the extended barrel was a suppressor and the pistol was firing subsonic rounds—as he dove to one side. Yasaman's response was more useful. She leapt to her feet as the pistol kicked. While Max was squeezing the trigger a second time, she was swinging the coffee urn by its handles. It connected, dropping Max like a wet towel.

The arc of the urn narrowly missed Joval, who slid from his chair. Mitch saw him reach into his jacket. Stabbing with his cane, he caught the consul in the ribs, making him yelp, just as Yasaman released the urn's handles. The vessel struck the edge of the table and ejected its lid in an explosion of steaming liquid. The consul screamed as scalding coffee splashed across his face and chest.

"Gun!" shouted Wells. The weapon Max had fired was lying on the creamy floor a yard from Mitch's feet. With a surge of adrenaline allowing him to ignore his sore hip, he dove like a runner trying to snag second base and got a hand on the grip. At the same moment, Max made a grab for the suppressor. Blood was streaming from a gash in his forehead, making his face a scarlet mask. He misjudged the grab, spinning the pistol away from both men.

They scrambled on hands and knees. The barrel pointed in Mitch's direction, giving him something to grasp but Max less to lose. Mitch felt the pistol's hot steel an instant before Max's palm closed over the back of his hand. Instead of trying to lift the gun, Mitch threw his weight into the other man's elbow. Max was caught by a boot to the face as Mitch went into a roll, landing on his back with the pistol pointed menacingly at Max's head.

Wells moved in, a small sidearm in hand. It must have been the weapon Consul General Joval had been trying to pull from his jacket. A kick from Wells sent the pseudo-spy Max sprawling. Mitch spared a glance at Joval, who was whimpering, holding his face with his hands. Outside, Neil was pounding on the automatic door. The shots had been almost silent. The clang of the urn and Joval's bellowing had likely informed Neil something was wrong. Leaving Wells to cover Max, Mitch went to the side of the sofa, where Yasaman crouched over Trent.

"I am sorry," she said. Her hands were dotted with blood. "I am *so* sorry. He's gone." She averted her eyes from Trent's ruined face; one bullet had entered his skull beneath the left eye, the second through his temple—both had created ragged exit wounds at the back of his head, through which the gray-pink of his brain spilled out.

Mitch considered looking for a pulse, but there was no point. Looking into the holes Max's bullets had dug in Trent's skull, he saw nothing pulsing, no signs of life at all. He felt a dark chasm open deep within his chest, and at once he was back outside the movie theater screaming for his wife and son. Quickly, swiftly, Mitch paved over the pain with purpose.

Wells screamed and lunged at Max, burying a knee in his chest. Neil paused in his pounding for a second.

"Don't kill him," said Mitch.

"Why not?" she snarled. Before Mitch could answer, she'd pistol-whipped Max across the face, adding a split cheek to his collection of injuries. "Switch up."

"Huh?"

"You watch him while I deal with the weasel." She tilted her head toward the whimpering Joval.

Not daring to argue, Mitch covered Max as Wells jerked the moaning consul by the collar. She spit into his pink and blistering face and pressed the cold steel of her gun against the ball of his right eye.

"Tell me who owns you or I swear to Christ I'll pound this in up to the guard before I pull the trigger."

"*Fugit hora*," said Max.

"What did he say?"

Max pushed up on his elbows. Mitch waved the pistol. Max eased back down.

"*Fugit hora*," said Max.

Yasaman said, "That's Latin for 'the hour flies.'"

"An abort signal," said Joval. "He's right. Our game is blown. You were all meant to die. Nothing personal. Please, I need medical attention. Take me out. Let me see someone. I'll tell you all I know."

Max said, "And what is that, fool?" He sat up as he said it, seemingly having forgotten about Mitch and the gun.

Mitch didn't fall for the act. He fired a muted shot into Max's arm. Max cried out, pressed the place the bullet had gone in, and flopped on his side. Too late, Mitch saw he was clutching something in the hand of the injured arm. The cylindrical device no bigger than his palm had appeared as if by magic. Before Mitch could repent his decision to wound instead of kill, Max clicked a button on the top of the device. The next instant, a roar swallowed every other sound.

The room shook and the window erupted in flame. For a span of seconds, Mitch was stunned. Before he had a clue what was happening, Max had leapt up and grabbed the gun, attempting to wrench it away. Even shaken as he was, Mitch was too strong. His opponent got the weapon pointed away but couldn't take it from his hands. Mitch spun him, shoving his back against the wall. There was smoke in the air and a smell like burnt tar. Mitch was sent back to the horrible day that should have been the last of his life. He'd caught the self-same scent then. An anchor, the linguist would have called it.

Choking, gagging, and wanting to retch, Mitch slackened his grip. Max slammed an elbow into his ear, followed by a forehead to the face. Mitch got a knee up to protect his crotch, but Max's own knee didn't go for the crotch. It drove into Mitch's weak hip with the pulsing power of an electric jackhammer. Mitch went down. With the help of the sweat on his wrists, Max twisted away.

He had control of the gun for only a moment before Mitch, his training kicking in despite the intense pain in his hip, grabbed it back once more. Two shots rang out from the spot where Wells was standing. One shot went wide. One went high. Both went into the smoke. Max followed. Mitch watched his feet leave the floor even as a third shot rang out. There was a thud from outside as Wells ran past Mitch.

"You're kidding me!" she said.

Yasaman cried out, "Agent!"

There was confusion, then, as Mitch followed Wells to where Yasaman and Neil blinked at the body of Consul General Joval, who lay on the floor with the last of Max's bullets in his brain.

18—Just Mitch

Yasaman didn't know how many explosions there had been. She didn't know how Max had escaped or what had become of the cane Mitch had wielded so deftly in battle. As far as she could tell, both had simply vanished in the tumult following the blast. Yasaman also didn't know the subject of Mitch's debate with Wells, only that it ended with Wells saying, "There's no time. We need to move." Wells and Mitch had looked at Agent Parker, who was busy wrapping his own jacket around the bloodied head of poor Trent with ritualistic slowness.

Wells stepped up to Yasaman's elbow. "I need you to help Mitch."

"I'm sorry. Help him how?"

"With a shoulder. Walking. Bad hip."

Yasaman hurried to the side of the waiting detective. He draped an arm without comment and hobbled with her out of the room. Wells emerged next, followed by Parker, carrying Trent. Wells clearly had a head for such adventures. She stopped at every bend, holding Joval's gun at the ready while she checked the coast was clear. In a few minutes they skirted around two squads of guards and a dozen fleeing office workers. A minute later, they located an isolated stairwell.

"How did he do it?" said Mitch.

"Bead of C4 around the window," said Wells. "What I want to know is how I missed the shot."

"It was smoky. Don't blame yourself."

Wells halted and rounded on the detective. "Oh? And who am I supposed to blame? Two bad pops on a standing target and he nails his in one?"

"Blame me for that last part."

Conflicting emotions clouded the face of the FBI agent. She tightened the cord restraining her braids. "No. You did all right."

They walked on. When they reached the ground floor, Wells took a glance outside the stairwell before gesturing them all to stay back.

"There's more going on than one blown-out window," said Wells. "Looks like the psycho set multiple charges. There's damage to the floor above, a line to get out, bodies. I'm going to scout ahead. Mitch, can you take charge?"

"Sure," said Mitch.

Wells shot a worried glance at Neil Parker, who was sitting on the stairs with Trent's body still in his arms. She then gave Yasaman a lingering look, as though she were transferring custody of the young agent into Yasaman's hands.

"I'll be a minute," said Wells, and left.

The stairwell was lit by yellow security lights. The main power was out. Lately, it seemed, darkness was bound to creep in whenever Yasaman was around. Setting her existential doubts aside, she focused on Parker.

"Agent Parker," said Yasaman. "Is your name Neil?" Parker didn't acknowledge he had heard. Yasaman went to him and laid a hand on his arm. "Neil?"

His eyes were kind, despite being red from crying. "That's me."

"Neil is a nice name. Friendly."

"I was—it was my granddad's name."

"A great-grandmother of mine was called Yasaman. You must call me Yasaman, Neil. Or Yaz, if you prefer."

"I will. Thanks."

A crack appeared in the door. Wells slid into the stairwell. "We've got an exit, but we'll have to move fast." Wells glanced cautiously at Trent's body, draped across Neil's lap. "Partner, I need you to carry Mitch."

"I can't," said Neil. "I can't manage both."

Wells said, "I need you to carry just Mitch."

Neil peered at the little crack under the door. Yasaman wished she knew him better. She could only guess how he felt about leaving Trent's body behind.

Wells said, "Those are US Marines out there. Our guys." Careful not to touch Trent, she squeezed Neil's shoulder. "They'll find him. He'll be safe."

"We'll get justice," said Mitch.

Neil's body clenched like it was a single muscle. For a moment, he trembled.

"I promise you, Park," said Wells, "we'll make this right."

With a sigh, Neil rose. He lowered Trent's body to the floor. With that done, Wells touched the body once, briefly, then rose and said, "No matter what happens, keep moving. Mix with the crowd. Walk out. I'll meet you across the street."

Wells moved so fast, Yasaman had to jog to keep up. Neil jogged too, trying not to bounce Mitch, who slung an arm around Neil's shoulders to preserve his dignity while Neil cradled his legs and back.

The lobby was a scene out of Dante, full of smoke and fire and bodies rushing about. Fallen victims were indistinguishable from broken beams and burning shrapnel. They existed to be tripped over by the living. Any survivor who got within arm's length of a guard was snagged and sent scurrying for the front entrance. The side-facing entrance was gone. Flames and twisted metal showed where it had been. The security desk Yasaman had passed on the way in had been atomized. At the far end of the lobby, the elevator bank appeared to be intact, but when she tried to trace the path of the car she'd ridden, she found a three-meter circle of sky where ceiling and wall had been. A woman's body hung over the edge of the circle. The hand at the end of her hanging arm was missing all the fingers but the pointer, so she appeared to be jabbing at the ground in accusation.

A guard stepped in front of Wells.

"Federal agent," Wells said. "I've got wounded." She showed the guard her badge.

"Move to the side," said the guard. "I'll need to check with—"

Wells's eyes darted to where Yasaman and Neil stood idle. Yasaman got moving as Wells said, "I know who's responsible for the bombing. There's evidence upstairs."

The guard reached out to Yasaman, but Wells caught his arm. "Never mind the civilians. Get me your commanding officer, pronto."

Then they were out. Yasaman and Neil crossed the street and looked back on the destruction from the corner. Smoke was billowing from the gap Yasaman had seen above the elevator bank. The blast had consumed the security entrance and radiated outward. Black ash extended from a crater in the pavement to the underbellies of two cars rolled on their sides and tossed on the sidewalk.

Neil set Mitch on his feet. Producing his phone, he began tapping commands, apparently to no avail. Yasaman didn't realize what he was doing until he said, "I'm going back for Wells."

"No need, Boy Scout," said Mitch. He pointed down the street. Wells was sprinting their way.

"Ditched . . . the CO. Had . . . to go around."

"Let's get off the street," said Mitch.

"Hotel," said Wells.

"Can you make it?" said Neil.

Wells replied by jogging off.

19—The Language of Instinct

The Hotel Manin was an easy six-minute hike. Trent had booked a suite as a venue for the debrief, before Joval had insisted the consulate was safer. The walls of the suite were thick, but not thick enough to block out the sirens of emergency vehicles swarming the consulate.

When Mitch got to the room, the first thing he did was turn on the TV. He muted the volume, since he couldn't speak Italian, and sat flipping channels while Wells and Neil retreated to the bedroom to put in calls to Baltimore and Washington. Yasaman retreated briefly to the restroom. Looking as stunned as when she'd left, she joined Mitch on the couch.

He let her get comfortable, then said, "How did you know Max had a gun?"

Yasaman sighed. Her eyes were tired. They also shone like polished stone. "Why do you think I did?"

"I watched him from the moment he left the window. I didn't see the gun 'til it was too late. The way you swung the urn, I know you beat me to the uptake."

"You watched him. But did you see his eyes?"

"I saw 'em bounce like he was watching a tennis match. I once knew somebody with eyes like that."

"I spent days with Max. His condition makes it difficult to know where he is looking, but in time I learned to distinguish a twitch from a glance. You remember what the consul asked?"

Mitch thought back, but most of the past hour was a blur. "Remind me."

"He said, 'Anything more you'd like to learn?' He wanted us to think he was talking about my research. Max didn't look at the tablet. That's how I knew he was up to something. I didn't know about the gun, exactly, but I'd already formed the opinion he was a dangerous man."

"You're a good judge of character."

Yasaman looked wistful. "I used to think so. To say I was suspicious of Max is an understatement. From the moment we met, I was sure he was pursuing some hidden goal. He moved me like a pawn on a chessboard. What I can't understand is why I let myself be moved. That's not like me at all, Mitch. I *challenge* authority. Why was I so meek around Max?"

"Don't blame yourself. Those spooky types are trained to get into your head."

"I'm sure they are." She didn't look comforted. "What happened to him, do you suppose?"

"He took a hard bump jumping out of the window. I don't figure you'll see him again."

"If I do, it will be too soon."

Mitch watched the silent TV for a minute or two. Something was tugging at the back of his mind, a hazy notion that grew hazier when he tried to focus on it. He let it drift around until the breaking news report on the consulate bombing went to commercial. He'd often found backing off an idea was the best way to make it crystallize.

"Let me ask you something. Did Max show you any video footage? Maybe something on his phone?"

"No. Wait. Yes, I think he did. A teleconference with his superior. At least, that's what he said. The superior—I don't know his name—was going to explain the wisdom of fleeing to Italy instead of Israel. What I actually saw on the phone, I've forgotten."

"Think back, then. Did you have more control over your will before you watched the video?"

She turned toward him. "Yes, the influence Max had on me dates to then. What made you think of that?"

Instead of wasting time explaining a trick he didn't understand, Mitch fished out his phone and showed the Mattoo Clip. Yasaman watched it twice. When she had finished the second run, Mitch asked, "How does it make you feel?"

"I should be sick. But, to be honest, I feel invigorated."

"Congratulations. Not everybody takes it so well. I nearly brained somebody on my first time through. Since then I've watched the clip more than anybody who didn't blow up a building. I'm at the point where I can take it or leave it, but it took hours and some serious adrenal fatigue."

"I'm sure. But, are you saying—? You are. You think Max made me forget. Whatever he showed me, it made me suggestible . . . and erased my memory. Do you understand what this means?"

"I'm not happy about it, but I do."

"I didn't choose, and yet I forgot. Agent Wells as good as accused me and Bizhan of pursuing mind control. That was never my intention, nor did I think our discoveries made it possible. The symbols amplify emotions. They speak to an already inherent instinct. But, if Max could compel me without my remembering what he'd done, what might he *not* have made me do?"

Neil came in from the other room, phone in hand, head slung low. He was taking Trent's death hard. Mitch wished to help, but his grief over Jessica and Ethan was too fresh.

He couldn't tell Neil he was going to be okay in a few months or even a few years. He didn't know when anybody was going to be okay.

Wells walked in after Neil, looking tired but not without purpose. "We have an eight thirty flight out of Malpensa."

"I'm all packed," said Mitch. His gym bag had been in the consulate's security lockup, along with the guns and the rest of the luggage. Wells glared, but her look had lost some of its bite.

She said to Yasaman, "I talked to the powers that be. So long as you come willingly, you're not under arrest."

"That's a comfort."

Neil was standing in the middle of the room, squinting at the TV. "What's going on?"

Mitch checked what he was watching, seeing the images of chaos flashing behind the heads of two anchors, a man and a woman. He raised the remote. "Let me flip around. Maybe I can find the BBC."

"No need," said Yasaman. As Mitch turned up the volume, she began to translate. "Buildings are burning. North Milan is an inferno. Those are his words." She indicated the male anchor. "It started after a riot at a futbol stadium, or perhaps after the consulate. It's unclear if the riot or the bombing happened first. There are reports of an explosion at the Duomo. The mayor is begging religious groups not to retaliate. The latest . . . atrocity, she calls it . . . is a gas attack. A truck parked in front of the Islamic Culture Institute vented an unknown gas. Casualty reports are coming in. There are at least eight dead."

Neil said, "It's like another—"

Mitch knew what he had been about to say, so he said it for him. "It's another Red Line attack."

"Is it just in Milan," said Wells, "or other cities?"

"I don't know," said Yasaman.

"Mitch, try another channel."

"Wait," said Yasaman. "The Carabinieri are looking for a woman who claims to be FBI. She was last seen in the company of two men and a woman believed to be from a hostile nation."

These last details were unnecessary. The photos on-screen were clear headshots of Wells and Mitch and Neil. A blurry shot of Yasaman looked like it had been cropped from an airport security camera.

"I'm getting a vibe," said Mitch. He had been feeling queasy for some time but had put it down to ordinary panic. "You feel it? An itch under the skin. The sense of being watched down a gun barrel."

"I feel it," said Yasaman. "Paranoia. Danger. A fear the walls are unsteady and the floor is about to collapse. I don't want to be here anymore."

Wells said, "Let's go with that emotion. This city's not safe."

Ten minutes later, Mitch was in the alley behind Hotel Manin, trying not to look at Yasaman and Wells through the glass door. Over Mitch's head, the bare limbs of a tree stretched skyward. They were lucky it was winter. Mitch didn't look too out of place in his heavy coat with a hood hiding his face. He rocked gently on his heels with hands in his pockets until an off-white Subaru sedan crept up the picturesque alley doubling as the hotel parking lot. A moment before it stopped, the glass door to the hotel opened and Wells stepped out, tugging Yasaman by the arm. Yasaman shielded her eyes as Wells walked her to where Mitch was opening the front passenger door. He smiled as Yasaman climbed in. Wells raised an eyebrow.

"You said to look casual," said Mitch.

Wells climbed into the back seat. As he made his way around the front of the car, Mitch spotted the bundle of wires drooping from the dash in front of Neil. The agent saw him looking and tipped up the reflective sunglasses he'd gotten from somewhere. He gave an exaggerated wink. Mitch took the show of good humor as a positive sign. In the room, he had been so caught up in grief, everybody had wondered if he was up to driving, let alone grand theft auto.

Mitch dropped into his seat, wishing not for the first time he'd managed to hold on to his missing cane. His place in the car put him across the seat from Wells, behind Neil, and at a diagonal from Yasaman. Wells had dictated the seating arrangements. With his eyes covered, Neil was the less distinct of the two agents. As memorable as Yasaman's appearance made her anywhere, at least in the fashion capital of the world she was one perfect face among many. Being the most likely of the foursome to be missed by Milanese who had watched the news, Neil and Yasaman rode up front, while Wells and Mitch kept their heads down in back.

"Seat belts on," said Neil. He backed the sedan into an empty parking space. Completing a three-point turn, he drove back the way he'd come in. Mitch held his breath. There was only the one way in and out of the alley. If the authorities were quick, they could cut off their escape route with a single car parked across the exit. No one lingered in the parking lot but a smattering of hotel guests, their faces pinched with fear as they rushed to waiting vehicles. It was clever of the Red Line masterminds to stoke the flames of the burning city with the NOT SAFE subliminal broadcasts. Ages ago, Mitch had watched a nature documentary about lions stalking a herd of antelope. Marching at right angles to their brothers, the young males of the pride had let out short, barking roars to maneuver their prey into the mouths of the other lions. The clueless civilians were being made to do a similar task, closing the trap around the fleeing Mitch, Yasaman, Wells, and Neil.

Neil turned right on Via della Moscova. Mitch was not the only one in the car who exhaled. At the corner of Via Daniele Manin, a handful of pedestrians stood having animated conversations with their phones. They looked flustered, genuinely perplexed. From their fine clothes, Mitch guessed they usually moved around town in cabs or Ubers. They were met with busy signals at a time when everybody wanted to be on the move. The news feeds they checked between phone calls would continue to make them antsy until they either got through to a driver or took to their heels.

As Neil took a left, Wells said, "Get down."

"Sorry?" said Yasaman.

"She meant me," said Mitch. He slumped in his seat, grimacing in the pain from his hip.

Yasaman gave him a sympathetic look. He considered telling her not to bother—he deserved all the pain he got. Before he could collect his thoughts, she said, "How long is the trip?"

In the distance, thin trickles of smoke wafted over the roofs of the buildings between them and the consulate.

"Forty-five minutes, usually," said Neil. "Today, who knows?"

"We have to avoid tolls," said Wells. "An hour five, minimum. Take a left, Neil."

Neil braked hard to make the turn.

"Right coming up. Watch the bus."

"It's like driving with my mom."

Yasaman turned in her seat to hold her hand out to Wells. "Perhaps I could help?"

"Be my guest," said Wells, placing the phone in Yasaman's palm. She returned to slumping low in her seat while Yasaman fitted the phone into the bracket the car's owner had suction-cupped to the windshield. They drove in silence until the GPS called for a left turn to circle around the west side of the Cimitero Monumentale. Neil executed a sharp right instead, nearly clipping the curb on Yasaman's side.

"What was that?" said Wells.

"Road block," said Neil. He gestured out the window. Mitch held his phone camera up to the level of his window, using the camera and screen as a periscope. A line of stationary traffic stretched toward distant, flashing lights.

Halfway through a right turn to take them away from the cemetery, Neil said, "We'll have to—" He was cut off by horns, a crunch, and a lurch that set fire to Mitch's hip.

20—Monumentale

A smell like charcoal and gunpowder sent Yasaman's mind back to the men's hostel, where she'd found Bilel caked in soot. It took a moment for pain to enter through her ankle, then dart to her nose. She felt like she'd tripped into a haymaker. Stars dotted her vision. Past the brilliant haze her vision had become, she saw Neil was no longer beside her. His door was hanging open. She heard his voice urging someone to take his hand. After she had blinked away most of her dazzled state, she saw he was talking to Mitch.

"Wait," said Mitch. "Yasaman. Yaz, you hear me?"

"I—yes."

"Can you make it? Do you need a hand?"

Yasaman turned to open her door and found herself meeting the glazed stare of a young man. His hair was permed into a million tiny braids and he was sitting in the driver's seat of a car whose front end had meshed with that of the stolen sedan. One of the eyes she was looking into was bloodshot. The airbag that dangled like a spent condom from his steering column had evidently struck his eye. Her own situation suddenly became clear.

"My ankle," she said. "It's wedged in a bend." She tried to drag it out of the accordion the floorboard had become, but couldn't.

"Move aside, I'll get her," said Wells. She was behind Mitch, having exited the car by means of her own door, which was jammed ruthlessly into the side of the other car. The angle of their collision had left just enough space for Wells to squeeze through. For Yasaman, such an operation was impossible.

Mitch said, "I got it. Yaz, drop your seat back."

"My seat?"

"There's a lever on the side. Pull."

She took his meaning and popped the release for her seat back. Pushing with her free foot against the dash, she turned the seat into a chaise lounge and was able to wriggle out of the accidental bear trap. Holding Mitch's hand, she pulled herself from the car.

Wells was in motion. "We have to split up."

"Can you walk?" said Neil.

Yasaman tested her ankle. It felt bruised but sound. "Yes."

"Go with Wells then."

Catching up to Wells, Yasaman hustled across a lane of stalled traffic. Together, the women passed through the cemetery gate. Yasaman shivered, not due to superstitious dread, but because she couldn't shake the feeling the drivers were watching them closely. Maybe they were thinking the accident had started a quarrel and the women were putting distance between themselves and the men. Maybe they were thinking, "They've had a brush with death. It's natural they should seek the company of angels." Or maybe they were thinking, "Aren't those the women the police are looking for?"

Yasaman hugged her overcoat tightly, wishing it had a hood like Mitch's. Fighting the urge to look back, she followed Wells to a junction, where they stood considering what path to take through the cemetery. An ornate statue of the crucified Christ surrounded by women in various comforting poses stood at the corner of a path on the left. Yasaman pointed it out. Wells nodded agreement. It was as good a place to start as any.

The only person strolling along the path was an old man in a wool cap. Yasaman felt better about their chances of making it through without being recognized. Many of the statues on display were breathtaking. She had to remind herself not to stop and stare but to keep hurrying after Wells. For several fruitless minutes, Wells ordered Yasaman down one path while she herself searched another for a break in the cemetery's high wall. Yasaman took a series of turns, deciding she had strayed too far. Turning back, she came across a monument that froze her in her slushy footprints.

Propped on stone pillows in a stone bed was the sculpted figure of a woman whose face and body were so lifelike, it made Yasaman's skin prickle. The subject was dead, without question. The sculptor had captured her spent mortality with excruciating fineness. Still, her beauty shone through. The hair splashing across the pillow was rampant as waves on a stormy sea. The woman's bedclothes had slipped down to expose small but perfect breasts. A crucifix had been placed on the fringe of the sheet that covered her abdomen, as if the priest who had spoken last rites had attempted to cover her nakedness, only to suffer a spasm, which had caused him to drop the emblem. Above the woman's head, praying angels flanked a heavenly choir. The choir, in turn, adorned a circular window dappled with stars.

Yasaman stared, unable to look away. She studied the features of the dead woman as she touched her own cheekbones, nose, and throat with her fingertips. There was no denying it. The model for the eternal dreamer might have been Yasaman herself, fifteen years ago. She had never attended a Christian funeral, so had never been so intimate with a dead face. Did death, like Botox, smooth worry lines? If so, there might be no span of time between her face and that of the sleeper.

"Yasaman?" Wells called from the next fork in the path.

"Coming."

"I found her," said Wells. She was speaking into the phone that had been clipped to the windshield bracket, which she'd remembered to retrieve. "We're on our way."

There was no break in the wall in the place Wells led Yasaman. A mausoleum had been built into a corner. After checking they were alone, the women scaled the structure and mounted the wall from there. A delivery truck was parked in the street on the other side. First Wells, then Yasaman, walked the balance beam atop the wall. They lowered themselves to the roof of the truck, climbed down to the cab and the hood, and at last to solid ground.

A woman was standing in an open doorway across the street. At the moment she caught Yasaman's eye, Wells grabbed Yasaman by the arm and jerked her away from the side of the truck. A burgundy-colored SUV hurtled past, missing Yasaman by inches. Tires squealed. The vehicle came to a halt. The driver had a shaved head and the build of a university wrestler. He hopped out, shouting an insult. Yasaman was too shaken to catch the beginning, but *troia straniere*—foreign slut—was near the end.

Wells was between her and the man before Yasaman knew what was happening. Thumping his chest with a fist, the man loomed over Wells. The next second, he folded in half as Wells buried her knee in his stomach. Pounding his back with her elbows, Wells tripped him to the ground. A second man emerged from the SUV. He was smaller and younger. His face was a mask of rage. He was brandishing a length of pipe, as if he meant to stove in someone's head. Yasaman shouted a warning an instant before he charged.

Bright spurts of crimson erupted from the man's chest. Each was accompanied by a thud and a gasp. After the third, the man fell face-first to the pavement. Neil said, "Got his partner?" from the other side of the SUV. Wells dropped onto the first man's back, pinning him to the pavement.

Neil jogged into view holding Max's silenced pistol. Seeing Wells had her situation under control, he ran over and felt the neck of the man he had shot. To Yasaman, he said, "Tell him to call an ambulance. If he doesn't do it right away, his friend will die." He motioned with the gun. "Walk while you translate."

Yasaman did as instructed, wondering with each step she took if she was implying a false hope. The young man wasn't breathing, so far as she could see. Three bullets had struck him. He looked in worse shape than either of the men Yasaman was sure she had killed. It took an eternity to pass the young man by, though the distance was less than twenty steps.

Beyond Neil and the SUV, Mitch was leaning against the rear quarter panel of a black Alfa Romeo. He limped toward her, extending a hand. She waved him back and went alone to the passenger seat. Mitch got in behind and sat watching her face in the mirror. She saw his eyes. Turning away, she hid her tears.

21—The Landslide

While Yasaman and Wells had been touring the cemetery, Mitch had done his best to keep up with Neil's course through the winding streets. He had been impressed by the young agent's ignorant American act, briefly marched out when a driver saw them fleeing the scene. The driver had demanded they explain themselves, first in Italian, then accented English. Neil had pretended not to catch a word as he steered Mitch through creeping traffic to the safety of the sidewalk.

They had put a block's distance between themselves and the cemetery before Neil started hunting for a new car. A black Alfa Romeo had caught his attention. It was old enough to be easily hot-wired and too old to stand out in traffic. The boxy sedan's best features were its rear windows, which were composed of two parts. Neil had asked Mitch to stand guard while he smashed the small, triangular window on the passenger side with a chunk of spark plug scavenged from the car wreck. A pedestrian had rounded the corner as the glass shattered, but she was too concerned with her own safety to stop a car theft.

From their parking space outside the cemetery walls, Mitch had watched a thick black cloud roll in from the west.

According to the news on his phone, gas tanks from stations blocks apart had been detonated in western Milan. The speculation was some sort of drone attack had caused the explosion. Officials refused to comment. Mitch was so absorbed by the streaming reports he hadn't realized Neil was out of the car until the man with the pipe was on the ground. With his heart in his throat, he had thrown his door open to help Yasaman.

When they were seated in the Romeo, he said, "Are you hurt?"

"No," she said and coughed, choked by her tears. "Is this what we are, Mitch?"

"The pot's boiling over. It'll cool down soon."

She turned to face him between the headrests of the seats. "I killed two men."

The confession was part of a larger story, but it didn't feel like the right time to ask for more. "I let my family die."

She blinked, stunned. "I am sure you—"

Neil opened the driver side door. Wells jumped in beside Mitch. The sedan launched like one of the rockets Ethan used to like watching online. Neil ground through the gears, braking hard when they reached a thronged intersection. Mitch waited for Wells to insist they find another way. Before she could, Neil shoved the sedan's nose into a nearby fender. The driver blared his horn, but Neil kept on pushing. The vehicles ahead and behind slowly gave way. In fits and starts, Neil got them through.

"Wish the old man had seen that," Neil said in a whisper.

The Alfa zipped through a few turns, putting on speed and losing it as Neil dealt ruthlessly with traffic. Minutes passed with only the thrum of the engine to fill the silence.

Yasaman said, "Do you think we can make Malpensa?"

"Yeah," said Neil.

Wells said, "No." At Mitch's prompting, she showed him her phone. The screen displayed a color-coded traffic map. The last time Mitch had seen so much red, it was Xs on a math test.

"Give me an alternative," said Neil.

"Maybe we should go to ground," said Mitch.

"Maybe we should."

Yasaman bristled. "If you mean you will hide me away somewhere, I won't go."

Wells said, "What makes you think you have a choice? We have orders to keep you safe."

"What is happening in Milan will not stop here," said Yasaman. "If hiding means staying out of the fight, that I cannot do. People are dying, Agent Wells. I must aid the fight if I can."

Mitch looked from one woman's face to the other. Both were iron. He brought the news stream he'd been watching and tilted his screen so Wells could see. "She's right."

In a live broadcast from Vatican City, a stiff-lipped reporter stood in front of St. Peter's Square. Over her shoulder, police in bomb gear hoisted a body through the smoking windshield of a delivery van. Heaps of discarded clothing lay strewn all around the van. Mitch watched for the exact moment when Wells realized they weren't just clothes but scraps of the dead and injured.

"Bombs, shootings, gas attacks. Not just Italy. All over Europe." Mitch cycled through phone alerts. Eight gunned down on French soccer field. Blown-out craters in Nuremberg, Rostock, and Essen. Commuters evacuating the London Underground as rumors spread about hundreds choked to death by poisoned air. "I'm changing my vote. We've got to get Dr. Karami to where she can make a difference." He paused, not wanting to push too hard, but decided he couldn't push hard enough. "It's what Trent would have wanted."

Again the engine noise was all the four of them could hear. At last, Neil said, "Your call, Noreen."

Wells stared out the side window. "I need a minute. Drive."

As Neil followed the frequently rerouted directions of the GPS, Wells studied her phone. Mitch watched discreetly as she scrolled through her contact list. She made a selection. A pause. Soft ringing from the other side.

"Mac?" said Wells. "I need an exit. Get on to the Pentagon. Urban retrieval. Right. ASAP." She hung up. "He'll call back. Head north, Parker. Back roads, side roads. Don't stop."

"Got it."

The Romeo navigated through the city like a mouse working a maze. At every traffic jam, Neil made a three-point turn, scenting the air before starting in a new direction. Whenever he smelled smoke, he went the other way. It was a slow, discouraging process. The only evidence they were making headway was the higher concentration of chaos behind, rather than in front.

Mitch got tired of listening to horns and watching buildings slide by. He went back to his streams. Almost immediately, he found an English-language news service from Belgium that triggered the same instinctual reactions he had felt in the hotel room. Yasaman's al-zban ghraza was on the move, pouring gas on sparks of fear. He showed the feed to Yasaman.

"So brazen," she said. "Who would have the resources to spread so wide a net?"

Wells said, "If we knew—wait. What's that buzzing?"

The car jolted sideways. A thundering sound like a landslide came from somewhere behind them. Mitch jerked his head around. Behind the Romeo was a truck-sized crater and a plume of smoke. Squinting, he managed to make out a gray crescent swooping at them out of the middle distance.

"Was that meant for us?" said Yasaman.

Neil said, "I don't mean to find out." He downshifted, roared around a slower car, and turned the wrong way down a one-way street. It turned out to be an access road for a nature park, empty of hikers in the time of crisis. The Romeo cut between trees and bumped over a curb. They passed into a neighborhood where an abandoned street market gave way to high-rise apartments.

"Any idea where it came from?" said Wells.

Surprised to know something she didn't, Mitch said, "Aircraft, small. I think it's a drone."

"Parker," said Wells, "turn right!"

Neil spun the wheel a split second before another explosion lifted the back tire off the ground. Mitch turned to see fire where previously a produce stand had stood.

"We're not gonna make it," said Mitch. It was the fear talking, fear flashed in pixels from his phone.

Neil said, "I've got an idea. We corner faster than it can. When I make this left, get ready to jump."

Several objections popped into Mitch's mind. He inadvertently looked over to Wells, his brown eyes wide with more fear than he normally would have let on. Wells slid across the seat, saying, "I'll help." As he worked the seat belt release, she reached past his chest to grasp the door handle.

"Leave your phones," said Neil. "Tracking."

Mitch tossed his phone on the seat. Yasaman's hands were empty. Wells glared for a second before letting her phone go.

"On my mark," said Neil. "Now!" He cut the wheel hard and slammed the brakes.

Wells pulled the handle while momentum was carrying them forward. With her pushing from behind, Mitch exited the car. He ignored the pain from his hip until it buckled. Wells ran into him, and they both crashed to the pavement

A buzz in the air was joined by a low-pitch hum. No sooner was Mitch aware of it than it was covered by the roar of the Alfa Romeo's engine. The car peeled away with Yasaman's arm still bracing her door. She hadn't made it. Neil hadn't tried. A sound like a thousand hissing cats screeched past them. Something sleek flashed overhead. The brake lights sparked. The car spun. A rocket dragged smoke through the air, barely missing the car and instead striking the corner of an apartment tower, exploding into a ball of fire, brick, and carnage. The thunderclap made Mitch's ears scream, though instinct had made him cover his head. Blind and deaf, he felt the ground shake. He looked up in time to see the high-rise tilt, dip, and crumble, spraying bricks from its middle.

Mitch had seen the show before. He went back to hiding his eyes, letting lives end without him for the second time.

22—Urban Retrieval

Some places in the badlands Bilel had shown Yasaman were as black at night as the one in which she found herself. She had glimpsed them only briefly, and from the safety of the Jeep. Locked in the closeness of smoke and rubble of the fallen building, she thought, resigned, "I am the statue. This is my tomb."

She heard nothing, but she suspected a sound akin to a teakettle whistle was coming from inside her head. A minute or a lifetime ago, Neil had shoved her hard enough to lift her from her seat and toss her out the half-open door. That was the last thing she remembered clearly. There must have been an explosion. She had been buried in the aftermath. Exactly how deep, she didn't know. Another question she wondered about was, what had happened to—

"Neil!" said a voice. The name was shouted at a register below the whistling in her ears. Still she barely made it out.

A lower voice said, "Yasaman? Yaz! Can you hear me?"

She felt pressure on one side of her body, and none on the other. That was how she knew up from down. She lifted her head and tried to say, "I'm here!" but choked. A few sips of coffee were all she had in her stomach. She vomited into her mouth, spat. With her throat burning, she said, "Here."

The voices repeated their calls. No one had heard her. Lacking the breath for a bellow, she began to grope in the black, trying to get closer to the sounds. Her hand found heat and pain. She recoiled, striking her head against a surface. Caressing her hand, she thought, shouldn't fire be bright?

The fear of being blind slashed away the last of her self-confidence. She gave up trying to grope her way out. Instead she dragged in what breath she could and shouted, "I'm . . . here!" They were two, tiny syllables, yet they exhausted her more than her last half marathon. She collapsed on what she supposed was ruined pavement. Dust and detritus had given it the texture of a dry grave.

Suddenly a light, blessed light, shone down from above. Mitch called her name and told her to come on; he wasn't sure how long he'd be able to keep it up. The black shifted, and she scrambled into brilliant sunlight. She clung to Mitch's arm, letting him drag her out. If not for her recent vomiting episode, she would have kissed him on the mouth.

For a moment it seemed Mitch was supporting the whole wall itself. On second look, she saw the light, which had seemed all-pervading a moment earlier, was merely a thin sliver between curtains of smoke and a plate of flat metal Mitch had lifted away. The abyss Yasaman had been trapped in was a corner of wall and a bit of roofing that had happened to fall together to shield her from other debris. The metal plate, whatever it had been before, had ended its life as the third wall of her triangular prison.

"Don't touch," said Mitch. "It's hot." His voice was gruff, his jaw tense. He had wrapped his jacket around his hand for use as an oven mitt, and she was keenly aware of the muscles under his thin shirt.

"Thank you," she said and moved away so he could release the plate. Blisters were bubbling on her fingertips, but she was so pleased to see them, she didn't mind. Her hearing had recovered, but her soundscape still included a phantom teakettle. She was lucky to be alive, so if she had to live out life with a whistling head, she would.

Mitch loped off in a shambling run, dragging her with him by the sleeve. They stopped at the edge of the burning nightmare that had been an apartment tower.

Mitch replaced his jacket, then slumped against a streetlamp. As he slid down, breathing shallow breaths, grimacing in pain, and holding his leg stiffly in front, he said, "At least this time I got somebody out."

Yasaman tried to assemble her thoughts. She had been in the car. Neil had shouted the signal. Her seat belt had jammed. By the time she got it loose, Neil had been accelerating down the street. He had spun the car and pushed her out. Then . . .

"Something hit the building," she said.

"A missile," said Mitch. "From the drone."

"It was sent for me."

"We don't know for sure."

"Did it fire on you once I was gone?"

Mitch didn't answer. He didn't have to. They both knew she was right.

"What happened to Neil?"

Grimacing, Mitch pointed. A single rubber tire, detached and flopped on its side, was all that was visible of the Alfa Romeo. The rest was under a heap of rubble. Agent Wells was on her knees, digging with her hands, cursing as spillage from higher up filled in whatever she excavated.

"I have to help," said Yasaman. Mitch tried to stand, thought better of it, and waved for her to go.

She dropped to her knees beside Wells, who paused only long enough to gasp. Her eyes were watery, the pupils dilated. As one, the women dug, shoving mounds of dust aside and piling brick fragments. The corner of a car door emerged.

"He . . . could have made it out," said Wells. Yasaman didn't answer. She helped Wells lift the door. It took all their strength to raise it a few centimeters.

"Can you hold it?" said Yasaman. "I'll look."

In the dim light, she thought she saw something, a shadow perhaps, wedged between the door and the pavement. She hunted through the pile of bricks, found a chunk a little larger than the gap Wells was fighting to maintain, and shoved it under the doorframe, working it deeper with pushes and kicks.

Mitch came limping. He sank to his knees, slid his fingers under the exposed portion of door, and heaved. With the brick as a pivot point, Mitch and Wells were able to tilt the door another few centimeters, enough for Yasaman to get an arm underneath.

She felt crushed stone and splintered plastic. Shattered glass was everywhere, but she felt around too gently for it to do her harm. She touched skin. It was warm, wet, and roughly the shape of a hand. The fingers were smashed flat, every bone in pieces. Feeling upward from the back of the palm, Yasaman found the wrist. She tugged to make sure it was still attached to a body. There was no pulse, no suggestion of a pulse. She withdrew her arm. It was bloody from finger to elbow.

Mitch said, "You're hurt."

"I'm not. Wells, I'm sorry."

Between them, they got Wells to stop screaming. She was up and walking seconds ahead of the approaching sirens. Huddling like children in a storm, the three survivors trudged along a street to shelter in an alley. Yasaman felt a chill. Paranoia had set in, and she expected Max to leap any moment from behind a dumpster. They were on their own, without phones, and with no idea who to trust.

In the end, it was Yasaman who thought of a plan. They walked high-rise to high-rise until someone answered an intercom button. An elderly man answered with, "*Lasciami in pace!*"

Yasaman told him she needed help. Would he turn away a weak woman? After a minute of sweet talk, he let her in, agreeing to let her friend use his phone. While Wells made the call, Yasaman sat with their host, holding a cup of weak coffee she couldn't drink. She wore Mitch's jacket to cover her bloody arm. To thank the old man, she embraced him, pressing her breasts to his chest so he felt the shape through his World Cup sweatshirt.

For the next three hours, they hid in the stairwell. Yasaman sat with Mitch. He told her his wife's name, and his son's. Jessica and Ethan had been his world. He didn't say so; she read between the lines. After he had said a little about his family, he let her cry against his chest, holding her lightly. He still sat stiffly, distant but not unmoved. Wells sat by herself on a landing one floor up.

When the sun had become but one orange glow among many on the Milanese horizon, they stood on the building's roof listening for the whir of helicopter blades. Right on time, the craft Wells had called—a Chinook helicopter—swooped low over the buildings to hover five meters overhead. The plan was to deliver them to Aviano Air Base, where the United States Air Force kept a fighter wing. From Aviano they would arrange a flight overseas.

A ladder descended from the helicopter. Wells mounted first. When Wells was secure in the Chinook, a man in a flight suit waved to Yasaman, giving the signal for the next climber to start. Yasaman turned to Mitch, but he wasn't looking. She called his name.

"Sorry," he said, limping closer to steady the bottom of the ladder. "I was trying to remember. Justin. That's it."

She could barely hear over the noise of the blades. "Who is Justin?"

"Agent Parker's—Neil's—kid. If we get through this, maybe I'll look him up."

"That would be kind," said Yasaman. She turned to the ladder, leaving the detective to stare into the distance, the reflection of distant fires in his eyes.

23—Out of Bounds

Baltimore-Washington International was abandoned, a ghost airport. Mitch wasn't a frequent flier. He didn't carry a card to track his miles. As a kid, he had flown a couple times to Oakland to see his grandparents. As a teenager, he'd gone to visit Grandma, Grandpa, and Mom. It had been on a flight back from California when he'd placed his hand on a stack of *Hemispheres* magazines as thick as a Bible and pledged never to fall out of love with someone like Dad had fallen out of love with Mom. After a week spent flinching every time Mom smoothed a crease in his shirt, it was the only way he could convince himself not to punch Dad in the face the next time they were together.

Every other time he had landed at BWI, he had tried to count the planes waiting to take off as his plane was coming down. He had always been on the ground before the count was finished. Today, there were only two planes sharing the runway as the charter carrying himself, Yasaman, and Wells touched down.

"Are you miles away, or years?" said Yasaman.

"Decades," said Mitch. "Airports make me remember my parents. Are yours alive?"

"Mother was, the last I called. Who can say, from day to day?"

They had hardly spoken on the flight and didn't speak again until they were inside the terminal. Wells, who hadn't uttered a word since Milan, mumbled to the geriatric minding the gate.

"Sorry, ma'am. I don't know. I'm just here to hold the door."

Before Wells could get too far ahead, Mitch asked the man, "Where is everybody?"

"You must have had one long flight," he said.

"We slept on the plane."

It was true, of course, though it glossed over all the times Mitch had woken in a cold sweat, gripping the armrests and panting for breath. Once, he had opened his eyes to find Yasaman sitting beside him, singing softly in a language he didn't know. She had stroked his cheek until he calmed down. His last memory before the pilot woke them all for touchdown was Yasaman swishing her hips as she returned to her seat.

"The stuff in Europe," said the gate attendant. "Euro Line or Red Line Two, whatever they call it. Did you hear about it?"

"Some," said Mitch.

"There were shootings, bombs, people killing each other in the streets. The news is saying it wasn't all terrorists. Regular people losing their minds, acting like animals. Flights are canceled. Most of our staff stayed home. We had to pull folks off gates to answer phones. I cycled from security to unlock the door. It was different with Red Line, you know? More of a slow burn. This is a forest fire."

Wells snapped her fingers. She was standing down the concourse, tapping her foot. Mitch thanked the old guy and hurried to catch up.

"'Regular people losing their minds,'" he quoted. "That's new."

"Is it?" said Yasaman, who had stood in earshot.

Now she'd mentioned it, Mitch wasn't sure. What he had done to Hanifa Mattoo, what he had wanted to do, wasn't that a little crazy? Yasaman stayed close by as they followed Wells, eventually offering her shoulder. Mitch held back for a moment. He had let her get too close already. But his hip was hurting. He wasn't sure he could make it out of the airport without help. He accepted Yasaman's offer, being careful not to lean on her too heavily.

Wells had built a considerable lead by the time they reached the fork in the Y-shaped concourse. As they approached the corner, she stopped, looking briefly in their direction. She let them catch up before walking on, and turned her head to the side to make it easier for them to hear her voice and harder for the cluster of FBI agents at the base of the Y to eavesdrop.

"Stay smart, stay quiet, and let me do the talking," she said.

When they were a stone's throw away, the wall of men and women in blue jackets broke into an inverted wedge. Agents flanked their trio, closing in as they passed to block a retreat.

"Noreen," said a tall angular man in a knee-length coat. Despite the lack of insignia, he couldn't have looked more like what he was if "G-man" had been tattooed on his forehead. He was neat, thin, and dour. There was something familiar about the shade of his skin and the shape of his face, but Mitch didn't figure out what until later. When he pointed at Wells, he jabbed with two fingers, as if one alone couldn't carry his meaning.

Wells took a wide stance and pinned back her shoulders. She looked like a prizefighter at the weigh-in. Her opponent held his hands up before dropping them down. He was flummoxed, not defeated.

"How did you do it, Noreen? Of all the assignments you could have landed, all the leads you could have run down, how did you get in the middle of this mess?"

"What mess would that be, sir?"

He chewed his lip before answering. "Euro Line is the name Fox is using. On CNN it's Red Line Two. I don't know what will catch on. What's more interesting is what's being said about you, a representative of the FBI and these United States. Care to guess?"

"No sir, I don't."

"'Unknown Fed at Heart of Euro Terror.' That's the *Daily Beast* headline. Do you need to hear *The Atlantic*'s?"

"I can imagine."

"Can you, Noreen? Imagine Trent Falwell is standing where you are now. What sort of a line do you think he'd feed me for busting jurisdiction?"

"We didn't mean—"

"Don't lie to me, Noreen!"

Wells fell silent. Mitch put in a question. "Those headlines. Is the press trying to shift blame on us for what's happening?"

Mr. G-man gave a chuckle through gritted teeth. "Oh, shift isn't the word. The pink sheets are outright accusing us of a cloaked invasion. They say Red Line was a false flag, a smokescreen to get US troops on NATO soil. Never mind the size of our usual presence. I would be inclined to say the press are idiots, except I don't know any better than they do why three of my agents crossed an ocean when they should have passed their intel to somebody else."

"There wasn't time, Dad," said Wells. "Dr. Karami was on the move. We had to act fast." She turned away, but whether in anger or in embarrassment over the family connection, Mitch couldn't say.

The man she had called "Dad" showed a badge to Mitch. "Deputy Director Steve Solomon. You're Falwell's pet contractor, correct?"

"Detective Mitch Wilson, Baltimore PD." He held out a hand. The deputy director arched an eyebrow and eyed the pied skin on Mitch's hand. He didn't shake.

"You're in over your head, Wilson. I was friends with Trent Falwell. I grieve for him and our other fallen agent. Russell, what was his name?"

"Parker, sir," said a man behind Solomon.

"I grieve for Agents Falwell and Parker, but Trent led you astray. You had no business leaving US soil."

"We never meant to leave it," said Wells.

"What you never meant to do," said Solomon, "was come home empty-handed. I know you, Noreen. You don't let anything go. Which is why I'm taking the professor off your hands."

"Sir! You can't—"

"Watch me, agent. Professor Yasaman Karami?"

Yasaman had been standing by quietly. With perfect coolness, she said, "Yes?"

"I'm going to assume you meant to apply for asylum. If the thought hadn't occurred, I implore you to give it a think. While the paperwork goes through, I'm placing you under arrest for improper entry into the United States. Agent Noreen Wells, I'm taking you into personal custody on a charge of aiding and abetting that entry."

A stream of profanities issued from Wells.

Mitch spoke up. "Deputy Director, the ordnance that dropped a building on our car and killed Agent Parker was fired from a drone aircraft. Such a weapon suggests a state actor."

"Does it?" said Solomon. "You might be surprised. It's also none of your business. Russell, make sure Detective Wilson's theory gets passed on to the Pentagon."

"Yes, sir."

"As for you, Wilson, consider your contract with the Federal Bureau of Investigation terminated. You were contracted for thirty-five hundred dollars a month, I believe. Russell, pay the man."

An amused Russell produced a stack of hundred-dollar bills strapped with a rubber band. He tossed the stack at Mitch's chest. It fell to the floor.

Solomon said, "I suggest you pick up those bills, Wilson. If you don't, I'll have to bust you for littering."

"He threw 'em," said Mitch; there was a distinct tone of desperation in his voice, as if he were hiding the fact he was doing his best to act tough.

Solomon's lips twitched. He shrugged. "I've decided you're not worth my time, Detective. Get out of my sight before I change my mind."

"Sure. I mean, yes, *sir*." Mitch had to fight to keep his voice steady. Inside, he was panicking. If he walked away now, he'd be cut off from Yasaman and the opportunity she offered to get his hands around the throats of the monsters behind Red Line. Without Yasaman, the only leads he had left were the names she had mentioned in her interview. He had instantly logged Bizhan Al-Kabir and Farbod Namdar in his memory, but he had no idea of the spelling. Even if he guessed right, would the names alone be enough? They would have to be.

There was also something else: a feeling Mitch had been fighting to ignore since he'd first been introduced to the Iranian—it was a niggling mix of longing and guilt that gnawed away at the back of his mind and teased him with thoughts of what *might* be, the likes of which he'd not experienced since his priapic adolescent years. There was just something about Yasaman, even though he was still not sure she was to be entirely trusted, that tugged at Mitch's primal urges despite the rawness of his emotions at having lost his beloved wife.

Maybe in another life, another circumstance . . .

But now, the asshole agent Solomon was taking Yasaman out of his life, and, along with her, all hopes of him discovering if his sentiments were to be reciprocated. And he was impotent to do anything about it.

Beaten, and with a reluctant nod at Yasaman and a grimace at Wells, Mitch stepped over the money he had no intention of lowering himself to pick up and limped away.

Halfway to the exit doors, he glanced back. Yasaman had tucked her chin and folded her arms as she listened to Solomon. Mitch could see she was defiant, unbreakable . . . and yet another loss for Mitch to deal with.

24—Foreshadowing

Only a few blocks away from the consulate where Mitch said his silent goodbyes to Dr. Yasaman Karami, Ada Fetterman stood stiffly behind the counter at the Rite Aid where she worked part time to top up the miserable police pension her husband, Ira, had left her when he passed.

Looking for all the world as if she had a steel pole stuck up the back of her drab blue company-issued shirt, Ada eyed the customer who'd just walked in with a glint of hope in her eyes; all she could do was pray he could tell something was terribly wrong. He looked to be in his thirties with brownish hair that covered most of his ears, and a large, beaked nose, which spoiled his otherwise handsome face. He had a swagger about him that had Ada believing her prayers had been answered—she'd recognize an off-duty cop anywhere.

"Excuse me," the man said. "Do you sell olives here? My wife had a craving, and here I am to get her some." He smiled.

"No," Ada replied shortly. "Sorry." She'd been told to get rid of anybody who came in, and not to say too much when she did so.

"How about pickles?" He moved a bit closer to her.

"We do. But we're out. Sorry. Truck didn't come in." Ada looked away.

"Well, maybe I'll just check out these Slim Jims. They're salty. Maybe she'd like some of these." He seemed to be deciding between flavors of the meat sticks.

Ada's lips quivered, and she knew the man could see the fear etched across her face. She looked pleadingly into his eyes, hoping he could read the silent message she was trying to convey. He glanced down and to the right. Ada's eyes followed his. He glanced down and left. Her eyes stayed put.

"Hey, you know what?" The man—Ada's hunch had been right—shrugged his square shoulders and gave her a forced smile. "She'd probably prefer some chips or something." Turning as if to walk down an aisle, he patted the counter casually.

Then, spinning around suddenly, he vaulted over the counter.

The off-duty cop came down almost on top of a young guy—teens or twenties, maybe—who squatted next to the cashier with a gun pointing at her belly. The cop thrust the kid's hands downward so if he pulled the trigger, it would only blow off the old lady's high heels. The kid pulled back and the cop held on to the gun. The kid let go and backpedaled in a crab walk. Then, as he dove around the side of the counter, he hollered, "Rod! Yo, Rod!"

"Shut up, asshole," said a voice.

There came the unmistakable *click-click* of a shotgun pump. "Get down!" the cop ordered the cashier but didn't wait for her to comply. Instead, he scrambled to his feet and tackled her an instant ahead of the boom.

The display behind the counter exploded, showering Ada and her savior with glass and shotgun pellets. The cop put his back to the counter, checked his three o'clock, and cocked the gun.

"I'm BPD!" he shouted across the store. "Drop the cannon, kiss the ground, or go out in body bags."

The shotgun's reply made it clear what its owner thought of that plan. The cop glanced up at the racks of candy and seemed amazed the gun's pellets hadn't gone right through them to pepper his back; thank God for Peanut M&Ms.

He scrambled to the end of the counter and made ready to take a shot. The kid who'd given up the gun huddled just around the corner of the counter, panting like he was having a panic attack. The cop reached around and dragged the young guy to him by a fistful of sweatshirt. He called out to his gun-toting buddy. "I've got your man here! He wants you to give up. Isn't that right, son?"

"Get off me," the kid snapped. Then, much to the cop's surprise, he skinned the sweatshirt and smacked his hand away. Impressive muscles bulged under the wifebeater the kid had underneath the shirt. Although he was short and baby-faced, he was strong, and panic hadn't made him completely helpless. In a desperate move, the kid grabbed for the gun. The cop put a bullet in the tile by his feet, which forced him to dance away. As he did so, he cursed and waved, presumably at the elusive Rod.

"Get down, idiot," growled Rod.

The cop threw himself sideways and fired three shots in front of the kid's face toward the source of the voice. There came a shrill scream from the kid and a gurgle from Rod, followed by a thud. The shotgun went off as it hit the floor, and packets of chips exploded, filling the store with scorched fragments that looked like bizarre confetti.

In the ringing silence that followed, the young would-be thug moaned, "No. No. I didn't mean it. I didn't mean it, Rod." He clutched his left hand with his right. There was blood on the wifebeater where he had pressed the hand to his chest. He turned to the cop. "I owed him money. He made me . . . I didn't mean for anybody to get killed."

He halted there, appearing to realize for the first time just how much trouble he was in. Glancing from the cop to the Rite Aid's door, he weighed his options, which were limited given he wasn't wearing a mask. Evidently, his partner in crime thought a hoodie was disguise enough for him.

The cop shoved the confiscated gun into his waistband and got to his feet. As he did so, the kid lunged forward and body blocked him hard into a magazine stand. The cop swayed but refused to fall. Grabbing the kid by his wifebeater, he shook him.

The kid's gave an incomprehensible, wordless growl, punctuated by attempts to rip himself from the cop's grasp. The two grappled, and without sleeves for the cop to hold onto, the kid was slippery. He tilted and wriggled, and though the cop was the bigger by far, the kid managed to wriggle free.

Finally, with a bellow of, "Let go!" the kid spun away. The cop lunged and missed as the kid darted off to snatch up the shotgun from the growing puddle of his dead partner's blood.

Instead of taking a shot at the cop, who was already reaching for the gun he'd secured in his waistband, the kid bolted for the door. With a reassuring nod at the terrified Ada, the cop started after him, only to drop and hug the tiles when the kid spun a one-eighty and pumped lead into the door from the street—he was fast as well as strong. "Just you wait until the next cycle!" he called as he ran away. "I'll be a survivor, and you—" Whatever he said was swallowed up by the wind.

When the cop looked up, the youngster had disappeared, although the sound of his sneakers slapped along the pavement for a few seconds more.

The cop checked on the dead man; he wouldn't be causing any more trouble. He went to the traumatized cashier next, helped her to her feet, and used the store phone to call the police.

Ada was glad of the company. Ira had often regaled her of stories of shootouts and bringing swift justice to the bad guys who terrorized the streets. They had made for fine, heroic tales back then, but now that she'd experienced it firsthand, she was pleased her husband was no longer around to bring back the memories.

25—Four Days to Go

It was getting late when Mitch finally reached Ben's townhouse. Before hailing a cab, he'd taken some time out to walk around in an attempt to clear his head of Yasaman, only to find he couldn't. He'd heard from the BPD guys that one of the cops had encountered a guy who mentioned "the next cycle," whatever that meant. He pondered that for a while—until his thoughts returned to Yasaman.

He climbed the townhouse steps with the help of his new cane—he'd stumbled across it in an antiques store and it was much nicer than his old one—and knocked on the door. The peephole blinked. A second later, Liza cracked the door and dragged him in by a sleeve. She set the bolt as soon as he was clear and turned the knob lock.

"God, what happened to you? You smell like smoke," Liza asked.

Mitch shrugged and offered her a half smile. "It's in my clothes." Mitch had gotten used to the smell himself. It had been with him across an ocean. "What's behind your back?"

Liza touched a finger to her lips. Down the hall, Therese laughed at the TV. Mitch nodded to show he understood.

Liza showed him a snub-nosed .38. "I have to look out for my own."

"Sure," said Mitch. "How are they?"

She waved him to the living room. Therese and Cella were sitting on opposite ends of the sofa. The older girl was tapping away at her phone while little Therese stared at the flat-screen TV. Mitch thought she was mesmerized, but she looked over at him when he poked in his head.

"Uncle Mitch!" said Therese.

"Hi, sweetie. You good?"

"I'm okay. Wanna watch my new show? It's on soon."

"Maybe later, sunshine."

Therese looked slightly disgruntled, but evidently decided it wasn't worth fussing about.

Cella looked over. She was wearing chestnut brown lipstick, a concession, according to Ben, after she had asked for midnight black.

"Did you fall in a trash fire?" said Cella.

"I didn't, but you've got your mom's nose."

"What's that mean?"

"Nothing bad."

Mitch retreated into the hall. Liza was dusting her hands beside the umbrella stand. The .38 was out of sight.

"You need a case. You should keep it locked up," said Mitch.

"We'll figure out something. Where have you been?"

He couldn't tell her the truth, but didn't want to lie. "I was part of an investigation. That's all I can say."

"Life of a cop's wife. Long days, lonely nights, no answers."

Mitch flashed back to Neil using his jacket to wrap Trent's bloodied head. Somehow, in his mind, it dovetailed with Yasaman blinking up at him as he lifted the plate she'd fallen under.

"Believe me. I'd tell you if I could."

Liza sighed. "Fine. Make it up to me. Ben's at work. I've got the girls distracted, watching everything but the news. Come play uncle."

Mitch didn't ask why she wasn't at work or the girls at school. Red Line Two, like the original, had changed everyone's lives. "All right," he said. "For a minute. Then I gotta work."

On their way to the living room, Therese said, "It's on, Mommy!" Liza sat between the girls, waving Mitch to a chair. He didn't sit but held up a hand, showing he was content to watch from the doorway.

The age gap between Cella and Therese was wider than Ben or Liza had intended. In private, they called Cella their "happy accident." Therese was their "miracle girl." A six-year battle with Liza's endometriosis separated the sisters. Mitch could relate, since he and Jessica had experienced their own infertility issues. At eight and fourteen, there were few interests the two sisters shared in common, but judging by Cella's rapt attention, the show just beginning was one of them.

"Heeeeello, friends and cousins, zips and buttons," said the man on the TV screen. Despite the gray in his hair and beard, he abounded with youthful energy, clapping his hands with ebullience at odds with the old-fashioned office he was in and the suit he had on. He looked slightly familiar, though Mitch couldn't place him right away. "Can you believe it? Only five days of waiting now. Then, such excitement. Such treasure! Such a day."

Listening to the rhythm of the speaker's accent, Mitch worked out where he'd heard him before. Countless internet and TV ads had shown him gushing about *Spex: Your Electric Friend* in the days leading up to the premiere.

Ethan had pointed at his beard, laughed at his accent. His name was unusual. It sounded something like one of the months. July? Jules? No. August. August was the month. The name was Aaugstad. He was rich, a tech mogul like Bill Gates or Steve Jobs, or the Facebook nerd. Lars Aaugstad, CEO of Stadion Technologies International, had stood in front of a crowd at last year's Consumer Electronics Show and debuted the J-Pad tablet Ethan had obsessed over until Christmas.

"Only five days," said Aaugstad. He showed five fingers to the camera, spreading his whole hand. "Five days more!"

The CGI character, star of the most analyzed children's movie in history floated on screen. Spex was shaped like an owl, with a fuzzy muzzle in place of a beak. Its cartoon body blended so perfectly with the real world, Mitch actually got goose bumps when it bumped into Aaugstad's shoulder.

"Eh?" said the billionaire. "Ah, it's you, Spex. Something to say?"

The swollen body jiggled, inverted, then righted itself. Spex was clearly agitated, but no sound came from him, apart from the whirring of wings.

"Calm down, Spex. Calm down. Think of the cousins watching. You don't want to get them upset. I know it is frustrating, not being able to use your voice. You remember, friends? Spex lost his voice. He won't be able to speak until the exciting premiere. Cheer up, Spex. Only five days to wait."

Far from being cheered, Spex's agitation peaked. Wings beating, he flew in spirals around the office, which Mitch thought looked a lot like Uncle Walt's from the old *Wonderful World of Disney* TV shows. Spex knocked books off bookshelves and toppled a telescope. Aaugstad gasped, making a show of ducking out of the way. Leaping into the air, he caught the frenzied creature by a booted foot.

"Spex, control yourself! What's the meaning of this ruckus?"

Spex sniffed. He held up a wing with the feathers spread. Since flying was impossible with only one wing, he was left dangling at the end of Aaugstad's arm like a cash bag carried by cartoon bank robbers.

"What are you saying? I told the cousins how long we will wait. Five days. I—"

Spex twisted free to fly in circles around Aaugstad's head. When Aaugstad made another grab, Spex caught his hand in its muzzle, clenching canine jaws around one of the planet's wealthiest thumbs.

"Ow, Spex! Ah. Of course! Forgive me. You're right. Do you know what Spex is saying, friends and cousins? I am wrong. I am bamboozled. Oops, I make a mistake!"

Therese laughed. Apparently, that last line was a catch phrase.

"There aren't five days," said Aaugstad, "but four." He pointed to his trapped hand. With the thumb covered, it showed the correct number. "Good job, Spex." Spex bobbed enthusiastically, still clamping Aaugstad's thumb. Aaugstad tapped the muzzle. "If you don't mind, please? Careful . . . thank you. I need it to text."

Spex looked ashamed.

"Oh, Spex, I'm not mad. In fact, I am grateful. Thanks to you, we know we're four days away. Only *four* more days!"

There was a cheer on the soundtrack. A blare of trumpets accompanied a rain of confetti from the ceiling. Aaugstad and Spex were soon covered in dots and streamers. Spex shook his imaginary body, spraying what looked like real confetti in every direction. Mitch was startled to hear himself chuckle. He had become so engrossed by the comedy that his end-of-the-world troubles had faded away.

Aaugstad dusted confetti from his hair. "Four days, friends and cousins. Think what adventures we can have in four days. It's hard on Spex not to speak, but the important thoughts, yes? They are known. Be sure to tune in for our final preview, in only four days. Something special may happen. Who knows? Now, are you ready for today's preview of *SteadyStream* by Stadion? What do you think, Spex? Shall we look in on what a certain stable of four-legged friends have been up to since they opened their new school?"

The camera zoomed out to show Spex flying in spirals. On the couch, Therese was trembling. Cella slid to the edge of her seat. Liza, who was sitting between the girls, sank back with a look on her face that didn't fit the situation at all. Her cheeks were flushed, her eyes narrow. She grinned at Aaugstad, beaming. If Mitch had seen her flash the same look at a man at a bar, he would have shoved her in a cab and warned Ben to keep her at home.

Something more than light entertainment was flashing on the TV screen. He broke the spell of his own interest in the show by studying those on the couch before him. Therese getting swept into a world of funny animals was one thing. Cella should have given Lars and Spex the teenage brushoff. Liza should have given the show a giggle, not given Aaugstad a "come on" stare. Mitch's own fascination with the segment was strange. He had all but forgotten the research he meant to do, the danger they were all in, the pain in his hip after the chaos overseas. Even his righteous quest for revenge had taken a back seat to watching some suit and his bird. If not for his awareness of al-zban ghraza, he might have settled in to watch the next cartoons without a thought for the chaos he'd seen unleashed on another continent and the statement the kid had made to the BPD cop about surviving the "cycle" about to hit, whatever it was supposed to mean.

On screen, an animated banner had been unfurled:
Four Days to SteadyStream!
~~Live Premiere~~
March 25th 8pm Eastern
Therese pushed up to bounce on the cushions, rattling the soapstone lamp on the table by the sofa. Liza didn't scold her, just sat content, drinking in the scene. Cella set down the phone she had been holding but never looked at, all through the previous segment, and fixed her eyes on a troupe of animated horses who were galloping across a desert as the banner faded away.

"How long's this been on?" asked Mitch.

"Huh?" said Liza. "Oh, days and days."

"It's a *preview*, Uncle Mitch," said Therese. "'Every day from ten to two, and four to eight p.m.!'"

"Got it," said Mitch. "Look, I need to make a call. Can I borrow a phone?"

Without looking his way, Cella said, "What happened to yours?"

"Lost it."

"God, that'd be the worst day of my life." She unlocked her phone and handed it over.

"I'll get this right back," said Mitch. Cella didn't glance his way. He returned to the hall. How long would the ladies sit together? To judge from their faces, "four to eight p.m." was the answer. Liza had forgotten the tension she had felt when she had jerked him inside, armed with a gun. The instinctual messages coming off the screen were strong; they'd told Mitch he was safe, he could relax, take a load off. He wished he could take them at their word.

On his first attempt to call Agent Wells, he got a busy signal. The second call was answered by an automated operator. Mitch didn't give the extension of his party, because he didn't know. The operator told him to hold for a human being. Then he got cut off and had to call back. He endured the machine telling him to call 911 in the event of an emergency for a second time. Finally, a woman answered.

She got out "Federal Bureau of Investigation" before Mitch interrupted. "Special Agent Noreen Wells. She was with the deputy director last time I saw her."

By using Solomon's title, he hoped to sell himself as an insider. Either the woman didn't buy the act or didn't care.

"Are you calling with information on a crime?"

"It's about Red Line. I need to speak to Wells."

"Transferring you now," said the woman.

Mitch was pleasantly surprised. He'd been ready to talk fast and make up lies.

"This is the FBI mass-terror hotline," said a man's voice.

"I don't want—I'm trying to get through to an agent."

"Are you calling with information on a crime?"

Mitch sighed. "Is this still the Baltimore field office?"

"This is a national hotline, sir. Are you calling—"

Mitch hung up. If his own phone hadn't been thousands of miles away and covered in rubble, he might have tried calling Trent's number, or Neil's. As efficient as he knew the FBI to be, they were probably monitoring the numbers. Having seen both only briefly, Mitch couldn't remember well enough to try dialing. He had never even seen the number to the surviving agent's phone.

Would Wells hate him less, having brushed death together, or more? There was no question; given the choice, she would have picked him to be the one lying dead in a marine lockup or under a crushed car, instead of either colleague.

Calling was no use. If he was going to get back in the game, he was going to have to do the work himself. He took a shower in the guest bathroom, dressed in smokeless clothes, and went out to sit at the kitchen table, where the Wi-Fi reception was better. He was still there two hours later when his host flipped on the overhead light and stepped back, clutching his chest.

"*Madre de Dios*! You trying to give me a heart attack?"

"Good to see you too."

Ben gaped at him. His suit was dusty, his eyes tired. "I tried to call. Where were you, man? I called like a hundred times."

Mitch motioned to a chair. "Phone's gone. The rest of the story will keep. I need your help."

"Whoa, whoa. You know what kinda day I had? 310s going down all over the city." Ben stewed for a moment. "Fine. You want my help, huh? Did my last 'help' get you anywhere?"

"Further than you know."

"You know what you put us through, man? After you disappeared, Liza was worried. Therese thought it was her fault. She cried, bro. You know I can't take that. If you want my help, I need to know what happened."

Mitch considered closing his laptop, making an excuse, and going back to the guest room. His access to NLETS, the national law enforcement network, had been suspended after he took leave. The truth was, Ben was the last of his resources. Without Ben's access, he would have nothing to work with but Google. No browsing databases of case files from law enforcement across the country and, via Interpol, around the world. No unpublished mug shots or surveillance photos, no inside tracks or insight on active case leads. He would be more on his own than ever, another widower pounding keys on a keyboard, waiting for the darkness to close in.

"Fine. I'll tell you. I'll tell you what you need to know."

Mitch spilled his guts. He told Ben how he had tracked Mrs. Mattoo down, how he had hurt her in a stupid act of negligence of his own making. He told him of the enemy he'd made in Noreen Wells, and of Neil Parker's kindness and Trent Falwell's enthusiasm and devotion. When he reached the part about meeting Yasaman Karami, he pulled up a photo. It hadn't been hard to find. A few minutes of searching had turned up a group photo of Yasaman attending a linguistics conference in France. Better yet, the man next to her in the photo was, according to the caption, none other than Farbod Namdar.

Pointing at the stout, bearded man, Mitch said, "We think this guy's a key witness to what happened on Red Line Day. That's what I need your help for, to look him up."

"Hold up. You're getting ahead of the story." Ben pointed at Yasaman with her intense, confident gaze. "Tell me about her."

"I told you. She was our contact in Milan. The one who wrote the paper about protolinguistic symbology."

"Yeah. What I mean is, how old is this pic? She still hot?"

"You might keep your voice down, bud, with the missus in the other room." Mitch nodded at the hallway through which cartoon noises filtered in from the living room.

The casual endearment had slipped naturally from his tongue. He realized the word carried a little less fraught emotion than the last time he'd heard it—used it. Had a tiny measure of healing taken place?

Ben smiled.

"What?"

"You called me 'bud.' Like the good old days."

Mitch drummed his fingers on the table. Yeah, but he didn't exactly want to have a conversation about it. "You wanna hear this, or not?"

In as few words as possible, he recounted the meeting. How the subliminal messages worked, he left vague, not wanting to alarm Ben more than necessary. He described Trent's shooting, the attack on Yasaman at the cemetery, and what had happened to Neil. The summary ended with Yasaman in Solomon's custody and Mitch stripped of his consultant status.

Ben looked puzzled. "This director guy. What's his deal?"

"What do you mean?"

"Go through it. He says he likes Falwell. He's pushing Falwell for results. Falwell takes you on, and bam! Instead of sitting on his thumbs, Falwell's chartering airplanes and interviewing persons of interest. If *your* team got targeted, *your* friend who got killed in the line of duty, would you cut loose a witness without taking a formal statement? Not to mention, you're the guy Falwell trusted enough to risk his career on your gut."

"Nah. I'm nothing. Wells made all the connections."

"She put the puzzle together, but you supplied the pieces. You've been leading from the front on Red Line for weeks. Every cop in the country has been chasing leads for this long, and none of 'em got even close to this far. Solomon needs you. If he doesn't see that, he's an idiot."

"He's not an idiot."

"Then he's what? If he's not an idiot, what's his angle?"

Mitch let the thought simmer. He spun the laptop to Ben. "Get me on NLETS." Ben typed and spun the laptop back. Mitch searched every spelling he'd thought of for Bizhan Al-Kabir, then tried Farbod Namdar. When nothing but old passport records showed up, he said, "Okay," and ran an information request on FBI Deputy Director Stephen Solomon. Public and police records came up at once. Mitch scanned what was available. He grunted.

Ben said, "What?"

"Nothing. Wells has a sister, Valerie. Younger. In college. Goes by her dad's name."

"And?"

"There's a link here, an active case . . . Valerie Solomon is a missing person. Last seen on campus over a month ago—on Red Line Day."

"A victim? Wow. Explains a lot about her sister."

"But not her dad. What about this? Say Valerie isn't dead. Somebody grabbed her before the attacks happened."

"An abduction? You thinking they're keeping her close to scare Solomon, make him behave. 'She dies if we hear sirens.' That sort of thing?"

"More than that. Tie his hands. Stop the investigation from making progress."

"He rides Falwell, but the moment something breaks loose, he jumps in to jam it up again. I like it, partner. It plays. Now prove it."

They tapped away, passing the laptop back and forth. At 7:57 p.m., as the girls down the hall were cheering some dramatic turn on the last of the night's previews, Ben smacked himself in the forehead.

"What took me so long? In my defense, I did check out the student body."

"You really need to keep your voice down. What's up?"

Ben pointed. "Look. Faculty photo, University of West Florida. Fall semester last year. See anyone you know?"

It took a few moments to scan the ranks of academics standing in rows on a set of library steps. The silver hair and beard is what caught Mitch's attention.

"Namdar. Yasaman said he disappeared too. It can't be a coincidence."

They searched a few minutes more. Liza came into the kitchen and started laying out leftovers.

Mitch found a captioned placeholder in the headshot section of the university's World Languages Program. "An alias. Fahim Laghmani," he read. "It has to be him."

"Definitely hiding then," said Ben. "What's our play?"

"*Our* play? Sorry, partner. We don't have one. I'm going to call the FBI until I get through. You are going to take care of your family."

Liza stopped pretending not to eavesdrop. "I like the sound of that."

"Don't you go cutting me out, Mitch."

"I'm not, bud. I promise. You broke the case. Now I need you to do what I wish I could, keep you and yours safe."

Ben sat back in his chair, frowning. He clearly wanted to hop in a plane—or a car, if none were flying—and head south with Mitch to confront Namdar/Laghmani. Pitted against his instincts were his lovely wife, standing in the kitchen with a fist on her hip, and his two lovely daughters feuding at mild volume down the hall.

"Don't make this hard for yourself, Benny. I'm telling you. Give some old guy the third degree with me or stay here with the girls? It's no choice at all."

Liza agreed. "That's right."

Ben sighed. "Yeah, okay. But this time, partner, wherever you go, you keep in touch. Deal?"

"It's a deal," said Mitch.

As Liza bent to kiss Ben on the cheek, Cella appeared in the doorway. "Hey, where's my phone?"

It was sitting on the table, at Mitch's right hand. As he handed it over, it rang. Cella exited, answering, "Hello?" A second later, she returned, holding the phone out to Mitch. "It's for you."

Mitch looked at the number, willing it to belong to Noreen Wells. "This is Mitch."

"Something's wrong with my dad," said Wells.

"Yeah? I bet I know what."

She was silent for a heartbeat. "I'll say an address. If you still want justice, be there at midnight."

"Sure," said Mitch. He concentrated all his energy on the next words to come out of the speaker.

26—Clear Heads

Forty blocks uptown, Darren McGann slumped to the floor of his house, barely aware of the Eagles tune rolling out from the stereo speakers. The bloodstained shotgun clanked when it hit the hardwood, despite being wrapped in a blanket. Hours ago, the blanket had belonged to a homeless man. Even in the ghost town Baltimore had become, it was possible to count on bums sprawling full length on the sidewalk in front of skyscrapers or out-of-the-way alleys. Darren had pointed the shotgun at the bum's head, told him to strip off his dingy work shirt, and made him hand over his blanket. With the shirt over his wifebeater and the blanket draping the shotgun, Darren had told the bum not to think of calling the cops, though doing any such thing was unlikely to have even entered the loser's mind.

"Rod," Darren said to the empty hallway. He sniffled, swiping sweat from his forehead and rocking back and forth, hugging himself with both arms. "I'm sorry, bro. I'm so sorry."

"Babe?" Ness called up through the basement door. "If that's you, babe, come down. Jer found us something to watch. It's so good, babe. You'll love it. Come down. Can you hear me, babe?"

Darren didn't answer. He had seen Ness twice since the arm incident, once to deliver the sling and aspirin, and once again to drop off food and a hot plate. She had barely said a word, then. Earlier in the morning, when Rod had shown up to tell Darren exactly how he could work off his debt, Darren had tried to give Ness the good news. She had yelled, "Whatever," up the stairs. Either her attitude had changed radically in the hours since, or she was trying to trick him again.

Darren was in no mood for games. He and Rod had spent half the day casing shops and bodegas, the other half knocking them over. Since the chaos overseas the day before, dozens of places had been left practically abandoned. And, with hardly anybody in the streets, including cops, so many business establishments sat like naked stacks of cash behind thin panes of glass, just waiting for someone to pull a smash-and-grab.

Rod had insisted it was easy money, right up until the point at which the off-duty cop had shot him dead.

"Babe, you okay?" said Ness. "Come down, or let me out in the hall. I was wrong, babe. I see it now. How about you let me make it up to you."

In happier times, "make it up" had meant sex. So long as it was only the two of them, he could have it any way he wanted. Ness wasn't stuck up, and she was very generous.

No way was the offer for real. She'd hated him when he left with Rod. Did she think he was so stupid he would believe she wanted him now? He glanced down at the bloody shotgun, felt a twist in the gut, and gagged.

Ness continued talking. "You sound sick. Come down and I'll take care of you. We'll bar the door, snuggle in, and watch *SteadyStream Preview* with Jer. Today's show is over, but we're lucky! There's a replay. It'll make you feel better, I promise. It's already, like, cleared up my head."

Ness had never been much of an actress; she'd always gotten by on her looks and hot body instead of drama. What was waiting for Darren behind the basement door? Nothing good. Darren swore to himself he wouldn't find out. Ness wouldn't trick him into letting her out or luring him into danger. The bait she thought she had held zero appeal. Darren had just seen his brother gunned to death—sex was the furthest thing from his mind.

Darren knew the cop in Rite Aid had been a Deep State agent sent to play head games with him; it was just too much of a coincidence they were in the same Rite Aid at the same time.

And now Rod was dead.

The raw memory of Rod's body jerking like a doll on strings as bullets ripped through it made him shudder. And the fact Darren had run away from the scene where his brother's lifeless body lay filled him with guilt. He had to face the fact he was weak, someone who ran when circumstances got difficult. He hated himself for that.

He covered his face with shaking hands as the reality of his situation sank in: the cop who'd shot Rod was likely to come after him next. Darren felt like crying, but the tears wouldn't come. Only a deep sense of fear. He felt like he was losing hold of reality. He rubbed his eyes, as if to clear away the vivid images that swirled about in his head; it was truly exhausting. Crawling to the farthest corner of the house, away from Ness's voice, which called out sporadically from the basement, Darren fell into a troubled sleep.

Upon waking, he didn't immediately open his eyes; he wanted to remain in the haze of clarity after slumber. He tried to assess his situation rationally. He knew people had been after him ever since the Trevor incident. That much was indisputable. But, the government was probably after other guys too. After all, the bomb in Baltimore hadn't managed to kill him, although it *had* killed others who seemed innocent. And he was correct in doing everything possible to protect his family. Yes, his methods might be questioned by some, but given the current state of the world and the fact his family was unsafe because of their relationship to him, his response was fully justified, righteous even.

Spending his time away from his wife and kid while they were locked in the basement was messed up. He needed to join them, to enjoy spending time with them while the world outside sorted itself out. The government would likely not have finding him as their number-one priority right now. He could afford letting his guard down a bit. He needed to find a way to join Ness and Jeremy without them striking out at him.

Ness wasn't the one thinking straight. Darren was. For the first time in days, he had lifted out of the fog where he had been groping around. The bombing, the place it had in the context of other attacks, and his running away from Rod—all these events had happened and were over. The way you lose to terror is by letting it change your life. The best thing to do, the right thing, is to go on living. Don't bow, don't bend, don't break. Don't care so much what your dad thinks.

As for the gun, he needed it gone. What good had it done Rod?

Darren stood up, though he was still tired, wrenched open the front door, and was about to hurl the shotgun out into the street when he remembered his fingerprints. They were all over the weapon, visible without dusting, thanks to the blood. He retreated into the house, shut, and barred the door. There would be time to set everything right later.

First, he had to be smart. He would wipe the shotgun down, find someplace to hide it, and clean up.

A faint knock on the basement door derailed Darren's train of thought. Was Ness still up to her tricks? He didn't blame her after all he had put her through. First, an apology. Then he would worry about the gun.

The reply was not his wife's. "Daddy?"

"Jer? I'm here." Darren moved to in front of the basement door. "Yo, get Mommy back, little man. I've got something to say to you both."

"Come here, Daddy. The show's ready. I've got something special set up."

"Uh, what's Mommy doing right now, Jer?"

Ness answered for herself. "I'm curled on the couch waiting for the show to start. I'm telling you, D. It's the best. You won't be disappointed."

"Daddy? It's not a trick. Come see."

Darren made his decision. After ordering Jer downstairs, he removed the padlock and set it aside. He was being invited to join them, so he would go out on a limb and take them at their word. He took a few tentative steps down the stairs, then reached the basement without incident.

Ness was curled up on the couch, as she had said. The scene on the rollable TV was set in some kind of office, with an old white guy in a suit talking to Spex, the cartoon character and VR sidekick of Jer's favorite game.

"What's up?" said Darren, still wondering if Ness planned to throw something at his head.

"Sit, babe. Watch. But don't get too comfortable. Jer wants to take it up a notch."

Darren sat. He watched. The Preview Re-View, as a box in the corner of the screen proclaimed it to be, was a clip show hosted by the suit guy. There were segments of kid shows interspersed with comedy bits featuring the two hosts. The more Darren watched, the more he liked it and, by the time the third host segment rolled around, he was sat at the edge of his seat, pointing at the screen and chanting, "Here we go! Here we go!"

Jer hit pause on the remote. "Time for a treat!" Standing up, he padded across the basement to retrieve a VR headset.

"Try this, Daddy."

Darren gave Ness a look. She winked. He was sure she wouldn't hurt him, unless he took too long and delayed the show. It was hilarious, moving, about the best however many hours of entertainment he had ever seen. He was so glad to be watching and couldn't wait for the live stream his family had told him about while the ads showed to hit the Re-View channel. Darren put on the headset.

"What's this about, Jer?"

But Jer didn't have to answer in words. The instant Darren asked, his son pressed something to make the dark headset light up. Darren blinked. As soon as he could focus, he saw he was in the very office he had been looking into in 2D a moment before. The human host, Cousin Lars, was there, as was Spex. Both were frozen, Spex hanging in air on motionless wings.

"Ready?" said Jer. He didn't wait, but pressed another button. Lars and Spex came to life. They moved around the room, fretting at each other in their comic way, Lars talking, the mute Spex zipping around, making mischief.

The weirdest thing about the setup was how real it felt. The edges of the desk and the shelves along the office walls were somewhat blurry, and the lines on the suit Lars wore were not as sharp as they had been on TV, but it didn't matter to Darren's brain. When Lars came walking straight at him, he stepped out of the way. When the ever so slightly blocky Spex came swooping his way, he ducked.

Darren heard Jer and Ness laughing. He heard them stop. No sound of movement replaced the laughter, only contented silence. Darren understood. He was content too, inside the VR simulation of the show. When the host segment ended, he stood transfixed, reading the schedule banner floating in front of him, in back, and to either side. He was delighted when the next cartoon started. It was a fresh reboot of a classic. Alien mice dropped down from overhead on motorcycles. The VR simulation of a domed alien city was something to see, but the visuals were not what Darren found so satisfying about the experience. Neither was the rock-and-roll soundtrack, although it really was something to hear.

There was an invisible quality to everything Darren laid eyes on in VR. It had also been on the TV screen, he realized. VR made it more noticeable. Every red rock he looked at and every flicking mouse tail made him feel calm. It remained true even when the villain of the cartoon clip showed up to menace the heroes. Not that the villain was scarier. He was a stupid, greedy land developer with a matted orange wig, and the voice actors for the alien mice didn't pretend to take him seriously. But even if the villain had been terrifying, Darren was confident he would have felt happy to be watching *SteadyStream*. It was so good, as Ness had said, such perfect family entertainment.

A digital Jer appeared beside Darren. "What do you think, Daddy?"

"Ah, it's great, Jer. How long did you say the streams are?"

"Four hours. There are four, now. There should be another tonight."

"We'll have to skip forward. We'll watch it, then back up. Or maybe we'll watch it a couple times. Do you think this review will last until then?"

"I don't know. If it doesn't, we can do last night's."

"Great, Jer. This is such a good show."

"So good. Daddy?"

"Huh?"

"Did you mean to leave the basement door open?"

Darren felt uncharacteristically charitable. He found himself making an unbelievable statement. "Oh. Yeah. If you want to go—"

"I don't. Mommy doesn't either."

"Is she still on the couch?"

"Uh-huh. Hit the button on the side of your controller. Where your thumb goes if you try to touch the baby finger."

Darren did. The cartoon faded, and the soundtrack went quiet. He saw a hazy live feed of the basement. Ness was curled on the couch, watching TV with a look of perfect contentment.

"This is where we need to be, Jer."

"You're right, Daddy."

Darren let off the button and was back in the cartoon, not really watching but turning slowly as the action progressed to glance at every object, savoring the feeling they gave.

"Jer? Do me a favor. Go bar the door."

"I'm not strong enough, Daddy."

"Aren't you? Okay, I'll do it."

He did, and came back. With the VR headset in place, he returned to feeling good about the closeness and seclusion of his family. It was nice to stay in and watch a show together. How different Ness seemed. How clever of Jer to find just what they needed to make safety and security complete.

***

If Darren's family had gotten a glimpse into how the rest of the world was responding in the time of crisis, they would have seen other families crowded around their TV sets. Families who usually lived in discord snuggled up in unity, beguiled and pacified by entertainment. Sibling squabbles across the country were fewer; arguments centered on who had the best seat for viewing the TV ceased once the program began. Competitive quarrels were tabled for another day.

At the nearby Target store in a Baltimore suburb, the aisles were strangely empty during the evening hours. A few baby boomers gathered items into their carts, happy because, for some reason, the crowds weren't bad. Teens employed as checkout clerks snuck glimpses of the *Spex SteadyStream* in between checking out customers when they thought their bosses weren't looking. They rushed customers through as quickly as possible to get back to the broadcast. Some even left the broadcast running on their cell phones while they served customers, catching snatches of the show as they could. Their conversations with patrons centered on the topic of *Spex*. Employees stocking the shelves juggled watching *Spex* on their phones while unboxing and arranging items on shelves. Phones took up residence on top of unpacked boxes so the employees could watch and unpack at the same time. Even managers took overly long breaks since someone had unwisely turned on the *SteadyStream* in the break room.

In office buildings, talk around the water cooler centered on *Spex*. Productivity hit a collective all-time low as large segments of workers, from secretaries to lawyers to CEOs, lost track of time after tuning in to watch "just a couple minutes" of the previous night's broadcast.

In Detroit, management at the Ford factory responded to the out-of-control situation of inattentive employees by mandating a "no cell phones while on the factory floor" rule.

Restaurants nationwide, at the request of their patrons, switched their TVs from NBA and NHL games to the *SteadyStream* broadcast. Customers stayed longer than usual, losing track of time as they watched the broadcast while eating.

Alyssa, a lone mother out taking a walk in Dallas, pushing her toddler and newborn baby in a double stroller, felt smugly satisfied she didn't allow her young children any screen time. She was aware other mothers had fallen victim to watching too much TV with their kids. Even her friend Ashley, who was usually dying to get out of the house, had declined the invitation to walk today. Alyssa had heard the TV playing loudly in the background at Ashley's house when she called. Although she missed saying hello to other mothers she usually passed on the sidewalk, she felt relieved she and her kids were avoiding the weird fixation the *Spex* show was creating. She vowed never to let her kids see the *Spex* show.

At Chase Center in San Francisco, the Golden State Warriors prepared to play a game to a stadium only half filled with spectators. The players argued among themselves why attendance was so low. Those who had seen the *Spex* broadcast named it as the reason, while those who hadn't proclaimed that to be a stupid thought. Some figured flu season must be worse than normal.

CNN reported on recent crime sprees running rampant throughout the country, even in sheltered enclaves usually safe from such incivility. Darren and Rod were far from the only thugs cashing in on the advent of stores empty of customers but full on cash.

But for now, Darren's family was the picture of harmony as they shared a bowl of popcorn around their shared fixation on the television screen.

27—Three Days to Go

A thump at her door startled Yasaman from a doze. She was lying on top of the bed sheets, fully dressed and ready for action. There had been no discussion, no plan. Intuition had told her she wouldn't be staying the night in the holding cell styled to look like a windowless hotel room, where she had been locked in by a pair of FBI agents. Grabbing a plastic toothbrush case from the end of the bed, she stood near the door with her back to the wall. The case was the only object she'd found in the room that was not bolted down. As a weapon, it wasn't much, but it was her only choice.

The lock clicked. The door creaked. Yasaman held the case like a knife. She was prepared to smash in the temple of the first person through the door. Then she would figure out her next move.

"Yasaman?" said Noreen.

Yasaman exhaled. She'd been hoping Noreen would appear but fearing Max would show up in her place. Earlier, she had watched Noreen storm out of a debriefing with her father, dropping the man sent after her with a judo throw. At that point, Yasaman had known her time in FBI custody would be brief. She chided herself for imagining it could have ended any other way.

"I'm here." She stepped into the doorway. A woman wearing a sidearm was laid out in the hall. Her mouth was gagged and her wrists and ankles bound with plastic cable ties. Yasaman helped Noreen carry the woman to the bed.

"How long do we have?" asked Yasaman.

"Not long."

Together, they jogged to the end of the hall. Noreen unlocked a door with her key card.

"I would have come earlier." Noreen gestured Yasaman ahead of her into the unheated stairwell. "Had to get enough footage to loop the security cams."

Yasaman began to descend, quickly but carefully, not wanting an accident. She thought she knew the answer to her next question, but wanted to make sure Noreen was on the same page.

"Why did you come?"

"Something's wrong with my dad. I told him about Barroso, the subliminal messaging, the bruiser Neil shot at the cemetery. It was like I was talking to a wall. Nothing I said got through."

"He cares about you."

"Who does?"

"Your father. In his body language, at the airport and the office, I could tell. He wants to keep you safe, Noreen, which is why he will not discuss—"

"No. Sorry. That's *not* it. I mean, he *cares*. But it doesn't get in the way of the job. There's something else. Mitch has a theory."

"You have spoken with Mitch?"

Noreen didn't answer at once. Yasaman fancied she actually *heard* the other woman's eyes rolling.

"You'll see him soon," said Noreen.

Yasaman left it there. When they reached the bottom of the stairs, Noreen produced a phone. After studying a video feed showing the other side of the door leading out, Noreen waved her through.

Outside, Yasaman got her first look at the building she had been forced into while wearing a hood. Four stories tall and sided with corrugated metal, it would have been impossible for anyone who did not know better to realize it was anything other than a nondescript industrial building on the outskirts of Baltimore. Noreen took her by the hand to conduct her across the parking lot.

"This place, is it all cells, like the one where I was kept?" There had been many doors along the hallway. Too many, in Yasaman's opinion, for a government agency not in the business of maintaining people who had vanished.

Noreen answered at once. "It's a warehouse. Nothing inside but fork trucks and cardboard boxes. You would know that if you'd ever been inside, but you never have been. Understand? You were never inside, Yaz. In fact you were never here, and you and I never had this conversation. You know where I keep my badge? Jacket pocket. Close to my heart. Are you clear on everything I just said?"

"Yes, perfectly." What wonderful loyalty! Yasaman's only hope was it would extend to her, if push came to shove.

On a ridge road a quarter mile distant, Noreen gunned the engine of her late-model sedan. The car looked a great deal like a hundred others Yasaman had seen at the FBI field office. The vehicle that had carried her from the office to the warehouse had been nearly identical, only with darker windows and a driver who didn't act like he was racing Formula One.

"I saw the end of your conference with the director, Solomon," said Yasaman. "What happened next?"

"Dad sent a senior agent to lock me up."

"I find it hard to believe there is an agent so experienced as to get the better of you." Yasaman spoke loudly to be heard over the sound of the racing engine.

"By senior, I mean old. A lady I couldn't slap a wrist lock on without breaking the wrist. She led me to an office, locked me up. It wasn't so bad. There was a window to look out, a computer I could use. I found a pack of crackers in a desk drawer. I would have stayed if they hadn't cut off my internet access. It's the first freedom to go."

"Oh, I know. How did you escape?"

Steering into a curve, Noreen lifted two wheels off the road. Yasaman gripped the door to steady herself and was happy to see a straightaway ahead.

"I banged on the door until somebody came. Dad and I had a knock-down, drag-out. He let it slip he booked me in with a counselor."

"Is this a bad thing?"

"Not for an alcoholic or somebody with PTSD. For an agent with intel on the next major attack? You bet it is."

They pulled onto a highway. Traffic was sparse, either due to the lateness of the hour or the fear the terror in Europe had engendered.

"Before I got cut off," said Noreen, "I got a lead on your professor."

"Farbod?"

"Facial recognition software says he's somewhere in the US."

"You believe he is alive?"

"I do."

"I—I was sure he had been killed."

Noreen gave her a moment, then said, "How well do you know the guy?"

"We are friends, colleagues. I know his wife. Are we going to rescue Farbod?"

"We're going to see him. I lost access before I could track him down, but Detective Wilson, like I said, he's got a theory."

"I thought the theory was about your father."

"Yeah. Turns out, it's about them both. The drive will be a long haul. Can you drive stick?"

It took a moment for Yasaman to decode the Americanism. "Manual transmission? Yes."

"Great. We can use you. Or I can, if Wilson doesn't show."

At a parking garage in sight of the highway, the women swapped cars. As Noreen was starting the zippy little soft-top convertible, she said, "Trent and I had plans for a rainy day. This is one. We'll change again at another place I know. Route I'm running and the car swap should fool the satellites."

Yasaman asked, "Whose car is this?"

"Mine. It was an old girlfriend's from college. I might have said something about wrapping it around a telephone pole—which might not have been the exact truth."

"Noreen! You mean we are reaping the profit of your criminal past?"

"Hey, if crime didn't pay, lawyers would go broke."

On their circuitous path through the city, Noreen proved to have an uncanny knack for spotting traffic cameras and diverting onto side streets. As they made one detour after another, Yasaman occupied herself by braiding her hair, the idea having come to her thanks to a set of elastic bands she found in the glove box. When she had finished, she coiled the braid and tucked it under her cap. The light was too dim for her to check her disguise, so she asked Noreen, who declared it, "Cute."

Near midnight, they pulled into a small garage on the city's north side. Noreen removed a blue tarp, revealing a battered, brick-red pickup.

"Grandpa Falwell's fishing truck."

"It would have to belong to an old man," said Yasaman. A memory of Bilel's jeep made her smile. "Will it start?"

Twenty minutes later, Noreen emerged from under the hood. "Try it now."

Yasaman pressed the clutch and turned the key in the ignition. The engine rumbled but didn't turn over. She gave the truck some gas and tried again. It roared to life.

"Good job," said Noreen, climbing into the passenger seat. "You can drive this heap?"

"It is familiar. Half the vehicles in my country are the same age."

They followed Noreen's directions to a filling station just off a highway. There were no lights on at the station, no customers at the pumps. A dusty gray sports utility vehicle had been backed into a parking space on the side of the building.

Noreen grunted but otherwise made no comment as the SUV's door opened and the tip of a metal cane emerged to prod the pavement.

***

Even at rush hour, the highways of America were sparsely populated. They were more like trickling streams than the perpetual logjams Yasaman had seen portrayed on TV news. The pickup had no built-in GPS, and Noreen and Mitch had disabled the tracking capabilities of their phones, so they navigated with the help of paper maps. It was like being back in time.

In the first several minutes of Yasaman's initial driving shift, Mitch detailed finding out about Valerie Solomon going missing the day of the Red Line attacks. How his detective partner, a clever man, had discovered Farbod working under a pseudonym at her Florida university. Farbod lived, according to police documents, in a picturesque town across the state border. For nearly five months, he had lived in the United States and been employed as a researcher in linguistics. What that suggested about his complicity with the Red Line attacks, she shuddered to think.

Per National Public Radio, the fires had gone out in Europe, but it would take weeks before anyone knew the full extent of the damage. The world was reeling again, and accusations were being hurled. International goodwill was promised after America's crisis, but it had dissolved the moment it became clear terror was contagious. Political tensions were high. Fear had the world by the throat. Countries large and small were following Iran's example of shutting foreigners out and their own citizens in. Their belief, unproven but primal, was that hiding at home would help.

After navigating the empty streets of Chattanooga and before crossing from Georgia into Alabama on Interstate 59, a patrol car trailed the pickup for half a mile. Tired after multiple driving shifts, Yasaman felt her heart thump. She considered pulling off, speeding up, or waking her companions, who were both asleep after their own three-hour turns behind the wheel. At the last Georgia exit, the patrol car exited, leaving Yasaman to calm herself with shallow breaths.

At noon, the group stopped for lunch outside Birmingham, Alabama. Noreen told Yasaman to stretch her legs—a cruel jab at Mitch —while she bought takeaway from a roadside diner. It was one of very few places they had come across that was open. Other than themselves, no one appeared to be out in search of food.

As they both leaned against the pickup, Yasaman asked Mitch, "What will you do when we find Farbod?"

She had avoided asking the question all day, though it had plagued her constantly.

"Why ask me? If we're right about Solomon, Wells is the one with family in danger."

Yasaman nodded. "I see. He believes his daughter is safe as long as he doesn't investigate too hard. On one level I can even understand. He only wants his daughter back."

"Yeah, I can too. But I can foresee only more death to come in the future if we don't stop whoever is responsible. And whoever is responsible killed my wife and son. If it's this Farbod guy—"

"Noreen has much to lose. Mitch, forgive me. You talk, sometimes, as a man who has nothing."

He didn't storm off, as she had been worried he might. Instead he tapped the tip of his cane against the pavement. "You know the last thing I said to my wife? 'See you in a sec.' I've been waiting for that second to be over ever since. Losing Jessica and Ethan wasn't the worst thing to happen to me. Waking up in the hospital? Much worse. When I meet your friend, I'm going to find out what he knows. If he's a ladder on the rung to the top of Red Line, I'll use him to climb up. If he's the top rung or the top I can reach—" He looked her in the eyes. "Don't get between us, Yaz. For your sake, don't even get close."

28—Life or Death

Fairhope, Alabama, looked like a nice place for a vacation. The restaurants were probably expensive—it was just as well they were all closed—but the clean streets, the spotless downtown, and the well-kept harbor spoke of a lively tourist trade in better times. The sun was setting when Mitch piloted the pickup into town. A handful of hardcore sunset junkies sat looking out over the water as he rolled past. On so mild a twilight, there ought to have been at least a hundred of them watching sheets of orange clouds bleed to pink as a golden glow sank past the horizon. Spotting a family with kids the same age as Ethan, Mitch downshifted and sped away.

The motel Wells had booked them in was a short drive away. The place was quaint, with white picket railings enclosing a second-floor walk. There was a hospital across the street. Mitch limped up the stairs to the second floor carrying boxes of Chinese food in plastic bags. At the window to the room shared by Yasaman and Wells, he paused. The curtain had been pulled back to admit a sliver of light. The two women were sitting on the floor, face-to-face, foreheads pressed together. Yasaman had an arm around Wells. She was mumbling something. Reciting a poem, maybe, or a prayer. Mitch backed away and waited until he heard movement inside. Only then did he step forward and knock.

While he'd been gone, Wells had changed clothes. She was dressed all in black, head to toe. Yasaman had changed too. She wore the jeans she had bought at Goodwill a couple towns back. Her hair was still damp from her shower, and she had yet to slip on the charcoal turtleneck folded up on the edge of the sink. Between her black bra and flat stomach, she reminded him of a billboard model for Agent Provocateur.

As Wells let him in, he said, "I think I got everything you asked for."

"Hi, Mitch," Yasaman greeted him with a coy smile; she made no effort to cover herself, which he found alluring given her culture.

"I hope you're hungry." Mitch watched as Yasaman made her way slowly over to the sink and slipped on the turtleneck, the unmistakable stiffness of her nipples protruding through her bra's flimsy material. He figured the decent thing would have been to avert his eyes, but there was something sensually hypnotic about the woman's smooth, olive skin and perfectly toned flesh.

Mitch also got the impression she *wanted* him to see her like that.

Breaking the moment, Wells took the bags from Mitch and began to unpack. "No fortune cookies?"

"Gotta make your own luck." Mitch smiled over at Yasaman; although the turtleneck covered her now, he thought she looked as stunning as ever, and he hated himself for the attraction that stirred within him.

Between bites of lo mein, they finalized plans.

***

It seemed darker in Fahim Laghmani's neighborhood than out by the harbor, even though there were more streetlights than on the oceanfront. The houses had been built neat; overgrown lawns made them sloppy. There were few signs anybody lived in the houses, aside from the firefly flickers of screens—TV, phone, whatever—in the windows.

Mitch whistled. "You'd think nobody goes outside."

Lost in her own thoughts, Yasaman kept quiet. Wells said, "It'll make our job easier."

The job she had in mind would be tough no matter what. If Namdar was a prisoner, he would be guarded. If he was one of the masterminds behind Red Line, he might have a small army in his two-story hideaway. Wells had training in infiltration and extraction, but with paid killers on the watch, there was no question of her going in alone. She would get close, using her skills to find blind spots in the security layout. Mitch would provide a distraction at the crucial moment. In addition to Yasaman's turtleneck, they had bought watches at Goodwill and synchronized the time. At 7:38 p.m. he would pound on the door, demanding to see Laghmani. Wells would take his racket as a cue to move in.

Wells parked the truck two blocks away and checked the supplies in her duffel bag. Satisfied, she climbed out of the truck's cab, giving Yasaman a nod. Her farewell to Mitch was a glowing watch face. Mitch made his watch glow to show it was keeping the same time.

When Wells was out of sight, Yasaman got behind the wheel of the pickup. Mitch shook his head. Both he and Wells had tried to get her to stay in the motel room. Not only had she insisted on coming, she had demanded to be part of the team. Getaway driver seemed the safest role to play.

"Would that be a smile?" said Yasaman.

Mitch had to touch his lips with his fingers to confirm it had happened. He had lost count of his post-coma smiles.

She added, "It is in bad taste."

He knew what she meant. While they were waiting for lunch, he had issued a warning that probably sounded like a threat to not get between him and Laghmani, as if he were still seeking revenge for his family's deaths. They hadn't been alone since then, and he hadn't wanted to mention it around Wells.

"Yaz . . . what I said before . . . I'm sorry."

"Are you? It is safe, then, to get between you and Farbod. I have no need to worry you will confuse justice and revenge."

The echo of his past conversation with Trent Falwell about justice versus revenge stung so deep, it ached. He reached for her shoulder. She stopped him with a glance.

"I know Farbod Namdar, Mitch. Whatever they have made him do, he is a good man."

"Sure. He was your teacher, your colleague."

"We were lovers. Does that shock you? I was young, a student. I wanted Farbod, so I took him. You imagine it was easy? No. It was not. Farbod loved his wife. I triumphed by hating her, deep in my heart. I made myself evil, Mitch. What else could I be? The contest was unequal. I was brilliant, beautiful, not at all vain. She was plain, middle-aged. She persisted in knowing nothing of me even when I sent her husband home, time after time, with lipstick on his collar. I couldn't ignore the injustice of my conquest. For so long, as I indulged in the spoils, evil was all I *could* be. Let other women appeal to love, to destiny. I seduced out of selfishness, a lust for my own glory. I did it with a hard heart."

The hand touching Mitch's was like ice. It warmed, slightly, as she drew his hand to the left side of her chest. He felt her pulse.

"Farbod couldn't stand to have his wife hated. He brought us together, Fatemeh and I, let me see her, let me know her. He called himself a weak man when he ended our affair. He apologized to me, begged pardon of the woman who had won him to wickedness, made him betray the man he was. Only then did I love him. Fatemeh too. They both became dear friends, as kind to me as ever I was cruel. That is how I know he is a good man, still. He could not have changed so much. If you meet him, remember, he is a good man. You must promise me, Mitch. Will you promise?"

"What exactly am I promising?"

"If the choice of his life or death is in your hands, you will choose life."

The possibility Farbod Namdar was a key figure in the bombing that had killed Jessica and Ethan tipped the scale in Mitch's head to one direction. Yasaman's earnest expression, barely visible in the light from the street, tipped it the other.

"If I could promise, I would. If there's any way—"

She released his hand. He caught a glint of tears as she motioned him to silence.

"If you can't promise, at least do not lie."

He nodded. She didn't see. According to his watch, there were four minutes to wait before he started his walk to the house. He decided to pass them in the cold. After ten minutes of waiting and walking, he turned off the sidewalk, leaning more heavily on his cane than he actually needed, and limped up the path to the only house in the neighborhood, if not the whole town, with manicured grass.

A quick check of the watch showed his timing was perfect. He knocked loudly, pounding the door with the side of his fist. Immediately, it opened. The man who greeted him was not Farbod Namdar. He was younger than Namdar. Younger than Mitch, for that matter, though not a kid. A twenty-something of middle height, with a bit of muscle and smiling eyes under dark eyebrows. Though his features made it clear he was from Yasaman's neck of the woods, he was dressed like a wannabe cowboy: jeans tucked into boots and a turquoise shirt matching the stone in his belt buckle. He had a nice layered haircut, black with the tips dyed red.

Looking pleased to see the visitor, he said, "May I help you?"

Mitch exaggerated the confusion he felt. "Uh, does Mister Laghmani live here?"

"Professor Laghmani does, yes. I'm his assistant."

"I need to see Laghmani. My niece is a student at West Florida University. She's gone missing. I hope he can help."

The pleased expression didn't change. "You're talking about Valerie Solomon. I know her. Great girl. Come inside, please. I'm not sure if the professor can help, but I'll be happy to do what I can for Val."

There was something off about the nightclub cowboy. He was clearly acting, and not doing much to disguise the fact. When he stepped back from the door, Mitch didn't enter at once.

"Just a sec. You say you're a friend of Val's? I don't get to see her much, but we talk. What's your name? Maybe she mentioned you."

"Oh, I doubt it. Friends isn't the right word. We share some circles. It's not a big school. Sorry, didn't you want to come in? The professor is home, I should have said. He's just upstairs. Come in and sit down. I'll fetch him. We can talk."

Having come so far, Mitch felt he had no other options. Wells would be creeping closer. The longer Mitch kept the cowboy talking, the better. He stepped across the threshold. The cowboy gestured at a round-topped doorway leading into a living room with leather furniture and plushy, white carpet. Mitch took a step and was stopped by a man in slacks and a sports jacket who appeared from behind the wall.

Mitch turned. "What gives?"

The cowboy was shutting the door. Concealed behind it stood another man. Neither bothered to greet their new guest.

The cowboy stepped aside. The bruiser from behind the door waded in and did what he knew best. Mitch's instincts and training kicked in as he dodged a punch, caught the bruiser's arm, and drove a knee to the guy's face. Hopping on his good leg, he rounded on the other man, only to find himself facing a pistol. There was a good yard or more between him and the shooter.

The cowboy had taken a seat on the stairs leading up from the foyer. "He's a good shot. I'd give up, Detective, if I were you."

"You're not," said Mitch. He lunged, aiming low. As the shooter's knee bent backward, Mitch heard a shout and a shot. Lead fire slashed through his calf.

The shooter fell on top of Mitch. His partner dragged him away and kicked at Mitch's flesh wound. Mitch rolled over. The bruiser dropped on him, swinging punches and driving knees. With a grunt, Mitch thrust him away. He spun to a knee. The pistol, wielded by the cowboy, whipped across Mitch's face.

For a second, he didn't know if he had been struck or shot. The former, he figured, since he was still alive. The bash from the gun barrel was followed by a boot stomp, also to the face, delivered by the bruiser. Then the bruiser and the shooter were both on him, their blows thick and fast. Mitch got his licks in, but he didn't rise from the tile of the foyer until the ceiling went fuzzy and his mouth filled with blood.

29—Not Forgotten

At precisely 7:38, from the open window of the getaway car, Yasaman heard the knock. She was shocked, a minute later, to hear a gunshot. The sound was muffled. It didn't echo like a shot in the open, but she had heard too many like it to mistake it for something else. At once, she slammed the pickup into drive. Fear gave her a lead foot. The truck spun around the corner without a flash of brake lights, wheeled left onto the street beside Farbod's residence, and squealed to a halt. Leaving the truck to idle, Yasaman dashed across a short stretch of lawn to the privacy fence.

The fence enclosed a patio and swimming pool. Yasaman had seen both in satellite photos of the property. The gate leading into the fence was normally secured with a padlock and chain. Tonight, the chain and lock were lying in the grass. Damage to the wood above the latch showed where Noreen had inserted the pry bar and bolt cutters. Yasaman didn't rush inside; she hadn't lost her good sense. Easing open the gate, she focused on the house's back windows.

Which window would Noreen have chosen to force open? Not knowing exactly where the cameras would be placed, Yasaman couldn't see any advantage that one offered over the others. She ran to the near corner of the house and tried the window there. It didn't budge. The fence enclosed two windows along the house's side. These, too, were locked. She was returning to the back of house at a run when a man wearing black slacks and a white tee stepped around, holding a pistol.

"*Kimildama!*" he commanded in a thick Turkish accent. Yasaman complied and held still. She faced the house with her hands on the wall as he patted her down, pausing to squeeze a breast.

Beneath her breath, Yasaman muttered *kirli domuz*—dirty pig—in his own language. The man laughed and thrust against her. Yasaman gritted her teeth, preparing to fight, to kill if there was no other choice than to be taken. Just then a second figure emerged from around the corner. Yasaman saw him from the corner of her eye so didn't recognize him at first. Before she could glance, the pig of a guard twisted Yasaman's arm behind her back, making her cry out in pain.

"*Waqef!* Don't hurt her!" The first word was in Arabic, but Yasaman recognized the accent, as well as the voice, of the speaker.

"Bizhan?" she said, looking. She was not wrong. Her gone-but-not-forgotten fiancé was standing before her shaking his head, as if he were the one who couldn't believe *she* was there.

Motioning to her captor, he said, "Careful. She is not a prisoner, but my guest. Yasaman joon. I have dreamt of this moment."

Yasaman dug her heels in the dirt, resisting the push of the man behind her and her own instincts to move forward. Bizhan's tastes had changed—he had tucked his jeans into boots and was wearing a button-down shirt of vibrant blue. He looked healthy, robust. She had imagined him dead, mostly. On the occasions she had pretended he might be alive, she had pictured pale skin on a body made skeletal after months in a hole. On the contrary, Bizhan was tan, fit, and obviously well fed.

"What is going on? Bizhan, why—"

"You mean, why am I here? To meet you, flower of my heart."

No sooner had he pronounced the pet name than Yasaman saw the truth. Breaking eye contact, she said to him, "Do not call me by that name."

"Why should I not, sweet one?" He didn't wait for an answer but led Yasaman and her guard through the patio door into the house.

"It has been you all along," Yasaman said as she allowed Bizhan to guide her; the way he commanded the guard belied his authority. "I should have known."

"Should you, now?" Bizhan appeared most amused by his old love's realization.

"I expected to find Farbod here—it was naive of me to have not expected you too, Bizhan," Yasaman said.

"You flatter me, flower of my heart."

Yasaman winced at his deliberate use of the pet name. "I wasn't flattering you, Bizhan," Yasaman spat. "I can think of no one other than you and Farbod who would be capable of decoding and weaponizing the al-zban ghraza in only half a year."

Bizhan nodded sagely as he soaked up what he appeared to be taking as praise. With one hand at the small of her back, he steered Yasaman toward the stairs.

"I should have put two and two together a long time ago," Yasaman chastised herself. "First you go missing, and then Farbod—and then all the research you both know as well as they did is used to destroy thousands of lives."

Had Bizhan appeared emaciated, damaged in some way, she could have fooled herself into believing he was acting against his will, as she still naively hoped was true of Farbod. But the hale man in cowboy *haute couture* was no captive. Yasaman found the undeniable truth appalling; Bizhan was her enemy. He was the demon responsible for the attempts at her kidnapping and the horrible terror acts.

"Perhaps you were blinded by your love for me?" Bizhan suggested with a lascivious grin. "Perhaps that is why your two and two did not add up, Yasaman."

For as much as she hated to admit it, there was a grain of truth in Bizhan's words—her feelings for him remained strong, even after all the time that had passed since he walked out of her apartment and her life. Perhaps it was simply a case of unfinished business, that she had not found closure to their intense relationship. Well, she was sure as hell finding it now.

"Let me go!" Yasaman protested as they neared the staircase. She'd deliberately raised her voice, hoping Mitch or Wells or even the neighbors might hear.

Bizhan said calmly, "Don't shout, flower. Your friend is upstairs. He is hurt enough. Do spare his ears."

They had caught Mitch. What about Wells? Yasaman declined to ask, hoping Bizhan wouldn't know of the agent's existence. With Bizhan ahead of her and the guard behind, she passed through a sunroom and entered a living space with garish white carpeting and a leather love seat and chairs arranged in a semicircle. A man dressed identically to Yasaman's guard, aside from a shoulder holster, stood in a marble foyer on the other side of the white carpet, shoving a fallen sports jacket around with his foot.

"Get towels, idiot," said Bizhan. "But not now. Drinks, instead."

The armed guard disappeared, leaving the jacket in a swirl of blood smears that brought a gasp from Yasaman.

"Oh, he's alive," said Bizhan. He sat and gestured her to a chair. "Rest, Yasaman joon, flower of my heart. You have questions, surely? Sit. Ask."

Released by her guard, Yasaman took a seat. "What have you done to my friend?"

"Only what he made us do. Detective Wilson said he came to see the professor. If he had not resisted, I would have let him see the old man's face."

"Farbod is here?"

"Of course. He is my other guest—an honored one. He has done as much for the world to come as anyone. As much as myself. Everyone alive owes him a debt."

"And what of those you have killed?"

"We killed no one. We merely let tyranny die." His face became grave. "I have missed you, my flower. Do you know how much pleading I have done to keep you alive? I have loved you, not wisely, but too well."

Tears had appeared in his eyes. Yasaman wanted to go on despising him, but the inconsistent weakness in his strongman facade made it impossible to be totally consistent herself. She settled in and let him assault her with flattery, wondering all the while what had become of Mitch Wilson and Noreen Wells.

30—It Means Victory

Alone in an upstairs room, Mitch heard Yasaman's, "Let me go!" He couldn't rush to a window because of the nylon ropes binding his wrists and ankles. A gag was pulled tight between his teeth. It made shouting back impossible, not that he figured shouting would do him any good.

A wad of fabric had been stuffed behind the gag. It had triggered his gag reflex, summoning acid from his gut, which had nowhere to go but his sinuses. His nose became hopelessly clogged, the wad bloated and slippery. At every moment, it threatened to close his throat. He had only managed to breathe so far by contorting his neck muscles in a way he had never known they could move. His throat ached, telling him in no uncertain terms that it wouldn't be able to keep up the trick for long. Pressing his forehead to the floor in the empty room, Mitch concentrated all his energy on staying alive.

A hard head had gotten him thus far. He was closer to the Red Line masterminds than he would ever have thought possible since losing Ethan and Jessica. Losing them had taught him there was only one impossibility—holding on to the folks you love. Revenge on an international shadow conspiracy was nothing by comparison.

He attempted to lever the wad away from his throat with his tongue. It jammed farther back. Mitch gagged, barely exerting the necessary throat control to keep the wad from closing off his airway. He didn't mind dying. He had figured on getting killed eventually. The injustice of going without getting his hands around the throat of a single mastermind made him furious. In his frustration, he thumped his head against the floor. Quickly deciding it was pointless, Mitch strained against the ropes instead. They flexed but didn't give, a sure sign he was wasting oxygen. Exhaustion made his muscles quiver. He sank into a slump, trying to think of what Mama would have prayed if she had been in something like his situation.

Spasms shook him. The walls closed in. He fought for dignity in death, then gave it up to rage quietly at the night. He saw, or thought he saw, a rim of perfect blackness orbiting a gray space occupied by fireflies. His ears whined, his nerves frayed, and the fireflies transformed from a dance of tiny lights to streamers of green painting the gray background so it glowed.

Mitch advanced toward the glow. His earthly concerns didn't seem as pressing as they had a moment earlier. He drifted, forgetting his bonds and his struggle. The glow was warm like a touch, not like fire.

A hand parted Mitch's lips. Fingers dragged something putrid across his tongue. Gagging, he tried to pull away, but the arms holding him were too steady.

Wells said, "What's wrong with you? Are you trying to die?"

No, he wasn't. Not die.

"God, you look awful."

If he'd had breath enough, Mitch would have said, "Nice to see you too." He settled for a grunt.

In as few words as possible, Wells brought Mitch up to speed. She had scouted the positions of the cameras before entering the backyard. Letting herself in by a window, she had heard his struggle with the bruiser and the firing of the gun. She had seen him soaking up blows and figured bullets would have been quicker if they wanted him dead, so she had searched downstairs discreetly while he was being taken up. With a high degree of certainty, she confirmed there were only the cowboy, the bruiser, and the shooter to worry about. Nobody else was present on the lower level, though it was possible someone could be up here. She had crept up the stairs and been searching a room across the hall when Yasaman shouted. She had entered Mitch's room with the intention of looking out a window and found him thrashing on the hardwood.

"What about Yaz?" said Mitch, who had recovered enough to speak. Even to his ringing ears, his voice sounded like he was gargling gravel.

Wells went to the window. "Truck's on the side. Gate is wide open. Can't see the patio. You armed?"

"Not anymore." The man who had tied him had taken his gun.

Wells drew her own weapon, a compact semiautomatic. "Stay here. I'll go down."

"I'm coming. I'll draw fire."

"Don't be stupid."

Wells began to leave. Wobbling into her path, Mitch caught her shoulder. "I'm serious. I'll go first, make noise. You come after me, popping shots."

"You want to be a martyr?"

"Better me than you. Wells, they've got Yaz. Let me help."

"You'll slow me down."

"Only if you're going too fast."

Without waiting for Wells to say more, Mitch went to the door and listened to sounds of voices from downstairs. At least one man's voice was audible, and one woman's. Though she wasn't speaking English, Mitch was sure the woman was Yasaman. He turned the door handle.

"Wait," said Wells. "Any twenty on Namdar?"

"No," said Mitch. In the hall, there wasn't much to see. Wells had shut the door she'd been in before coming to the rescue. Three additional doors led off the hall to Mitch's left. Two were on his side and one across, all the way down. Dim light streamed out from under the most distant door, from where faint music seeped.

Mitch looked a question at Wells. She shook her head. They couldn't do anything about the music lover. The prospect of alerting another hostile was too great. Before he left the room that had almost been his morgue, Mitch took off his shoes, the better to glide to the head of the stairs. Wells shrank out of sight.

With his back against the wall, Mitch advanced. His hip hurt, but the general agony of his face, calf, and everything else made it seem trivial. At the end of the hall, he got down on all fours, crawling forward with his head under the level of the banister. When he saw no one below, he descended step by step to the first floor on hands and feet.

The conversation was lively. Sometimes the speakers shouted. Sometimes they spoke in hushed tones. Always, they spoke with passion. There were clearly two participants, the cowboy and Yasaman. The position of the bruiser and shooter were impossible to tell. Mitch had hoped he had dislocated the shooter's knee with his tackle, but he hadn't heard a car engine or any sounds of someone administering medical care.

He reached the bottom step, inches above the marble tiling of the foyer. Even from his vantage point, the only thing he saw was one turquoise arm of the gesturing cowboy.

He had a decision to make. He could rush into the room and fling himself at the first enemy. Or he could limp outside, through the door ahead, hoping the guards would follow instead of shooting straightaway. A third alternative presented itself. He could show himself briefly, then retreat to the dining room. The entry was across the foyer opposite the living room. Figuring his hip into the equation, the third option was likely to put the most distance between Yasaman and anyone with a gun.

As the cowboy slapped the arm of his chair, Mitch lurched from the last step, trying to make it look like he was fleeing in panic. Momentum sent him into the heavy exterior door, which he made a point of thumping with his shoulder. The cowboy rose, shouting. Yasaman was sitting opposite him, her eyes gleaming, looking fragile.

Responding to an order from the cowboy, the bruiser took a run at Mitch. Mitch turned his back and ran as best he could into the dining room. The bruiser got as far as the foyer before a shot rang out. Wells.

Mitch would have felt triumphant had the shooter not appeared through the door separating the dining room from the kitchen. He had lost his jacket and was holding a drinks tray, which he tried to balance while fumbling at a shoulder holster. Praying his hip would hold, Mitch grabbed the chair at the head of the dining table. He swung it at the shooter, who had to drop the tray to save himself.

As glasses from the tray shattered, Mitch grabbed the gun still in the man's holster and flipped the safety with his thumb. It was a Glock 19—a common law enforcement piece—that felt natural in his hand. His opponent shoved the chair, but Mitch kept a grip on the gun. He drew. In time with rapid gunshots from the foyer, Mitch pulled the trigger three times. The ex-shooter was tossed into the doorframe by the impact of bullets to his belly and neck. Somewhere between shots, Mitch took a knee. He fired several more shots as the man fell through the swinging door, dropping the chair that had failed to offer any kind of protection.

As Mitch struggled to rise, a shot echoed from the foyer. Wells said, "Show me your hands."

"What a waste." The cowboy's voice was laced with contempt.

With the help of the table, Mitch climbed to his feet. The man who had shot a gash in his calf lay in a bloody heap. Mitch remembered the flesh wound's sting and thought he ought to feel good about the payback. He didn't. He felt empty. He wished the fight had gone another way. If he had knocked the shooter down with the chair, he could have turned him over to the FBI, or local PD, and it would have been a job well done. There was nothing good about killing. It left him cold.

He went to the foyer, where Wells was straddling the body of a man she had shot. Her eyes and gun were on the cowboy, so it was lucky Mitch lost his balance as he stumbled from the dining room. Tilting at random, he saw a gunman appear upstairs.

"Wells!"

She spun and put four bullets in the man's chest. As he skidded face-first down the stairs, the cowboy tried a move that was doomed to failure. He was halfway to tugging a gun from his waistband when Wells spun to shoot him once through the chest and once in the belly. He fell, shrieking in pain, as Yasaman leapt to her feet.

"Bizhan!" she cried. "Oh, Bizhan."

Wells said, "Get the gun."

Mitch stooped beside the fallen cowboy and lifted him by the belt to fetch the weapon. It was, in fact, his own confiscated pistol. Once he had shown it to Wells, she gave him a nod and left to sweep the premises.

Mitch crouched on the far side of the cowboy from Yasaman, holding the gun in his hand. Tears flowed freely from Yasaman's dark eyes.

"You're not hurt?" said Mitch.

"I'm fine." Her voice had no life or energy to it. "This is the man I spoke about, Bizhan Al-Kabir. He is my—we were engaged."

Bizhan was in the process of bleeding out. A bullet had punched a hole in his rib cage; it pulsed blood and sucked air. Mitch removed his own pullover, folded it over, and used it to cover the wound.

"They wanted me here all along. They sent Farbod to fetch me, but he betrayed them. Max, Milan, the acceleration of the Europe timeline, it was all so they could get their hands on me."

"Who are they, Yaz?" Her sadness dampened his excitement, but not completely. A few sobs less and he might have shaken her for an answer.

"Bizhan, the people he works for. He won't say names."

"Ask again."

"He won't say."

He seized her wrist. "We have to know. It's why we're here. Lives are at stake."

She blinked at the hand holding her wrist, at Mitch, at Bizhan. When she spoke, her words sounded more like pleas than demands. Bizhan didn't answer, apart from groaning.

"Tell her," said Mitch. Bizhan looked at him, lips twitching, as if to resume the smirk he had worn when they met. Releasing Yasaman's wrist, Mitch plunged the gun barrel into the hole Wells had made in Bizhan's belly. Bizhan screamed.

"Stop it," said Yasaman. She seized Mitch's wrist. "Stop! Isn't it enough he's dying?"

"It's *because* he's dying. Ask him again."

"I won't."

"Ask!"

Yasaman got to her feet. "He speaks English. Ask yourself."

Rocking back on his heels, Mitch pulled the gun away. The dying man's eyes flashed to Yasaman. His lips, still twitching, shaped a word. Yasaman knelt again, leaning close. For what seemed an eternity, Bizhan whispered to her with his eyes half shut, his breath too weak to stir the hair straying from her ball cap. When he fell silent, Mitch didn't have to check for a pulse to know it was the final time.

Wells was looking on from the foyer. "What did he say?"

Yasaman removed her cap and shook her braid loose. She covered her face but didn't sob. She seemed to have run out of tears.

"He said a name."

Mitch said, "Only one?"

Yasaman nodded. "A name or a word. A concept, repeated as many times as he was able. Verethragna. A Zoroastrian deity. The name means victory, the doom of foes."

Wells let a moment of silence pass. "It's clear down here. Mitch, come with me upstairs."

The two climbed the stairs, Wells much more quickly than Mitch, to approach the still-closed door. The music played at the same volume, so there was a chance they were worrying about an empty room. Mitch didn't think so. He leaned on the cane he'd retrieved from downstairs and kept his back to the wall while Wells, gun pointed, opened the other doors along the hallway, finding an empty bathroom and closet in addition to the rooms she had already visited. As she faced the door to the room leaking strains of jazz and muffled French vocals, Yasaman ascended the stairs. Wells signaled for her to stay put.

Mitch threw the door open while Wells pointed her gun at the interior.

"I'm a federal agent," said Wells. "Show me your hands."

The only response was a plink of piano strings and a stutter like a needle skipping on vinyl. Though Mitch couldn't see into the room from his position by the door, he smelled signs of life in the form of stale coffee and fresh body odor. Wells led with her gun. Mitch followed her in. He still wasn't able to see much, as a desk lamp on the other side of the room that provided the only light was blocked by Wells. It made a shadow of her fierce form and drew a halo around her silhouette.

"Keep still," said Wells, not to Mitch. Over her shoulder, she said, "Call Yasaman in here."

Mitch returned to the hall and signaled to Yasaman. He noted a light switch on the wall beside the door. After getting the nod from Wells, Mitch flipped the switch and found it wasn't connected to an overhead light, but an outlet, into which a standing lamp had been plugged. The naked bulb had a red tint to give the walls a bloody hue. When Wells stepped aside to reveal an elderly man strapped to a chair, the pajamas he wore looked purple because of the light; Mitch would later find out they were blue.

The pajama wearer's limbs were slack. His chin was resting on his chest. If not for the occasional shudder, Mitch would have sworn Farbod Namdar was dead. His breathing was covered by the music coming from a record player on the desk. The player wasn't for Namdar's benefit, as much of his head, including his ears, were enclosed in a virtual reality headset. Wells toed his slippers. He didn't respond.

Yasaman darted past Mitch and Wells. "Farbod. Farbod, it is Yasaman. Do you hear me?" She looked back at Wells, desperately. "We must help him. What can we do?"

Mitch said, "The headset. It's got to be some variation on the messaging we've seen before."

"Can we remove it without hurting him?" said Wells.

"All the videos I watched, it didn't hurt me to quit. But I was never that far in."

Wells circled to Namdar's back. After frowning for a moment, she lifted the needle off the record player. "Do you hear sirens?"

Mitch listened for the electronic howl. It was soft, but growing louder.

Wells said, "You're our expert, Yaz. You make the call."

Mitch moved to the wall to get a better view. It was hard to believe the pathetic figure in the chair had once been the target of her romantic interest. He had obviously been younger then.

"Be careful," said Mitch as Yasaman reached for the headset. "We don't know what he can do."

"This can be said about anyone," said Yasaman.

After drawing a breath, she lifted the headset away. Namdar stirred, and his entire body commenced trembling. He swung his head like he was trying to locate a sound. The ringing had left Mitch's ears, but he remembered what it was like to have noises in his head. Namdar covered his ears and rocked in his chair. He shook so violently, Wells reached forward to restrain him from falling out. The sight brought Mitch back to a flash of bloodshot, staring eyes he had first seen almost two months ago. He couldn't see Namdar's eyes through his hands, but suspected if he could, they would have held the same bloodshot stare.

"I'll help you, Wells," said Mitch.

"Please," said Yasaman. "Stay where you are."

Her tone was icy. Even knowing she was mad, her voice took Mitch off guard. His willingness to torture Al-Kabir had damaged the trust they shared. Would he be able to patch things up, or had he burned a bridge, as he had done previously with Wells? He was momentarily puzzled, and oddly pleased, that he cared.

Mitch held a hand out to Yasaman. "I won't hurt him. I promise. What happened downstairs wasn't me."

"Was it not?"

Mitch groped for an answer. Wells said, "I pulled the trigger, Yaz. After Milan, if it had been me in Mitch's place, I can't tell you I would have done differently. I might have done worse."

Yasaman gave it some consideration as the sirens swelled. Finally, she nodded. "We are all fighting instinct. It's not an easy battle."

Wells firmed her grip on Namdar's left arm while Mitch took the right. Together, they forced Namdar's hands apart. Yasaman fell to her knees in front of him, stroked his chin, and spoke kindly to him in their language.

Yasaman said, "Do you know me, Farbod? Oh, Baba!"

"Fa—Fatemeh?" said Namdar.

Yasaman didn't correct him. "Doctor Farbod Namdar. You know that name?"

His voice quavered. "Is it—it is my own."

"Yes, Farbod. You were being held against your will. Compelled to act. I must know. Who compelled you?"

The old man tried to cover his face again, but was not allowed. "The young man, is he here? Like a son to me. Very dear."

"Do you mean the young man in this house?"

"House? Yes. We have worked together, here. Bizhan is his name, as mine is Farbod. But you, you are not my Fatemeh."

Outside, the sirens blipped and a car door slammed. Wells and Mitch exchanged a look.

"You know me, Farbod," said Yasaman. "Are you not my *baba jaan*?"

Namdar looked troubled. As his expression cleared, a knock sounded at the front door. Wells went into the hall, swearing liberally.

Yasaman pressed her cheek lightly against Namdar's beard stubble. "You know me, Farbod. I need your help. Yasaman joon needs help."

Downstairs, a policeman commanded Wells to put her hands up. Namdar inhaled. His eyes went wide. Mitch was sure he was about to go into a fit. But instead of thrashing, Namdar said, "Joonam? I know you."

Beaming like it was her own uncle she had gotten back, Yasaman fell on Namdar, hugging his neck.

"You have come, my child," said Namdar. "Tell me, what is today? We have little time."

31—Two Days to Go

The interview room at the Fairhope Police Department was as comfortable as the holding cells, so Yasaman made no effort to leave. She sat smiling pleasantly while the female detective called the sheriff departments of several counties, asking what translators they had available. Pretending she didn't speak any language the locals were likely to identify was part of her plan. It kept the wheels spinning while Mitch hedged and Wells got in touch with her contacts.

While the detective who had been attempting to conduct her interview took a wellness break, Yasaman sifted through her selection of languages, challenging herself to cobble several together into a believable patois. She needed the distraction to keep from worrying about Farbod. How thin he had looked! Even more than when she had seen him on the bridge. Confidence and intelligence had returned to his face mere moments before Mitch had been shoved against the wall and handcuffed by police. Yasaman hadn't had time to feel hopeful of Farbod's recovery. She had also not asked what he meant by "little time." Plying her linguistic skills was pointless, but it kept her mind off the two men who'd been taken to the hospital under guard.

With a scrape of the metal door, the Fairhope detective returned. She was accompanied by Noreen and the detective's captain, along with the agent whom Deputy Director Solomon had called Russell. After a brief, unenthusiastic apology, the detective bid Yasaman goodbye.

"Let's keep in touch," said Yasaman as she left. They were the first words she had spoken in English since entering the station. She chided herself for finding the detective's stunned expression gratifying.

In the parking lot, Russell opened the back door of an SUV. The father of Noreen Wells and Valerie Solomon sat in the back on the far side of the bench seat.

Deputy Director Solomon acknowledged Yasaman with a nod, then issued an order that took his lackey by surprise. "Russell, get the boys in blue to give you a lift. Noreen can drive."

"Sir?" said Russell.

"It's not complicated, Russell. I want a word in private with my daughter and Dr. Karami. Find your own way to the hospital."

"Sir." Russell shrugged at Yasaman and offered to help her into the SUV. She took his arm, though only to make him feel better. With Noreen in the driver's seat and Solomon staring at his hands, the vehicle left the station.

Yasaman said, "You had a pleasant flight?"

The deputy director declined to meet her eye. He had been humbled, evidently, but by what? If his secret was out, if it was known he had acted to slow the Red Line investigation, he would surely be under arrest. Instead, he was sitting beside her. A dutiful daughter, Noreen had found a way to enlist her father's aid without destroying his career.

"There was nothing I could do," said Solomon. "They let me know—never mind how—what would happen if I didn't play ball. They wanted you locked up, Doctor. Said it wouldn't be long. I swear, getting you out of the game is all I've done for them since they took Val."

Noreen said, "What about cutting Mitch out?"

"It . . . seemed like what they would want me to do. These people are serious, Noreen. If we want to get your sister back, I have to make them think it's all going their way."

"Like it isn't, Dad? Tell me you had an endgame. Tell me you have a way to trace back these messages you've been getting you're not telling me about. Tell me you've been playing them as much as they've been playing you."

"I can't."

"You can't be ser—"

"I can't, Noreen. All right? I've been playing for time, and that's all I've got to show for it. I don't even know—I don't know if Val is alive."

The deputy director clenched a fist and pounded the finish on the inside of his door. As the SUV flashed past streetlights, Yasaman saw tears on his cheek. She considered what to say, decided discretion called for silence, and let the silence stretch out. The trip to the city hospital, which was across the street from their hotel, took less than five minutes.

Noreen found a bright patch outside the emergency entrance to let them off. Before climbing out, Yasaman took a good, long look at Solomon. He was completely in control. He showed no signs of stress or emotional pain. Like Noreen, when he had a job to do, he could shut out all else.

On their walk to the sliding emergency doors, she said, "Farbod is here, yes? Did he say something? A warning, perhaps."

Every muscle in Solomon's angular face tightened. "Yeah. Something's coming, a new attack. There will be a third Red Line, bigger than the others combined. We have days to stop it, maybe hours. So far as I know, your friend is the only one who can say how. I don't know your politics, Doctor. I don't know how you feel about the thousands of people who lost their lives in this country and in Europe. I don't need to tell you there are enemies of the Western world who would like to see more of a death toll. Per your friend, they are about to get their wish."

A pair of uniformed police officers flanked them as they were admitted to the emergency floor proper. On the way to Farbod's room, Yasaman spotted Mitch sitting in a hospital bed. He was talking to a man with a laptop. A woman with recording equipment sat in the only chair of the little room.

Yasaman said, "Is Mitch under arrest?"

Solomon looked apologetic. "For shooting terrorists with a legally registered firearm? Of course not. We're taking his statement on everything from Milan and after. I've got people cutting clips from the feed keeping your friend Namdar in VR limbo. Detective Wilson has agreed to decode what they play. Don't worry. I've renewed his contract and doubled his salary."

More uniformed police were stationed outside Farbod's room. Solomon waved at them impatiently. "That's your time, gentlemen. Tell your boss to give us the room."

The policeman in charge of the others glared but did as he was told. A moment after he had disappeared through the door, Solomon returned, following an angry woman detective. Solomon told her, "We'll keep you informed," and gestured for Yasaman to come inside.

Propped on pillows, with a plastic tube in his arm, Farbod looked more pitiful, though less haggard, than before. When Yasaman approached his bedside, he clasped his hands as if in prayer. She bent to kiss his forehead, then sat in a chair offered to her by a man in an FBI windbreaker.

Farbod wasted no time. He spoke in Persian, which Solomon must have anticipated, as he didn't object. The man in the windbreaker scribbled notes on a pad. He was evidently a translator.

"Time is short," said Farbod. "My time especially. Disease of the kidneys, I am told. An operation is possible. I have refused. There is dirt on my head. The deeds I have done are too terrible to mention, to say nothing of what I was made to do."

"What do you remember?" said Yasaman.

"Everything, my child. I have disgraced myself. I thought I was strong, Yasaman joon. I fought nearly a month after I was captured, but in the end, I proved weak. But that was early on. With the refinements to the technique I helped introduce, no resistance to the language of instinct is now possible. After a few hours of exposure, there is nothing our enemy cannot make a man do."

Yasaman pictured Mitch lifting his head like a bloodhound scenting the wind. "Who is our enemy, Farbod?"

"Legion. Businessmen. Politicians. Radicals from all nations. Some are capitalists, some socialists. There are atheists, fundamentalists, jihadis, luddites, and technocrats. Shut up in a room with knives, they would make sausage of each other's entrails. So long as they are kept apart, they can count money as a common cause. What they despise most, what all agree they must oppose, is the globalization of economic interest."

It seemed an abstract concern to Yasaman. Her face must have conveyed the feeling.

"You think this a trivial concern. Tell me, why does a worker in Bangladesh now expect the same housing conditions as a worker in the UK? Because the global economy says he should. Why are Bangladeshi factory owners investigated by EU journalists? Because the global internet carries news to all. The powers who despise globalism are fundamentally disunited, except in their opposition to unity. Their grandfathers scaled great heights on the backs of slaves. They will do anything to ensure those slaves are never free."

"Even kill?" said Yasaman.

"Who cares for life, eh, when money is to be made? There have been two cycles so far, the attacks you call Red Line and Red Line Two. These were to prove a global stance against terror is impossible. The only sensible foreign policy is to close the borders, shut foreigners out, and restrict communication with the outside world. No single outside group can be shown to be behind the attacks. Therefore, all outside groups are suspect. You have seen the results in only two months! Global culture is breaking down. In another month, individual nations will be set free of common restraint. The oligarchs can go back to dominating their local slave masses without worrying about international outrage."

Yasaman heard Solomon make a sound between a groan and a growl and turned to look at him. He failed to notice, so intent was he on reading Farbod's words over the translator's shoulder. Noreen came in, not bothering to knock. She leaned against the doorpost, watching her father with her arms crossed.

Concentrating again on Farbod, Yasaman said, "You speak almost as if you wish to persuade me."

"Before I saw you on Pol-e Tabi'at, dear heart, I was a true believer. Like Pavlov's dog, I was conditioned to crave the achievement of the conspiracy's goal. Catching sight of you returned me to myself. I recognized my foolishness too late to save the victims, but soon enough to help you keep your freedom.”

Yasaman’s trigger finger twitched. She pictured Farbod’s minder spraying blood as he fell for the thousandth time.

“The—*the conspiracy*. Is that what they call themselves?”

“It doesn’t begin to capture their arrogance. The Godhead. *That* is what they call themselves. The allusion is to a trinity of powers: finance, technology, politics. Their membership is diverse—strange bedfellows, as they say. Do you know what Bizhan discovered when he was drafted to the cause? A delivery system for the language of instinct already existed. Methods for implanting thoughts in the brain were developed in the early days of the Cold War. The Soviets used these methods in Korea, the Soviets and Americans in Vietnam. Our own countrymen were spurred to revolution by subliminal proddings buried in our news broadcasts. The men who created this technology profited outrageously. They are part of the Godhead today.”

Yasaman exhaled, feeling suddenly winded. “But they did not have the language of instinct.”

“Correct. They could not control hearts, only make suggestions. Your research, and Bizhan’s, was the key they were missing all those years.”

Sinking back in the chair, Yasaman attempted to digest the information. Controlling hearts was more than she had thought possible.

Having caught up to her in the translator’s notes, Solomon interjected, “What’s this about a key?”

Switching to English, Farbod answered, “There was only so much the Cold War messages could do. Besides, with the invention of the VCR, it became impossible to hide readable messages in broadcasts without them being detected. The subliminal influence program had to be suspended. But, when Yasaman discovered the al-zban ghraza, everything changed. Combined with the techniques the Godhead knew well, it became the perfect weapon for evoking action on a mass scale and being able to direct it. Displayed correctly, the symbols are potent, irresistible. Yet their appearance is subtle; they are hard to catch, even at slow speeds, and are not readily comprehended."

"So the Godhead approached Bizhan," said Yasaman. "They wanted to use his knowledge of the language to help adapt their techniques."

Farbod nodded. "I fear money is all it took to win him over. He went into hiding immediately and began experimentation. Flashing the ancient symbols proved effective, but his skill at crafting complex manipulations was limited. I was kidnapped to supplement the deficiency. We achieved much, in little time, though progress would have been faster if we had brought you in at the start."

"Why did you not?"

His smile was rueful but honest. "Bizhan forbade it. I was lost, by then, joonam, but your bold Hafez never did lose himself. He had his own agenda, his singular focus."

His reference to her ex-fiancé as the ideal poet-lover raised a flush to Yasaman's cheeks. It also caught the ear of the translator. He looked askance at her.

Noreen made an impatient noise and crossed the room to tap the translator's shoulder. "Take a walk, okay? We can handle the rest." When the translator was gone, Noreen faced Farbod. "What about my sister? Valerie Solomon."

For a moment, Farbod looked blank. "Ah! One of the university girls, yes? They were test subjects. It was part of my role to try out our techniques on campus. Sometimes I would program a girl to go to the house so Bizhan could test them further. The Solomon girl was not one of mine. Bizhan had orders to seek her out."

The professional restraint holding back Solomon broke. He surged forward and grabbed the front of Farbod's hospital gown. "What happened to her?"

He barely reacted. "She was conditioned, like the rest, as a sleeper agent. The process takes a day, but this girl stayed longer. Three days, I think. She left, oh, nearly as long ago. I don't know where she went."

Between the snarl Noreen wore and Solomon's pulsing jawline, Yasaman was afraid for Farbod's life. She said, "Agents, you have your answer. She is alive. She can be found."

Solomon released the gown and stepped away. Noreen said, "You have to have a way to contact the people you work for, this Godhead."

"There is a protocol. Any who know how can call a meeting."

Solomon said, "Who would be at this meeting?"

Sallow and weak though he was, Farbod managed to look cunning. "In this instance, there is one man who matters more than the others. Bizhan said it was because he possessed the necessary infrastructure, as he put it. If we can draw this man out, we can prevent the Third Cycle from occurring."

"How?" said Yasaman.

"His is the hand that holds the key. If he can be persuaded not to turn it, there will be no Red Line Three."

"Again, how?" asked Solomon. "Using these symbols?"

Farbod shook his head. "No, Director. He is not entirely immune to these devices, but he will not be easily persuaded simply by flashing images at him." He paused then asked, "Have you noticed anything about the pattern of these Red Line events?"

"Of course," said Noreen. "The first wave was limited to the United States and seemed to be a response to the *Spex* movie. It targeted people, institutions, and businesses that were connected to it in some way. The second expanded to Europe but was still connected to the entertainment industry for the most part."

Farbod fixed the agent with a raptor gaze. "That is the most visible pattern. But there is another hidden within it. The Godhead's stated intention is to upend the global community by shattering the links between its component parts. But think of it: If this is random and widespread, it would also cut the corporations off from both their international consumers and their cheap labor. If they destroy entire economies—especially of the most wealthy nations—who will purchase their products and services? The pattern has been calculated to achieve the goal in such a way the financial players involved still have markets and a workforce when this is all over."

Yasaman shook her head. "Yes, but how does it affect this . . . head of the Godhead?"

"Remember, I told you Bizhan had his own agenda? The members of the Godhead are, as I said, strange bedfellows—people who have great disdain for other members of the cadre. This was not lost on Bizhan. He saw the promises made to the radicals in the collective were not going to be served by the Godhead's end game. Bizhan observed the business interests in the Godhead had, how do you say it, rigged the game in their favor. So, he undertook to change the rules of the game. The third Red Line event will not be the targeted strike the Godhead planned it to be. It will be far-reaching, random, and devastating to every nation, every layer of society, every institution, every linkage in the global network. What the man at the top of the conspiracy does not know is what Bizhan and his cohorts in the Godhead have planned will ruin him and everyone like him."

The stillness in the hospital room was punctuated only by the steady blip of Farbod's heart monitor. Yasaman was stunned by the sheer hubris of the assumption that an army made up of inveterate enemies could be trusted to serve the same master. Ultimately, they must betray each other. She suspected the others in the room were harboring similar thoughts.

Director Solomon broke the silence. "How do we get to him?"

"If the deputy director will loan me his best computer analyst, I can invoke the protocol at once, then spend the rest of the evening drafting a coded message. Though Bizhan told me our target is resistant to the symbols, I still recommend we might use them to . . . impress upon him the urgency of his decision. What is the time?"

Solomon checked his watch. "Thirteen minutes past ten."

"Four-thirteen, UTC," said Farbod. "We will send the message at seven, if you agree."

Solomon searched Farbod's face with the intensity of a surgeon exploring the aorta. "What would be in the message?"

"A request for a meeting. An introduction for the participant, signed with the personal code phrase of Bizhan Al-Kabir."

"Participant in the singular?"

"We can send only one. That is the protocol."

"I'll go," said Noreen.

"No, that won't work," said Farbod. "Forgive me, agent. Only one person will be welcome. Only one will be believed."

"Me," said Yasaman. "I am the one you mean, Farbod, am I not? I am the one this man will trust."

The man who had gone from mentor to lover and back again, all without losing her respect, lifted a hand for her to take. "Bizhan spoke often of your genius, of the value you would bring to the Godhead. He persuaded his masters to seek you out, to pursue you even when the risk of exposure was great. When I failed them, they wished to abandon you. When the FBI expressed interest, they wished to kill you. Bizhan negotiated a plan. The agents you met in Milan were to kill your fellow travelers but to spare you, Yasaman joon. That was the purpose of the Milan operation. I thought it madness. I thought his entire treacherous plan madness. It was this disagreement that moved Bizhan to have me put in the headset. No words can say how pleased I am you survived."

Yasaman spoke a revelation even as it bubbled into her brain. "Bizhan wanted to turn me, to make me one of your 'believers.' You mean to tell the man you were speaking of succeeded?"

"Turning me was Bizhan's proof of concept. Turning you was to be his masterpiece. With your unique genius, he could perfect his conditioning technique. You were to be his final test subject. You see? You would have been living proof the technique had achieved perfect control. It is very swift, very hard to resist. But we have not been able to make it impossible to set aside. Bizhan was convinced he needed you for that. He said as much to anyone who would listen."

Yasaman said, "If I go to this man, Farbod, will he believe I come from Bizhan?"

"He will accept your very presence as proof." He turned to Solomon. "If you will please record me repeating what I just told you about Bizhan's betrayal, Yasaman joon can embed the al-zban ghraza into the video. In addition to the proof of her own person, she can offer that proof. Once this man understands the attack to come will be world shattering—to him as well as to those whose suffering he is willing to cause—he will not wish it to take place. No sane man would. If you convince him the technique has been perfected, and reveal what Bizhan has done with perfection, he will abort the Third Cycle. If he is reluctant, the al-zban ghraza must convince him."

Noreen spoke up. "Then what? No way will he let her catch the next bus home."

"We won't leave you in the cold," Solomon told Yasaman. "That's a promise. I don't care how big these people are. We'll knock them down and get you out."

Yasaman lied. "I don't doubt it."

"She will be tracked the moment the protocol is activated," said Farbod. "You must alter the satellite imagery to hide any evidence of the FBI's presence in Fairhope. I suggest we get to work."

"Fine," said Noreen. "It happens I'm the best analyst. What do you need?"

32—Last Request

The FBI interviewer had abandoned the single chair by the time Yasaman entered Mitch's room. Mitch was surprised at the sheer depth of his relief to see her. Surprised and confused. What exactly was he feeling? Jessica had been gone a little less than two months, and the empty place in his being she had occupied was agonizingly empty. And Ethan . . . he couldn't think about either of them without wanting to sleep for a hundred years.

He was certain a psychologist would be able to explain to him in volumes about why he was attracted to the dark, mysterious, cosmopolitan woman he had, at first, wanted to strangle; he felt it went far beyond the physical, that he had forged a strong bond with her. Yasaman was a strong-willed, spirited woman, one who had taken a much older married man as a lover just because she could; she was pretty much the polar opposite of his dear, sweet Jessica, who would never have even dreamed of such a thing.

Mitch had saved the Iranian's life; she had saved his. They shared a common cause. On some level, Mitch understood theirs was a bond forged in crisis, one that could not possibly survive the realities of normal, day-to-day life. Yet . . .

Yasaman didn't look at him or speak for a full minute, only sat in the chair by his bed. At length, she reached up and took his hand.

"I would have died alone in the dark, if not for you," she said; her eyes glinted with what only could have been tears.

"In Milan? Nah. You would have made it out. You're like a cat. Nine lives."

"I was lost, Mitch. Trapped in dark and heat and with too much noise for my voice to be heard. Did you know it was *all* my fault? Everything that happened—all the destruction and death. All because Bizhan wanted to make me a conspirator in the Godhead's apocalypse."

"The Godhead?"

"It is the name of our enemy, what the conspirators call themselves."

Mitch allowed the information to sink in. She knew the enemy—knew the identity of the masterminds he wanted to exterminate. Although, at that moment, it didn't seem nearly as important as it had mere hours ago.

"Milan wasn't your fault. None of it was. Don't take that on yourself."

"The men I killed—"

"You were defending yourself."

"You weren't there."

"I'm here now. And don't tell me I've got you wrong. You're not a monster, Yaz. You're one of the kindest people I've ever met. Also the bravest. It's crazy, you know? I've wanted to kill the people responsible for taking away my family. Now you come here with a name—and I'm guessing, a plan—and all I want to do is sit and hold your hand. I told Trent I was after justice when I really wanted *revenge*. Now I don't care about either. What I want is peace. To be left alone. I want all this madness to stop."

Yasaman squeezed his hand. "You are also not a monster. And I think we have a way to make it stop—Farbod and I."

Mitch exhaled. "How?"

"They—the Godhead—made me the key to their opposing agendas." Her expression let Mitch know the very notion disgusted her. "It is clear I am to be the one to take Farbod's message to the head of the conspirators—the man who holds the key to the Third Cycle. I have been part of the message all along."

Mitch understood what she was telling him. All of it. And he understood she was the only one capable of ending the terrible conspiracy before the Third Cycle occurred. He also understood he would have to stand on the sidelines and wait it out.

Still, he wanted to argue against it—against Yasaman putting herself back into the line of fire. That was supposed to be *his* job. She was a linguist, a college professor, not a cop or counterterrorist agent, and she was also someone he so desperately wanted to protect, since he'd been unable to protect Jess and Ethan.

Mitch's epiphany stopped his internal processes. Was *that* what it was all about? If he was unable to save Yasaman Karami, he'd believe he had failed *twice*? Had protecting her become some form of redemption in his tortured soul?

As if reading Mitch's mind, Yasaman explained, "Deputy Director Solomon is already planning my extraction, should it become necessary. But we believe, Farbod and I, the head of the Godhead will comply: he will not want his empire destroyed."

"What if he only *postpones* the Third Cycle until he can undo whatever it is Bizhan has done? What if he wants you to help him?"

"That is where Mr. Solomon comes in."

Mitch squeezed her hand. "Yaz, I know this is probably inappropriate, but I've . . . I've come to care about you a great deal."

"And I, you," Yasaman replied with a sad, wan smile.

"You're so very different from Jessica." *Jesus, Mitch! What is wrong with you? Why would you even say that?* "I thought, maybe, when this was over—"

"When this is over, I am supposed to return to Tehran and hopefully take up my teaching post again."

Mitch eddied for a moment in confusion, his heart sinking. "I guess I thought you'd stay here . . . in the States."

"This is not my home, Mitch. My life is in Iran." Yasaman hesitated, then added, as if preempting his next thought, "Yours is here."

"Here, I have so much I want to forget."

Yasaman gave Mitch a look, which was at once incredulous and shrewd. "You want to forget your wife and child? You want to forget how much you loved them? You want to forget your friends, your work, your passion?"

The woman was right, Mitch didn't want to forget any of those things. Tears welled in his eyes. "I guess I mean I just want to forget I *lost* my family."

"Mitch," Yasaman said softly, "if I were in your life, I would be a constant reminder of your loss. I am a result of it and, in many ways, a *cause* of it. Do you think you could deal with that?"

Mitch knew that—knew the truth of it. But Yasaman was here, and real, and she offered him something to hold onto; he reckoned with her by his side, yes, he would be able to deal with it . . .

There it was again—Yaz was someone he felt compelled to protect for reasons that had little to do with her needing his protection.

"Yes," he said. "I know, and I would deal with it all. If only . . ."

"When this is all over, I do have one request for you, Mitch: When you get back to Baltimore, find the most beautiful woman you can and ask her to dance."

"I don't dance."

"I know you do not, with your hip."

"I didn't dance even before the hip. I hate dancing. Drove Jess crazy. She got me to slow dance exactly one time—it was on our first anniversary. My lack of dance was a bone of contention between us." He smiled at the memory, and Yasaman smiled with him.

"You can still ask. Will you promise me?"

"No."

"Why not? You need to relearn how to have fun, Mitch."

"Dancing is apparently fun for you. It's not for me. You promise me you will dance, and I'll promise you when I feel . . . *whole* again and find a woman I feel good with, I'll ask her to go fishing."

Yasaman laughed. The sound was like the trill of a tenor sax, throaty and warm. She let go of his hand and rose to leave. "That does sound quite idyllic." She met Mitch's eyes with hers, and there was the hint of promise in her voice that gave him a thread of hope. "I would like to go fishing with a man who cared as much about me as you cared for your wife."

"Maybe someday you will—if you ever find him." Mitch sensed hesitation in Yasaman's tone; she had no more desire to leave the room than he had in watching her go.

"Perhaps I already have." Yasaman stepped toward Mitch and reached for his cheeks with both hands. "And perhaps once all this is over, I may have to find him again."

The kiss was soft, warm, and tender, filled with promise and a longing for some kind of future. Mitch melted into Yasaman's heavenly lips and relished the feel of her body pressed against his, their breathing in perfect harmony, and he imagined he felt her heart beating against his chest.

All too soon, the moment was gone. Yasaman broke the kiss and took a half step backward. Her eyes remained fixed upon Mitch's, her lips still slightly parted.

"Thanks," he said.

"For?"

"For helping me take a next step in healing. For helping me feel something besides rage. For making me realize being in the world means protecting it, that it always will, and it's well worth the pain. And for giving me a little hope for the future."

Yasaman smiled. "You need sleep," she told him. "And I have work to do."

33—One Day to Go

Seven hours later, Yasaman was riding east in a taxi on Marsh Causeway Road, headed for Knotts Island, North Carolina. As a site for the meeting, it would have set off Noreen's alarm bells. It was remote, with only the single road to the mainland plus a ferry with fixed disembarkation points. If the conspirators decided they didn't want Yasaman to leave the island, they could easily guard the exits.

She had been picked up at a private airstrip and flown to a large commercial airport in the state of Virginia. Like the airport in Baltimore, Norfolk International had been all but abandoned. Yasaman hadn't gone inside, but waited on the plane until her taxi arrived. The pilot and copilot had been surprised to be called out so early, but they expected a rich bonus for their trouble. Yasaman didn't suspect either man was part of the Godhead. They were fellow slaves, doing the will of their masters.

The taxi driver seemed to have no knowledge of where they were going, apart from the address. He was a tall man with a kind face, somewhat past middle age.

"How long can you wait with the meter running?" she asked.

"All day," said the driver. "You might have to bang on the glass to wake me up. It's been a long night."

In Yasaman's purse was a stack of twenty-, ten-, and five-dollar bills. The FBI had given the Fairhope police a receipt for petty cash. After riffling the bills with her thumb, she held up two twenties.

"Here is your tip as it stands now. It will grow every hour you don't wander off."

The driver winked in the rearview. "They'd have to drag me out."

In the darkest hour of morning, after the moon had set and the sun had not yet broken the horizon, they passed over open water to the island. The taxi hugged the Virginia state line before dipping down into North Carolina. The address, per the mapping software in Yasaman's phone, was a semiretired horse farm with property stretching a kilometer eastward from Knotts Island Road to the Atlantic. The driver pointed out the modest farmhouse, which was all but invisible save for a single light in the upper story. As taxi tires crunched along the gravel drive, a spotlight snapped on. It wasn't pointed at them but at a parking space outlined in white paint on the gravel. The driver mumbled something Yasaman didn't hear, then pulled into the space.

"Would you please ask somebody to turn that off?"

"At once," said Yasaman, shielding her eyes. She passed the pair of twenties over the seat. "Keep the meter running."

"Wouldn't dream of any—"

A sudden crash shattered the windshield. The driver's head jolted. Part of his cheek was torn away. Ducking a spray of blood, Yasaman heard the driver gurgle. She saw only a ragged pit of gore and exposed, shattered teeth where the side of his face had been. A crack from outside made his body jolt. The driver slumped against the headrest, quite clearly dead.

Yasaman was too breathless to scream. Panting softly instead, she tore at the door handle and threw her full weight against the door. Rather than springing open, the door swung forty-five degrees and halted. A gloved hand reached in to clasp her by the arm. It dragged her from the taxi. Fighting to rise, to flee, she was tripped by her captor from behind. She put her hands out to save her face, and gashed her palms on the gravel. The foot that tripped her lightly kicked at her ribs. She rolled over and found the barrel of an automatic rifle pointing at her head.

In the glare of the spotlight, the shooter glowed a spectral white. Yasaman knew him from the long, black overcoat he wore. She didn't have to see the darting eyes.

"*Kheili vaghte ke azat khabari nist*," said Max Barroso.

"I would have been happier," said Yasaman, "never to see you again."

Max stepped to the side and motioned her up. Her hands were bleeding. Jagged pebbles stuck to the blood. Glancing at the taxi's open door, Yasaman remembered her purse. The phone given her by the FBI was inside. She took a step, reaching for the door.

"You don't need a thing," said Max. He motioned her back with the gun barrel.

"Bizhan has sent me," she said. "Bizhan Al-Kabir. His message is on my phone."

"You think me a fool? I know not to look at a screen."

Yasaman's heart sank. Without the phone, she had only herself to rely on, her words and her lies. She had no hope of persuading Max to do anything without al-zban ghraza. Only . . . was he the person she was meant to convince?

She asked, "Shall we speak out here, then?"

"What?"

"I will give you the message. Then I will leave. I will have to walk. I trust you can clean up this mess?"

"Don't be stupid," said Max. "I'm here to do a job. The man you want is in the house."

Her emotions fluctuated from a thrill almost as hopeful as her fear had been dire, giving her confidence. "Of course. Forgive me. You're playing your accustomed role. Well, he will want to see my credentials."

She held her breath, knowing it was her only play. If Max refused the bait, she had nothing more to say.

He stepped back, glaring. "Go on."

She took a silent deep breath to restraint her instinct to cheer with relief. As she scooped the purse from the taxi, she whispered to the murdered driver, "I'm sorry."

With the purse under her arm, she preceded Max along a curved path to the house. Two steps admitted her to a porch with a roof directly under the lighted window.

"Please, may I wash off the blood and pebbles?" she inquired of Max, displaying her bloody palms.

Max grunted his approval and pointed to the restroom. "I'll find something you can use as a bandage." The chandelier in the bathroom where she went to wash her hands was hung with thick, octagonal crystals glimmering through a coating of dust. Her contact had clearly not brought a cleaning staff to the island house. He was making a special effort to meet her, which would have been more encouraging if he hadn't chosen Max Barroso as a bodyguard. Callous disregard for life was not a trait she wanted in proximity to the man whose sympathy she hoped to kindle.

Max was standing outside the bathroom when she came out. He held in his hand a brightly colored kitchen towel, not far from new. When he held the towel out, she hesitated, thinking it rude to spoil good linen.

Max made a noise in his throat. "He can afford it." Taking the towel in both hands, he tore it in two. He dropped each wadded half onto her bleeding palms.

With her fists wrapped like a boxer's, Yasaman mounted the stairs. At the top, she found herself facing an open space occupied by a narrow cabinet. To the right of the cabinet was a hall with two doors, one each to the left and right. While she had been in the bathroom, Max had deposited his rifle somewhere. He now covered her with a pistol. Waving it irritably, he indicated she should go down the hall.

"Which door?" said Yasaman.

"I'm here," said a man behind the door on her right. He spoke in English, and even in his curt phrase, she was able to detect a Nordic accent.

She opened the door in response to Max's gesture. The speaker sat in an armchair, looking out a window that had been pushed up to give him an unobstructed view of the parking lot. A cool, salty breeze was wafting through the window. With no vents and no fire in the room, and only a Tiffany lamp, which provided little heat, the speaker had covered himself with a blanket to ward off the chill.

"Welcome," he said.

Between his face and his accent, she knew him at once. He was the outspoken technologist she had seen interviewed, the adventurous billionaire who had supposedly survived the collapse of the Chicago Board of Trade. Some sleight of hand had been employed there, no doubt. She remembered seeing Lars Aaugstad on her lost phone's screen, while she waited for Bilel to arrange their passage out of Iran.

How strange to recall her initial impression. She had enjoyed Aaugstad's outspokenness and been attracted to his energy. When, later, he had defended the dangerous depiction of Muhammad in his children's movie, she'd felt sick to her stomach; he was part of the conspiracy behind the terrorist acts. He was head of the Godhead.

Max prodded Yasaman with the gun. Her host rose, draping his blanket over the chair.

"Gently, Max," said Aaugstad. "Don't mistreat the good doctor."

Swallowing the abuse she would have liked to heap on him, Yasaman extended a toweled hand. Instead of shaking it, Aaugstad turned it lightly, examining the two sides.

"I saw you fall. Accept my apology on behalf of my associate." Waving her to a chair, he said, "Max, you may go."

Max rested his darting eyes on Yasaman for an instant. "I'll be outside," he said as he shut the door.

Yasaman sat with her purse on her lap. "He is a dangerous man."

Aaugstad shrugged. "All men are dangerous. Are you cold?"

"You may certainly leave the window, if you prefer."

Smiling, Aaugstad seated himself. He wrapped up in the blanket, evidently giving no further thought to her comfort. "It is good to feel the cold, I think, if one has a remedy at hand."

The blouse Yasaman had changed into before boarding the plane was thin, and she had left her jacket in the taxi. Fighting the urge to shiver, she returned Aaugstad's smile.

"I feel I know you," he said. "Bizhan is an excellent friend. He has sung your praises often. Max, too, has told me of your time together. How wonderful to finally meet you. I understand from your summons, you have some information to offer. Something touching the Third Cycle?"

"Very much so."

"Tell me, why is your information relevant? Some weeks ago, you fled our representative. Am I to believe you have gained knowledge, since then, which convinced you to support the cause?"

It was a test. Farbod had said it would come. The message he had sent in Bizhan's name first told the tale of Yasaman's conditioning, the perfect control it promised, then detailed Bizhan's betrayal, interwoven with the protolanguage symbology. Yasaman was expected to rationalize her mental shift, confidently asserting it had been made of her free will.

"I did gain knowledge, which I owe to a new technique Bizhan theorized and Dr. Namdar and I implemented and tested. I admit, I worked at first in a state of skepticism. Then, I learned what the Godhead intends. I learned what the cycles will accomplish. If I had known the wonderful shape you meant to give to the world, I would not have fled. I must admit, I have admired you, personally, for some time. I am pleased to be able to make common cause."

"I'm flattered. Please, call me Lars. What is the 'wonderful shape' we mean to give?"

Yasaman frowned, arching forward, tucking her forearms under her breasts and lifting. Aaugstad's attention was fully engaged. He shrugged out of the blanket and shifted forward in his chair, lips compressed. Outside the window, a subtle pink hue showed the sun was rising on the other side of the house.

"You intend for sovereign nations—nations with borders that are more than lines on a map—to be empowered to build their economies and their cultures upon the distinctive qualities of their people. You understand a nation that opens its borders subsumes the identity of its natural citizens. In the natural world, organisms evolve by opposing their neighbors, not by taking them in. Species benefit each other without intermingling." She let her voice become breathless with feigned passion. "These plans, Lars, they will restore Iran and nations like it, who have long been under the thumb of more powerful and more wealthy adversaries, to the sovereignty that should be theirs."

Aaugstad's eyes dilated, as though he'd been stung by electric shock. He was practically trembling with excitement as he leaned toward Yasaman. He was a zealot, as Farbod had said. The women of mother's kenesa had not looked so ecstatic when the rabbi read the Torah.

"Yes," he whispered. "Bizhan has taught you well."

They had come, at last, to the crucible. Either Aaugstad would melt at the argument she introduced, or the plan to stop the Godhead would go up in flames. Yasaman leaned closer to him, until they were virtually nose-to-nose. She drew his gaze and held it.

"When I had come to believe as I now do," she said, her voice low, "Bizhan shared something with me and Farbod. His secret jihad."

Aaugstad frowned. "Secret jihad? What are you talking about?"

"Bizhan saw a pattern in the Red Line events. He realized you were sheltering the economic interests and assets of your cohort within the Godhead."

Aaugstad tilted his head to one side, his expression wry. "Yes? And so?"

"It was a pattern he felt betrayed his own interests. Using this new technique, Bizhan has altered the content of the messaging for the Third Cycle. When the cycle begins, the entire world will burn, not just the parts of it you are willing to sacrifice."

She sat back suddenly, leaving him to stare at empty air. She let the revelation lie for a moment, then said, "The method surpasses expectation. Perfect control over a subject can be achieved in minutes, permanent transformation in under an hour. One need only compose a clear statement of ideas, and transmission from eyes to brain is simple, effective, and irresistible. Bizhan has encoded it in his software as shades of emotion in the language of instinct, and it is calculated to cause universal, random, and wanton devastation. He meant to destroy you."

He caught the past tense, and looked up at her, his already pale complexion ghostly white. "Meant?"

She lobbed her grenade. "Bizhan is dead. I killed him."

"You?"

"I shot him. Twice. Once in the heart and once in the stomach. If you doubt me, try to reach him, but Lars, there is little time. Can you stop the Third Cycle from here?"

She rose and he stood with her, meeting her gaze again.

"No, it must be stopped from our research facility. If what you say is true . . ."

"It is, Lars. Bizhan has betrayed you." She leaned hard on the word "betrayed," tilling the soil for Farbod's video.

"Do you have proof?"

"I have a message on my phone, from Farbod Namdar. He understands Bizhan's betrayal even better than I."

"Your phone?" His eyes narrowed with suspicion. "Why did Dr. Namdar not come here himself?"

"You'll understand when you see how he made this video from a hospital bed." She let her anger show. "Farbod was injured during our . . . mutiny." She glanced down at her purse. "Will you see it?"

Aaugstad jerked his head at the side table between their chairs. "Empty your purse."

She did, carefully picking the phone out of the pile of contents and waking it. She queued the video and held the phone out to Aaugstad. He lifted a hand to take it, then hesitated.

Dear God, what would she do if he simply refused to believe her? She kept her expression solemn, even angry, showing none of the raw fear threatening to close her throat.

"You realize," said Aaugstad, "I am resistant to Bizhan's . . . methods."

"Bizhan's methods are irrelevant. You need to hear Farbod's words."

Holding the phone for them both to see the image of the frail old man sitting in his hospital bed amid myriad snaking IV tubes and blinking monitors, Yasaman moved to stand next to Aaugstad, pressing herself close to his side. She felt his bicep tense beneath the weave of his sweater. He took the phone gingerly from her hand, his lips pursed wryly.

"Surely, you are not afraid of what Farbod might say?" she prompted him. "He will verify what I've said. Please, Lars. The stakes are so very high. If the Third Cycle plays out as Bizhan intended, it will ruin you. It will ruin us all."

"This was made on your phone?"

"Yes. I recorded it myself." She didn't mention she'd also edited it herself.

He looked down into her upturned face in an attempt to read her eyes. "And how do I know you have not doctored the recording?" Aaugstad eyed her with deep suspicion. "You are clever and infinitely resourceful, Dr. Karami. I am sure you wouldn't find it too taxing to edit such a recording to have it say precisely what you want it to say."

Yasaman forced herself to remain relaxed; was it possible the man was reading her mind or that he saw duplicity reflecting in her eyes? "I suppose I could have," Yasaman bluffed; leaning in a little closer under the pretext of looking at the still image on her phone's screen, she felt the heat of Aaugstad's body, the quickness of his breathing. "All I can do is assure you I have not," she lied. "It is in your best interests, and those of the Third Cycle, to trust me, Lars."

Aaugstad screwed up his face as if in pain. Then, with a long exhale, he pressed the Play button on Yasaman's phone.

Farbod began to speak. He spoke briefly about the efficacy of their new—mostly fictitious—methodology, then reiterated what he'd told the FBI agents.

As Aaugstad watched Farbod, Yasaman watched Aaugstad; she noted the moments in which the language of instinct registered with him subliminally: Here, a quick breath. There, a widening of the eyes, a flushing of the cheeks, a quiver at the corner of his mouth.

When Farbod condemned Bizhan's treachery for the third time, Aaugstad cried out. "My God, it's true! That Persian son of a bitch has betrayed me!" He turned to Yasaman, his expression thunderous. "We must abort the Third Cycle! We must—"

The door banged open.

Max, who had clearly been listening in on their conversation, burst in. He hesitated but a split second to take in the situation—then aimed the pistol and fired. Aaugstad dropped as if his legs had been deboned; blood arced out from the ragged holes in his neck.

Yasaman spun away from the gruesome sight, seeking some shelter, but before she could find any, she felt a searing pain slice along her hip. She bit down on the pain, let it galvanize her. She leapt for the open window as one who expects to fly, her outstretched hands bursting the screen from its mounts. She tumbled out onto the roof of the porch, skinning her elbows and shredding her blouse as she skidded over the shingles. She rolled sideways, swung her boots over the gutter, and plunged to the dead grass of Aaugstad's lawn, grunting as she tucked into a roll. By a miracle, her ankles survived the fall.

She ran for the taxi. The driver's door came open seconds before Max emerged onto the porch. The driver was still buckled in his seat. Yasaman didn't have time to drag him out, so she straddled his lap and turned the key. When she punched the gas, the car roared but didn't budge. A shot through the shattered windshield exploded the driver's headrest. Thankfully, his head had flopped to one side. Yasaman sat up, put the car in gear, and stomped on the accelerator. Gravel flew as she spun the steering wheel. A bullet ricocheted off the hood.

She drove with her head down and the door open, sitting half in and half out of the dead man's lap. With grim determination, she steered directly into the gunfire. Something man sized and wrapped in black bounced off the hood of the car with a horrible thud of flesh on metal, then rolled off the driver's side. Yasaman spun the steering wheel and floored the accelerator. Gravel flew as the taxi sped away.

She stopped some distance down the road, only long enough to push the poor taxi driver into the passenger seat. Then, tears all but blinding her and the pain in her hip tearing at her, she drove north with the rising sun off to her right.

Our research facility, he'd said. A Stadion research facility. She prayed that among the effects the FBI would find at Aaugstad's seaside retreat, they would discover the facility's exact location.

34—Zero Hour

The strike team had barely passed the front desk before the first shots were fired. Mitch loped along beside Noreen Wells, stiflingly hot in the body armor and chilled to his core at the same time. Noreen flattened her back to a wall. He did the same. While she listened to a report from the team leader, he checked his FBI-issued weapon, ensuring the safety of the high-caliber pistol was off.

"How's the leg?"

Mitch blinked at her. "Huh? Fine." The brace he had been fitted with was a huge improvement on the cane. It was motorized to do some of the walking for him. Though his hip still burned, it didn't slow him down.

"Good to hear it. Going in three . . . two . . . *one*!"

They jogged around the corner, Wells leading, Mitch covering her back. A man in business casual ducked out from a cubicle, wielding an MP5 rifle. Mitch put him down with two pulls of the trigger. He didn't think about what he was doing, he only pointed and shot. The firefight wasn't what he wanted. He wanted millions of casualties even less.

Wells skirted the cubicles, gunning down hostiles on the way. The team was moving efficiently, clearing corridor after corridor, but there were too many desks and portable divisions to flush every enemy out.

How many of these people were true believers? Mitch didn't want to know. He wanted to believe their instincts were at fault, that the rottenness driving them to terrorism went to the core. As he shot a woman who came at him with a machete-sized weapon they called a zombie-killer, he prayed it was true. Not that it mattered. He was there to save millions more lives than he could take. He made up his mind to do his job and ask God for mercy later.

They had reached an isolated corridor where the strike team leader, a woman named Gant, and Conway, the demolition expert, were setting charges around a heavy steel door. At Conway's signal, Gant waved everyone away. While Wells and Mitch ran, Gant jogged, and Conway backed up and crouched down. Following another three count, the putty around the door blew with a thunderous *whomp*. Gant checked on Conway, then called on her headset for a battering ram.

While the ram did its work, Mitch and Noreen had a minute to breathe. They didn't waste breath talking, but Wells let Mitch make eye contact. Moving his lips without making a sound, Mitch said, "Parker." Silently, she nodded and answered. *Parker. Trent. Val.*

The mangled door broke away from its frame. The strike team rushed through. Wells leapt through the door, then turned to give Mitch a hand. Shots, smoke, and shouted orders filled the room. Mitch was sure he was about to flash back to the Senator, but he stayed in the moment, kneeling to pop shots at the new wave of defenders, who flooded in through a side door. The newcomers were in body armor as sophisticated as the strike team's own. The first part of the fight had been easy, and it was over.

The room they were in was long and straight and filled with screens, just as the floor plans and elevations they had studied indicated. Screens hung on the walls and from the ceiling. Screens sat clustered on the two parallel lines of desks flanking the room. Some screens stood on stalks in the open. With so many bullets flying, it was impossible not to bust a few screens, shattering plastic and spewing sparks. Mitch was faced with a fresh dilemma. How could he defend himself without destroying every piece of technology in sight?

The strike team had struck hard and fast. Meanwhile, the best minds in cyber defense had been working to assure no signal escaped the Stadion Remote Research Station to cause another terrorist facility to take over as Third Cycle broadcast command. The files seized from Aaugstad's personal laptop and Stadion's Silicon Valley HQ had gone into detail about failover procedures, which included the failsafe protocols. So far, it seemed, the government brainiacs had managed to keep the strike force invasion a secret. If they were interpreting the secret instructions correctly, if they stopped the broadcast there, they would stop it everywhere.

All they could do at that point was hope their assumptions were correct and they were not on the receiving end of some heinous double bluff.

An armored gunman got a bead on Wells. Mitch shot him in the arm a second too late. She twisted to the side as a bullet thudded against her vest. It didn't pierce through, but it did wind her. Bracing against a wall, she told Mitch to give her a minute.

"I'm right here," he said.

"No. Don't wait for me. Go."

Ahead, a strike team member was waving. Over the headset, Gant said, "We've breached the server room. Package team, you're up!"

There were exactly two members of the package team. Checking the strike team had the hostiles pinned down, Mitch left the other member and ran to the waving officer. Each man held the other's elbow as they dashed behind the rightmost line of desks. Overhead, rifle blasts blew divots in the concrete. A screen exploded to shards as Mitch ran by, narrowly escaping small pieces of plastic peppered into his body.

He passed through a glass door into a cold, narrow room filled with vertical server racks. Gant was standing by a terminal.

"You're alone?"

"Wells is stunned. Better send somebody." As she gave the order, Mitch unzipped a pouch. Inside was the thumb drive Wells had prepared for the high-stakes hack. He hunted for a suitable dock.

The terminal was built into a cabinet with no visible means of making a physical connection, but it featured a corded keyboard fixed to a tray. Mitch followed the cord of the keyboard to a rectangular dock positioned in the back of the cabinet. There he found several spare USB sockets. He picked one and inserted the thumb drive. When he returned to the front of the cabinet, the terminal screen was flickering. Stark, white text scrolled against the black background, streaming multitudes of characters far too quickly for anyone to read.

The screen flickered again, and the black of the terminal display was replaced by dark green. A gray box appeared, hovering in front of the background. It dissolved into a login screen complete with small, rectangular boxes for the username and password.

Mitch typed *BizMoYa* as the username. Farbod had explained his given name was Mohammad, as was the case with many of his faith. The username was a mash-up of names of the three former colleagues. As soon as Mitch hit

Tab to advance to the password field, the text of the login changed from English to what he assumed was Persian. That was good. The terminal recognized the username and was prepared to be helpful.

The password was random nonsense gleaned from Aaugstad's files using FBI cracking software. Mitch unfolded a paper from the pouch in his Kevlar vest and typed. The login box bounced. The password line turned red, and a red triangle containing an exclamation point appeared above it. Below, a message warned of a password error.

Damn.

He tried again. Again, the bounce. A "3" appeared at the end of the message. Did it mean three tries to get the password right? If that was the case, he couldn't afford to waste even one.

Noreen Wells arrived on the arm of a fellow agent. Both were panting, like they'd dodged bullets all the way.

"No good," said Mitch, knowing the agent's intolerance for small talk. "Yes on user, no on pass."

"Caps lock?" said Wells.

Mitch turned his attention back to the terminal. There was no light to indicate if caps lock mode was on or off. He struck the key, typing the password again carefully, making sure it was accurate.

"Still no. There's a countdown. It just ticked from 3 to 2."

Wells had her phone in hand and was tapping at the screen before Mitch could make the suggestion. A moment later, her father's grim face appeared onscreen. "Don't talk, Dad. Listen," Wells said. "We're in. But the password didn't work. We need another. Looks like we have two chances—no take backs. Can you get with Yaz and Dr. Namdar and see what they've got?"

"Yes, but you need to listen to *me* now." Wells's father's tinny voice replied through her phone. "According to some texts we just decrypted, Yaz's old flame arranged for the cycle to go up ahead of schedule. I suspect it was an extra layer of safety."

"How far ahead of schedule?"

"Ten minutes." His sigh was audible and heavy. "It's as if he expected a last-minute attempt to shut it down."

Mitch felt a chill trying to settle in his chest, but he couldn't say he was surprised. Bizhan might have been evil, but he sure as hell wasn't stupid. He must have figured there was some chance Aaugstad or others in the Godhead would tumble to his plan and try to stop it. Mitch glanced at the phone. It was 7:57. The Third Cycle had already begun.

"Give us to Yaz." Mitch struggled to keep his voice steady. "We need her and Farbod to think what else Bizhan might use for a password. We're underground, behind locked doors and armed security. He wouldn't have bothered making it too cryptic. What might be meaningful to him?"

Seconds later, Solomon's phone was in Yaz's hands. The deputy director had apparently been in her hospital room when Wells called.

"I have an idea, but how do we know Bizhan has not set a trap? If we use his login, we may lose all hope of stopping the broadcast."

"We can't know, only try," said Wells. "If we can't stop it this way, we'll have to blow the whole facility and hope for the best."

Mitch shook his head. "That won't silence the repeaters. Please, Yaz. I trust you."

"Very well," she said. "Try this . . ."

35—Presence and Light

At 7:53 on the night of Wednesday, March 25th, the shotgun was in Darren's hands. He stood at the top of the basement stairs wondering why he was there and why he had taken the weapon from its place behind the couch.

He saw blood on the shotgun. The dried stains from Rod's last heartbeat were there, but the blood was fresh and wet, from a fine spray. What remained of the VR headset was bloody too. Darren was wearing the headset. The visor had been torn off and the wires ripped out. Red droplets were collecting on the rim of hard plastic above where the visor had been.

Darren looked at his clothes. Blood stained his shirt, the front of his jeans, and the Timberlands he had put on after showing Jer how to perfectly apply a polish-and-alcohol shine. His last clear memory was of Jer admiring his reflection. That had been hours ago. From the hallway, Darren saw through to the living room windows. Outside was dark. The street lamps were lit. What had Darren been doing from afternoon to night?

Watching the *SteadyStream Preview*, of course. Just like yesterday and the three days before that. Ever since Ness had lured him back to the basement, he had been putting in at least eight hours watching *SteadyStream*, with only meals and games with Jer to break it up. And why not? It was the best thing ever, as Uncle Lars, Spex's buddy, liked to say. Nothing could be better until the *SteadyStream* service itself premiered.

It was happening tonight, wasn't it? Panic ripped through Darren as the thought occurred to him he might miss the first minute, when Spex was supposed to get his voice back. Forgetting the busted headset, the blood, and the gun, Darren thought about running downstairs. All was quiet down there. Before he could run down to Ness and Jer to ask why, something tugged his leg.

Darren spun. There was something on the staircase, something small or oddly twisted. Darkness made it a shadow among shadows, a humped, fleshy heap lurching his way, extending a tentacle. Or was that a hand?

"Da—" said the heap, an instant before the shotgun answered with a boom. As the heap flew backward, the muzzle flash gave Darren an impression of its shape. It had arms and a head. Had it been saying his name? The mumble might have been Darren, or it might have been . . .

Darren had the sudden urge to run outside. In the blink of an eye Darren was out the door, running from the row house and whatever lay within. He pounded his polished boots on the pavement and held the shotgun across his chest. He traveled a whole block without seeing anyone, though he heard plenty of shots, shouts, and screams. As he was stepping on the curb of the next block, a crash and screaming sounded overhead. Two women, one strangling the other, plummeted from a fifth-story window. They fell so fast, the glass was still twinkling as one woman hit the lamp light; the upper woman pounded her body like a hammer.

The upper woman didn't die instantly. A snapped bone from the lower woman's leg stabbed up through her abdomen. She lay moaning as Darren crept up. He aimed the shotgun at her head and heard it boom. How did it keep happening? Darren didn't remember pulling the trigger. He didn't remember working the pump to clear the chamber and loading shells from his pocket into the breech. He didn't even remember pocketing the shells.

He turned at the corner and ran another half block. A middle-aged man stood framed in a doorway, shirtless. With the shirt, he was swabbing clean a knife in his hand. The shotgun swung at him and boomed. The man was knocked back but not killed. He lunged at Darren, slashing with the knife. The shotgun boomed again, and then it ran out of shells. Darren's hands broke open the action. He watched as his fingers loaded shells as easily as a military man who practiced the skill every day. The knife caught his forearm before the shotgun boomed again.

The man fell. He looked dead, but just to be sure, the shotgun rested its barrel in the gap between the two halves of his clavicle. Boom.

There were sirens, flashing lights. Driven by instinct, Darren McGann leapt over the man's body, then his head, into the man's row house. The layout was unfamiliar. There were no basements on the block. In the living room, a woman sat in an armchair watching TV. Or not watching. Blood from a number of cuts had congealed on her chest. On the flat screen in front of her sightless eyes, a countdown ticked from 1:53 to 1:52 to 1:51. There were less than two minutes until the *SteadyStream* premiere. Darren could hardly believe the great day had finally come. He wanted to sit, but the armchair was the only piece of furniture facing the TV. The sofa was for watching the window. Darren sank to his knees in front of the flat screen. Laying the shotgun on the carpet, he lifted the broken headset from his head.

More than anything in life, he wanted to be here, watching the *SteadyStream* premiere. Earlier that evening, just a few minutes ago, in fact, he had something else he had to do, but he couldn't think what. The first live-action intro, the first words spoken by Spex, and the first surprise show from Stadion were his reasons for living. In the back of his mind, he saw images of Ness and Jer and the improvements he had made to the house. He remembered the urge to dig in, to shelter at home after the horrors he had witnessed. Those impulses seemed trivial compared to the wonderful gift he was about to receive.

On screen, Uncle Lars appeared. "Can you believe it, friends and cousins, zips and buttons? Let's count down to the end together. Five! Four!"

A police officer entered the house, holding a gun and shouting to see Darren's hands. Darren saw him and heard him but didn't budge.

"Three! Two!"

The cop said, "Hands!" Darren felt for the shotgun.

"One!" screamed Uncle Lars.

A blare of trumpets, a bang, and a boom sounded from the television, followed by at least one flash. Darren lay on his side. The cop was on the floor, toes pointed up. The trumpets stopped blaring on the TV, and the brilliant owl eyes of the great, praiseworthy Spex swelled huge in close-up.

They were wonderful, those eyes. Full of wisdom and beauty surpassing all earthly splendor. Darren was happy to do their bidding. He waited expectantly for the command from Spex.

"Happy!" said the beautiful, animated being. It flew in circles, like a tornado. "So happy to say—"

A louder bang than the previous one shook the room. The screen cracked and went silent. Darren surged to one knee. He expected the shotgun to aim at the second cop, the cop who had shot the TV. For some reason, it failed. Glancing down and to his side, Darren saw his shoulder was a bloody mess. He wasn't holding the shotgun. He couldn't hold it. The first cop's bullet had torn muscle and shredded bone.

He looked at the second cop, who was a woman. Young, tall, and good-looking, she reminded him, against his will, of Ness.

"Praise Spex," said somebody. It sounded like Darren, and he did agree. Spex was wonderful, perfect. It did deserve praise. Many were unworthy of Spex. Though not as many now. Thinking back on what the shotgun had done, Darren felt an impulse to be proud, to be happy, as Spex had said.

He couldn't bring himself to follow the impulse. He had done no work for Spex, only carried the shotgun in his name. He had not raised the weapon. He had not aimed or fired the instrument of wrath. What the shotgun had done to the people in the basement, and to the woman and the man and the cop, it had done on its own, working the will of Spex. Darren had been a vessel and he was poured out, emptied. The divine face of Spex had vanished. The divine voice was silent. The instincts driving Darren were nearly spent.

He had one instinct left. He focused on the cop aiming a gun at his heart as she glanced fitfully at the body of her partner. She was shouting something. Darren couldn't hear it anymore. He lunged. She shot him, calling forth bullets by pressure from her finger, driven by her own will.

Darren lay on his back in the unfamiliar house. The ceiling was popcorn plaster, not smooth like his ceiling at home. The slopes and peaks reminded Darren of a mountain range. He pictured climbing mountains on a quest to meet Spex in the Library of Burning Souls, where the books are alive and flutter from shelf to shelf, pausing only to drop into the hands of readers. Jer had discovered the way to the library in his last VR play session, but he had been too busy watching *Preview* and *Preview Re-View* to enter. What a shame, what a shame.

Darren hoped Spex would welcome Jer to the library. He hoped Ness and Jer would be there when he arrived. How badly would his failure as a husband and a father count against him? Only Spex could judge. When he got to the library, he would sit down with Jer on his knee and finally finish *The Hobbit*. They had read through the end of the troll scene, in which a kid-sized adventurer triumphs over monstrous bullies. Jer had loved it, but Darren had set aside the book when he got the idea to show Jer the cartoon classics and never taken it up again. Well, there would be time. An eternity in the Owlish Presence, watched over by the Light of Lars.

The edges of the ceiling had gone dark. It looked like it was on the verge of winking out, like his phone did before he cracked it, and like TVs used to when Darren was little. And Ness would have said, "You're little now." And Darren would have said, "Small and mighty." And Jer would have jumped into their waiting arms and giggled as his mom and dad let him wrestle them down to the ground.

If Darren had been able to see how the moment played out in the rest of the world, he would have seen loving families watching the *Spex SteadyStream* take up arms against one another. Fathers shot sons, and mothers attacked daughters. Siblings gouged each other's eyes out. The more hours of viewing the family had spent, the more intense their violence. Screams of terrified victims filled the streets.

At Target, the few customers happily oblivious to Spex roamed the aisles. But several teen workers left their checkout stations at 7:57, hunting down humans like heat-seeking missiles. One grabbed a pack of kitchen cutlery from the housewares; another seized a glass olive oil bottle. Shirley was happy to see an employee approaching, as she was having trouble finding her favorite hair coloring to rid her of those pesky white roots. She smiled and gave eye contact to the employee to beckon him over. "Dear, I was hoping—" she began. Then she screamed as the employee raised the glass bottle, shouted something that sounded a lot like, "Praise Spex!" and slammed it into her skull.

Marvin, shopping two aisles away, left his cart behind in his haste to assist the screaming woman. He never saw the teen employee who accosted him from behind. Marvin fell to the ground, a knife in his chest, blood gurgling from his mouth.

An employee at a law firm in a high-rise in Kansas City had chosen to watch the broadcast by himself while working late. The Spex show was so intoxicating; he didn't realize he'd done no work. Instead, he felt more and more energized as the program continued. At 7:51, he felt wound up, angry. Why did he have to work late? Why had Susan gotten the promotion and not him? He kept watching the broadcast, almost physically unable to turn away. His anger turned to rage. A desire to set the record straight, to hurt those who had hurt him flooded his veins. At 7:57, his fury reached the breaking point. He needed to hurt someone. He grabbed a vase sitting on a side desk, dumped its contents on the floor, and took off down the hallway. He'd taken only three steps when someone shrieked and leaped on his back. He grasped at a piece of rope the attacker was tightening around his throat. Smelling perfume, he sensed his attacker was a woman. Susan! He recognized the scent. He was much stronger than her, but she knew exactly where to place the rope and how to tighten it. He fell to the ground as she yanked the rope tighter. He kicked and flailed, using up his oxygen supply in the process. His world went black.

At Buffalo Wild Wings in suburban Cleveland, infants screeched while parents and older siblings sat transfixed by the communal TV screens, mindlessly chomping on their wings. At 7:57, a busy server noticed a change in the atmosphere. Arguments broke out between tables. Patrons rose as the arguments turned physical. One guy secretly packing heat shot three people at his own table. The server dashed to the back room to dial 9-1-1, locking the door behind him.

Alyssa in Dallas sat quietly reading a book to her toddler while her newborn slept in her lap. At 7:54, her husband ran down the hallway from the home office where he'd been working. "Hon! Did you hear that? It sounded like a gunshot. Get down!" He raced over to lock all the doors, pull the blinds on the windows, and turn off the lights. The young family huddled together, keeping as silent as possible.

The Golden State Warriors led the Utah Jazz 42–35. At 7:55, Johnson went for the three-point shot to further extend the lead. As he ran back to the other end, he was knocked cold by a punch from an unruly Jazz fan who had run onto the court. Pandemonium erupted as fans in the audience picked fights with those sitting near them; multiple fistfights broke out. Managers and coaches reacted quickly by ushering players into the locker room, locking the door behind them.

CNN had the story by 8:07, reporting on widespread violence with an unknown cause.

36—United We Stand

"Verethragna," Yasaman said. She lay back against the reclining head of her hospital bed clutching Director Solomon's phone as if it were a lifeline. She saw everything Noreen Wells could see in the faraway Stadion facility.

"You'll have to spell that for me," said Mitch. He was standing before a computer terminal in the facility's server room. On the screen in front of Mitch was a prompt demanding a password.

There were several possible spellings of the last word Yasaman's late fiancé had whispered to her. From what she knew of his studies, Yasaman chose the most likely, a variant used by the Persian cultists who worshiped vengeance incarnate. Slowly, she dictated the spelling to Mitch, careful not to make a mistake, secretly fearing they were doing the wrong thing. Ending the violence of the Third Cycle was worth the risk, but could she trust Bizhan had honestly meant to help her in the end?

He had claimed to love her, and then betrayed her for financial gain. He had wanted her aid in committing another act of betrayal, one resulting in indiscriminate mass murder. His idea of love was evidently very different from her own. Initially, Yasaman had thought him unlike the other men who had sought to possess her, to conquer her feminine power with their masculine will. Indeed, he *had* been different. She had defended herself from the others, throwing up barriers against them. Bizhan had deceived her as only a lover could.

When she had knelt beside him, holding his hand as they waited for his organs to fail, she had remembered the man she had loved and whose heart she thought she knew. But did she ever? Had that man ever existed?

She imagined nothing more terrible than the Third Cycle, but it certainly didn't mean something worse might not exist. Bizhan could have prepared contingencies, as might others in his motley organization. With Bizhan's cooperation, they may have disguised a destruct code as a kill switch in the broadcast control. With his dying breath, Bizhan may well have been manipulating her into letting loose unimaginable carnage.

Verethragna.

Had he meant it as an apology, or a trap? Doubt made Yasaman pause her recital a few letters from the end.

"Is that it?" said Mitch.

"No," said Yasaman. "Mitch, you were there when Bizhan died. Am I a fool to think he was offering aid rather than threatening death?"

Wells chipped in, "We have to—"

Mitch said, "You're not a fool, Yaz. Come on. Whatever happens, we'll get through it together. We'll fix this, whatever it takes."

They were already out of time. "The last letters," Yasaman said, and then spelled them out.

Mitch typed them and pressed Enter.

"Shit."

That one simple word signified so much.

"Perhaps you mistyped?" Wells's attempt to help fell on stony ground.

On the tiny screen, Yasaman saw Mitch staring in disbelief at the tiny warning triangle; adjacent to it, the "2" had clicked over to an ominously blinking "1." "Try it again, Mitch." She suggested.

Mitch's eyes loomed large on the phone's screen as they stared out at Yasaman; she saw a hint of craziness in the man's desperation. "We have one more try, Yaz," he growled. "Just. Fucking. *One*."

"There's no time for this, Mitch," Yasaman heard Wells say in the background. "You have to try."

"And do what?" The despair in the cop's voice came through to Yasaman loud and clear. "Trigger the rest of the Third Cycle and be the guy who destroyed humanity?"

"It's going to happen if you don't try," Wells's sage voice echoed in the background.

Yasaman felt the poor man's agony. If ever there was a case of *damned if you do, damned if you don't*, this was surely it. "She's right, Mitch," she told him. "Even if you try and fail, it's all going to happen anyway. At least this way, you will know you tried."

"Fuck it," Mitch snarled as he turned the phone back to the screen, where Yasaman could see the password box.

"You got this, Mitch." Yasaman knew it sounded corny as hell, but she felt it better than saying nothing. By the way Mitch stabbed at the keyboard, she could see the weight of the world had rested upon his fragile shoulders and was slowly, but surely, crushing him.

After what felt like an age, Yasaman was staring at eleven tiny white asterisks in the password box. "Just hit the damn Enter key already," she muttered beneath her breath.

On the cell phone's screen, Yasaman could see the keyboard. Over it, Mitch's hand hovered with his index finger pointed at the Enter key; it was as if some invisible—yet infinitely powerful—force was holding his arm back. Yasaman's heart pounded hard in her chest, and there was the unmistakable acid tang of bile stinging the back of her throat; the fate of the civilized world literally depended upon the push of a small, unassuming computer key.

"God help us all," Mitch grunted and went for the key.

"Wait!"

Mitch's hand pulled away from the keyboard as if the thing had suddenly sprouted teeth and bitten him.

The suddenness of Yasaman's voice had startled even herself. "Try it with an 'e,'" she said.

"Pardon me?" Wells's voice chimed in.

"It makes Verethragna plural if you add an 'e' to the end," she told the invisible Wells. "I think Bizhan would have made the word plural for his password."

"Why the hell would he do that?" Mitch's tone was accusatory. "Was there more than one?"

Yasaman shook her head before realizing Mitch wouldn't be able to see her doing so. "That's the point, Mitch," she told him. "It's Bizhan's final test."

"If the asshole wasn't already dead, I'd kill him," Mitch said, oblivious to the emotional pain it caused Yasaman.

"Are you sure about this, Yaz?" Wells asked.

"As sure as I can be," Yasaman replied with as much self-belief as she could muster. "Bizhan was nothing if not sly, I learned that the hard way. When he whispered Verethragna to you, I believe he reckoned I'd be involved in deciphering it to deactivate the Third Cycle. He wanted the burden of civilization's fall to rest with me."

"Sweet guy." Wells's sardonic tone cut through Yasaman like a hot knife; how in God's name could she have been so naive?

"Here goes, shit or bust," Mitch said and jabbed at the 'e' key, which made a cold, ominous *click*.

"Do it, Mitch," Yasaman prompted, sensing the man's reticence once again.

Then, without hesitation, Mitch hit the enter button; Yasaman heard his sharp intake of breath over the phone and fancied he'd closed his eyes too.

The password prompt disappeared.

The screen fell black.

A screen of Persian text took its place—another layer of Bizhan's betrayal of his masters. Wells passed Mitch the phone and elbowed him out of the way. Yasaman could no longer see the terminal's display. Noreen didn't ask for help reading the text. The files seized from Stadion International told her enough to feel confident.

Yasaman wished she felt the same.

Wells stepped back. "That's it." The screen divided into two columns of black boxes, lines of text scrolling within each. Abruptly, every light in the room Mitch and Noreen were in flickered out. The terminal went dark. Yasaman was left looking at a small screen glowing a dim gray.

"It's done," said Wells. The outline of her face was vaguely visible on Yasaman's phone, being lit only by the phone sending the image. "It's a total blackout here. Hold on."

She turned away. A voice off-screen spoke.

"We're sure?" Wells asked. "Cable and satellites?"

There was an audible "Yes, yes, and yes" before Noreen's shadow returned to the screen. Her next words sounded tired. "It's over. You did it. Red Line Three—the Third Cycle—ended in roughly eight minutes. We have to hope it was soon enough."

Yasaman was too stunned to say anything meaningful. Mitch's voice floated to her through the dimness. "Good work, Yasaman. Thank—"

Mitch's voice was drowned out by the sudden burst of a Klaxon, a brutal, shrieking sound that could only have been a portent of something terrible.

"We gotta get out!" Wells's voice rose above the rhythmic wail of the alarm, which reminded Yasaman so much of the Imam's Call to Prayer back in her hometown.

"What's going on over there?" Yasaman demanded to know.

Mitch's face appeared on her screen, blind panic etched across his face. "Looks like your old lover left us one last surprise, Yaz." He turned the phone around for her to see the computer screen—it was lit up like Times Square at Christmas. "I'm no expert in Persian, or Arabic, or whatever the hell this is supposed to be, but I'd say he built in a self-destruct code for anyone who cracked his password."

"Damn you, Bizhan," Yasaman growled beneath her breath. Of course he'd left one final snub to her and anyone who dared get in the way of the Third Cycle—thinking about it now, she'd have been surprised had he not. "I'm so sorry, Mitch."

"Come on, Mitch!" Wells's voice urged.

"Gotta go, Yaz," Mitch said into the phone. "Wish us luck!"

The first of the explosions cut the phone signal, and Yasaman was left staring into a black, dead screen.

***

There were new lights outside Yasaman's window. Her FBI bodyguard had risen and was looking at them with obvious concern. Yasaman joined him silently in listening as sirens pursued orange flames from downtown Portsmouth, Virginia, southwest to the Great Dismal Swamp. Smoke blanketed the harbor outside the hospital, covering the moon and stars. She craned her neck to watch the billowing clouds, willing them to blow out to sea.

When they got the all clear and were allowed to watch the news, it told tales of a thousand disasters. Across the world, cities and towns were burning. There had been shootings and stabbings, violence of all kinds. Not in movie theaters or other entertainment venues, though—almost exclusively, the war of the Third Cycle had been fought in homes and random public places.

A grief-stricken newscaster with crooked makeup told of finding her husband being bludgeoned with a bat by her teenage son. She had called his name, begged him to stop, and defended herself with a stool when the son came after her. The son and the husband were both in the hospital. The husband was in critical condition, but talking about her son was what shattered the newscaster. Weeping, she was half carried off camera by two of her colleagues.

The man who replaced her wore a button-down shirt but no tie or makeup. Sitting straight as a pole, he smoothed his hair without looking away from the camera. He gave his name and identified himself as the station manager.

"We're lost over here. We don't know what's happening. We don't know what it means or what we should do. We know it's not aimed at any particular subset or group, any party on one side of a dividing line. Whatever has come has come for us all. Black and white. Gay and . . . we are together in this. In what we have done, what has been done to us? We are not broken. We, the People of These United States—"

He choked. As he turned to clear his throat, Yasaman saw the jagged gash where his earlobe had been and ribbons of dried blood where he had been scratched on the side of his neck.

"We stand together, America. Against all enemies, foreign and domestic, we stand."

She flipped through channels and found no more stirring sentiment. The BBC had the most sweeping coverage. It was the least personal and the least emotionally charged of any live English news broadcast, and still the anchors brushed away tears between segments and watched stripped-down fire brigades putting out fires in London, Peterborough, York, and farther afield—Dublin, Paris, Berlin, Moscow, Budapest.

In the US, a former presidential candidate was found dismembered on his lawn. In shadows against the skyline of a burning New York City, a man hung from a noose secured to the arm of a crane. In The Hague, someone had set fire to the seat of the International Court of Justice. The scenes blended together in time.

Yasaman switched off the television and considered asking for a sedative so she could sleep. She decided against it, not because she feared nightmares, but because the FBI had assigned her a personal nurse. She felt guilty taking the woman's time when so many others needed her time and attention.

"Would you please dismiss the nurse?" she asked the bodyguard. He was skeptical but went to check the hall, where the nurse was meant to be sitting.

"She's gone," the bodyguard reported.

"Good for her," said Yasaman.

By dawn, the sky was clearer than Yasaman's conscience. How many fires had they prevented? How many wouldn't have been set if Noreen Wells had been able to call ten minutes earlier? As the clouds of smoke drifted, she hoped she could find it in herself to be as forgiving and warm-hearted as Mitch.

37—The Right Bait

On a tepid, cloudy afternoon, Mitch Wilson swung his ax at a log of dry cedar. The log split. The ax bit deep into the stump he was using as a base. Days of practice had taught him to counterbalance his hip when he split the wood, but the effort exhausted the new muscles he had never had to use before. That was fine. He was getting stronger. These days, he hardly used the brace.

When he had come to the cabin, he'd found a pile of aromatic timber staked under a blue tarp. For the present, his sole ambition in life was to replace the chest-high jumble with a neat, split stack. It didn't much matter how long it was going to take.

His phone rang. He checked, saw Ben's name come up, and answered. "Benny boy."

"Bud, it's a beautiful day in Baltimore. I'm taking my ladies to the waterfront. You want to come down?"

"I'm good here. How are they?"

"Perfect. I mean, schools are still closed so we're all going stir crazy, but the roads are clear, and most of the cleanup's done downtown. Traffic's still slow, but what's new, right? Hey, did you get the pic?"

"Yeah."

Mitch swiped to his texts and brought up the shot of the Martinez coffee table. Resting on it was a Lego model of an old prop plane, the kind a stunt flier would have flown before World War II.

"It's cool, bud. She do that by herself?"

Therese spoke into the phone. "I did, Uncle Mitch."

Ben said, "All I did was open the package."

"Hey, little girl. Great job. I can't wait to see it in person."

"When are you coming, Uncle Mitch?"

"Soon," he said. It wasn't a lie if he didn't know for sure. "I'll get there when I get there, okay? Put some more stuff together to show me. Now go and check on your sister or something. I've got something to say to your dad."

"I miss you, Uncle Mitch."

"Yeah. I miss you too. And Ben . . ."

Ben said, "What?"

"Just that you're a good man, Ben Martinez. You listen real good. You kept those kids away from screens when it counted."

"I'm gonna take the praise because it wasn't easy. There were some nasty withdrawal symptoms your friends at—what did you say they call themselves?"

"The Godhead. No friends of mine."

"Me neither, partner. Hey, seriously, come back soon, will you? We need more like you back here. The force is decimated. I mean that literally. Every tenth officer, man or woman, is gone. Another two-tenths just out of the hospital. The statistics are worse outside the boys and girls in blue. And yet, somehow, seems like a lot of crackhead carjackers made it through. I gotta think they don't watch much TV. We need good cops, Mitch. I was looking into the righteous shooting of yours. The guy with the shotgun, the kid—"

The rumble of an engine drew Mitch's attention to a bright-red pickup climbing the dirt drive to the cabin. The driver wasn't in a hurry. If Mitch had been worried about his safety, he could have fetched the rifle leaning against a tree trunk in the time it took the pickup to pull in range.

"Hold up, partner. I'll have to call you back."

"Make sure you do. Adiós."

"Vaya con Dios, bud."

Mitch picked up the pieces of split log and walked them to his stack. After that, he lifted the tarp and rolled out a new log to chop. The pickup parked. The engine cut off. Noreen Wells got out.

"You ain't scrapped that old bucket yet?" said Mitch.

"It gets me from A to B."

"Sure. Atlanta to Baltimore. One way was enough for me. That's why I flew."

"You flew because Dad comped your ticket."

"How is the old man?"

She gave a shake of the head. They still hadn't found Valerie . . . or all of the remaining members of the Godhead. These were people who knew how to hide. Some of them most likely in plain sight.

Mitch set the new log on the stump. "I was just talking to my partner."

"Must be nice," said Wells.

"What is?"

"Having people who care about you. Friends who want to help you move on."

"Do you want to move on, Wells?"

"I can't. Not yet. And it's Noreen."

Mitch lifted the ax high, wobbling on his way to the crest. With a grunt, he brought the ax down. The wood parted but didn't split. He lifted the ax and the log together and bashed the log against the stump a few times, battering the halves apart.

"What are you here for, Noreen?"

"Two reasons. First, to apologize."

"You had plenty of reasons for treating me like you did."

"Yeah, you're right. I'm not apologizing for that. I'm apologizing for letting you come out here to the woods, all alone, when we could have used you back at the office. There's plenty to sift through. Have you seen the DeLuca Cut? It's eleven hours of subliminal chemistry training. Recipes for explosives and Molotov cocktails. It took a week for the software and our people to flag half the thing. DeLuca came close to a breakdown. He lost his mom on Red End, so he won't quit."

"Good for DeLuca. 'Red End' is sticking?"

"Let's hope it does. Red Line. Red Line Two. When you stop counting, you've done a good day's work."

The sun poked out from behind a white, fluffy cloud, and far along the road came the distinctive glint of sunlight on a windshield. Mitch bristled before he remembered he had no reason to: the war was over, for now at least, and there was no need to be looking over his shoulder so far out in the wilds. Even so, Mitch's sixth sense caught the slightest feeling it may just be more than some random day tripper.

Shrugging it off, Mitch returned to the tarp and told Wells, "Your insincere apology is noted. You didn't let me go anywhere. I left. What's the other thing you wanted?"

Noreen folded her arms. "Your help. What else?"

"Sure it's a good idea? The last time I tried helping, three-and-a-half million people died."

"It would have been worse, if not for you. I was lying about the apology. I want to say I'm sorry for trying to push you off the case. You brought us the video. You got us most of the way to Yaz. It was you and your partner who tied Namdar to Valerie."

"I got Trent killed. Did you forget? Trent and then Neil."

"They died doing their jobs, Mitch. *Our* jobs. We ended Red Line. You and me and Trent and Parker and Namdar and Yaz. We stopped it cold. The Third Cycle still happened, but we shut it down as quickly as anybody could. We did more than anyone else to save lives."

"Maybe. All right. Apology accepted."

"What about my other request?"

Instead of answering, Mitch set up the next log.

Noreen sighed. "We're up against it, Mitch. We can't trust our eyes, now we know what can sneak past in a blink. Dad's putting together a special joint task force. Investigators, law enforcement, and academic types. It took eleven days to do DeLuca's cut because we've got nobody as good as you at picking out al-zban ghraza."

"What about the computers?"

"In another month, maybe they can learn. But can we trust them when they do? The whole tech sector is compromised. Who knows what Stadion or the rest of the Godhead built into the networks? We need people, Mitch. People we trust. We need you for Dad's task force. And I need you to help find Val."

"You'll find her, Noreen. You're the best."

She looked him in the eye. "Sure. But *we* are better."

He didn't know what to say. It was too much, too soon. He couldn't go back to the outside world, where the stink of his failure was on every burnt-out building. Every bloodstain on the sidewalk remained him of a chalk painting done by Ethan's hand. He knew Noreen was right. They hadn't prevented the final attack, but they had kept it short. The death toll was unimaginable, but it could have been much worse.

"I brought you a visitor," said Noreen, turning to look at the truck.

"Are you serious?" There was nobody visible in the passenger seat, or in the back seat of the extended cab. "Not a tall one, obviously." His eyes flicked to the vehicle speeding along the long, straight road toward the cabin; it wasn't often he saw cars go by, let alone bright yellow ones.

"He's about right for his age," Noreen said with a warm smile.

As Wells returned to the pickup, Mitch's heart gave a thump. He saw little hands appear above the tilted back seat, a hatted head resting on Noreen's shoulder as she lifted the boy out. A child a little longer than Noreen's torso clung to her like a bear climbing a tree. She crossed the space between them and turned to show him the sleepy face.

"This is—"

"Justin," said Mitch. "I know." Neil Parker's son was the spitting image of his father.

At the sound of his name, Justin blinked. He looked Mitch over. A bold kid, he didn't look away.

"It's good to meet you, Justin."

Several phrases sprang to mind to follow up. *I knew your dad. He was a hero and a fast friend.* What he said was, "I hear you like fishing."

Justin brightened with interest. "There's a stream over the hill. I bet I could find a pole. What do you say, Noreen?"

"That depends," she said. "Can you promise I'll catch something?"

Mitch sighed. "It's complicated." He studied the burden in her arms. The world the kid was going to grow up in, the challenges he would have to face, were mountainous. If his generation couldn't trust their eyes, if they couldn't trust their instincts or their minds, what was life going to be for them but an endless lonely struggle, chased by fear and smothered by doubt?

"Aunt Ree," said Justin. "I wanna fish."

"It's up to your Uncle Mitch," she said. "Well, Mitch? What is it going to be?"

"You know how to bait a hook," he said. "How about we cast a few lines? Then we'll see."

"Perhaps later." Noreen ruffled the kid's hair and screwed up her eyes against the sunlight as a taxi cab swung into the driveway. "I think Uncle Mitch has company."

As Mitch spun around to see Yasaman exit the cab, his heart quickened. Had she come to tell him her final goodbye?

"No need to wait," Yasaman said to the cab driver and absently gave the car a double tap on the roof.

"Have it your way, lady," the driver grunted and, without further ado, reversed back along the driveway using only his rearview mirror.

"Hello, Mitch." She nodded to Noreen. Yasaman's greeting was cordial as she made her way toward Mitch— one of old friends rather than would-be lovers. Mitch's heart sank a little further.

"Bad timing—we just were planning a fishing trip." Mitch nodded toward Justin, who was still beside himself with excitement at the prospect.

"That sounds fun. You can show me how to bait a hook," Yasaman replied with a smile filled with promise. "And then maybe we could dance together later?"

And then she was in Mitch's arms, her lips pressed against his, her body warm and inviting as she kissed him with a rough, urgent longing—despite the sour faces Justin pulled at them.

Mitch held Yasaman tight, like he never wanted to let her go; her presence in his life would never erase the memories of the family he had lost, but she would certainly help toward his healing and provide him with a future he could finally look forward to.

About the Author

Blake Rudman enjoyed a former, successful career in executive management, building his own companies from the ground up.

Success or not, Blake's heart has always been in the written word, and the myriad ideas he spent much of his spare time jotting down in notebooks, Post-Its, and scraps of paper whenever the inspiration hit him.

Now a breakout author of five noir thriller novels – all to be published in 2023 – Blake's destiny of becoming a writer of some renown is well under way.

When he's not working diligently on his next novel, Blake spends quality time with his family and tropical fish.

Follow Blake's blog at: https://blakerudman.com
Facebook: @BRudmanThriller
Instagram: @BRudmanThriller
Twitter: @BRudmanThriller

For all Blake's books, visit him at:
www.hellboundbookspublishing.com/authorpage_rudman.ht
ml

Blake Rudman Novels from
HellBound Books:
Available in Kindle, paperback, hardcover, and audiobook.

The Gentleman's Choice

"Caught in a whirlwind of adverse publicity following a viewer's death, the streaming show, The Gentleman's Choice becomes the target for a sadistic killer – and it's up to PI Vanessa Young to put a stop to it before more young women are murdered."

A sleazy internet dating show blamed for a viewer's death, a host with a dark, secret past, and a killer with a sadistic grudge…

Someone is kidnapping and murdering previous contestants from the popular streaming show *The Gentleman's Choice* – a strictly-for-adults hybrid of *The Bachelor* and *Love Island*. Private Investigator, Vanessa Young, is hired by a victim's family to infiltrate the show as a contestant to expose and capture the killer.

Vanessa and the show's charismatic star, Cole Gianni, begin to fall romantically for each other, until Vanessa's plan goes terribly awry when they're drugged and taken to a remote location to take part in their captor's own brutal, ultimately fatal, version of *The Gentleman's Choice*.

With the clock ticking toward their fateful final night, Vanessa and Cole are forced into a battle of wills to survive their tormentor and escape with their lives before it's too late…

Tessa and Kristin Morgan are identical twins, exquisitely beautiful, and have the world at their perfectly pedicured feet; they are also profoundly different beneath their stunning facades.

Tessa is the laser-focused academic with her eyes firmly fixed upon a career in neurology, while Kristin exploits her striking looks and undeniable power over men to carve out a single-minded path to fame and fortune as a model and actress; an ambition she also holds for her sister.

But, on the night of the pair's debut as top-tier models, and with a high-profile movie role in the bag, tragedy strikes the twins in the form of a cruel acid attack by an unknown assailant. Thus, a gruesome chain of events begins - one that leaves a trail of blood, death, and devastation behind both Tessa and Kristin.

As Tessa fights to rebuild her life and uncover the truth behind the attack, she finds herself getting closer and closer to an uncomfortable truth about her sister and her search for the truth turns into a nightmare struggle to stay alive.

"As with *American Psycho*, Blake Rudman's *Goodbye Stranger* has a wealthy, successful man whose wonderful family life masks a much darker side. Throw in a once-trusting, increasingly suspicious wife, and the stage is set for twists and turns you'll never see coming!"

Danielle Harrington has the life many women envy: She's beautiful, rich, has two wonderful children, and is married to *the* Preston Harrington - the handsome, charismatic, retired quarterback who won two Super Bowls.

Unfortunately, something is very wrong with Preston. Having suffered more than his fair share of injuries and concussions, he becomes quiet, withdrawn, and distant. As Preston spends more time away from his family, Danielle begins suspect an affair without realizing her husband is involved in something much, much worse…

Following a series of tragic incidents and the return of an old nemesis from the past, things begin to spiral out of control for Danielle as Preston's dark side puts her and their children in terrible danger.

"If Lee Childs' Jack Reacher or Clive Cussler's Dirk Pitt tackled a terrorist scheme that utilized subliminal messaging to sow social and economic chaos on a global scale, it would look a lot like *Red Line*." Baltimore Police Detective Mitch Wilson wants a nice day out with his wife and son. Instead, they are all caught up in a catastrophic terrorist attack that has repercussions across the USA and triggers events that could alter the course of civilization.

Having lost everything, Mitch sets out to seek justice – and revenge and stumbles upon a global conspiracy.

On the other side of the world, renowned linguistic professor, Yasaman Karami, flees her native Iran for the freedom of the west; she holds one of the keys to defeating the terrorist organization.

Yasaman and Mitch's worlds collide as, alongside federal agents and allies, they race against the clock to hunt down the terrorist masterminds and prevent worldwide catastrophe.

The Slow Plague killed billions of women and girls worldwide. The gender-targeting infection without cure drove the remaining, sparce female population into an insane supply and demand situation in which they are treated as valuable commodities.

Though their "market value" is high, paradoxically, women's rights take a nosedive as they have become more desirable than the most precious jewels. Women are objects avarice, awe, and worship – to be owned or won in high-stakes games.

Kutri Chandigarh, one such "prize" and a rare beauty, is shipped from her native India to Los Angeles, a shattered metropolis barricaded behind a radiation-repelling wall. Within the city stronghold, a bleak, broken society comprised mostly of men is mesmerized by the stupefying programs pumped out by Little Angel Studios: an endless parade of reality TV shows.

The studio's #1 hit is "Good Breeding", in which a bevy of ethnically "pure" young women compete to marry a chosen suitor and produce a family in the spotlight of the public eye.

Like all women, Kutri has dreamed of wining the competition since her early childhood. But, when she arrives in LA and meets Jakob Freeman, her assigned matchmaker, the fantasy is turned on its head. It quickly twists into a horrific nightmare that extends far beyond Kutri and the man she chooses for herself.

As Kutri tries to escape the fate she once coveted, Jakob is swept up in events that threaten him body and soul and spark memories of a past he has deliberately tried to forget.

www.hellboundbookspublishing.com

Follow Blake's blog at: https://blakerudman.com
Facebook: @BRudmanThriller
Instagram: @BRudmanThriller
Twitter: @BRudmanThriller

For all Blake's books, visit him at:
www.hellboundbookspublishing.com/authorpage_rudman.html